Charlotte Moore grew up in Sussex and now lives with her husband and their two sons. She has a degree in English from Oxford University and in Art History from London University and until recently taught at Westminster school. She now reviews in *The Times* and the *Spectator* and has contributed articles to a number of publications including the *Independent on Sunday* and the *Daily Telegraph*, in addition to her writing. *Martha's Ark* is her second novel. Her first, *Promises Past*, is available in Arrow paperback.

Praise for *Promises Past*:

'Immensely enjoyable . . . I could not put it down . . . A
talented first novel of great promise'
Titia Sutherland

'Like Jane Austen, Charlotte Moore directs a sharp and
sympathetic gaze towards people whose comfortable lives seem
somehow insulated from the dangerous outside world of
politics, strife and financial anxieties . . . A well written and
enjoyable story'
*Sunday Telegraph*

'A story of infidelity and marital malaise with an old-fashioned
twist and what emerges, with its gentle, gossipy manner, is a
simple, loving reassertion of family life . . . Moore has a good
ear for dialogue and the small details of family life give it a
universal edge'
*Evening Standard*

'Charlotte Moore's debut is a cautionary tale about the crisis of
a middle-class marriage with a good eye for the petty
misunderstandings and jealousies that can drag a marriage
down . . .'
*The Times*

Also by Charlotte Moore

Promises Past

# MARTHA'S ARK

## Charlotte Moore

ARROW

Published by Arrow Books in 1996

1 3 5 7 9 10 8 6 4 2

Copyright © Charlotte Moore 1996

The right of Charlotte Moore to be identified as the author
of this work has been asserted by her in accordance
with the Copyright, Designs and Patents Act, 1988

First published in the United Kingdom by
Century Books Limited
20 Vauxhall Bridge Road, London SW1V 2SA

Random House Australia (Pty) Limited
16 Dalmore Drive, Scoresby, Victoria 3179

Random House New Zealand Limited
18 Poland Road, Glenfield
Auckland 10, New Zealand

Random House South Africa (Pty) Limited
PO Box 2263, Rosebank 2121, South Africa

RANDOM HOUSE UK Limited Reg. No. 954009

A CIP catalogue record for this book
is available from the British Library

Papers used by Random House UK Limited
are natural, recyclable products made from wood grown in
sustainable forests. The manufacturing processes conform to
the environmental regulations of the country of origin

ISBN 0 09 955351 1

Printed and bound in Great Britain by
Cox & Wyman Ltd, Reading, Berkshire

For George and Sam

I would like to thank my agent Sarah Molloy, my editor Mary Loring, my family for their support, my husband Min for a great deal of help, and Eva Littna for salvaging my manuscript.

# CHAPTER ONE

On the night of the harvest moon Leo Antrobus left home. Martha Antrobus lay on her bed, gazing at the moon's creamy, brimming face through the uncurtained casement window. It seemed to tilt towards her, leaning at an angle to the fathomless sky like a badly hung mirror. Martha fixed her eyes on it as she listened to Leo slamming the front door and revving the motor. Which car has he taken? she wondered idly. She hoped it wasn't the green one because her Wellingtons were in the back. It would be a bore to have to buy new Wellingtons, on top of everything else.

The noise of the car melted into the empty night. Martha lay motionless for a long time. She watched as the sky clouded and thin strips of vapour drifted across the surface of the moon like flimsy purple scarves. The wind was up, the lime trees shook their brittle August leaves. Martha began to shiver. She shivered because the window was open, and she was naked. During their final argument Leo had torn her nightdress from her body. It dawned on her moon-dazed mind that she and Leo had just finished the last argument about money that they would ever have.

Martha swung her heavy fifty-year-old body over the edge of the bed. She leaned her hands on the windowsill, looking out on the fields that by day were as trim and comforting as a child's picture book but which now in darkness had lost their friendly detail and looked alien, a planetary landscape. A fox barked; an owl shrieked. From deep within the house Bella wailed in her sleep.

As usual, thought Martha, I'm the one who isn't howling.

She closed the window. On her way back to bed she noticed a pool of something white on the bare wooden floor. The remains of her nightdress. She picked up the soft heap and shook it out. Not worth mending, she thought, but all the same she dropped it into the laundry basket. Still naked, she made a

1

cocoon of her sheets and blankets, and tried to keep her eyes closed.

Sixty miles away, in a smart St John's Wood flat, Martha's daughter Jess was restless. It wasn't the kicking – now the pregnancy was nearly at an end the baby seemed to have settled down a bit – and it wasn't heartburn either. She had fallen into a wretched habit of waking in the small hours and thinking, thinking, thinking. She thought about the birth and the pain quite a lot, but that was interesting rather than worrying. What disturbed her was the thought of the baby's face. Would she love her baby straight away? Would she even recognise her own baby? If they took it away from her in the hospital how would she know that they brought the right one back? It was such a silly, nebulous fear that she couldn't tell anyone about it. She had tried to explain what she meant to Nick but he'd just looked baffled and faintly bored. So now she had to lie awake for hours, imagining the blind, angry face squashed in its red darkness, longing to be free of it so that she could have her body to herself again.

Sometimes she just didn't manage to go back to sleep at all. Then she panicked, because people kept telling her how little sleep she would have once the baby was born, and she kept thinking she ought to grab as much as she could now, like hoarding tinned food in a store cupboard against future dearth. Jess shifted her bulk, trying to find a comfortable position without disturbing Nick. It was very important that he should get his eight hours; a couple of startling displays of ill-temper when he'd had to do with less had convinced her of that. He was sleeping with his back to her now. They had had an argument that evening over supper – their usual argument, about nannies. Jess didn't want a nanny. She wanted to be all in all to this baby. Nick said she needed a nanny so that she could go on painting, but Jess had a private vision of herself working in a sun-filled studio while the baby watched and gurgled and played with its toes. She didn't tell Nick this in case he was scornful; she simply said she didn't want a stranger in the house, she only wanted Nick. Nick said that if they had a nanny they'd spend more time together, not less, because the nanny would baby-sit. And so on.

In the end she had burned the crêpes and burst into tears and Nick's comforting had been more perfunctory than usual. It will be better when the house is ready, Jess reassured herself. They were still living in Nick's bachelor flat, waiting for the work on their new Islington house to be completed, and the flat was really too cramped. They were bound to get on each other's nerves. Once they were in the new house, everything would be fine.

Jess felt terribly hot on this August night. Her long honey-coloured hair, always abundant, had thickened still further during her pregnancy. She twisted it into a coil in an attempt to cool her neck. She wished Nick didn't insist on sleeping with the windows shut and the thick curtains closely drawn. She manoeuvred herself out of bed as surreptitiously as she could and padded next door to the living room, where at least she could see the moonlight falling through the blinds in stripes on to the deep pale carpet.

Martha wrote, 'Dearest Lila, Your father has left me.' Then she crumpled the sheet of paper and threw it into the parlour grate, where it joined several earlier efforts in the pile of wood ash that she should have long since cleared away. She let her gaze travel round the room. The low ceiling crossed with blackened oak beams and the deep-set, small-paned, fly-spotted windows meant that even on a bright morning like this one the parlour was cool and shadowy. Very little had changed since the day when Martha had first seen it more than twenty-eight years before. The deep-red turkey carpet had been faded and worn even then; now, patches of floorboards a foot square showed through the holes. The armchairs had never been reuphol-stered. Instead, rugs and shawls had been thrown over them to hide the bald patches and stains. The air smelled of old books and dead fires and the dried lavender and rose petals that filled the ceramic bowls dotted about the place. Martha loved the bowls. Some belonged to her mother-in-law, plain but elegant 'thirties creations glazed in sea green or pale ginger. Some Jess had made as a schoolgirl; they were prettily decorated with leaves and flowers, not at all bad. The thickest, most functional, least decorative ones Martha had made herself. They were dipped in glaze to halfway; she liked the contrast in texture as well as the colour of the fired earth.

She forced her attention back to her writing pad. 'Dearest Lila,' she wrote again. Overhead she could hear the sounds of Finian getting up. Odd that in her long night's vigil she'd given so much thought to breaking the news to her daughters, so little to the more immediate problem of informing her thirteen-year-old son.

Martha thought, I'll cook him some breakfast. She retied her dressing gown belt – Leo's dressing gown belt, actually – and strode into the kitchen, her broad feet bare. Bella was up, of course, poking about in the deep enamel sink. Bella liked to wash things up before breakfast, before the germs were awake. She liked to catch the germs by surprise.

Martha unhooked the black cast-iron frying pan and set it on the heat with a dab of lard in it. When the lard began to smoke she laid three rashers of bacon across the bottom and fetched two eggs from a straw-filled basket on the floor of the pantry. In passing she brushed against Bella's bony back. Bella turned round and smiled vaguely.

'Leo's gone,' said Martha.

Her cousin looked at her with pink-rimmed eyes. 'Good,' she said.

'Good?' Martha had always thought Bella was rather fond of Leo.

'Yes, good. One less mouth to feed.'

Martha turned the bacon, and cracked the eggs open on the rim of the pan. Finian appeared in the doorway, his fox-coloured hair standing in stiff peaks. 'Cooked breakfast!' he said. 'Is this a celebration?'

'No, Fin. A consolation. You see – Dad's left us.' Of all ways of putting it, Martha thought, that was possibly the worst.

'I know,' said Finian, 'I heard.' He fetched a plate, knife and fork from the draining board. 'Like I said, a celebration. You forgot the fried bread.'

Bella let slip a china egg cup. It shattered on the stone floor of the scullery. She screamed, briefly, piercingly. Martha said nothing. She reached for the brush and dustpan and swept up the scattered fragments.

4

# CHAPTER TWO

'Chandler?'

'Jamie,' said Jamie, and was immediately furious with himself. All the way to his new school that morning he'd been muttering 'Jack, Jack' like a mantra, so that he'd almost forgotten to change on to the Circle Line. Not even 'Jack' actually, but 'Jac', because his initials were J. A. C. James Alexander Chandler.

He was sick of Jamie. It sounded so babyish. Jamie was what his mother called him, along with the kinder teachers and better-disposed boys at his prep school. All the others had called him Chandler. To his father he was usually James. Now, entering his new school, he had had his chance to become Jac, and he'd blown it. Blown it right away.

In his confusion he forgot to concentrate on finding out what the other boys were called. The form master was reading through the list of surnames in alphabetical order, and each boy had to call out his first name so that the master could write it in the register. Jamie had told himself to remember as many names as possible; if you knew who someone was it gave you a tiny amount of power. Now the master – Mr Nethersole, he'd written it on the blackboard – had reached the P stage, and Jamie had failed to take in anything.

'Thomas.'

'Ranjit.'

'Ben.'

'Alasdair – A-L-A-S-D-A-I-R. It's Scottish.' Some boys tittered at the earnestness of small, freckled Alasdair. Mr Nethersole smiled, quite kindly, and moved on.

'Joshua.'

'Amir.'

'Christopher.'

'Sasha.'

Sasha! That was a girl's name. Jamie looked with pitying amazement at Sasha Webster, last in the alphabet. He quickly

5

realised that he could spare his concern. Sasha Webster wore thick-soled boots with luminous green laces and his hair was cut so close that you could see the whiteness of his scalp through it. He slouched in his chair with his long legs stuck right out in front of him. Most boys, Jamie included, sat upright, their black polished shoes tucked round the legs of their chairs.

Mr. Nethersole closed the register and handed round time-table forms. Jamie felt a surge of panic. He knew he would never be able to understand how to transfer information from the computerised sheet to the little boxes allotted for each day of the week. His neighbour on the right-hand side was a clean, efficient-looking Chinese boy. Jamie decided to copy whatever he did.

'No, no, Chandler.' Mr Nethersole loomed over him, scratching his sparse beard. 'You're down for Route Two. You're electronics, not ancient Greek.' Jamie cast him a glance of mute appeal. Teachers, in his experience, had proved less treacherous than classmates. 'Don't worry,' said Mr Nethersole to the brown, anxious face, 'I'll get you a new sheet. Look, Route Two subjects fit in here –' The pieces of the jigsaw fell into place. 'You've picked up quite a tan. Been anywhere interesting?'

'Only St Lucia,' said Jamie. 'With my father and –'

'Only St Lucia!' Mr Nethersole chuckled. '*Only* St Lucia. Well, well.' A buzzer sounded. He raised his voice. 'Time for break. I hope you all know what you're doing now. Any queries, come and see me. Oh, and Webster, stay behind, will you? Off you go, the rest of you.'

It was double maths after break. The first proper lesson. Jamie was dreading it, but not as much as he was dreading break itself. In his pocket he turned a small shell over and over, a brilliant pink shell he'd found in St Lucia. It was a lucky one, or that was what the old black fisherman had told him. He followed the crowd down the stairs and out into the school courtyard. Here the pack dispersed and little knots of boys formed and reformed all over the huge sunlit space. Everyone else – even tiny Alasdair – seemed to have some idea of where to go and what to do. The only place Jamie felt sure about was the lavatory. He headed off, almost running, and locked himself in.

6

Eliza Antrobus lay in her single bed in her small east Oxford house, reading. She was impatient to get going – as always she had a tremendous list of things to get through – but she thought she'd give her new lodger a chance to do whatever he had to do in the bathroom first. She was trying to fill the time usefully by reading a new life of Eleanor of Acquitaine as background for her special subject, but it was pointless. Her growing feeling of irritation made it impossible to concentrate.

She slipped on her dressing gown and went to turn the handle of the bathroom door. Locked. She listened for a moment, hoping that the occupant was only brushing his teeth, but prolonged sounds of splashing indicated otherwise. Now there wouldn't be enough hot water for her own bath. Eliza thought, bother that lodger, not for the first time. She padded downstairs to make herself a cup of tea to take back to bed.

The lodger had a name, of course; he was called Graham. But Eliza had talked for so long to her friends and family about getting someone to share the rent that even now she'd finally done it and he was thoroughly installed she still thought of him as 'the lodger'. She lit the gas, and looked with distaste at the small saucepan half full of tinned tomatoes that he'd left on the hob. He hadn't washed the grill pan, either; it was thick with white grease. The lodger tended to get home late at night and cook himself dirty little suppers. Eliza shoved the pan back under the grill. Maybe she should only have accepted a female.

A squeaky scrape on the window pane alerted her to the needs of Sylvia, her black and white cat. She unlocked the garden door and Sylvia dashed in, pushing briefly against Eliza's legs before making for her food bowl that sat on a newspaper in one corner of the cramped kitchen. Eliza reached for the tin opener, but as she did so she heard the post flop on to the doormat. It was her twenty-eighth birthday in a few days' time; the arrival of the postman gave her a childish little thrill.

Sure enough, there were two early cards – both addressed in the familiar handwriting of long-standing female friends who never forgot – and a letter, in a reused brown envelope stuck down with Sellotape and covered in her mother's large scrawl. She opened this one first.

7

'Dearest Lila,' she read, 'I'm afraid I've got some rather dramatic news for you.'

Eliza's scalp prickled. She read to the end, then replaced the letter in its envelope and pushed it into her dressing gown pocket. She felt the squeeze of fierce anger. How could he? she thought. Just before the baby's born. Couldn't he even stick around for that?

The kettle screeched and the aggrieved cat meowed, circling her food bowl with righteous indignation. As she bent to pick up the cat's bowl Eliza felt the edges of the unopened birthday cards, shoved into her pocket along with the letter. 'How could he?' she said aloud. 'Just before my birthday.'

'Everything all right?' Graham, glowing, in boxer shorts and besloganned T-shirt, filled the door space.

'Did I say something?' Eliza essayed a little laugh. 'I must have been talking to the cat.'

'Bathroom's free,' said Graham, shaking coffee granules into a mug. 'Want some coffee? Our new neighbour's moved in, by the way. I saw him yesterday.'

'Oh,' said Eliza automatically. 'What's he like?'

'Thirtyish, divorced, got a kid. Very Green – cycles everywhere, and he's making a proper compost heap out the back.'

'You found out a lot.' Eliza wasn't very interested, but Graham's stream of talk diverted her attention from her mother's news.

'Oh yes, we had quite a chat. Nice bloke. He's a gardener at one of the colleges. I forget which.' Graham lit the grill. The smell of melting chop fat seeped through the kitchen. Eliza managed a wan smile before retreating to bed.

'I don't know why you should think that,' said Susan Chandler into the telephone. She drummed her fingertips on the marble worktop. Her nails were filed and polished but not painted. 'I can't see why you think that would be a good idea,' she repeated. 'He should have more time to settle in at school.'

'I'm only talking about one night away, for God's sake. From the way you go on one would think it was a lifetime. And the agreement was, weekdays with you, weekends with us.'

'You've only just had him in Barbados for two weeks. I don't see why –'

'St Lucia. That was holiday. Now Pippa and I want him to get to know his new home.'

'Tony, his home is here.'

'Not for much longer.'

Susan put down the phone. She knew what it meant to seethe. Hurt feelings bubbled and tumbled inside her like a boiling stew. Or line a mound of maggots dissolving a carcass.

She switched on the answering machine. Sure enough, there was soon another ring, followed by Tony's voice filling the kitchen. 'As you haven't the civility to speak to me in person, I'll have to issue instructions. I'll call for James at ten o'clock on Saturday morning and I'll expect him to be packed and ready.'

Susan smoothed lotion on to her long, thin hands and eased off her rings. She placed them in a clean cut-glass ashtray and pulled on rubber gloves. She was going to clean the whole kitchen. It was true that Estrelia had gone over it that morning, but she always left corners and crannies untouched. Behind the taps, for instance. Susan opened the cupboard under the sink and pulled out bleach, disinfectant, cream cleaner, scouring pads.

Jamie's first week at his new school, and his father was taking him off to his rural love nest for the weekend. For take him he would; Susan knew that her protests were token. Tony always got his way. 'Pippa and I want him . . .' Susan felt that painful seething again, like a physical symptom. She thought of Pippa's pink cheeks and silver charm bracelet and scoured the aluminium draining board until her elbow ached. She didn't hear the sound of her son's key in the door.

Jamie swung his heavy school bag into a corner with relief, but his heart sank when he saw that his mother had her rubber gloves on. He considered slipping quietly upstairs to his room, but he knew he'd only get into trouble for that, so he said, 'Mum,' loudly, because of the noise of the taps. His mother wheeled round with a little yelp of surprise. 'Oh, darling, it's you! How was it? Tell me all about it.'

'It was all right. Can I have a Coke?'

'Of course. Are you hungry? You must be starving.'

9

'Can I have some pizza?'

Susan frowned. 'I was going to make a proper meal for us later. If you have pizza now you won't want it.'

'But I'm hungry now.'

'Well, what about a sandwich?'

'I'd rather have pizza.'

'Jamie, I said a sandwich. Cheese or peanut butter?'

'Pizza.'

'Jamie . . .'

'I don't want a sodding sandwich,' said Jamie, and burst into tears.

Susan was appalled to hear her voice, like an automaton. 'Don't talk to me like that. Go to your room.'

'Don't worry, I'm going.' Jamie stumbled up the stairs to the shelter of his duvet.

Susan peeled off her gloves, and took a pizza out of the freezer. His first day at school, she thought, why on earth did I have to be like that? What damage had fifteen years of marriage to Tony Chandler done to her? Her thoughts wandered back to Pippa Watts-Davison and her blonde ponytail and her innocent, confident little laugh. This time Susan felt a kind of grim satisfaction. Just you wait, my girl, she thought. Just you wait.

# CHAPTER THREE

'Where are you going to, Fin?'

'Just to see how they're getting on with the barn.'

'I thought it was finished.'

'It is. They're moving their stuff in tomorrow. I want to see it empty just one more time.'

'All right. But I'll need help this afternoon. We need to muck out the stable. Pharaoh's got laminitis again, I'll have to bring him in.'

'Sure thing, Ma.' He squeezed her quickly round the waist and moved off, making dark tracks through the deep, dew-heavy grass. Martha stood in the kitchen doorway, watching her son's loose, easy stride, his swinging arms, his tufty hair bright in the sun. How tall he had grown this summer! As tall as she was, nearly – taller than Eliza by now. And yet there was no trace of adolescent gawkiness. With his jeans and faded checked shirt and his grimy tanned skin he looked completely at ease, a prince in possession of his kingdom.

A deep, shaky female voice, its accent pure pre-war BBC English, called her from the heart of the house. Martha shook off her reverie. 'I'm coming, Sibyl,' she called. She guessed what had happened. Her mother-in-law, eighty years old and suddenly showing it, would have embarked on the stairs unaided and become gripped with panic halfway down. How much longer could they manage without a lift? Martha wondered. And would the council pay?

Sibyl Antrobus still looked dignified, even when she stood clutching the banisters with one liver-spotted hand, prodding the staircase for weaknesses with her rubber-tipped walking stick. She was tall, and held herself upright; she wore a tweed suit and a string of pearls, and her hair, still plentiful, once glorious blonde, now faded to a soft cream, was plaited and pinned to the top of her head. Her face softened with relief at the sight of her daughter-in-law. 'Ah, Martha. Would you lend me an arm, dear? I don't know how it is, but I've got it into my head that beneath this carpet the staircase has quite rotted away.'

Martha took her arm. 'I think it's sound enough. But we can take the carpet up and have a look, if you like.'

'Oh no. I wouldn't want to put you to the trouble. If you took the carpet up you might never get it down again.'

Martha led the old woman to the parlour. Sibyl, reared in an age of servants, had never got used to sitting and eating in the kitchen. Increasingly she took her meals alone, eating off a tray with little folding legs. Martha lowered her into an armchair and opened the shutters before going to make her mid-morning coffee. 'Bring a cup for yourself, won't you?' called Sibyl as Martha turned to go. This was more of a command than an invitation. Sibyl, doubtless, had something particular to say.

'Thank you. I will.' Martha suppressed a sigh. So many things to do, so many demands on her time. Above her head she could hear Bella bumping up and down with an ancient carpet sweeper. Bella hated vacuum cleaners – hated and feared them. Martha made the coffee and fished a few unbroken digestive biscuits out of the tin. She carried the tray back to the parlour.

Sibyl said, 'I don't suppose you've heard from Leo? I thought not. He'll be abroad by now, I expect.'

'Abroad?'

'Yes. When he's in trouble, his instinct is always to cross the Channel. Surely you've noticed?'

Martha pondered. Her mind ran back to the early years of their marriage, when a romantic weekend in Rome or a family holiday in Switzerland had been his panacea for all ills. 'Yes, I suppose you're right,' she said, stirring her coffee.

'By the time he gets back,' said Leo's mother, 'I may be gone.'

'Gone? You don't mean –'

'Not in body, no. Though of course that's possible. No, Martha, my mind may have given way. I can already feel it happening.'

'Oh no, Ganna, no.' Martha felt a rush of affection. She laid a hand on the tweed-covered arm. 'Don't talk such morbid nonsense.'

'I saw it happen to my mother,' Sibyl replied, 'and I would be foolish to ignore the same symptoms in my own case. At first

12

Mamma forgot where she had put her glasses – she got through six pairs in as many months. By the end she knew no one, and nothing seemed to have any meaning for her except certain hymn tunes. Leo was very good about singing them to her, I must say. Over and over again.'

'Oh, Ganna –'

Sibyl raised a hand. 'No more. I don't wish to talk about this any more at present. I want to talk about Jess.'

'She's due any day now.'

'I know. Poor dear. Martha, I don't like that young man of hers.'

'Nick? What's wrong with him?'

'I don't like him, dear. He has a mercenary mind.'

'He's done very well in advertising, if that's what you mean. A little business sense is no bad thing in a husband, in my opinion.' Martha's tone had an edge to it.

'You misunderstand me. I have no objection to money *per se*. But that young man is tainted by it. He bought Jess to add to his collection of possessions, and when he's had enough of her, that will be the end of that.'

Martha was stung. 'Ganna, I don't think it's very helpful to think these things, let alone to say them. Nick is the father of Jess's child. He adores her – who wouldn't? – and he'll adore her baby. I agree he's not exactly my type, but –'

'I would not say things to Jess, of course,' put in Sibyl, 'but as I near my end I see less and less reason to beat about the bush. You and I must be on our guard. Jessamine's well-being is of paramount importance.'

Martha, carrying the tray back to the kitchen, found herself smiling at the old lady's melodramatic tone. Jess and the unborn baby were the brightest spots on her own horizon right now. And Nick would do. True, she hadn't particularly warmed to him, and it had all happened rather quickly, but he was a powerful, efficient, intelligent man. He was a coper, and he would give Jess a structure to her life. That was what she had always needed.

Upstairs, the bump of the carpet sweeper had stopped. Listening hard, Martha could just hear the squeak of Bella's rocking chair. She would be knitting, most likely. It was 'something for the baby', she said, but she never allowed anyone to see her doing it. Martha took a bucket, and set out to hunt for eggs.

Finian's trainers and the bottoms of his jeans were soon drenched with dew, but he didn't mind. He liked the feel of things – the damp of his shirt, sticking to the middle of his back, the mild throb of nettle stings on his hand where he had reached through a tangle of undergrowth to grab a scuttling toad, the heat of the sun, sitting like a cap on the top of his head. Such things made him feel alive.

He soon reached the old barn, now a barn no more. The Antrobuses' farm had been sold long ago, but they'd hung on to the barn and the yard it stood in, just because the liked it. It wasn't worth anything as a farm building – the man who'd bought the farm had quickly put up some structures made of breeze blocks and corrugated iron in far more convenient positions. The tile-hung barn, which with its arching rafters had always made Finian think of the skeleton of a great whale, had remained virtually unused for years. Martha stored hay and straw in one end of it; rats and barn owls used it, and the Antrobuses' cats littered in it if you didn't catch them and shut them up in the house in time. And Finian used it, of course, but that wasn't thought to count. He had swung for hours on a knotted rope from one of the great beams, he'd lain in the straw reading, he'd even spent a night there once. Half a night, actually. When the third rat had run over his sleeping bag he'd decided to slip back into the house and his own less public bed.

But now the barn had finally been sold, to pay off some of his father's debts, and it had been bought by a rich London lawyer who was having it converted into a luxurious holiday home. For months Finian had watched the builders almost daily; now the work was finished. People tried to make the best of it, by saying how many of the original features the architect had managed to retain, and how nice it was to have the building put to good use rather than have it slowly disintegrate, but to Finian it felt like a death. He'd become friendly with the builders, Colin and Ray, and had even quite enjoyed helping them – and he'd loved clambering all over the scaffolding, especially at night. But he couldn't stand the architect, with his brightly coloured shirts and pretentious haircut, and he hated with a deadly hatred Tony Chandler, the new owner. When either of those two appeared, Finian made himself scarce.

Ray, the nicest builder, was there today, collecting up some odds and ends. As usual, he'd set down a small radio on the paved terrace that now framed the barn. Ray always liked to be abreast of the travel news. 'Terrible snarl-up at the Wedgebury intersection,' he announced, as he caught sight of Fin. 'They won't get that sorted out before dinner time.'

'Can I go in?' asked Finian.

Ray looked doubtfully at the boy's jeans and trainers. Fin was soaked almost to the knees. 'They've got the carpet down,' he said.

'I'll take my shoes off. Please, Ray. It's the last day today.'

Ray liked Finian. He only had daughters himself. 'Go on, then,' he said. 'I'll unlock. Get them wet shoes off, though, and keep yer fingers off the paint.'

Finian left his trainers on the terrace to dry in the sun and rolled his trousers up as far as they would go. He explored the house slowly, holding his breath almost, as though he might be caught, though there was no one but Ray to hear him. The white-painted doors with black iron latches were hard to push open because of the thick new carpet. They'd put carpet almost everywhere, even on the stairs. Even in the bathrooms! Finian couldn't believe his eyes. He was used to curling lino tiles and a crumbling cork mat.

One bathroom – the one that opened out of the largest bedroom – had a jacuzzi. Ray had told Finian about it, otherwise he wouldn't have known what it was. Despite his contempt for the conversion, he was intrigued by the jacuzzi. Perhaps he could sneak in one day and try it out. Ray and Colin seemed to think that the Chandlers wouldn't be down very often. 'They won't like the winter,' Colin had opined. 'You don't get real winters in London. One burst pipe and they'll be off.' Finian certainly hoped so.

There were four rooms that seemed suitable as bedrooms – three smallish ones in a row, then the big one, the one with its own bathroom, separated by a little flight of steps. This one had the biggest windows – windows on three sides – and the best view by far, over the farm and the dark woods beyond to the gap in the distant hills which Finian knew was the sea. Would they even know that, though? They probably didn't have a clue about the sea. At least this bedroom didn't face the farmhouse. Finian hated the idea of being overlooked.

This room already contained a bed – the only piece of furniture in the house so far, except for the kitchen stuff. That was because they'd had a bed specially built. It was vast, set on a kind of platform, and though it wasn't quite a four-poster, it had a railing round the top from which curtains could be hung. It was like a room within a room, really. The poncey architect had designed it, and Ray's mate Paul the carpenter had built it. Paul had complained a lot about the architect's finickety criticisms, fuelling Finian's dislike. The mattress was already in place, though it was still covered in plastic. Finian was thirteen, not too old to be tempted by a potential trampoline.

Ray switched off the radio and called up the stairs, 'I'll just nip up to the garage. I've run out of cigs. Be'ave yourself. All right?'

'I will,' Finian called back. He waited for a few seconds and then took a flying leap into the middle of the mattress. No one had ever used this bed before, he thought. He enjoyed that idea. He was so used to things having a past. His great-aunt had died in his own bed, he knew, and she probably wasn't the only one.

He turned a few somersaults, backwards and forwards, and then tried to do one in mid-air. He bounced until he was breathless, then lay flat on his back, his arms and legs stretched out as far as they would go. He listened to the drunken stumblings of an overheated bluebottle trying to find an exit. He closed his eyes.

'Darling,' said a deep voice, 'look at this spider's web. Absolutely unbroken.'

A shrill giggle; 'Gosh no, Tony, I hate spiders.'

'Sweetheart, you're so sensitive. Come here.' Murmurings.

'Ooh, Tony, don't. Not here.'

Finian slithered to the floor and crawled towards the window. The voices came from the terrace below. He raised himself slowly and, pressing his back against the wall as he had seen people do in Hitchcock films, swivelled his eyes sideways. He could see the tops of the intruders' heads – the bald patch in the curly dark hair of the new owner, the black velvet Alice band securing the smooth fair locks of his young lady, as Ray called her. Chandler was kissing her, elaborately. Jesus, thought Finian, how gross can you get? This man was about the same age as his father.

'Ton-ee!' The woman removed his hand from the front of her dress. 'You really mustn't.'

A husky laugh. 'I'm sorry, my love. I'm getting carried away.' A pause. 'What on earth – ?' Tony Chandler had spotted Finian's trainers.

The woman said, 'Ugh!' as if she had stepped on a slug. 'Tony, what are they doing here?'

'Must belong to a tramp, I suppose.' Tony pushed them off the terrace with his foot. 'Or to one of those bloody cocky builders.'

'I thought they were rather sweet, those men.'

'Sweet? They take bloody liberties. All builders do. Give them an inch –'

'Tony, you don't think there could be a tramp in the house?'

'I'll check. Don't worry, Pips. I've handled this kind of thing before.' Finian froze. 'For Christ's sake, the door's not locked.'

'Tony, you will try not to swear when the baby's here, won't you?'

Tony ignored this remark. 'Wait here, Pips.'

'No, I want to stay with you.'

Their brief argument on the subject gave Finian a little time. Under the bed's platform was a hollow space – storage space for suitcases, as Paul the carpenter had told him. He crept in, and lay flat, trying to regulate his breathing.

He heard them searching downstairs, then opening the doors of all the bedrooms. 'No sign,' said Tony's voice. 'I expect it's just the builder.'

'I do hope so. I'm scared of tramps.'

Scared of spiders, scared of tramps! It wasn't worth her being alive, thought Finian, trying not to breathe in dust.

They were in the master bedroom now. 'Nothing in here either,' declared its owner. 'Nothing, that is, except a rather comfortable-looking mattress.' The murmuring noises began again.

'Oh, Tony –'

'Come on, darling. Let's christen our very own bedroom, shall we?'

Giggles, and thuds. The platform shook. Finian thought, It might all cave in on me. What a way to die.

The blessed relief, at a distance, of Ray's whistling! 'Tony, stop, I can hear someone.'

'Who cares? It's my house.' Tony's grumbling voice.

'No, no, no, I couldn't.'

'All right, angel. Paradise postponed.'

Ray's whistling had stopped, presumably because he'd caught sight of the unexpected car. Tony's heavy tread sounded on the stair, closely followed by the girl's lighter footsteps. Finian heard Tony's angry voice quizzing Ray about the unlocked door, and Ray's reply, conciliatory, revealing nothing. Finian grinned with relief. He'd make it up to Ray, somehow. He wriggled out. It might be safer to stay under the bed, but on the other hand they might come back . . . He nipped into the bathroom, limping because of pins and needles. He'd sussed out all the possible exits and entrances long ago; the bathroom window was a cinch. He crawled out of it, skimmed down the drainpipe, paused to check that the conversation was still going on at the other side of the building, then ran barefoot through the builder's yard that would one day be a garden, and vaulted over the fence into the strip of woodland that separated the farmhouse patch from the Chandlers' site.

'What was that?' Pippa sounded nervous. 'I heard something rustle in the bushes.'

'A fox, I shouldn't wonder.' Ray had caught sight of Finian's bright head disappearing into the darkness. 'He'll be after Mrs Antrobus' chickens. They've got so bold, these days, they'll rob in broad daylight.'

Pippa wanted to asked whether foxes were dangerous to babies, but she could tell from Tony's tense breathing that it would be best to say nothing.

# CHAPTER FOUR

Jess dreaded telling Nick. She spent most of the morning lying on the black leather recliner, staring out of the window, her mother's letter in her hand. She didn't cry. She didn't feel particularly sad, even. But she did recoil from the necessity of telling her husband.

Jess had married Nick four months earlier. Or rather, Nick had married Jess; this, like all important decisions, had been his. She had dreaded telling him she was pregnant, too, and put it off for several days, until her unaccountable tears and dizzy spells led him to coax the information out of her. Once he knew, he took charge, magnificently. 'Then we'll get married, mermaid,' he had said, removing the tears one by one from her cheeks with his fingertip and kissing the end of her nose. 'I've been looking for an excuse to marry my mermaid for ages.' Jess assumed that he'd meant a quick dash in and out of a registry office, but no, not at all. Nick liked to do things in style. He wanted it done in the crypt of St Paul's; this meant waiting several months, until after Lent. 'But I'll show by then!' Jess had protested, but Nick said she should wear her bulge with pride. He took down a book about Botticelli and found the *Primavera*. He pointed to one of the gauze-robed, round-bellied figures: 'I want you to look like *that*.'

And she had, more or less. Her dress was made of whispering silk chiffon, edged with embroidered bands of a kind of golden green. She'd worn her hair down, but with ribbons plaited into it and a half-circle of white jasmine – her name flower – to keep it in place. The flowers she'd carried were cream and pink – lilies and roses intertwined with dark, glossy ivy leaves. Her feet, bare in their gold embroidered slippers, felt the chill of the flagstones, but she looked and felt enchanting. Early on, she'd felt a pang not to be marrying in the tiny church at home, which was what she'd always imagined, but when she'd mentioned that to Nick he'd said he wanted to keep her family out of the

19

proceedings as far as possible, and that was perfectly under-
standable. They could be difficult, if you weren't used to them.
And he'd been so energetically supportive about the pregnancy
that she hadn't felt inclined to argue.

The wedding had happened at the end of April. It was a grey,
drizzly day, and as she stood on the cathedral steps having her
photograph taken Jess felt her skin tighten with cold beneath her
filmy dress. But when she stood by Nick's side later at the altar,
flanked by two immense stands of firm-throated Madonna lilies,
listening to the priest intoning the magic words, she felt the
baby bubble inside her and had to close her eyes just for a
second, to cope with the hot gush of dizzying excitement. Never
had life seemed so full of sweet promise.

Now, at the fag end of the summer, that neat little curve of a
stomach had become this colossal mound, pale and bumpily
irregular like a Christmas turkey ready for roasting. A dark line
ran down from her navel like a zip; her unrecognisable breasts
were networked with blue veins like string bags. Her eyes looked
smaller in her newly round face; she had developed a double
chin. Here she lay, still in her dressing gown at noon, spilling
over the edges of Nick's elegantly narrow *chaise-longue*. And in
her hand she held a letter telling her that her father had left her
mother, apparently for good.

The telephone rang. 'Jess?'

She recognised the rather thin, clear voice of her older sister.
'It's me. Have you heard from Ma? Well, I don't know about
you but it makes me bloody angry.'

Jess paused before replying.

'I don't know, really. I don't know what I feel about it.'

'Jess, how can you be so –'

'Oh, Lila, don't expect me to *feel* anything right now. I've
turned to soggy cotton wool.'

Eliza's tone softened. 'What does Nick say?'

'I haven't told him yet. I don't want to disturb him at work.'

'Why ever not?'

'I think he's out at a meeting anyway.'

'Oh. Well, what are you going to do about it?'

Jess said weakly, 'Is there anything to do about it?'

'Doesn't it occur to you that Ma may need our support?

Things may be a little difficult at home, don't you think?'

Jess paused. 'Are you going to go down, then?'

'I think we should both go down.'

'Lila, it's only ten days to go. I don't think I should risk it.'

'There are doctors and hospitals in Sussex, you know. It's not especially convenient for me, either. I'd counted on getting my Henry II lectures ready, but I think we should show solidarity with Ma.'

'Why don't we talk to her first, and ask her what she wants?'

'Because she'll say she's fine, of course.'

'Well, maybe she is.'

'Jess, how can you be so selfish?'

Jess burst into tears.

'Oh God,' Eliza said, 'I can't cope with this. I'll ring you back later.'

'No, no, it's all right. I'll ring you.'

The first time Nick Gascoigne had seen Jess Antrobus had been at her degree show. Nick was looking for talent; part of his job was to commission artwork for the advertising company which employed him, and he also wanted a large, colourful, interesting oil painting for his rather pallid St John's Wood flat. His friend Rob Weeks had a younger sister just finishing at the Slade. Rob was going to the degree show, and suggested Nick should come along.

They had started with Megan Weeks' display, naturally. Megan was tiny, with a spiky cap of jet-black hair and colossal clumpy boots. You could see her ribs through her black vest. She made installations out of rusty bicycles and fishermen's nets. After ten minutes in her company Nick felt a pall of irritation and gloom fall upon him. He left Rob to it, and wandered off through the high-celinged, interconnected rooms, looking for something to lift his spirits. The lapsed grandeur of the building formed an ironic setting for the unappealing work on display, he thought. Room after room of dingy, scruffy, mono-chrome constructions – why didn't any of these students paint *pictures* any more?

Then he saw Jess – or rather, he saw one of Jess' paintings. Apricot-coloured paint had been laid streakily across a large canvas, as a backdrop to a standing female nude. She was constructed very simply, out of almost geometric shapes – triangles for her small breasts, cylinders for her limbs – and yet the different elements cohered to create a warm, graceful female presence. The head was turned to one side, and her long hair – a rich biscuit colour – hung thickly over three-quarters of her face. One hand rested on what was probably a windowsill; natural light seemed to suffuse the painting. 'I'll buy it,' said Nick aloud.

'Do you really mean that?'

Nick turned. At his elbow stood a slender young woman. It was a warm summer evening; she wore a long black dress, close-fitting, with a lacy white bodice over the top, and on her feet black plimsolls, the kind schoolchildren wear for gymnastics. Her abundant hair was piled on top of her head.

'Is it yours?' he asked. 'How much do you want for it?'

'But are you sure? Don't you want to look at my other stuff first?'

It was Jess he really wanted to look at. She wore a thin black ribbon round her creamy throat. Her eyes were grey, the colour of a raincloud; round each of them she had drawn a smudgy charcoal line.

'I think it's marvellous,' he said. 'Has it got a title?'

She said simply, 'It's a self-portrait.'

'Then I'm having it. I'll give you a thousand pounds for it. And when I've hung it, you must come and tell me what you think.'

Eliza paced unseeing through the Ashmolean museum. Small and slight, inconspicuous in jeans and blue cotton shirt, her light-brown hair shaped into a neat helmet, she would have appeared utterly harmless to anyone who bothered to look at her at all, but her external condition in no way reflected the simmering confusion within. The telephone conversation with Jess sent a tremor of restlessness through her. She felt as if she had snagged a torn nail on something woollen, and she knew that it would be impossible to work, or to settle to anything, before she'd filed down the rough edges of her mind. So she jumped on her bike and made for the Ashmolean, hoping that on a weekday morning out of term she would have the place to herself.

She was right. Attendants – some of them undergraduates employed for the Long Vac – dozed on their chairs, and a wave of Scandinavian tourists surged in silence past the Pre-Raphaelite paintings, but there was virtually no one else. Eliza tramped the length of one gallery after another, using the stairs and corridors as a caged mouse uses its wheels and ladder. She tried to think rationally and constructively about her father's defection, her mother's plight, but the image that crystallised in her mental crucible was of her sister and Nick the last time she had seen them. A summer weekend at Powdermill, blazing hot; navy-blue shadows lying like cutouts on sun-bleached grass. Garden chairs and sun beds grouped higgledy-piggledy under the mulberry tree on the back lawn. Jess gazing up at the heart-shaped leaves, wafery discs of purest lime; the unripe fruit, darker green, knobbled like tiny fists. Jess rubbing her back cat-like against the rough, rust-red trunk, her straw hat lying by her side, her beachball of a stomach scarcely veiled by the flimsy pleats of her white muslin dress. Nick, upright in a wicker chair, immaculate linen trousers, one slim brown ankle balanced sock-less on the other knee. Nick's shirt sleeves were folded neatly to the elbow, his dark glasses were designed almost out of exis-tence. He held the newspaper up in front of his face, as always. Eliza in a deckchair a little way off, half reading, half watching, thought he looked like an advertisement for – well, for after-shave, or cars, or expensive watches, or for any other bloody thing an aspiring young idiot would find desirable. Eliza's dan-gling hand tugged at a blade of grass; it parted from its sheath with a clean little squeak. She chewed the white end. What, in the name of all that mattered, was Jess doing with a husband like that?

Jess turned with a little purring noise and reached for her husband's hand. He put aside the newspaper with reluctance. Jess didn't appear to notice. 'Nick,' she said, kissing his finger-tips, 'isn't this perfect? If I could make time stop now, I would.'

'Very nice,' said Nick. There was a sharp, straight crease between his eyes, just above the bridge of his sunglasses. He glanced at his watch – another top-of-the-range aspirational icon – and allowed Jess to play with his fingers for a few seconds

23

more, then withdrew his hand and rose. 'Got to make a phone call,' he said over his shoulder. 'I'll bring you a cold drink when I come back.' He made his way back to the house.

Jess closed her eyes and yawned and stretched luxuriously. She looks like the cat who's got the cream, thought Eliza, removing her glasses and wiping the sweat off the sides of her nose. How can she be so blind?

Now, hastening without purpose through the museum, a fug of irritation circling her head like a cloud of insects, Eliza thought of her sister's weak plea of that morning – 'Oh, Lila, don't expect me to *feel* anything right now.' And then the ugly, aggravating sound of weeping. Was it really the end of pregnancy that had reduced her to that state? wondered Eliza. Or had Jess begun to see through her mail-order handsome, heartless husband?

Eliza had been woken that morning by a strong, unfair dream, and she couldn't rid herself of its flavour. She had dreamed of Oliver, the married don with whom for the last four years she had conducted a shameful, intermittent, largely secret affair. Oliver who was by turns so passionate and so indifferent, but who was undeniably clever, easily clever enough to wriggle unscathed out of any number of half-formed promises. It was at Jess and Nick's wedding that Eliza had vowed to break with Oliver once and for all. She had many doubts about the wedding but as she sat in the front pew, breathing in the holy scent of lilies and listening to her sister's sweet, bell-like voice repeating the magic words, she had told herself that if this all meant anything at all then she must in all honour retreat from Oliver's life and leave him to his eminently repairable marriage and his three invisible, clamorous children.

She found it easier than she expected to bury his memory. She filled her days with routine and order and nipped incipient moping in the bud with bouts of frenetic activity. But then last night – or this morning, rather – Oliver let himself right into her dream and climbed into bed, and all the things she thought she'd forgotten, like the sound of his voice and the texture of his skin, were with her again as if he'd never been away. That dream had undone months of hard, careful work. And then there was her mother's letter and her conversation with Jess . . .

I could be wrong about Nick, thought Eliza, striving to be rational. Some people would say I was jealous, because I wanted a handsome husband of my own, because the best I've been able to do was borrow someone else's husband on terms that suited him, not me. But – how long did it take Ma to see through Dad, I wonder? Impossible for a child to know, because until you're more or less grown up you have no criteria for judging your parents' marriage. Your parents set the standard. Whatever their marriage is like, it's your norm, and therefore unquestionable, unfathomable.

She had circled and spiralled through the antiquities, the Middle Ages, the Renaissance, and now she found herself back with the Pre-Raphaelites. She came to rest in front of Collins' *Convent Thoughts*, where a clean-faced nun, rigid with bliss, contemplated a passion flower, while at her feet bright goldfish hung, jellied in glassy water. The simplicity of the painting, the minutely painted, brilliant-coloured garden, like a child's view of heaven, always made Eliza smile. Today, those snug, excluding convent walls looked particularly appealing. You've got a point, she said to the nun, almost out loud.

# CHAPTER FIVE

Hugh and Sibyl Antrobus bought Powdermill Farm in 1938. Hugh was a writer, a philosopher really, or at least an able critic of the philosophical writings of others. He supplemented his income with journalism and by lecturing at a London college. Sibyl, ten years younger than her husband, was a beauty of the least self-conscious kind. Her pale, smooth skin and aura of stillness meant that she was in demand as a studio model, and sat for some of the major artists of the day. She drew a little herself, sang rather well, and spasmodically wrote poetry. Hugh first met her at a party in the white-walled Hampstead studio of an artist friend. He saw her standing beside a piece of sculpture, a polished shape of blue-grey stone, twisted in the middle, taller than a man and as graceful as a woman. Sibyl was talking to a stranger, making polite conversation, but as she talked her long, pale hand caressed the stone as if her fingertips could communicate to her the essence of its cool beauty. The sight of this tall, golden-haired girl with her hooded eyes and her air of remoteness and her shoulders like smooth marble seized Hugh with a sudden jealous desire and he interposed himself between her and her unknown, hated companion with a decisiveness that was quite uncharacteristic. Hugh Antrobus had always prided himself on his rational stance, but there was nothing rational about the passion that now possessed him. It took him twenty-four hours to ask her out to dinner; when he did so, her quiet, unhesitating acceptance caught him unawares. The siege was over before it had begun, but Hugh did not value his prize the less. All his life she never ceased to be a source of wonder to him.

When he fell in love with Sibyl, Hugh did not know that she had money. He was always glad about that. He had none of his own, and it had never particularly concerned him. Sibyl treated her money like a magic wand. Hugh was stirred by a painting; she bought it for him. Sibyl admired a lapis lazuli necklace in a shop window; she made herself a present of it. Driving through

Sussex one green and gold May morning they caught sight of a rippling tile roof and twisted chimney stacks crouched behind whispering banks of chestnut and cherry trees. Three weeks later Powdermill Farm was theirs.

Their intention was never to farm; the land was let. Powdermill was to be a retreat from London for Hugh and Sibyl, a place for weekends and holidays which they could fill with their bohemian, socialist, artistically inclined friends. But weekends began to stretch to include Mondays and Fridays, and holidays sprawled beyond their allotted span. When war broke out they gave up the London flat. Sibyl immersed herself in country life with an ease that would have surprised her husband had he not long since ceased to be surprised by the natural, fluid transitions she made from one state of living to another. She kept poultry, grew vegetables, sewed blackout curtains, and accepted his decision to abandon his pacifist creed with graceful concern. Once he had joined up, his long absences left Sibyl alone in the house for much of the time. There was a housekeeper and a gardener, but they lived in a neighbouring cottage, and war made travelling difficult; the endless flow of visiting friends and relations diminished to an irregular trickle. But solitude suited Sibyl. Each time Hugh returned on leave she seemed to him to embody more and more the spirit of the place. When he was at the Front, the image he most often conjured up was of her pale shape in the orchard at twilight, moving noiselessly between the apple trees, beckoning to him to follow and watch young badgers at play. His clumsy feet had crushed some rotten stick or other and the badgers had fled, but the sense of harmony remained, a cool, safe retreat for him to contemplate in the worst of the war.

Leo was born on VE Day. In the midst of labour Sibyl caught the yearning in the midwife's eyes and willed the baby to hurry so she could release the young woman to enjoy the celebratory village bonfire. It worked; everything was over by teatime, Sibyl had her mother with her, and the midwife departed with a spring in her step and a twinge of guilt in her heart. Sibyl, too tired to sleep, held Leo for hours, trying to fathom the expression on the crumpled little face. Night fell; she heard drunken shouts and singing in the lane – like church bells, a pre-war

27

sound. Her son had been born into a new era, she realised, her heart full of hope.

Leo was their first and only child. Sibyl had almost stopped thinking about children when she discovered she was pregnant. Hugh, not yet demobilised, missed the first few weeks of his son's life. When he returned he found Sibyl, her mother and the nursemaid drinking tea on the lawn under the mulberry tree; the baby in its wicker basket waved its limbs in gentle rhythm, like a strange life form on the ocean bed. The sense of completeness that emanated from the group was almost tangible; it occurred to Hugh with revelatory force that he would never again have pride of place in his wife's heart.

The pattern of post-war life soon established itself. Hugh wrote, Sibyl ran the house and garden. The war seemed to have demonstrated that housemaids and cooks were no longer necessary or even attainable, but Mr and Mrs Avan in the cottage continued as cleaner and gardener and the Antrobuses employed a nanny for Leo. Old friends came to stay again; Sibyl's mother, newly widowed, became a permanent fixture. Hugh and Sibyl talked idly of a return to London, but there was no real question of it. Sibyl's tall figure thickened, her golden hair faded, but she glided through her domain with an air of authority and contentment. Her's was a dignified and placid middle age.

Hugh died, quite suddenly, when Leo was twelve. Leo, who had spent his childhood twisting everybody round his little finger, had been about to go to boarding school, to a progressive, liberal-minded establishment housed in a Jacobean mansion in the West Country where eurythmics and pottery and self-expression were encouraged and Latin and physics and obedience to one's elders were left to the individual conscience. Sibyl, bewildered by her unexpected widowhood, could make no decisions about her son's future, so he made his own. He flirted briefly with the idea of staying at home and looking after his mother and grandmother, but the boarding school had its own fully equipped stage and green room, and Leo was stage-struck. The school had no uniform; he packed his own trunk, vaguely supervised by his grandmother. He survived the first half of his first term with only one pair of socks, sustained by fourteen of the novels of G. A. Henty, which he brought from home with a plan of rewriting them for the stage. He never got much further than the cast lists.

Despite the socks, Leo was immediately popular at school. He could act, he could sing, he was a skilful mimic; the school kept organised sports to a minimum, but Leo cut a graceful figure on the running track or on horseback. From fourteen or fifteen he started filling Powdermill Farm with his friends every holiday, their wise-cracking, larky adolescent energy bursting in on the quiet female world of his mother and ailing grandmother. 'Leo could do anything if he puts his mind to it,' said his final school report, and both Leo and Sibyl tended to behave as though putative successes had already been attained. He was at Oxford briefly, but left after failing to turn up for Prelims. He moved to London, sleeping on friends' floors, working in bars or restaurants, eventually charming his way into spear-carrying roles at the Old Vic.

And then, on the night of his twenty-first birthday, Leo met Martha O'Hare.

# CHAPTER SIX

'Hello, mermaid.' Nick always had his jacket off the minute he was through the door. 'Rob rang me at work. He wants to try out some sushi bar tonight, somewhere in Soho. Anna will be there. I said we'd go along.' He tugged off his tie and undid his top button. 'That's better. He said eight o'clock, so I'll just have a shower and . . .' He caught sight of Jess's face, puffy and somehow fearful. 'Hey, what's up? You haven't been frightening yourself about the baby again, have you?' His tone was one of affectionate impatience.

Jess shook her head, and handed him her mother's letter. All day long she'd been rehearsing ways of broaching the news and had come up with nothing better. She retreated into the kitchen while he read it and poured him a drink.

'I can't say I'm entirely surprised,' he said, throwing the letter on to the sofa and accepting the proffered glass. 'I mean, your father's weak, but even he couldn't be expected to put up with that amount of hen-pecking for ever.'

Jess said nothing. She folded the letter and slid it back into the envelope. A little involuntary shudder ran through her body. 'A goose walking over your grave', Ganna called it.

'But hey, mermaid, come here.' Nick put down the drink and opened his arms. Jess stepped into his embrace. There was nowhere else to go. He nuzzled his face in her hair. 'What a bastard, to do it just before you had the baby. Poor darling. Go on, cry if you want.'

Jess didn't cry. She clung on to him, hiding her face, squeezing succour out of the physical manifestation of comfort, trying to forget his cold words. Nick swung her gently from side to side, making a crooning noise. Over her head, he glanced at his watch.

'I guess you won't feel like eating out tonight, my poor little one?' He released her, holding her shoulders.

'Oh Nick, I couldn't.'

30

'Do you mind if I go? It's too late to reach Rob now. I don't want to let him down.'

Jess looked away. 'It's OK,' she whispered, 'I've got to ring Ma. I'd rather be alone.'

'Good girl.' Nick smacked a kiss on to her forehead. 'I'd better take that shower. I wonder if your mother will be pushed for cash now? Let her know we'll help out if necessary, won't you?'

In fifteen minutes he was gone, and Jess was left to derive what comfort she could from his generous offer.

The removal vans had been and gone; the Chandlers' goods were all installed. From behind a tangle of elder bushes, their black fruit glistening like little eyes, Finian had watched. With Tony Chandler barking orders, it hadn't taken long for the removal men to sort it all out. Now it was Saturday, and Finian's eavesdropping had told him that they were returning today, just for one night. Finian was starting school again on Monday. It seemed fitting that his farewell to the barn and to the summer should come together in this way.

Both his sisters were in the house. They'd only arrived the evening before, but Finian had already had enough of them. It was funny how much more he enjoyed seeing them separately. This time, they'd descended with some misplaced notion of supporting their mother – Lila had said so, in so many words – an idea Finian found silly and embarrassing. Nick had come too, of course. Finian didn't mind Nick – they usually kept a respectful distance from each other – but he didn't like having a stranger listening to discussions about his family life. And Nick still was a stranger, even after a year. It was as if he'd chosen to be.

So Finian left the women slumped round the kitchen table, cradling endlessly refilled mugs of tea, and slipped out to spy on the barn-dwellers again. The weather had changed; it wasn't cold, but the even grey cloud turned the sky into a giant saucepan lid, pressing down. It was the kind of still, lightless day that both muffled and magnified sound.

Car doors creaked and slammed. The Chandlers were un-loading the Mercedes. Tony Chandler told the blonde woman

31

not to carry anything too heavy; she simpered idiotically in response. Then the door of the hatchback was flung open, and out bounded, to Finian's surprise, a dog. It was quite large, tan and black with a thick ruff, and a lot of energy to shake off. Finian guessed it was mainly sheepdog, with perhaps a little Alsatian in it somewhere. He had to admit it was a pretty cool dog.

It leapt at Pippa and puts its paws up on her white trousers. White trousers – for God's sake! They made her bum look big, too. She expressed dismay. Tony opened the car door and bellowed, 'James! Come and keep your animal under control.'

A boy, smaller than Finian, but probably about the same age, disengaged himself slowly from his seatbelt and pulled off his headset. 'Samson,' he called, and the dog bounded to his side.

Finian had heard there was a son, of course. He'd been down to look at the barn once or twice, according to Ray, but Finian had never seen him before. He was very brown, and skinny; he had sleek black hair and he looked younger than he probably was, not just because he was small but because he had big dark eyes and a narrow, pointed face. He ran his hand over and over the dog's head, playing confidently with its ears and muzzle. Finian thought he didn't look too bad.

The blonde woman – Pippa – said something about preparing lunch. 'I'll just take Samson for a walk, then,' said the boy. 'He needs some exercise.' He was told to be back by one, to which he grunted surly assent.

Finian watched him cross the Home Patch and open the gate into the Thirteen Acre. He raced back to the stable and released Linford, his own dog, a wiry-haired lurcher now somewhat stiff in the joints. He had been named after Linford Christie and indeed he had one been a very fast runner, but his zest for life had dwindled with the onset of arthritis, and Finian now felt a little shy about his name. 'Come on, Linford! Rabbits!' he lied. Linford displayed a vestigial enthusiasm, and they both set off across the fields.

'What are you going to do about money, Ma?' Eliza asked.

Martha snorted. 'Save it, if anything. You didn't imagine your father had been contributing anything to the exchequer lately,

32

did you? With him gone it's just one less mouth to feed, as Bella put it.'

'Did she really say that? I thought she liked Dad.'

'Apparently not. Bella's mad, but she's not daft.'

Martha's bitterness frightened Jess. She cast about for some means of assistance within her power, and took up her sister's theme. 'But about money, Ma. I mean, what are you living off? Nick said we could help. We've got lots – at least, I think we have.'

'It's all right, poppet. We've got what I earn from the college, and Ganna's pension, and Bella's living allowance. And I get something for looking after her. Oh, and Fin still qualifies for child benefit. It's not much, but . . .'

Eliza frowned. 'It's not ideal, all this living off the state.'

Martha was aware that she tended to favour her younger daughter, and whenever she saw the two of them together she vowed to rectify this. But really Lila's remark was, at best, unhelpful. Her tone was clipped as she replied, 'No, it's not ideal. But then, not much in this particular situation is.'

'Wouldn't it be better – fairer,' Eliza persisted, 'if you were to take some money from Nick and Jess, in lieu of some of your handouts? I mean, Jess has offered.'

Martha smiled, a little grimly. 'I know. And it's sweet of her – and of Nick, of course. But Jess will find that the baby and the new house will absorb an alarming amount of money. And anyway, Lila, Robin Hood economics are not the solution to the problem. As I said, money isn't really an issue. There's no reason why we shouldn't go on managing.'

'I was only trying to be helpful.' Eliza was stung. 'And what would be the solution to the problem, then?'

'It remains to be seen,' said Martha, 'how much of a problem there really is. I can hear Ganna's bell. She'll want me to take her to the lavatory.' She rose to her feet.

'I'll do it,' said Eliza. She had come down to help; finding ways of doing so was harder than she'd imagined.

'Thanks,' said her mother, 'but I don't think she'll let you. She's really – changing – quite quickly now.'

'Since Dad left? She's got worse since then?'

'Well, yes. Even though it's only a few days, yes, I think so.' Martha made for the door. 'Coming, Sibyl!'

33

Eliza took the mugs to the sink. 'Selfish bastard,' she said, half to herself.

'Do you know,' said Jess, 'I've only just realised that I hate him?'

'I don't think you do,' replied Eliza. 'I don't think you know how to hate anyone.' She turned on the taps full blast as she spoke. She wasn't sure whether Jess had heard what she said. Certainly, there was no reply.

On 8 May 1966 Leo met Martha O'Hare in an Irish pub in Kilburn. She was there for her bearded boyfriend, who was employed to play the fiddle. She had pale red hair and clear blue eyes and she was drinking Guinness and smoking Capstan Full Strength; she was nothing like the doe-eyed dolly birds with whom Leo had consorted so far. She was an art student, and shared a flat with a girlfriend in Camden Town; Leo moved in, and the bearded Irishman disappeared without trace. They spent the summer getting drunk and sharing dreams. In August he took her home to Powdermill. She was pregnant before Christmas, but it didn't matter; there was no way, he told her, that he could ever marry anyone else.

The Camden flat didn't even have a bathroom, let alone space for a baby. Leo was between jobs, and money was scarce. Martha's youthful optimism began to sag. 'Let's move to Powdermill,' Leo suggested. 'Mother adores you. She can help you to look after the baby. She's been lonely since Granny died.'

'And you?' said Martha. 'What'll you do? There won't be anywhere to act, in deepest Sussex.'

'I'll write,' said Leo. 'I'm sick of the theatre. It's such a shallow world.'

'But what will your mother say? She might not want us.'

Leo looked at her in surprise. 'Oh yes, she will,' he said. 'All she wants is for me to be happy.'

'And that's all I want, too.' Martha, beaming, embraced him. 'So we can't go far wrong.' Martha was an orphan; the prospect of Sibyl's supportive attention was attractive to her. As for the art degree – well, she could always pick that up again, some time. In any case, since meeting Leo she'd let it slide.

Leo was right about his mother's response. Sibyl accepted the

34

new order with perfect equanimity. Martha carried with her an air of timelessness and self-reliance that Sibyl admired. She was so different from the nervy, skinny little girls Leo had favoured in the past. Martha had spent her childhood in rural Ireland. She soon adjusted to the slow pace of life at Powdermill and established her own quiet routines there, separate from but compatible with Sibyl's.

Martha and Leo were married in January 1967, quickly and privately at a London registry office. They celebrated with oysters and Black Velvet and a handful of friends; a big party was planned for the future but somehow it never materialised. As Martha's pregnancy progressed so her desire for activity of any description diminished. Not that she was lazy. She always pulled her weight, and more, in the running of the house. But the urge to socialise, to be daring, to experiment, quite left her; as she sat in the sun cutting out baby clothes or knitting or simply dreaming, she seemed older than her twenty-two years. Her docility would have made Leo impatient, except that she never seemed to mind what he did. Often he'd spend the night in London after an evening's carousing, knowing that back in Sussex Martha and Sibyl were together, safe and content.

And he did write, too. Sibyl paid for everything at first, of course, but it wasn't so very long before Leo started to earn. He wrote scripts for radio and later for television; he had a knack, and he prospered. His gift for friendship, or at least for entranced acquaintanceship, provided him with the openings he needed, and at first he used them to good advantage. Offers of work flooded in. Martha and Sibyl, tending the infant Eliza and keeping a cheerful, comfortable home for Leo, were pleased and proud.

Eliza took her parents rather by surprise. She was a pale, thin, judgmental child, cautious and precocious. Martha wanted her to paint, model clay, make mud pies in the garden, but Eliza disliked getting her hands dirty. She followed her mother about her daily tasks, always holding the hem of Martha's voluminous skirts; she was nervous of the geese and ducks and hens that Martha had taken to raising. The collie dog, too, with its grin and its sudden bark, unnerved her. She preferred the cats, their quiet, deft little movements, the neatness of their tucked-in paws. When Leo played tickling games with her or tossed her in the air and caught her, Eliza would squeal and giggle, but when he had finished she would smooth down her frock and admonish him gravely: 'Silly Daddy, that's very dangerous. Don't do that.' Her favourite times were when Ganna got down one of Andrew Laing's fairy books, or *Old Peter's Russian Tales*. She loved to sit on a little embroidered footstool, leaning against her grandmother's knee and gazing at the fire, seeing caves and rivers and mountains form and crumble in its shifting black and orange heart as she listened to the familiar fairy tale rhythms.

If Eliza was the rather unlikely by-product of early, heedless passion, Jessamine, three years younger, was the planned, looked-for child of moderate prosperity and confident domestic contentment. Jess, or the idea of Jess, was adored from the moment of conception; perhaps as a result, she was always adorable. There was nothing precocious about Jess. She walked late, talked late, showed no ambition – she had no equivalent to Eliza's infant wail, 'I want to do it by mine self.' She sat, plumply beaming, crowing with pleasure at flowers or kittens or pretty beads, her round little head dancing with flaxen ringlets, her long eyelashes curving delightfully against her peachy cheeks. She was her father's special pet. The demands she made on him were only of the most direct, physical kind. He could satisfy her so easily with a hug or a tickle or a pretty trinket. And as the years went by Leo found it harder to satisfy anyone else. He became careless with deadlines, and lost some contracts; as the arrogant charm of youth hardened into a stubborn refusal to tackle his own inefficiency, agents, editors and producers turned away from him in favour of more malleable talents. In London the number of his drinking companions dwindled as families and mortgages laid their claims, and at Powdermill he was confronted by a steadily thickening wall of female disapproval. His mother and his wife, united in their rarely voiced sense of grievance, were joined by Martha's cousin Bella, who came to convalesce after some kind of mental breakdown and who put down roots faster than ground elder. 'What can I do?' said Martha. 'She's got no one else. And it's not as if *you* have to look after her.' In that emphasised *you*, Leo read the implication that poor mad Bella was less of a burden than he was himself, with his failing career and his love of risk-taking. Bella's pale energies could be harnessed to some of the more routine household tasks. At least she tries to earn her keep, said Martha's firm-set jaw, and broad, folded arms. Whereas you . . .

When Martha fell pregnant for the third time, she hardly knew how to tell Leo. She kept the news to herself for two months, almost hoping she would miscarry. For this baby had been con-ceived in a forced reconciliation following an ugly row, and Martha felt that it carried no one's blessing. She felt sick, too, sicker than before; in the dun-coloured winter dawns, trudging out to the hen-houses carrying her slop bucket, with the sickness forcing prickles of sweat on to her brow, she felt old, used up, dead to colour and life and joy and pain. The first two babies had glowed inside her; this one hollowed her out. But it clung on; there was no miscarriage, and now way of avoiding the subject with Leo for ever.

He was pleased – surprisingly pleased. His writing might have ground to a halt, but here was something he had achieved. He was good at making babies, he thought, beaming fondly at Eliza and Jess, so graspable in their corduroy smocks and woolly tights. His enthusiasm encouraged Martha. The sickness began to ease; she picked through the drawers of baby clothes and tried to think about the future. Sibyl and Bella were excited, and little Lila prattled endlessly about the new sister, who, she insisted, was to be called Rosebud – Rosebud Mattel, because that was the name stamped in raised letters across the back of the neck of her large plastic baby doll. Leo, as the provider of the excite-ment, found himself reinstated at the warm centre of their female circle, and as his frozen talent thawed he began to write again. He rediscovered his boyhood passion and adapted a rol-licking Henty adventure for the BBC. It was perfect family viewing for Sunday teatime. Commissions flowed once more. Martha did her best to suppress her sense that this pregnancy wasn't right, but the private, exultant, internal dialogue she had experienced so strongly with the other two babies was missing. People expected her to hope for a son, but she failed to envisage a boy – failed to envisage anything. When she tried to think about the baby, she never got beyond the birth.

37

It was another girl, born a month early after the most difficult of the three labours. That there was some damage was obvious from the start, because the baby wouldn't suck. But it wasn't until six months later – six months during which, Martha felt, she had done nothing at all but struggle to insert milk into this floppy, unfocusing bundle – that the realisation broke over her in a cold wave that things would never be very different. Clare Antrobus would grow larger and heavier and harder to handle, but her consciousness would never develop beyond that of the swaddled, cradle-bound infant, vaguely watching the shifting shadows.

Martha had read of mothers who fought like tigers for their handicapped children, endlessly seeking out therapies and stimuli and special equipment, but she found no such such instinct in herself. Her inclination was to let Clare be. She washed her and fed her with infinite care – with far more attention to detail than Eliza or Jess had ever received. She dressed her snugly and propped her where she could see moving leaves or a bright fire. She sang to Clare when she bathed her, and sometimes she held a pinch of lavender or a crushed bayleaf under her nose, but she could never tell whether the flickering grimaces that wrinkled the child's countenance were a reaction to what she heard or saw or smelt or merely a meaningless and involuntary twitching of the facial muscles.

Martha never doubted that she loved her silent, sprawling daughter, but she recognised her love as akin to that which, as a child, she had felt for a bald and limbless doll, the vulnerability of whose grimy pink torso used to make her ache with pity. She knew that Clare did not know her, would never know her. She rejected all cheery, supportive remarks from friends and relations who thought that they detected smiles or tiny movements towards sound or light. And what she never told anyone, what she never dared investigate properly herself, was a superstitious belief that Clare's condition was the result of the love lost between herself and Leo.

As for Leo, he avoided Clare. She looked very much like Jess, except that her hair was properly red, and it broke his heart to see Jess' beauty stretched and blurred on Clare's empty face. He felt that the likeness insulted, invalidated Jess. The older girls liked to have Clare propped between them on the sofa while they watched television. Leo hated to see her lolling head, a monstrous puppet with its orange woolly curls, so like and yet so unlike the other two with their shining alertness. He tried to compensate for his neglect by doing more for the older girls, sparing Martha some of the heavier tasks, keeping the money supply going, but when he turned away from Clare in pity and distaste, Martha watched him with cold eyes. He was shut out of her heart, and he knew it.

When Clare was two, an American film company bought the rights to one of Leo's scripts, and a big-budget production was talked of. Leo insisted on celebrating by taking Martha on holiday. A recent, secret, brief affair had turned sour; remorse and a sense of panic at the way his stock was falling with his wife led him to book two weeks in a hotel in Venice. Sibyl was to supervise Bella, a nurse was hired to look after Eliza and Jess and Clare, and a neighbouring farmer's wife was to minister to Martha's poultry. On the eighth day of their holiday, Leo and Martha, drinking grappa and espresso on the hotel terrace, were interrupted by a waiter; there was a telephone call. Martha drained her glass slowly, didn't hurry to her feet. She knew that these were her last moments of freedom, freedom from the woeful guilt that would hold her in thrall for the rest of her life.

It probably wasn't anyone's fault. It could have been the nurse's fault; Clare choked alone in the garden while she popped in to answer a ringing telephone. But the nurse had not left her with food in her mouth. Clare choked on her vomit, as the inquest confirmed. Leo said, half-heartedly, that it was his fault – 'I should have insisted we got two nurses. Then there'd have been no need for her ever to have been left alone.' Martha hardly listened. Her brain was trapped, chained to the treadmill of 'if only . . .' with no prospect of release.

Martha's depression, which lasted for at least five years, was of the invisible kind. She went about her daily tasks, she was civil to people around her, she showed affection towards her daughters. Leo found her easier to live with, now. There was no nagging, no reproach. There was a bedrock of indifference, though, and he, accordingly, lived his emotional life elsewhere. One of his affairs threatened to turn into something serious, but he looked at his wife's stately solidity as she doled out bread and butter to the girls in the low-lit kitchen, and he looked at his mother, sitting in the rocking chair reading aloud to them from *The Jungle Book* as they ate, and he thought that passionate excitement was a poor exchange for such permanence. So he stayed, and they never knew how nearly they'd lost him.

Finian was an accident. He was born seven years after Clare's death, when Martha was thirty-seven – absurdly old, as she smilingly told people, to make a mistake like that. Eliza, aged fifteen, found this evidence of the continuing carnality of her parents shocking and repulsive; it wasn't until Fin was toddling after her, calling, 'Li-li come,' that she felt able to take much interest. Jess, twelve when he was born, doted on him, and he on her. 'I'm going to get married and have babies as soon as I can!' she announced, her forefinger locked in his tenacious new-born grip. Eliza, who was reading Simone de Beauvoir, snorted. Martha said, mildly, 'I hope not, darling. It's not really such a good idea.' Jess asked, 'Why not? You did. Wasn't having Lila a good idea?' and Martha was about to explain that it hadn't really been an idea as such at all when Leo flung the door open, ushering in friends whom he'd brought to admire his tiny son, and the conversation got no further. But Eliza remembered it, and pondered its implications many times.

The advent of Finian brought about a renaissance of family unity, but it didn't last long. For by now Leo had found a temptation more potent than drink, than women even. I thought we'd weathered all the storms, Martha was to think bitterly in later years. How could I have foreseen that a man in his late thirties would be bitten by the gambling bug? Martha knew about gambling; her long-ago Irish childhood had been overshadowed by it. How had she failed to notice the symptoms in her own husband? But the chrysalis of depression that had spun itself round her after Clare's death, and from which she had only partly emerged, prevented her from noticing such things.

It was cards, mainly, in expensive London clubs, but virtually anything would do. Horses, dogs, general elections – she found him putting a bet on the outcome of the Eurovision Song Contest, once, and he'd only just been able to see that it was funny. There wasn't much else to be amused about. By the time

Finian entered his teens Leo had sold the farm, the silver, a couple of Paul Nash paintings that had been Sibyl's pride and joy.
The barn was the last thing to be sold. After that, it was Leo
himself who went.

Linford and Samson met before Jamie and Finian did. Jamie
had got as far as the pond, shaped like a fat heart and overhung
by oaks and sycamores, that lay in the middle of Church
Pasture. Samson had dashed in, and was struggling to swim in
the thick brown water; Jamie stood on the edge, absently stripping a bush of its blackberries. Linford bounded up to the pond.
He hated water, but he was fascinated by the sight of Samson,
who whooshed out to meet him, casting off slimy weed and
soggy leaves as he did so. The two dogs instantly became entangled. Samson was by far the heavier and stronger. Jamie pulled
him off, and looked up to see Finian striding towards him.

'Is he yours?' asked Finian, without introduction. 'Has he got
Alsatian in him?'

'Yes. A quarter.'

'Thought so. He's strong, isn't he?'

'Yeah, really strong. He pulled my dad through a hedge once.
But he's calmed down a lot now. What's yours?'

'Mainly greyhound, with some deerhound. That's why he's
so tall. He's a lurcher – that's what you call a greyhound cross.'

'I know. What's your name?'

'Fin.'

'I'm Jac.'

'Oh? I thought you were called James.'

Jamie turned his head, pretending to watch the dogs. He
hoped he wasn't blushing. With his dark-olive skin he didn't
blush easily, thank goodness.

'That's just what my dad calls me. I'm Jac, really. How did
you know who I am?'

'I was watching your mum and dad unload the car.'

'That's not my mum!' Jamie said hotly.

'Oh.' Fin didn't seem interested. 'I live in the farmhouse. It
used to be our barn.'

Jamie looked at him sharply but there didn't seem to be any
rancour in his voice. 'Is your father a farmer, then?'

41

Finian snorted. 'My father's a gambler. But he's not around any more. Have you gone back to school yet?'

'Yeah. Last Wednesday.'

'Mine starts on Monday.'

'Oh.'

A silence fell between them, but it felt companionable. Finian pulled off a couple of blackberries and ate them. 'Will you be here for Bonfire Night?' he asked.

'I don't know. When is it?'

'November the fifth, of course. They have a massive bonfire in town and people chuck bangers and things. It's brilliant. You can come with us if you like.'

'OK,' said Jamie, 'cheers.' He knew he had to be back by one, and it was almost one now, but he didn't want Fin to see that he was obeying someone who wasn't even his mother. 'Here, Samson,' he called, 'better get you cleaned up.'

'I'm going on,' said Finian, setting off. 'See you around.'

'See you.'

The bleak, empty ache that had settled inside Jamie on the journey down had lifted. Fin wasn't at all like the boys at school, but he was none the worse for that. As Jamie trudged back to the barn he wondered whether Fin meant what he'd said about Bonfire Night. He had a feeling that he probably did.

# CHAPTER SEVEN

Martha scraped leftover porridge into an old Tupperware box and threw toast crusts in on top. She looked in the fridge to see if there was anything else the hens might relish, and found a half-empty tin of spaghetti hoops. The hoops, congealing in their orange sauce, made a cold, glopping sound as they slid into the plastic box. Nick Gascoigne glanced at what his mother-in-law was doing and quickly looked away again, shaking out the news section of the Sunday paper in front of his face.

'Are you going to feed the birds, Ma?' asked Jess. 'I'll come too. Can I borrow your Wellies?'

'I'm afraid not, darling. I haven't got any.'

'Why on earth not?'

'They were in the green car that Daddy took.'

'And he didn't even leave you your Wellingtons?'

'He wouldn't have thought about it. It was what you might call the heat of the moment.'

'Well, you won't see those again. You'd better buy some new ones.'

'Oh, these'll do.' Martha indicated the ancient plimsolls she was wearing.

'Don't be daft, Ma. You live in boots.'

'They're expensive, Jess. Fin needs new shoes for school this week. I'll wait till the weather gets worse. These are fine for now, really.'

Jess dropped the subject. By the back door her mother handed her a bucket of grain, and she followed her, picking her way in her soft leather sandals through the detritus of the back yard where a dozen or more coops, hutches and flights leaned shakily against each other. Underfoot was cracked bare earth, speckled with bird droppings; nothing green stood a chance, though some resilient bushes – holly, elder, dogrose, bramble – provided shade, or perches. The yard looked like a miniature twelfth-century village; when Martha flung open the doors of the coops it was instantly filled with noisy citizens, chattering, quarrelling, bargaining, as the contents of the grain bucket were scattered.

The soft, heaving mass of poultry that had instantly formed round Martha gradually dispersed. Jess admired the birds with an artist's eye. She noticed the way the cocks' combs glowed when the sun caught them, as bright as cocktail cherries; she took in the neat, embroidered detail of the bantams' neck feathers, the deep icing-sugar white of the doves' breasts. Martha shook out her leftovers under the questing beaks of half a dozen ducks with bottle green heads and smooth caramel bodies. A peacock and his consort, tailless now at the end of the summer but with some dignity left in the poise of their iridescent necks, eyed the spaghetti hoops with interest; the ducks moved aside in deference.

Martha collected the various receptacles strewn about the place – oval pie dishes, rusty baking tins, plastic ice cream cartons – and filled them from the tap in the corner of the yard. Jess leaned against the stable door, enjoying the rough, sun-warmed wood. 'Do you remember when Fin was little?' she said. 'How he used to shout "Heli-copters!" when the doves whirred their wings?'

Martha smiled. 'I bet you don't remember what a job I had when *you* were tiny, keeping you from eating the hens' food. You always had your hands in the grain sacks.'

The air was full of the pulse of bird sounds. Coos and clucks and quacks and the peacocks' soft 'pok' – no screeching at this time of year – drifted in and out of each other in warm currents. For Jess, these sounds formed the very fabric of childhood. 'Ma,' she asked suddenly, 'how do you know when you're about to go into labour?'

'It takes people different ways,' replied her mother. 'I started nesting like mad.'

'Nesting?'

'Yes; tidying cupboards and airing blankets in a compulsive sort of way. You know the way the cats look into everything when they're about to produce? With one of the babies – you, I think – I insisted on making the most colossal fruit cake, and then things really got going and it was found in the Aga a couple of days later, looking like something dug up at Pompeii.'

'Well, I haven't done anything like that, so it can't be.'

'Why? Do you think – ?'

'I felt strange in the night – restless.'

'Worried?'

'Yes, but only about unimportant things. Like whether it was time to renew our resident's parking permit.'

'Oh yes, I remember. One time I became obsessed by some overdue library books – I went on talking about them through labour, apparently. I think that was when I had –' Martha stopped herself. 'Any other symptoms, Jess? Is the head engaged?'

'I don't know. I don't think so.'

'You would know if it was. Like sitting on a coconut. But it doesn't always happen. You're not due yet, though. I thought it was another week.'

'It is. But –'

'And first babies are usually late.'

'I know. But – oh, *Ma*!'

The change in her daughter's voice had Martha by her side in an instant. 'What is it, darling?'

'I can feel – it's warm. I'm bleeding. I must be haemorrhaging. Oh, Ma, *help*.'

'Nonsense, Jessie. You're not bleeding. Your waters have broken. That means it's on the way.'

'What – just like that? My waters broke just like that?'

'Any why not? Come on, love. Let's get you indoors, and I'll ring the hospital. No need to panic. It'll be a while yet. Are you all right to walk? Lean on me.'

'Wait, Ma, wait. I think I'm going to be sick.'

Eliza sat by the telephone, trying to read. She was surprised to find how much she minded about this baby. Her feelings about her sister had always been, to say the least, mixed; Jess' dreaminess, her unspoken assumption that other people would take care of her, her unshaken faith in her own lovableness, all produced a sense of frustration in the precise, independent, unsentimental Eliza. Being a fair-minded woman, Eliza had of course asked herself whether Jess' prettiness underlay the exasperation she could provoke, but she was almost sure she'd gone beyond that. As a child, yes, certainly she'd minded. She remembered her father taking them to London for a treat, and a woman on the train leaning forward and saying, 'What a lovely face your younger daughter's got'; even now she could call to mind the pink face powder stuck in the pores of that woman's nose, and the tortoiseshell buttons of her bouclé suit – she still felt an aversion towards buttons of that kind. But even at that stage, she thought, her resentment was against the woman, and perhaps against her father for not qualifying the remark in any way; it had not been directed against Jess. At a tender age Eliza had prided herself on her rational mind; she had always acknowledged that the cloud-shaped hair, the pale-gold skin and sea-grey eyes were not Jess' fault. No, what galled her adult self was the way Jess' appearance made her so passive. It was as if her looks made her decisions for her.

'They're chalk and cheese'; that peculiar expression had often been applied to the Antrobus girls in childhood. It was true that to all appearances Eliza the reserved academic and Jess the sensitive artist had little in common. But despite this, despite everything and anything, now that Jess was in labour Eliza couldn't concentrate on her newspaper, nor could she move away from the telephone.

A car came up the track that led to the farmhouse; Eliza could hear it jolting over the ruts, and the faint throb of music. She hurried to the door. Nick's car! It must be all over, then. She flung open the door in welcome.

Nick switched off the stereo and pressed the button to close the electric windows. He was the only visitor to the Antrobus house who always locked his car. Eliza scanned him for signs of excitement or relief, but found none. He moved his tall, lean body in its pale-blue linen shirt and light flannel trousers as casually as ever, and his dark, bony face was immobile. When he saw Eliza he smiled his usual smile of social acknowledgement.

'Well?' demanded Eliza.

'No news,' he said. 'Everything's fine. But it'll be a while yet.'

Eliza stepped aside to let him pass. 'Have you come back to fetch things for Jess?' she asked. They had left that morning in rather a hurry.

Nick stared. 'No,' he replied coolly. 'She's got what she needs.'

'Doesn't she need you?' Behind her glasses Eliza's eyes flashed.

'She'll be all right,' said Nick. 'I've got some work to do as it looks as though I won't be in the office tomorrow. Not in the morning, at any rate.' He moved towards the stairs.

Eliza ground her teeth. She knew her mother would be in the garden, reading to Ganna. On fine days Ganna sat outside under the mulberry tree with a rug over her knees. Bella often joined her, equipped with a little knife to dig weeds out of the lawn. Martha read to them; they were currently working their way through Mrs Gaskell. Martha laid *Mary Barton* aside as soon as Eliza stepped through the French window. She was tingling for news.

Eliza shook her head in answer to the unasked question. 'Ma,' she said, 'Nick's come back from the hospital. But there's still a long time to go. He's come back' – she was almost spitting – 'he's come back to do some *work*.'

Sibyl, in the wicker chair, clicked her tongue. Bella made no sound, but dug fiercely at a dandelion root. Martha said, 'Well, it's their business I suppose,' but her voice was heavy with disappointment.

'I'm going,' said Eliza. 'She shouldn't be left alone. She's not even in the hospital she thought she'd be in. She just shouldn't be on her own.'

'That's a good idea, Lila. Ring us if – just ring us, won't you? Have you got coins for the telephone? I'll be indoors from now on. Fin can shut up the animals. Oh, and Lila – take these.' Martha broke off an armful of Michaelmas daisies. 'They're not very special, but there's not much else at this time of year.'

Sibyl stood up and folded her rug with shaking hands. 'I don't approve of fathers being there at all,' she remarked, to Bella. 'But if he's started something, then he should see it through.'

Upstairs, in the room Jess and Eliza had shared in childhood which was now the main guest room, Nick stared out at the garden, drumming his fingertips on the windowsill. This house was so bloody uncomfortable. If he sat downstairs he would be pestered by Jess' lunatic relations, but in this room there was nothing to sit on, except the high iron single bedsteads pushed together to look like a double, or the old cabin trunk in the corner that housed the sisters' soft toy collection, lovingly preserved in mothballs. When Jess had first shown him the teddy bears, rabbits and rag dolls, and named each one to him, he had found it enchanting; now, a year later, he thought it idiotic.

He laid his briefcase on one of the beds and took out his mobile telephone. He had no intention of adding to his mother-in-law's burdens by increasing the size of her phone bill. During the six hours he'd spent with Jess at the hospital she had constantly reverted, between contractions, to the need to buy Martha a new pair of Wellingtons. 'Hard-wearing ones – Dunlop, probably – size seven. She likes them a little too big so she can wear thick socks. You won't forget, will you, Nick?' And however much he had assured her that he'd look for them in Broadhurst tomorrow, she couldn't seem to shut up about it.

Nick, diary and telephone to hand, sat down on the edge of the bed. The counterpane gave off a puff of dust. Nick thought, I'll give myself an hour and a half, and then I'll go back. I was just in the way, anyway. He opened the diary.

'But I'm her sister!' protested Eliza. 'And she's on her own. You've got to let me in.'

'I'm sorry, but we can only allow admittance to designated birth partners. And your name is not mentioned in Mrs Gascoigne's notes, which have been faxed down from London.'

'No, it wouldn't be.' Eliza changed tack. 'You see, there's been an – emergency. Nick – the baby's father – has been called away urgently, and he specifically asked me to take his place. I know that you have to be terribly vigilant about security; I do understand that. But please, won't you just ask my sister about it?'

The nurse looked Eliza up and down. She had a young child herself; she remembered how unbearable it was during labour to have the least of one's wishes thwarted. 'I'll make enquiries,' she said, 'but I must ask you to remain right here in reception. Please don't move.' She glanced meaningfully in the direction of the security camera.

'Thank you very much indeed.' Eliza's frank and heartfelt manner told in her favour. She sat holding a copy of *Woman's Realm* with all the money-off coupons cut out, trying her best not to look like a baby thief.

The nurse returned, her face considerably relaxed. 'Your sister says she'd like you to be there,' she said. 'And I've cleared it with the powers that be. She's almost fully dilated; won't be long now. This way, please.'

The delivery room was in the basement; there was no natural light at all. Jess was half sitting, half lying on a high, narrow couch, propped up by vast pillows. She was naked except for a white T-shirt. Her hair was darkened with sweat but her teeth were chattering.

'Jess, you're cold! Can't they get you a blanket?'

'I'm not really cold, it's just my feet. I wish I had some socks.'

'Have mine. They're fairly clean, I think.' Eliza pulled them off and rolled them on to Jess' feet, which were puffy and mottled purple. 'Shall I do something about your hair?' she asked.

'Oh, yes – please. Only don't sit on the bed. The midwife sat down next to me and the jolt was agony.'

Eliza smoothed back the tangled mass as best she could, and was about to look in Jess' bag for something to tie it up with, when a shriek from the bed made her jump.

'It's just terrible,' said Jess when the contraction had finished. 'I'm never having another one.'

'Haven't you got any pain relief? What about that oxygen thing?'

'That gas-and-air stuff? Doesn't make much difference. Oh shit – here it comes again. Don't talk – don't touch me.' Jess' groan was followed by convulsive retching. Eliza saw a kidney dish by the bed and held it under her sister's mouth to catch the thin dribble of bile. She found a tissue and dabbed at her chin, as gently as she could.

'Nobody told me,' said Jess when the crisis had passed. 'Nobody ever told me that I was going to throw up all the way through.' Her face was white, clown-like, with red circles round each eye. 'Oh, Lila, I'm glad you're here.'

The midwife came in. 'Time to have a little look, dear.' She glared at Eliza. 'Could you move, please? I need to give Mum an internal.' She rolled on slippery clear gloves.

'Not another internal – please. That's the worst thing,' Jess wailed.

'Shan't be a moment, dear. We need to find our where baby's got to.'

Eliza turned away as the rubber hands delved. She busied herself looking for a receptacle for the Michaelmas daisies. Fat tears slid from under Jess' closed eyelids.

'Goodness, things have come on!' The midwife beamed as she peeled off the gloves. 'Fully dilated, Mum! You're in transition now. I'll tell Mr Price.' She bustled out.

'Jess, you're nearly there!' Eliza dabbed at the wet cheeks. 'You'll see the baby before supper time. The last bit doesn't take long, does it?'

Jess was sobbing weakly. 'I don't care about the baby. I just want it to stop.'

Eliza said, 'There must be something they can give you. For the pain. I'll ask the doctor when he comes in.'

'They said it didn't warrant an epidural. Oh, Lila, my mouth's so dry.'

'I'll get you some water.'

'I'm not allowed it.'

'Just swill it round your mouth and spit it out.' Eliza filled a plastic beaker at the sink.

'No, I'm sorry.' The midwife, returning with the consultant, spoke with triumphant firmness. 'If that water is for Mum, then I have to say no.'

'Nurse, she's very uncomfortable. Just one mouthful can't hurt.'

'Mr Price – ?'

The consultant looked up from his scrutiny of Jess. 'Mm?'

'Could you explain to this lady that the patient is nil by mouth?'

Mr Price looked bored. 'A little water won't hurt,' he said. 'Just a sip.'

Eliza charitably avoided the offended midwife's eye. 'Jess,' she whispered, 'shall I call Nick?'

Jess hesitated for a moment. 'No,' she replied, 'just you.' She craned her head forward. 'Oh, Christ,' she said, 'I can feel it. I can feel it knocking. It wants to get out.' There was wild laughter in her voice.

The next half-hour was a blur of instructions. Another nurse appeared from somewhere, and joined in the exhortations to Jess to push, to breathe out, to hold on, to stop pushing. Jess' eyes were round and terrified, but there was an excitement in the fear. Eliza stood by her head, murmuring encouragement. She felt that to spectate at the lower end would be somehow equivalent to driving very slowly past a motorway pile-up. Then, 'Cut!' called the doctor, like a film director, and the grumpy midwife handed him his instruments. The new nurse said soothingly to Jess, 'The doctor's just going to give you a little episiotomy, to help the baby out. You won't feel a thing.'

'There we are,' said Mr Price, a note of professional satisfaction in his voice, 'the head's out. Want to put your hand down and have a feel?'

'Oh, no, no!' shrieked Jess. 'Lila, tell him I don't want to touch it,' and as Eliza shushed and soothed her, Jess' body was shaken by one more heave, and the baby seemed to leap into the doctor's hands. Time stood still for Eliza as she stared at the lithe, filthy monkey shape; she thought its purple head had been crushed. Then she heard a noise like a Siamese cat and the doctor chuckled and said, 'Nothing wrong with you, young feller,' and placed the creature on Jess' huge, billowing stomach.

'It's wriggling!' squealed Jess. 'Oh, Lila, take it off.' But Eliza had caught sight of something petrol blue and twisted and was frozen to the spot. The first midwife laid a white towel over one arm and scooped up the baby, while the other clamped the thick and pulsing horror that Eliza now recognised as the umbilical cord.

'I want him now,' said Jess, struggling to get up. 'I just wasn't ready before. It's a boy, isn't it?'

'It's a beautiful bouncing boy.' The midwife placed the swathed shape carefully in the crook of Jess's arm. The furious dark face rolled blindly from side to side, its tortoise mouth opening and closing.

'He knows his mum,' said the nicer nurse, helpfully. 'Do you want to put him to the breast, dear?'

'Shall I?' Jess almost giggled. She manoeuvred the little head into place. 'My God, Lila, he knows what to do!'

'Isn't nature wonderful,' said Eliza, and they both laughed. Eliza reached out a finger to stroke the sticky top of the baby's head. 'Welcome, nephew,' she said.

'I must ask you to wash your hands,' said the midwife. 'It's all too easy for newborns to pick up infections.'

Things were still happening at the other end of the bed. 'Do you want to see the placenta?' the doctor asked as he stitched.

'Do I?' said Jess to Eliza. Eliza glanced at the enormous brightly coloured pancake. 'I wouldn't have thought so,' she replied doubtfully.

The doctor shrugged. 'Some women do. Now, I've stitched you nice and tight, Mrs – Er. Your husband will be pleased about that. Should heal up nicely; you can take paracetamol if it's uncomfortable.'

Jess was stroking the baby's tiny, corrugated forehead. 'Don't frown,' she was saying. 'Don't frown, little Louis. I'm your mother.'

'Louis!' cooed the amiable nurse. 'Ah! That's nice.'

Eliza wondered whether any choice of name ever elicited any other response. She took her hoard of coins from her bag and went in search of a telephone.

In the corridor she met Nick. He raised his eyebrows.

'Congratulations,' she said with a tight smile. 'You've got a fine son.'

'You mean it's happened? So soon? Why didn't you call me?'

'I was busy,' replied the new aunt drily. 'As were you, I suppose. She's still in the delivery room. I expect they'll let you in.'

'It's happened!' Martha turned to Sibyl from the telephone with shining eyes. 'Sibyl, it's a boy, and she's fine, and everything's fine. Just under seven pounds, and sucking already, apparently.'

'Oh, my dear.' Sibyl leaned on her rubber-tipped stick and rested on the back of one of the hall chairs with the other hand. At the sound of the telephone she had hurried from the parlour, and now her breath rasped a little. 'Oh, my dear Martha, how simply wonderful. I expected a boy, didn't you?'

Finian could be heard at the scullery door, whistling and

kicking his boots off. Martha called to him.

'Wow, I'm an uncle,' he said, trying not to grin too broadly. 'What's his name, then? Did she go for Louis?'

'Yes, so far, though knowing Jess she could change her mind.'

'She'd better not. She was talking about Alexis last night.'

'Alexis is a good name.'

'No it's not, it's poncey. I'm going to make her stick to Louis. Have you told Bells?'

'Not yet. We've only just heard.' Martha gave her son a fleeting hug. 'Will you call her, darling? And put the kettle on while you're about it. I'm absolutely dying for a cup of tea.' She took Sibyl's arm. 'Come and sit in the kitchen with us, won't you, Ganna? Or Great-Ganna, I should say now.'

The old woman patted her daughter-in-law's hand. 'Congratulations, my dear. How lucky that it all happened while Jess was here. I must say it will be simply splendid to have a baby at Powdermill again.'

# CHAPTER EIGHT

Susan Chandler couldn't get out of bed. It was gone eleven and the October sunshine had long since made its way through the chinks in the buttercup-coloured curtains, but Susan turned her head away from the dust motes that spun and glinted in each shaft of light. Dust was dead skin, tiny particles of other people, living and dead. She resented the fact that she was obliged to inhale other people.

Susan set her alarm for half past seven every day. She used an ordinary alarm clock now. Tony had liked the radio alarm, but Susan felt more relaxed without a stranger's voice in her ear pouring out news of other people's misfortunes. She set her alarm so she could get up with Jamie, chat to him over breakfast, make sure he had everything he needed for school, bid him goodbye and good luck for the day. But over the last few weeks this routine had been eroded, little by little. Jamie seemed to prefer getting his own breakfast. He worked his way through cereal variety packs, two little boxes every morning, always avoiding the bran flakes. There was quite a stockpile of bran flakes in the kitchen cupboard. What on earth was she keeping them for?

She still got up to see him off. She came down, long-limbed and bony in her lavender silk dressing gown, made herself a cup of boiled water with a squeeze of lemon in it and asked if he'd got everything – he always just said, 'Yes, Mum.' But as soon as the door had clicked shut behind him she'd retreat back upstairs and lie on the bed with her face to the wall. Sometimes she couldn't even be bothered to pick up the post.

Susan didn't really know why this should be. When it had become obvious that Tony was going to leave her she had decided to rejoice. Her friend Polly had encouraged her to rejoice. 'The marriage has been dead on its feet for years,' Polly told her in her characteristically uncompromising style. 'You're better off without him, Suze. Make the most of it.' And Susan had agreed with her, in principle. She no longer had to put up with Tony's temper, his swaggering need to prove himself, his infidelities, his deceitfulness – though towards the end he had stopped bothering to lie. She no longer had to think about his creature comforts or play the elegant hostess for the benefit of his business associates. She could build up her own career – she'd done some interior design work – and entertain her own friends. She could make life easy for Jamie, cushion him as far as possible from the tremors the end of the marriage must be sending through his small world, smooth his transition from the dreary but familiar prep school to the scary unknown quantity of the large, prestigious public school, full of confident, academic pupils and enriching, challenging activities. All these things she had decided on in the long sleepless nights that followed Tony's final departure; she had been able to fill up the blankness of those nights with bright images of success and fulfilment and control.

Why wouldn't it work any more? Why did her visions of Tony and his plump blonde no longer charge her with energising rage but instead drain her of spirit, tie lead weights to her limbs so that she could feel their heaviness as a physical fact? Perhaps, indeed, there was something physically wrong with her. Polly would say she needed to change her mineral intake, that she lacked some trace element or other. Maybe Polly was right. Susan looked at the bottles and jars of tablets on her dressing table, supplements of all kinds, in such a muddle. They were certainly due for an overhaul.

The telephone rang. Susan left it for five rings before picking it up. She was tempted to ignore the phone altogether these days, but she never could, quite, in case Jamie had had an accident at school. She braced herself for Tony's voice, for his words like angry insects released into the room.

It wasn't Tony. It was Polly.

'Darling!' she said, husky as ever. 'I've got such good news for you. You remember those people I told you about, who are doing up are that place in Islington? The Gascoignes? Well, they're definitely interested in having you sort out their living room for them, and possibly other bits as well. The building work's virtually finished – they want you over there as soon as possible to talk about colours and things. Money's virtually no object, as far as I can see.' Polly paused, and listened to her friend's silence. 'Suze, darling, aren't you pleased? It's a fabulous opportunity.'

'Oh, Poll – I don't know. I don't think I've got the time.'

'Time? Time is something you've got heaps of, surely. Susie, you're not going all feeble on me again, are you? I bet you're not eating properly.'

'Maybe not. I just – I can't seem to think straight.'

'It sounds as you need a little shaking up, my girl. Doing anything at lunchtime? I'll call round for you and take you out somewhere. One-ish. OK?'

'Polly, I'm not hungry. I don't – '

'You can watch me eat, then. See you at one! Bye for now.'

Susan stretched, and smiled. Polly was right; she did need shaking up. She would get up and shower in a minute. She listened to Estrelia bumping the vacuum cleaner up the stairs, and drew her dressing gown modestly round herself. Estrelia was inclined to open doors without knocking.

'Mrs Chandler? You OK? You still in bed so late?'

'It's nothing much, Estrelia. I'm not really ill; I just need to take things easy.'

'Time-a the month, huh? You don't worry, Mrs Chandler; I get you a cuppa coffee.'

Susan managed a smile. 'Thank you. Coffee would be perfect.' Estrelia made her exit, bumping and singing down the stairs.

Polly Cruse was large, but she managed her size with aplomb. Her clothes were well cut, fluid and understated; she favoured muted colours of slate and chocolate and charcoal, and enlivened them with outsize slabs of jewellery and hand-blocked silk scarves. She wore her black hair in a neat chin-length bob – 'No woman over thirty-five should let her hair grow below her chin,' she proclaimed – and was never seen without her trademark vermilion lipstick. She'd been Tony's friend originally – or rather her long-since-discarded husband John was an old friend of Tony's – but she'd taken to Susan as soon as she met her fifteen years ago or more, and had noisily championed her cause ever since. She was a little older than Susan, childless, with a successful career in advertising. Her patronage was an almost entirely unmixed blessing.

She ordered a seafood salad for them to share. 'You need zinc,' she had announced. 'You can't have too much zinc.' She'd insisted on champagne too. 'Just a half-bottle. To celebrate.' And indeed, after a few sips Susan had felt as if there might be something to celebrate. The Islington job would be easy, Polly said. A youngish couple, with a tiny baby. He was an advertising whizzkid, up and coming in the company Polly worked for. The wife was an artist. 'Dripping with ambition,' was how she described Nick Gascoigne. 'He'll be setting up his own company before long, and making a success of it too. He's an extremely sharp customer.'

'If she's an artist,' said Susan, peeling a prawn, 'I'm surprised she doesn't want to do the interiors herself.'

'She's too busy, I think. She's got a minute baby. Only a few weeks old. And I haven't met her, but I got the impression from him that she was the sweet and dreamy type, quite happy to let people do things for her.'

'And what's the house like?'

'Oh, you know. One of those tall, skinny Georgian ones. Flat front, two rooms on each floor, a hundred thousand stairs. Not ideal to tramp up and down with a baby, I imagine, but that's not my problem.'

'Babies grow bigger quite quickly.'

'True. Then they start falling downstairs, don't they? Anyway, you'll be seeing the house for yourself soon. I've arranged for you to go over it with them on Thursday evening. You've nothing on, have you?'

'No, but – Jamie.'

'What about Jamie?'

'He'll be home from school.'

'Can't you leave him in front of the telly?'

'Of course not, he's only thirteen.'

'Could you ask Tony to have him?'

'No thanks.' Susan's eyes narrowed.

'Well, take him with you then. Or something. Here's their number; you can rearrange it if you like. Take some more mussels, I'm sure I've had more than my fair share.'

\* \* \*

'Tony?'

'Mm?'

'You know those chocolate truffles?'

'Mm.'

'Well . . .'

'You want me to fetch them for you?'

'We . . . ell . . .'

'Of course I will, love bunny. Are they in the fridge?' Tony heaved himself out of the cream-coloured leather sofa with difficulty. This remarkable piece of furniture took up a good deal of the living room in his London flat. Once one was cocooned in its slippery acreage it was quite hard to work one-self free.

He fetched the chocolates, and a glass of Armagnac for himself. Pippa had never been a great drinker, but now she was pregnant she'd more or less cut it out altogether. She rewarded him with a pouty kiss and waved one of the dusty bundles of chocolate goo in front of his mouth. He shook his head. 'No, darling, they're all yours. Indulge your craving.' He squeezed her thigh. She was putting on weight quite fast, but it was not unbecoming; she'd always been plump as a little partridge. He thought fleetingly of his former wife's lean shanks and dismissed the image with revulsion.

Pippa snuggled against his shoulder and draped her legs over his lap. He loved her warm weight, and the clean smell of her fair hair. He remembered the smoky, oily hair of Thérèse, his last mistress. Thérèse had astonishing hooded eyes, as black as human eyes could be, and a superb feline elegance, but she was nearly forty and a hard-nosed bitch to boot. Little Pippa Watts-Davison was by no means the best-looking woman he'd ever been to bed with, but she was certainly the sweetest.

The television was on – some detective drama – but they weren't really watching it. 'Tony,' said Pippa, ruminatively, 'do you think we should ask the people at the farmhouse over? For a meal, or something?'

'The Antrobuses? Certainly not.'

'Why not?'

'They're a bunch of lunatics.'

58

'I didn't mean that strange one – I don't think we could ask her.'

'They're all strange.'

'No, but there's one who – mutters. But I didn't mean her. I meant Mrs Antrobus, really. The main one. With ginger hair.'

'Yes, darling, Martha Antrobus. Great big hulking woman. But why are you talking about inviting her on her own? What about her husband?'

'Oh, Tony – didn't you know? He's left her. Jamie told me.'

'*James* told *you*?' Tony sounded peeved.

'Yes, sort of. I was asking him about the boy – Finian. They really seem to get on well. And Jamie said Finian's dad had left.'

'Thought I hadn't seen him around. He's a scoundrel, that chap.'

Pippa said, 'You mean he's a scoundrel because he left his wife?'

Tony looked at her swiftly but there wasn't a trace of irony in her expression. 'More for getting through all the money,' he replied. 'I'll bet he's left her with a whole pile of debts. The barn was the last thing he had to sell – apart from the house itself.'

'I thought he seemed quite sweet,' said Pippa, 'but then I only met him once.'

Tony smiled at the schoolgirl limits of Pippa's vocabulary. 'Quite sweet, hm? Well, he was something of a charmer, I suppose. But gamblers often are. Totally unstable, I imagine – like the rest of the family.'

'If we invite them – or her – over,' persisted Pippa, 'then they'll probably invite us back. I'd like to see what their house is like.'

'What for? That ramshackle dump!'

'I love seeing other people's houses. I'm nosy, I suppose. I love finding out what they do with their kitchens, and things like that.'

Tony chuckled. 'I very much doubt that the Antrobuses "do" anything with their kitchen at all,' he said. 'The whole place is like something out of the Middle Ages. I shouldn't think any money's been spent on it since before the war.'

Pippa popped the last chocolate into her mouth. 'And I'd like to see the baby.'

'Baby? Oh, yes – the grandchild. I'd forgotten about the baby. It doesn't live at Powdermill, though. They live in London, don't they, that couple?'

'But they'll be down a lot. She'll want to be with her mother while the baby's tiny.'

'Hm. Pretty girl. Pips – will you want to be with your mother a lot too, when our baby's born?'

Pippa looked at him with round blue eyes. 'Oh yes,' she said in all simplicity, 'of course I will.'

Tony picked up the remote control and flicked through the channels to catch the news headlines. He took a large swallow of his Armagnac. He couldn't allow his heart to sink.

Jamie recognised the car. He nearly always remembered cars. A smoky-blue Porsche with matching leather seats. Two years old, or less. He'd have known whose car it was in any case, and the baby seat draped with a fluffy white shawl confirmed it.

'She's coming at half past six,' Nick had told Jess that morning. 'I'll go straight there, as early as I can, but you'll have to let them in. Sure you've got the keys?'

'Chandler,' Jess had said. 'Isn't that the name of the people who've bought the barn?'

'Could be. It's a common enough name.' Nick wasn't interested. 'She should be good. Polly Cruse usually knows what she's talking about.'

Jess hated driving the Porsche. She hated driving in London altogether, but the Porsche made her extra nervous, ever since she clipped a wing mirror and Nick had been coldly angry. That was about six months ago. That evening Nick had failed to kiss her good night, for the first time. Now he sometimes forgot to kiss her goodbye in the mornings too.

She toyed with the idea of taking the bus to the Islington house with Louis in the sling, but it was a longish walk from the bus stop, and if she took the car at least she'd be able to give Louis a feed if he started to yell. Five weeks old, and he was still utterly unpredictable in his demands. Sometimes he'd sleep for four blissful hours at a stretch; other times he'd wake every hour, apparently wild with hunger, all through the night. Nick had taken to sleeping on the sofa bed. It would be so much nicer when they had moved into the new house.

She arrived at Lennox Square at six; she'd allowed lots of time because she knew she'd have to stop every five minutes to check the A to Z. Nick had been surprised when he found out about her sense of direction – or rather about the absence of it. He'd assumed, he said, that someone with so acute a visual sense would understand maps. Jess explained to him that it was cities she didn't understand. Out of London she saw landmarks, she saw roads following some kind of geographical logic; in London the logic was man-made, and it was beyond her.

So here she was in the new living room, half an hour early. Just as well – Louis was beginning to make his angry seagull noises. There was nothing to sit on except the floor, and Jess didn't think she could manage that; her stitches were still tender. She looked about her. The radiator under the window had been newly housed in a smart wooden box, crisscrossed at the front. She perched on that, unbuttoned her blouse, and drew Louis' dusky crimson face towards her.

He was a demanding baby. He couldn't bear to be ignored. People told her that it was because he was bright, always wanting to be at the centre of things, but Jess thought they were just saying that to reassure her. Her private fear was that he was difficult because he was unhappy. He knew that he'd been born in the wrong place. He knew that his father hadn't wanted to be there. He knew that even she, his mother, had declared that she didn't care about him at the very moment when his struggle to escape from her had been at its height. And he knew, now, that she was afraid of him.

It didn't occur to Jess, any more, to ask herself whether she loved her baby. To say that you loved something implied that you had some kind of independence from it, some kind of objectivity. And Jess had no objectivity about Louis; she lived and breathed him. She didn't have any choice. She remembered a Russian fairytale from her childhood, about a witch baby with iron teeth who grew bigger than a house. The tiny shape in her arms was like that; when he pulled at her breast and fixed her with his lashless, shining eye he seemed to swell and stretch till he loomed over her like a shadow cast by the candlelight.

Susan and Jamie Chandler arrived a little early, too. Jamie

61

didn't mind coming. He was glad his mother had some work; maybe it would stop her asking questions every evening about what he did at school, which was all she seemed to find to talk about these days. He'd brought some homework along to do while she talked – just French vocab, to learn for a test. And then he saw the car, right outside the front door, and he'd clicked that the house belonged to Finian's sister. The sister with the hair. He didn't tell his mother. Hearing about anything to do with the barn upset her. He didn't want to put her off this job.

Susan, pausing on the pavement, looked up at the silhouette in the uncurtained front window. The girl was nursing her baby, her hair falling forward like a veil. The sight gave Susan's heart a squeeze. She hated to disturb her. She checked her lipstick in her handbag mirror and ran a comb through her short spiky hair before knocking.

Jess was still fumbling with her buttons when she answered the door. Louis had dozed off; she'd left him on the floor, well wrapped in the enormous purple blanket Bella had knitted for him. Deep, royal, ugly purple. It was a mad colour for a baby, but then, Bella was mad. She always had been. Jess didn't mind.

The discussion progressed satisfactorily. Susan felt drawn to this pretty, untidy young woman, pale with maternal exhaustion, apologising for her post-natal vagueness. She wanted to work well for her, to help make the house into a proper home for her and for the tiny scrap in the appalling purple blanket of whom nothing was visible save for one balled fist and a peak of black hair. Jess, for her part, respected the thin woman in the black cowlneck cashmere. She was direct and practical, decisive without being bossy. Talking about something other than the baby made Jess feel as if she was uncurling after hibernation.

Jamie sat in the opposite corner to the baby, learning his French. He wasn't afraid of being recognised. He'd watched Fin's sister leaning against the stable door, her hands on her huge belly, but she hadn't seen him. Then the following weekend he'd been sitting by the pond in the afternoon sunshine with Fin, throwing green acorns in and chatting a bit, and she'd come by with her mother – Fin's mother – the two of them walking slowly, Mrs Antrobus carrying the little white bundle. 'It's the first time she's been out,' Fin had said, jumping up. 'She's weak, she lost a lot of blood.' He'd introduced them, and the mother had given Jamie a careful looking-over, but the sister had looked kind of dazed. And he hadn't seen her again. Finian had talked about her; he'd gone on about how beautiful she was. Jamie was surprised by this simple pride with which Fin had said that, about his own sister, but he was surprised – and delighted – by quite a few of the things Fin said. He'd spent time with him every weekend, which made up for a lot that happened at school. But he was sure the sister wouldn't know him.

The two women talked on. They stood by the garden window, discussing whether a conservatory would be a good idea. 'Maybe one day,' Jess was saying, 'but I can't bear the thought of more building work just yet. I'm just dying to move in.' Jamie let his French book slide. He looked with admiration at her hair, curlier than Fin's, and a softer colour. Fin's hair was bright like marmalade. He didn't know what to call the colour of Jess'. You couldn't say it was ginger, but you couldn't say it wasn't. She was wearing long floppy clothes, a silvery-grey shirt over a drifting black skirt, with a shapeless cardigan hanging loose from her shoulders, but you could tell that if she hadn't just had a baby she'd have a good figure. And Fin had said that she did.

The roll of purple wool jerked; odd sounds, not crying, came from inside. The women, immersed in conversation, didn't notice. It might be important. Jamie got up. 'Excuse me,' he said, going hot, 'your baby's – he's making a noise.'

Jess hurried over and picked up the blanket and its contents. She smiled. 'It's only hiccoughs,' she said. 'But thank you for telling me.' She gave him a second look. 'I know you,' she said. 'The barn boy. Fin's friend.'

Jamie could not deny it. He was too overcome by being called Fin's friend to think of a reply.

'How amazing,' Jess turned to Susan, beaming. 'I said to Nick this morning, isn't Chandler the name of the people who've bought the barn? I knew I'd seen him before. I remembered his beautiful skin. What do you think of the barn? Are you happy there?' Talking of Powdermill made Jess ripple and glow.

Susan said, 'The Barn belongs to my ex-husband.' Her dark lipstick made her mouth look thin and hard.

'How stupid of me. Yes, of course.' Jess seemed about to say more, but the sight of Jamie stopped her. A wail from the blanket cut the subject short. Susan leaned forward, glad of the opportunity to make encouraging remarks about the baby. This barn connection made her more determined than ever to make a success of the house. She wanted Tony to hear, in casual neighbourly conversation, of what a stylish, competent, professional job she'd done.

They heard a key in the lock. Susan had almost forgotten about the husband. He introduced himself. Shook hands cordially, put an arm round his wife's shoulders, seemed pleased to find how far they'd got. A handsome man, thought Susan. A saturnine face. Was that the word? She wasn't sure what saturnine meant, but she thought it applied to Nick Gascoigne.

He didn't even look at the baby.

# CHAPTER NINE

Michaelmas Term began with Eliza poorly prepared. She had a course of eight lectures to give on social changes in England during the reign of Henry II; it was appalling to begin term without having completed work on them, but such was the case. Eliza, as a performer, was not a good lecturer. She relied on solid and scholarly groundwork to compensate for her lack of presence and panache – but this term, it looked as if the undergraduates would be cheated of both.

And it really wasn't her fault, she reflected as she unlocked her bicycle. Eliza hated to feel out of control, but circumstances had conspired against her lately. Her father had left home, without a word to anyone. Jess had given birth, not in a predictable and organised way in London, in the private wing of St Mary's, with Nick having a prearranged week off work, but suddenly in Sussex, on a hot Sunday at the end of August, with no bag packed and no baby clothes to hand and no one to know her at the local hospital. And above all, with no Nick. He had gone back to London the day after the birth, and had ended up staying there most of the week. His time off started on 5 September he said, and there was nothing he could do to change it.

It was left to Eliza to be furious. She had spent the first couple of days trying to work other members of her family into a suitable state of indignation – sparing Jess, of course, who was still in hospital anyway. Martha just shrugged, and said that they could cope without him; she said she was glad Louis would be a country baby, at least for the first week of his life. Ganna was as angry as Eliza, but she showed it in dark silences and slow head-shakings. She said Eliza's outspoken rage made her tired. Finian said, 'Why should Nick be here anyway? There's not a lot he could do. He'd just hang about looking bored.' Eliza knew this was true, but she rounded on her brother none the less. 'How do you think Jess feels, with her husband taking no interest? It's not natural. It's his *duty* to be here.'

Fin said, 'I dunno how Jess feels. But she'll feel a whole lot worse if she hears you going on about it.' He picked up a colander and wandered out to look for mushrooms.

It was Bella in the end who changed Eliza's mind. Bella made no comment on any of Eliza's outpourings. She just sat on the high-backed settle in the kitchen, knitting – she'd brought her purple wool out into the open now – and beaming, rocking herself a little and saying, 'A baby. A baby. A lovely little baby. I'll make it nice for him when he comes home.' Eliza looked around the squalid kitchen. 'You're right, Bella,' she said, 'the baby deserves a decent homecoming.' And she found a cleanish apron and set to work, throwing out piles of yellowing newspapers and used envelopes, removing Biros and paperclips from the fruit bowl, collecting up the encrusted feeding dishes that circled the Aga and putting them to soak. 'Bella,' she said, 'when the baby's here, the cats ought to be fed outside. Can you make sure Ma does that?' Bella nodded, vigorously. Eliza smiled to herself. Once an idea had penetrated the vapours of Bella's mind, it was impossible to dislodge. She knew the cats would never be fed indoors again.

Cycling through the familiar Oxford streets on this warm October day Eliza allowed the anxiety about her lectures to fade. Her mind ran over the events of that extraordinary week. Louis and Jess had been released from hospital on the Wednesday. Martha picked them up; Eliza and Bella and Finian laid tea in the parlour, with a tablecloth and a ginger cake and all the roses left in the garden arranged in Jess' favourite silver bowl. They even lit a fire, because Louis was used to the warm hospital. Eliza filled up the gaps between the roses with ferny tufts of southernwood. She knew Jess loved its bitter, spicy smile. They installed Ganna on one side of the fire and then stood by the front door to wait, Bella clutching the purple blanket. Eliza thought with satisfaction of the tiny cardigans, relics of Fin's infancy, that Martha had dug out of a drawer somewhere; newly washed, they hung like lamb's fleeces, airing over the Aga rail. Eliza had bought four plain white babygros in the hospital shop, too. When little Louis returned to London he would doubtless be showered with garments from Jacardi and Baby Gap, but for now he had the basics at least. Finian had bought a teddy bear,

66

quite a nice one, with a red bow tie. Eliza knew it had cost most of the money he'd earned doing odd jobs for the farmer who had bought their land.

And then the car had pulled up – extra slowly because Martha was trying not to let it bump – and Jess had seen them all at the door waiting for her and Eliza had seen her face twitch because she was trying not to cry. And it had taken Eliza by surprise, but the moment when Louis was carried over the threshold, his slate-dark eyes already wide and enquiring, and Bella said, 'Welcome home, baby' and handed over the blanket, had seemed overwhelmingly important, a moment which survived in perfect clarity in Eliza's mind, in portentousness even superseding the birth itself.

Eliza swerved to avoid a dog as she turned into Woodstock Road. The tidal wave of summer tourists was ebbing; Oxford was filling up with lost-looking freshers wearing brand-new college scarves that most of them would abandon in a week or two. In her own college there would be homesick girls sobbing into the pay phones and blasé second years displaying their ease and insouciance to the newcomers with loud shows of public affection. The college Eliza belonged to was unglamorous, founded for women only but now awkwardly co-educational, an unspectacular muddle of Victorian red brick and sixties grey concrete, but it suited her. It was aloof, businesslike, unhampered by tradition, and besides, the pink belladonna lilies and dark clots of dahlias glowed richly in the sunshine as she dismounted at the lodge. It all looked trim and friendly. She had work to do; she could put behind her the chaos of her family life, the emptiness of her personal life, the aggravation of Graham the lodger who had little by little eroded the order of her small, neat house.

She greeted her colleagues in the Senior Common Room, collected a cup of coffee, and inspected the contents of her pigeon-hole. A circular from the Mediaevalists' Society, an invitation to the Principal's beginning-of-year drinks, and a postcard of the Piazza della Signoria in Florence. She turned it over.

'Dearest Lila,' she read, 'I'll be in Oxford next Saturday, 16th. Meet me outside Blackwell's at twelve noon, and we can talk. Ever your loving Dad.'

No we can't, she thought. No, Dad, we can't talk.

67

She read the message again, then ripped it in two as if it were an invalid credit card and dropped the pieces in the bin.

'Yes,' said Jess, 'yes, I did like her. I think she'll be very good. But the price! We don't have to have anyone. There's no reason why I couldn't do it all myself.'

Nick pointed at Louis, who slept, wedged between two sofa cushions. 'There's your reason.'

'But I could manage. Other people manage.' Jess jutted out her chin in a way that was unfamiliar to Nick. 'After all, I am an artist. I never thought I'd employ someone else to make my aesthetic decisions for me.'

Nick smiled and took her hands. 'Yes, sweetheart, we all know you're an artist. And if only you'd agree to hiring a nanny you could go back to being one. But one thing you're not is a superwoman, which is why we'll pay Susan what's-her-name an arm and a leg to get our house ready for us.' He pulled her down into an armchair and arranged her on his lap. He coiled a strand of her hair round his forefinger. 'And it's just as well you're not a superwoman, because if you were, I'd never have married you.'

Jess fiddled with the knot of his tie. She sniffed, and blinked. 'Nick, would you have married me if I hadn't been pregnant?'

Before she was pregnant, thought Nick, I never saw her cry. These days she never stops.

He planted a kiss on her forehead. 'Jessie, you're being very silly. Now cheer up. The house is going to look fantastic – like its mistress. And the cost is nothing. That's what money's for.' He drew her closer. 'Now kiss me, mermaid.'

'Oh God,' said Jess, 'I'm leaking.' She wriggled off his lap and pulled two drenched white squares out of her bra. She made a face at Nick. 'He's due to wake soon anyway,' she said. 'Sorry.' And she disappeared into the bedroom.

Eliza spent the day in the library, in a frenzy of hard work. One thing she had learned over the years was now to put anger to good use. Her father's postcard had broken the back of the twelfth-century feudal system, in a manner of speaking.

She gathered her books and folders together in the Common

Room. The garden also benefited from her energetic rages; her interest in it was intermittent, but it was high time she tidied up the last vestiges of summer and put it in order for its long sleep. If she hurried, there would still be enough daylight left for a good stint.

Graham was out, thank God. As she changed into jeans and Wellingtons Eliza wondered for the umpteenth time whether she could manage without his contribution to the rent. She didn't think she could, really. Whatever her mother said, Eliza was sure that the family would soon run seriously short of cash. She wanted to try and save a portion of her own small income so that they could at least have some sort of Christmas.

The garden was long and narrow – a useless shape, really. It was fenced, not walled, which brought Eliza into closer proximity with her neighbours than she would actually have chosen. Not that she had anything against the Afshars, who lived to the right of her. They were civil, never interfering; their many children played obscure, private games in the garden, involving collections of stones and beads and feathers, and they had a pleasing habit of leaving huge flat baskets full of chillies to dry in the sun. The house to the left had been empty for some time. Graham the lodger had had several long conversations with the new occupant, this divorcee gardener, but Eliza had so far only glimpsed him.

She was disappointed, now, to find he was also taking advantage of the fine evening to do some work in his garden. In the six weeks or so that he'd been in residence he had transformed his strip of nettles and dandelions; there was now a patch for flowers, a smaller patch for vegetables, and the wooden-framed compost heap about which Graham was inclined to wax lyrical. Not much was growing at the moment, of course, but Eliza could see that everything was just as it should be, awaiting the coming of spring. He seemed to be clearing the toolshed now, stuffing the rubbish into sacks.

Eliza didn't look at him for long. She didn't want to start a conversation. She turned to a shrub that had long since ceased to produce its small, dull white flowers and snipped at it with her shears. She didn't know very much about gardening, but her instinct was always to cut things back.

From the other side of the fence, Tom Winchcombe watched her. Not with any particular interest, though her small-boned body and neat mousy head looked pleasant enough as she bent over the bushes. Tom watched her as he would have watched a robin or a dragonfly or a changing cloud; he had a lifelong habit of watching. She clipped away, making an efficient job of it, apparently intent upon her work. It surprised Tom when he heard a sigh escape her, a sigh that was almost a sob.

He looked away; he didn't want to embarrass her. She straightened up, rubbing the small of her back. Out of the corner of his eye Tom could see that she was preparing to go indoors. Seized by a sudden urge to communicate, he picked up one of his black sacks. 'Hello,' he called.

Eliza frowned, and wiped the shears on the edge of her padded plaid shirt. 'Yes?'

'I wondered if you'd like any of these?'

Eliza had taken her glasses off because they slipped down her nose when she was gardening, and now felt at a disadvantage. She had to move closer to the fence to see what he was offering.

'I've been dividing the irises,' Tom said. 'They were just about all that was left in this garden, and they were all over the place. Would you like some? If you don't plant them too deep, they'll thrive. Leave the tubers showing a little, see?' His voice had a slight Oxfordshire burr.

'I remember the irises,' said Eliza. 'Yes, I'd like some. Thank you.' She had sneaked into the garden, then unoccupied, last May, and had helped herself to an armful of the snaky, furry flowers, purple and tortoiseshell on their juicy, bulbous stems.

Tom passed the bag over the fence to her without further comment. He smiled, and Eliza noticed that he had a front tooth missing. His eyes were bright, the colour of conkers. He didn't say anything else to her. Eliza liked him for that.

Eliza had resolved to stay at home on the day of her father's visit to Oxford, but when that Saturday dawned she was struck by a new possibility. If she didn't meet him at Blackwell's, he might come round and seek her out. She couldn't think why she hadn't thought of that before. He knew perfectly well where she lived – he'd even visited her there. She didn't know why he'd written to her at the college. Perhaps he'd lost his address book – or left it at home. He would not remember the number of her house without it, but it would be like him to march up and down the street ringing doorbells until he found her.

Safer out than in, she decided. She'd just walk and walk. It was an absolutely marvellous day – a Pre-Raphaelite day, she thought, with every berry and brick and turning leaf burning with colour in the autumn sun. She walked to the river and through Christ Church meadow and round the Botanical Gardens and into Magdalen deer park. She walked all the thoughts out of her head and feasted her eyes on blue sky and golden stone until her head was spinning. She walked up the sweep of the High Street and, much to her surprise, found herself looking across Broad Street in the direction of Blackwell's just as the many bells of the city sung out for twelve noon.

She really hadn't meant to do it. It frightened her, the way her body seemed to have acted independently of her mind. She stood in the shadow of a doorway and peeped out. People crossed and recrossed the front of Blackwell's like beads on an abacus, but nobody was standing still. Perhaps he'd forgotten. That would be typical. He'd forgotten to be there, once, when she'd sung the most important solo in a school concert. She'd been very keen on singing, up till then.

She stepped forward a little, craning her neck. All of a sudden there he was, whirling across the road like an autumn leaf. Whatever he was doing, Leo Antrobus gave the impression of restless activity. His clothes always seemed to flap on his tall, lean frame. Whereas Martha was solid and still, stately like one of those women Picasso painted, with heavy ankles and white drapery and calm Grecian profiles.

He must have come down Turl Street too; he must have passed very close to Eliza. She watched, heart thumping, as he fidgeted in Blackwell's doorway. He was too far away to see, but Eliza knew that his long fingers would be twisting and turning in his baggy pockets, scrumpling bits of paper and jingling loose change.

He would probably stand there for half an hour, waiting. He would have to, having come all this way from – wherever it was he'd been. Eliza knew she had to escape, though her legs felt like

71

jelly. He turned to scrutinise the window display. She darted out of her doorway and was back down Turl Street in a flash, making for the Covered Market.

She immediately regretted this choice. The Market on a Saturday morning would be full not only of flowers and fruit and stripy sweaters and hanging pheasants, but also of everyone she knew in Oxford. The air was thick with the odours of coffee, cheese, hot bread, butcher's sawdust; the roof seemed to hold and amplify the hum of voices. It threatened to overwhelm her, but she had to go somewhere. One café alone had resisted any attempt at trendiness; the smell of frying fat and the dingy Formica tables, each with its cluster of salt, pepper and malt vinegar in encrusted plastic containers, was enough to deter most of her acquaintance. She sat down in a corner and ordered a cup of coffee. She was astonished to find tears pouring down her face.

'Who are you hiding from?'

Eliza recognised the voice. She looked up. 'How did you know I was hiding?'

'You'd hardly be in here on your own if you weren't.' Tom Winchcombe noticed her wet cheeks. 'Oh, Jesus, I'm sorry. I wouldn't have said anything. I didn't think you were really upset.'

'I'm not. I'm just . . . I've never cried in the Covered Market before. Sorry.'

'Well, I won't tell.' Tom, smiling, handed her a paper napkin. He was still on his feet. Eliza didn't want to tell him about her father, but she didn't want him to go either. He looked comfortingly familiar in his holey Guernsey and muddy brown corduroys, even though she hardly knew him.

'Are you hiding too, then? Or would you come in here anyway?' she asked gruffly.

'No, I'm not hiding. I'm filling time. I went to pick my son up for the weekend, but he's got chicken-pox and he can't go out today. His mother could have rung to tell me, but it's kind of typical that she didn't. So I thought I'd come in here for a sandwich. I didn't feel like going straight home.'

'Don't let me stop you.' Eliza had regained her composure.

'Thanks.' He pulled out a chair opposite to her. 'Man

trouble?' he asked, glancing at the stiff little menu in its dirty polythene cover.

'Yes, but not what you think. My father. But I don't want to talk about it.'

'Fair enough.' He ordered a cheese and tomato sandwich, toasted. 'Anything for you?'

'I'm not hungry.'

'Another coffee, then?'

'All right. I've got to wait until the coast is clear.' Eliza didn't mean to sound ungracious.

Silence fell, but it didn't seem to make Tom uneasy. It was Eliza who felt obliged to break it. 'How old is your son?' she asked.

'Dickon? He's five.'

'Dickon? That's a peculiar name.'

'His real name's Richard, but Dickon just sort of developed. Do you like children?'

'No, not really. At least, I thought I didn't, until I became an aunt six weeks ago.' Eliza found herself telling the gardener all about Jess and Louis and the culpably unresponsive Nick. Her pale face was still blotchy from crying, but her light, girlish voice was expressive.

'Maybe he'll come round to the baby,' Tom suggested. 'Some people have to learn how to be natural. It took me a while. I was worried sick at first, because I didn't feel anything for him. He seemed just like any other baby to me. Then Linda left me in charge of him one evening so she could go out with a friend. I was running his bath, and I left him on our bed. I heard a thud, and I was across the landing and holding Dickon before I even knew it. That's when I found out that he was the most important thing in my life.'

'And had he fallen?'

'No, I never knew what the noise was – a door slamming, maybe. Or perhaps something, somewhere was showing me how to care for my son.'

Eliza had never met a man who talked so simply and directly about himself. She wanted to ask more, but her self-defensive instinct made her say, 'You're very familiar, for a neighbour.'

Tom laughed at her. 'What do you want me to say? Should I

ask if I can borrow a cup of sugar?' He unhooked his jacket from the back of the chair. 'Is the coast clear yet, do you think?'

'I don't know. He'll probably have gone to look for me at home.'

'In that case,' said Tom, 'you'd better stay out a little longer. I'm going to buy some spring bulbs. Want to come along?'

Eliza assented. It was good to be taken care of.

The autumn sun was too warm for the thick cape he was wearing, but Leo kept it on none the less. The cape, full and black, had been left behind at the end of a film shoot years and years ago; Leo, the scriptwriter and friend of the producer, had thought it too good to waste. Of course that wasn't stealing. Leo would have laughed to scorn any such bourgeois notion. He had always enjoyed this cape, the small drama of its swirling and flapping. He was glad that he had had the presence of mind to seize it from the hat stand in the front hall, that moon-bright August night. That night was nearly two months ago now, and he felt an increasing attachment to the cape. Such an attachment might be childish, but Leo had always admired childishness. Most people were just too damn adult.

He didn't doubt that Eliza would meet him outside Blackwell's. She was a little late but, well, there could be any number of reasons for that. Eliza was sensible, organised, cool; by far the best person to approach for news of the family. It was only news he wanted. He did not in the least regret his decision to leave. Home had become impossible, a place where he had felt both crushed and excluded. He knew Martha could cope without him. She had always made a point of the limitlessness of her capacity for managing, implying by contrast that any contribution of his must almost by definition be peripheral and inept. He thought of his mother more than he thought of Martha; his eyes would mist over, sometimes, at the thought of how much his mother must be missing him. That was something he wanted to discuss with Eliza – how he could arrange a meeting with Sibyl that didn't involve going back to Powdermill. His mother hardly ever left the house, he knew, but perhaps Lila could drive her to somewhere nearby, to a teashop or something. He was not going back to the house, not on any account.

The one he missed the most was Jess. She would have had her baby by now. He was glad he had missed that grisly postnatal bit. He was curious to know about the baby, but his curiosity was easily quenched by his reluctance to associate his adorable fairy princess with all that pain and squalor and cow-like heaviness. Lila would bring him news of the baby, and when the time was ripe he would visit Jess in London – in the daytime, avoiding his cold-fish son-in-law – and bask in the welcoming smiles of mother and child. He thought fondly of the trusting grip of small babies, of their wondering, watery smiles. And as the child grew, what an exotic, colourful treat his – or her – grandfather's visits would be! Leo was good at enlivening the lonelier moments of his exile with such sunny imaginings.

He examined his reflection in the shop window, and was quite pleased with what he saw. A tall, spare frame – too thin, perhaps, but how infinitely preferable to the soft expansion of so many of his contemporaries. Lots of hair, too – grizzled, certainly, but still the rough curls had a certain wayward charm. His face was angular, hook-nosed, corrugated now with deep lines that added character if not gravitas. The collar of the cape stood stiffly up; he looked like a highwayman, or Doctor Who, or even Sherlock Holmes, though with a more mobile, sensuous mouth. Not, above all, remotely like your average fifty-year-old Englishman. He gave his own reflection a wry, approving smile.

He checked the time. Eliza was twenty minutes late. He turned and scanned Broad Street, a raised hand protecting his eyes from the sharp, defining sunshine. It was possible, of course, that his postcard hadn't arrived. Posting it from Florence might well have been a mistake; Italian posts were notorious. But that had been at least two weeks ago . . . Leo shifted his weight from foot to foot, jingling the contents of his pockets – some coins, lire still mixed irritatingly with English currency, car keys, and the key to his old friend Rufus Williamson's Hammersmith flat. Rufus, twice divorced, was a man of enormous appetites. He had become that rare thing, a highly successful restaurateur. He spent most of the time playing mine host in his flagship Knightsbridge restaurant, and was more than happy for Leo to camp in his spare room for as long as he chose. Leo had spent only a week in Florence, fruitlessly pursuing a director who had shown a flicker of interest in a project of his, and telling himself that he was recapturing his youthful freedom amongst the piazzas and churches and trattorias, but in fact he had cut his visit short. He couldn't settle, so far away. If there was any urgent news – about Jess, for instance – Martha would surely think of Rufus.

He looked at his watch again. Now he thought about it, sending a postcard from Florence was a crazy thing to do. It would probably turn up in Lila's pigeon-hole at least a month late. He could go and look her up – he couldn't remember her address, but he'd recognise the house once he was in the right street – but . . .

The King's Arms was open. The pavement tables were crowded with shouting, sprawling students, downing pints. The sight drew Leo like a magnet. How he relished this exhilaration, of living like a student again! It would be unfair to drop in on Lila unannounced. She had her own life to lead, and there was always another day.

# CHAPTER TEN

Finian meant what he said about Guy Fawkes Night. The part of Sussex where he lived had once been famous for the manufacture of gunpowder, as the name of the Antrobus farm testified. As a result, 5th November was commemorated with unusual vigour in this part of the country. Even small towns like Broadhurst managed torchlight processions and impressive firework displays. It was the highlight of Fin's year; better than Christmas, because it suspended family difficulties, whereas Christmas brought them into focus. Fin loved all four elements, but was most strongly attracted to fire; for him, 5th November was a festival of fire.

He had communicated his ardour to Jamie, who lived on tenterhooks in case his father and Pippa decided to give the Barn a miss that weekend. Jamie was only mildly interested in the fireworks. What he wanted was to cement his friendship with Fin.

At school, Jamie had fulfilled his aim. He had become invisible. The dreams of social success he had briefly cherished at the beginning of term had been quickly forgotten; instead he pursued the more attainable goal of utter anonymity. He wasn't completely solitary; that would have been counterproductive. He associated with a couple of bland, inoffensive boys who said little in class and usually gave their homework in on time. He sat near them in lessons and walked with them to the sports field or to the art block. He'd even been to the cinema with one of them, to see the latest Schwarzenegger. They were his cover; to be a loner would be to be classed as eccentric, and therefore conspicuous. Jamie had no objections to Simon Wilson and Matthew Fellows but if they fell off the face of the planet tomorrow he wouldn't mind very much.

So he got through the weeks at school comfortably enough, coming about two-thirds of the way down the form order in most subjects, shivering on the sidelines as reserve in the house football tournament, amassing an average sum for charity on the sponsored run. At home, in the evenings, he avoided his mother, got his homework out of the way, then pored endlessly over his Wildlife Fact-Files. These were ring binders which you ordered by post and filled with cards about every living creature there was. Jamie was unmoved by the poetry that he'd been made to read in class, but he found his own kind of poetry in these wonderful files: The Saltmarsh and Its Wildlife, Save the Great Apes, Conserving Peat Bogs, How Bats See In the Dark. He knew about dholes and warthogs, the Virginia opossum and the American quarter horse, the Glanville fritillary and the Loligo squid. Nature was Jamie's guilty secret. No plant, insect bird or reptile had ever failed to fascinate him, and the higher mammals could touch his heart.

In Finian Antrobus, for the first time ever, Jamie had found someone who understood his passion. Finian's attitude towards the natural world was different from Jamie's – less reverential, more practical – but that was a welcome antidote to what Jamie recognised as his own uncomfortable intensity. Fin was adept at spotting slow-worms, frogs, harvest mice and the like; he was good at catching things too, because he had little sense of the passing of time and could keep wonderfully still. Fin knew their habits and their habitats through long association with them, but it was Jamie who could reel off the facts about almost any living thing. Not that he ever did reel them off, of course – though he had shyly slipped in a few titbits that to his joy had surprised and impressed Fin. Unlike anyone else Jamie had ever known, Finian accepted things as they were. He assumed that Jamie would want to handle a grass-snake or pick mushrooms; he taught the city boy the lie of the land without comment. The weekends at Powdermill Farm had become the focus of Jamie's life.

Jess, too, was anxious to be at Powdermill that weekend. Not especially because it was Bonfire Night – she assumed that with Louis in tow, it would more or less pass her by – but just because she was, as usual, longing to get out of London. Work on the Islington house was progressing satisfactorily, and she had every confidence in Susan Chandler's taste and judgement, but there were still several weeks to go before it was finished. Jess had suggested that they should move in anyway and put up with the decorators' mess, but Nick said, 'No. Let's wait till it's perfect. After all, there's no pressure this end, since I'm not selling the flat.' The St John's Wood flat was to be let in the New Year. Some of Jess' friends had expressed surprise that Nick could afford the distinctly up-market Islington house without selling the flat first; Jess hadn't really thought about it, but she assumed that he did have capital as well as a substantial income. Having been brought up in a family where the approach to money was, to say the least, chaotic, Jess had almost no interest in it. Eliza had gone to the other extreme, squirrelling away tiny amounts and worrying in the small hours. It had always seemed to Eliza that she had to do a lot of Jess' worrying for her.

Jess had never like Nick's flat much. The first time he had brought her there had been a week after the end of her degree show; as he'd promised, or threatened, he invited her to see the newly hung self-portrait. Jess at that stage shared a terraced house with art school friends in an ungentrified part of Hackney. She wasn't used to entry phones that worked properly and clean carpeted stairs. Not that they used the stairs; Nick's flat was on the third floor, and there was a noiseless lift, disconcertingly lined with mirrors. Nick had guided her out of the lift by putting his hand under her elbow. She had been expecting him to touch her at some point, of course, but when he did it made her jump.

Inside, the flat was an exhibit, not a home. There was lots of glass and metal and smooth black wood. Three bird-of-paradise flowers jutted fiercely from a square glass vase on the mantle-piece. They looked as though they were pecking at their reflections in the mirror behind. The compact disc player, the television, the VCR, were all state-of-the-art designs, sleek and snug-fitting; everything operated at the touch of a button. While Nick fetched her a drink, Jess turned with relief to the only part of the ensemble with any sense of personality – the books. There was a whole wall of them; classic literature, not just for show because it had all obviously been read, a few smart modern novels, mainly in hardback, and dozens of immaculately produced books of art and photography. Byzantine mosaics, Piero della Francesca, Velasquez, Man Ray . . . Nick's taste appeared to be catholic.

Nick returned with a bottle of champagne and a pair of fluted glasses. When Jess protested, he said, 'I regard your presence here as a cause for celebration.' He apologised for the flat: 'Very impersonal, I know. I've been too busy to really live in it yet. Buying your picture is the first stage in what I hope will be a transformation.'

Jess remembered what she had come for, and looked around for the painting.

'It's in the bedroom,' said Nick, fixing her with his level gaze. 'I see it as a private picture. I didn't like the idea of friends sitting round in here discussing it.' He refilled her glass. Jess wondered at first whether she liked the idea of her naked self looking down on Nick's bed. She didn't say so, but a little later, when he led her in to see it, and, standing in front of it, took her in his arms and kissed her with great passion, she decided she had no objections whatsoever.

He had taken her out every single night for a week after that, and after a month they had gone on holiday together, to join some friends of his in a Tuscan villa. They were bright, witty, confident people who ate and drank and laughed and fêted Jess with unflagging energy. Nick and Jess shared a room with a cool stone floor and a painted ceiling. Lying next to her on the high white bed, both of them staring up at the birds and grapes and putti intertwining overhead, Nick had told her that he loved her.

She hadn't moved in with him straight away; not until after she was pregnant, in fact. But she came to spend at least two-thirds of her time at St John's Wood, and her influence crept over the flat. Nick seemed charmed to find bunches of raggedy cornflowers spilling out of milk jugs; he loved the little sketches she made of him on the backs of envelopes – Nick asleep, Nick reading the paper, Nick seen through the shower curtain. She bought fresh prawns, plump olives, bunches of dill and coriander; she piled oranges high on a blue glass plate. They ate croissants in bed on Saturday mornings; she kept forgetting to retrieve her earrings from the soap dish in the bathroom. The shared house in Hackney seemed sadder and shabbier every time she went back there, so she went back less and less.

One Sunday afternoon Alison and Jenny, her housemates, were expecting her to do her share of the monthly clean-up, a sensible arrangement which none of them had ever shirked. It was a dank, chill day; Jess and Nick had had brunch at a pretty local restaurant, and had gone back to bed, wobbly after their Bloody Marys, with coffee and a pile of newspapers. Three o'clock – she knew the girls would be waiting for her. She crawled out of bed, rummaging for her clothes.

'It seems absurd,' said Nick, 'that you should have to trek halfway across London to clean up a house that you've hardly set foot in for weeks.'

Jess was tempted to agree. 'But I'm still living there, officially,' she said, falteringly. 'And it's not fair on Jen and Ali, I suppose.'

Nick reached out and stroked her flank.

'But you'd rather stay?'

'Of course.'

He opened his arms.

'Then stay.'

At five o'clock Jess said, 'I really must go. They'll kill me if I don't.'

Nick sighed. 'I'll drive you, then.' He put on his jeans.

In the Hackney kitchen, Jenny and Alison, nursing mugs of tea, stared balefully at Jess and Nick. They ignored their jaunty greetings.

'We started cleaning up at two o'clock, as arranged. We've left you your share.' Alison spoke but didn't move. Jenny pointed wordlessly at the cooker and fridge, both of which had been pulled away from the wall. Clearly, Jess was expected to get rid of the mess that had accumulated beneath them. At the sight of the sticky mounds of debris Jess' stomach turned. She looked at Alison's unforgiving face; her cropped hair and heavy eyebrows gave her an aggressive look that her ragged black mohair sweater did nothing to soften.

'Sorry I'm late,' she murmured, pulling on some rubber gloves.

'Oh, come now,' said Nick, 'surely this can wait.' He wrestled both cooker and fridge back into position, and smiled at the girls. 'That's better. Jess and I are going out this evening,' he explained, 'and we just don't have the time now. Take those gloves off, darling.'

Jenny and Alison, pinched and rigid with rage, spluttered out protests. Nick extracted a wad of money from his pocket and peeled off a twenty-pound note. He laid it on the kitchen table. 'There now,' he said, 'you can pay someone to do it, if that'll help. Come on, Jessie.' He led her back to the car, closing the door firmly on the ensuing stream of obscenities.

In the Porsche, Jess burst into tears. 'I should have stayed,' she wailed. 'They're my friends.'

Nick shrugged. 'With friends like that . . . I never could stand women who swear.'

'You shouldn't have done that, Nick,' Jess continued, biting her nails. 'It wasn't really your business. You shouldn't have got involved.'

'I know,' said Nick. 'But I think you're glad I did.' They stopped at a red light. He reached over and kissed her on the mouth.

Now, not even a year later, Jess had come to think of the Hackney house with nostalgic affection. Her initial dislike of Nick's flat had turned to claustrophobic loathing. Her early efforts to humanise it had tailed off; now, it seemed that all she did was mess it up. She and Louis slept in the bedroom, Nick on the sofa bed. Even though Louis' nights had improved considerably, Nick made no attempt to move back. Weekends at Powdermill were a blessed refuge, despite the cold and the discomfort and the unpredictability of the inmates. She kept some spare things for Louis down there, so that she could go by train with just a small bag if Nick didn't want to come. And more often than not he didn't.

He didn't want to come this time. He had a lot of work to catch up on, he said. In fact, he'd got a business dinner on Friday evening which he'd go straight on to. Why didn't Jess take herself off Friday lunchtime, so that she would arrive before it got dark?

Why not, indeed? Jess took a toothbrush and a change of clothes for herself, and a changing bag for Louis, and boarded the 1.50 from Charing Cross. Louis seemed to like the train. She propped him up on her knee and he stared out of the window, puzzled and intent. It was a soft, grey, windless day, perfect for Guy Fawkes if the rain held off. Leaves of purest lemon clung to the damp black branches. On the cuttings brambles, no longer bearing fruit, looped their purple stems like an arterial system. Jess bent to nuzzle her baby's head. 'Listen, little Lou,' she murmured, 'it's Guy Fawkes' tomorrow. Remember.' And she whispered in his ear the Bonfire Hymn.

The old man in the corner seat looked on, enjoying the graceful sweep of soft hair falling round the tiny child. When the train reached his station he unfurled Louis' fist and pressed a fifty-pence piece into it. 'Where I come from,' he told Jess, half apologetically, 'they say you should cross a baby's palm with silver. For luck.'

'Oh, thank you!' cried Jess, charmed. 'I'll keep this.' She waved Louis' arm up and down in an imitation of farewell. 'For luck,' she said aloud when the old man had gone and she and Louis were alone in the carriage. 'You'll need luck, little Lou.' And she twisted her wedding ring round and round her finger.

Finian and Martha were both at the station to meet her. They embraced her as best they could without crushing Louis, who dangled against her chest in his padded sling. Finian had come straight out of school. His uniform was far too small for him; his bony wrists stuck out of the sleeves of his blazer by several inches. I'll give Ma the money for a new one, thought Jess. With a pang she saw how large Fin's hands had become, how like a man's.

# CHAPTER ELEVEN

'Leave him with me, poppet, he'll be all right.' Martha cradled her infant grandson on her lap. 'I can't go to the bonfire anyway, because of Bella and Ganna, so it'll be no problem to have Louis as well.'

Jess hesitated. Fin's enthusiasm had filled her with a childish longing to see the fireworks, and the prospect of a few hours away from Louis had its own appeal. 'But what about feeding? I've never given him a bottle yet.'

'Feed him just before you go. He'll last four hours, won't he? And if he doesn't, well, it won't hurt him to cry for a while. He won't be the only one crying.' Martha rolled her eyes expressively up to the ceiling, indicating Bella's room. Bella detested Bonfire Night. All afternoon she had been piling furniture to form a complicated barricade against her bedroom door, and sticking brown wrapping paper over the windows. Once darkness fell she would lie under her bed, sobbing and moaning, until the early hours. She would neither eat nor drink until the following morning. Finian asked, once, why she was so afraid, since the noise of the fireworks could barely be heard at the isolated farm, but Martha explained, 'She knows they're there, Fin, she hears them in her mind.' Martha had never attempted to coax her cousin out of her self-immolation. Unlike many of Bella's strange behaviours, the origin of this fear was easily traceable. As a tiny child, Bella had endured the Blitz.

Jess looked at her mother sitting squarely on the ladder-backed kitchen chair, her broad feet planted on the flagstones, her grey woollen skirt spread wide to make a lap for Louis. Her pale-ginger hair was full of silver threads now, but her back was straight and her light-blue eyes were as clear and steady as ever. The line of her jaw, strongly shaped like Finian's, was only a little softened by the soft pouches of skin beginning to pucker beneath it. 'I'd like to paint you, Ma,' Jess said, 'with you holding Louis like that.'

Martha smiled. She found it easy to smile at Jess. 'I'm glad you want to paint again,' she replied. 'You haven't wanted to for a long time.'

'Don't wear Wellingtons,' said Fin, 'in case someone throws a banger into one. Oh, and keep your hands in your pockets so that people can't stuff lighted fireworks in. Can you ask your dad for some change because they go round collecting?'

'Sure,' said Jamie. He did not like the idea of a firework in his pocket at all, but he would have died rather than say so. 'You're not taking Linford, are you?'

'Christ, no. "Keep pets indoors." I expect Ma will let him stay in the house for once. It doesn't matter if he howls, he'll drown out Bella.'

'How do you mean?'

'Bella screams all night when there's fireworks. It makes her think of the bombs.'

Jamie had been wanting to ask for a long time. 'Fin, who is Bella? I mean, why –'

'She's my mother's cousin. Ma looks after her. She's lived with us for years, don't ask me why. She's all right – I mean, she's crazy, but she never hurts anyone.'

Jamie admired his friend's insouciant attitude to mental illness. As far as he could remember he'd never met a bona fide lunatic. 'But why is she crazy?' he persisted. 'Was she always like that?'

Finian didn't sound very interested. 'I dunno. Suppose so. No – I remember, Ma said she got married to someone once and he walked out on her or something, and she never got over the shock.'

Jamie swallowed. 'My father walked out on my mother,' he said. His voice sounded young and shrill.

'Yeah,' said Fin, 'I know. And so did mine, don't forget. It doesn't mean that much. I reckon Bella must have always been a bit . . . Oh well. What are you going to do with Samson?'

'Dad'll look after him, no problem. Is your sister coming?'

'I hope so. She can drive us. It'll be a laugh.'

Tony Chandler made supper. He had taken to doing this on Saturday evenings, partly as a way of spoiling Pippa, and partly

85

as a way of tactfully avoiding her cooking. Most weekday evenings, Pippa popped something from Marks and Spencer into the microwave. Such meals were edible if a little monotonous, but at weekends she seemed to feel she ought to make more effort, so Tony had had to sit through some appalling messes without complaint. The recipes had been provided by Pippa's mother, and were recommended as 'easy'; they lived in a little floral plastic folder, and tended to sauces made with condensed soup or bottled mayonnaise. Desserts always seemed to involve tinned mandarin segments and crushed sweet biscuits. Why, thought Tony as he turned the swordfish steaks in their lime juice and chilli marinade, do I always end up with women who can't cook?

Actually, that wasn't really true of Susan. In the early days she'd been quite an ambitious cook. With her exquisite taste – and you had to hand it to her, Susan did have taste – she wasn't capable of serving up a really grisly meal. But as she became more and more neurotic so the food became plainer and plainer, until there was virtually never anything but skinless grilled chicken and salad. The same thing had happened to her clothes – well cut, immaculately clean but for the last few years nothing but black and navy and grey. Tony thought of Susan's shoulder blades, sharp under her grey cashmere pullover. He looked across at Pippa, snuggled in the corner of the sofa, her little feet tucked under her. She'd learn how to cook, he thought fondly. She was young and her tastes were still rather infantile. But she made the place cosy. How right she had been to insist on a sofa in the kitchen!

Pippa was flicking through an encyclopaedia of pregnancy and childbirth. She was already well acquainted with most of its contents, and had made Tony stick pieces of paper over the gorier illustrations. Samson, lonely without his young master, clambered on to the sofa beside her and thrust his muzzle against her hand. She responded automatically with a caress, and then jerked her hand away.

'Tony!' she called, 'I've just been reading about diseases you can get from dogs.'

'Rabies?' said Tony absently, throwing the mangetouts into boiling water.

86

'No, silly. Something beginning with T – where is it? – that can make the baby blind or brain damaged. So, really, we shouldn't let Samson sit on the furniture any more.'

'He's not supposed to anyway. Susan must have been too soft with him. He never did when – But Pips, darling, sometimes I wish you'd never bought that book. It just gives you new things to worry about. Here, boy.' He dislodged the reluctant Samson.

'No, but it's serious,' said Pippa, uncurling. 'It's quite common, apparently. Much commoner than people think. Perhaps we shouldn't have Samson here any more.'

Tony set the candlesticks on the table. 'James wouldn't be too pleased.'

'And after the baby's born,' continued Pippa, 'Samson might be jealous. Even the sweetest of family dogs sometimes turn against babies. Jamie would get used to it – I'm sure Susan wouldn't mind keeping him at weekends too.'

'I'm sure she would.'

'Or he could go to a kennels. Oh, please, darling, I do think it's important.'

Tony sighed. 'Well, if I raise it with James I'll have to tell him about the baby. It's about time he knew.'

'Oh no,' said Pippa, 'that wouldn't be kind. To tell him we weren't having Samson *and* about the baby – it would be bound to make him resent the baby. And I do so hope he'll love her.'

'*Her?* What –'

'No, sweetie, I don't know. But I always imagine a little blonde girl, don't you?'

Tony transferred the fish to an oval platter and scattered chopped coriander. 'Let's put it off for a little, Pips. Just steer clear of Samson for the time being. I'm sure you're worrying about nothing.' But one glance at Pippa's pink, mutinous face, the blue eyes welling with tears, told him that Samson's rural weekends were numbered. 'All right, darling, if it's going to upset you, I'll tackle it tomorrow. Now let's eat.'

'Thank you, darling,' Pippa reached up to plant a kiss on his cheek. 'This looks scrummy. You're such a clever cook!'

Broadhurst High Street was unrecognisable. Windows were boarded up, shops and houses stood in darkness. Only the pub doors stood open, disgorging their customers on to the street. People wandered in groups, shouting and laughing and slopping bitter out of plastic glasses. In the market square a colossal bonfire was piled in readiness, the Guy lashed to the top was almost invisible in the mist that had begun to gather. From the far end of the High Street the drums of a brass band could be felt rather than heard.

'Up here,' called Finian, scrambling on to the churchyard wall. 'You get a better view from here.' Jamie followed him. The church loomed darkly behind them; shapes moved in the mist. Jamie knew they were people really – every now and then a torch would flash out, and besides, he could hear their laughter. But when the church bell struck the hour it made him start.

'I don't think I can manage the wall,' said Jess. 'I'll stay down here.'

'Oh, come on, sis, I'll pull you up. Jac, give us a hand.'

Jamie grabbed Jess awkwardly by the elbow. It was the first time that he'd ever touched a girl – at least since nursery school or whatever. And Fin's sister wasn't really a girl. She was married, with a kid. As old as Pippa, probably. But tonight, with her long hair loose and her scarf trailing and her face alive with the excitement of being out, babyless, after dark, she looked like a girl.

Once on the wall she perched between the boys, and Jamie loved and feared the slight unwitting pressure of her arm against his.

Jess handed round a bag of hot chestnuts she'd bought from a street vendor, and they drummed their heels and waited. Figures in fancy dress flitted in and out of the thickening crowd. Faces were painted like skulls, or ghouls. Even quite tiny children were dressed as devils and goblins and there was a liberal sprinkling of Saxon warriors. This was, after all, 1066 country. Bangers, hurled across the street, skittered along in a trail of sparks before exploding. Each time, Jamie steeled himself. He couldn't quite get used to the bangs, loud as gunfire in the packed street.

'Here they come!' said Fin, and Jamie turned to see the procession at the top of the High Street, holding their flaming torches high. From this distance it looked like a river of fire flowing down the hill. The thump of the drums was like the crack of doom. The smoke from the torches mingled with the mist: the flames, the shrieks, the painted faces, caused Jamie's chest to ache with a painful kind of excitement.

The procession consisted of brass bands, dressed-up members of all the neighbourhood Bonfire Societies bearing banners, and, rumbling along at the end, floats bearing tableaux got up by the Young Farmers, the Scouts, or the local hospital. Despite the intrusive presence of spectacles and training shoes, the sheer number of marchers in fancy dress made Jamie feel that the 1990s had been suspended, replaced by an ancient, pagan past. A gaggle of boys processing with streaked faces and black cloaks whooped and yelled. Jamie thought of *Lord of the Flies*. Fin said, 'See them? They go to my school. I'm going to go with them. Coming?'

'I'll stay put,' said Jess. 'You can find me on the way back.'

Jamie hesitated. He was torn between avoiding the boys, which would mean undergoing the exquisite humiliating thrill of staying on his own with Jess, and proving his courage and solidarity by going with Fin. 'Coming?' repeated Fin, with an edge of impatience in his voice. Jamie slithered down.

Close up, the boys looked less threatening. Through the war-paint Jamie could see ordinary schoolboy features like recent haircuts and orthodontic braces and large ears. They greeted Fin warmly, and when Fin said, 'This is Jac,' they grunted acceptance, breaking ranks to make room for the newcomer. A man rumbled by with a metal wheelbarrow bearing several flaming torches. Fin grabbed one for himself and urged Jamie to do the same. The torches were like giants' clubs, with bundles of rags soaked in something flammable tied to the top. Jamie loved holding his. Now he felt validated, no mere onlooker any more. All he had to do was march down the street and concentrate on not jumping away from the bouncing bangers.

Alone on the wall, Jess felt conspicuous. She eased herself down – more than two months after the birth, and her body had still not regained its old suppleness – and stood with arms folded, wrapping her duffle jacket more closely round herself. She loved watching the watery movements of the flames and the smoke, loved the jagged outline of the tiled rooftops against the

89

night sky, the shadows of the marchers cast gigantic and angular on the wall of the church. Jess could look and look for ages without thinking about anything. At school she had been in endless trouble; twenty minutes of Latin and Chemistry could go by and she would still be staring through the window at cloud banks or bright berries or new leaves. It wasn't really possible, of course, but Jess felt she could remember her own babyhood, lying in her cot in a shaft of sunlight, watching her own hands move in front of her face.

A crowd of revellers brushed past; young men, with loud, rich voices and beery breath. They were dressed as Vikings with horned helmets and shaggy belted jerkins. One, hardly pausing, kissed Jess full on the mouth. In the split second it took, his laughing eyes, his white teeth, the brown hair curling out under the absurd helmet imprinted on her mind. He said nothing, gave her a flashing smile, and moved on. Jess stood stock still, relishing the reverberation of the kiss, that seemed to carry her back to a time before adulthood, before responsibility, before Nick.

In an expensive, intimate Notting Hill brasserie, Nick allowed his fingers to brush against those of Dominique, his dining companion that Saturday night. Dominique was sleek, French, dark-haired and well tailored; Nick looked for aesthetic contrasts in his life. 'And your wife?' Dominique asked, returning and amplifying his caress, her fingertips resting for an instant on his wedding ring.

'I'm waiting for the divorce to come through,' he replied. He shook his head. 'She was far too young. It was all a terrible mistake.'

'No children, then?' Dominique wasn't going to waste her time.

'No children.' Nick was pretty sure he'd tidied away every trace of Louis' existence from the flat. Still, perhaps it would be better to go back to her place, to be on the safe side. He summoned the waiter.

'Two glasses of your best Cognac, and the bill.' He turned to Dominique. 'And then?' He took her hand in both of his, and kissed the pulse in her wrist.

'Why not?' said Dominique. 'Come home with me. It's not

far.' She had no intention of waking, dishevelled, in a stranger's bed. She liked to be in charge of her Saturday nights.

Jamie woke late, in a panic he couldn't immediately account for. He groped through the recesses of his mind, searching for the horror that he knew lurked somewhere. Then it bounded out at him. What he'd heard Pippa say to his father last night.

He'd come back at ten, exhilarated by the fireworks and the bonfire. He and Fin would have stayed longer, but Jess had to go back and feed the baby. He'd gone straight to bed after greeting Samson, wanting to feast on the evening in private rather than give a pale, watered-down account to the uncomprehending adults. As he lay in bed, his mind still thumping, he heard Pippa and his father on the stairs. He remembered Pippa's squeaky voice, plainly audible despite her stage whisper:

'So you won't forget, will you, Tony?'

'Forget what?'

'To tell Jamie that we'll have to get rid of Samson.'

A tiny pause, then:

'Leave that to me, darling. I'll deal with it tomorrow.'

It was hours before Jamie fell asleep. And now he'd slept so long, it might be too late to avert disaster. He pulled on the smoky clothes he'd worn the night before and ran out of the house, breakfastless, pausing only to release Samson from the utility room where he had been shut up.

Jamie found Fin in the stable, feeding Pharaoh. The horse's breath curled dragon-like in the raw November air. While the two dogs gambolled round their feet, Jamie recounted the overheard conversation. When he had finished, to his horror, he burst into tears.

Fin put down the feed bucket. He didn't touch Jamie, but he stood by him shoulder to shoulder. 'Well,' he said, 'she can't get rid of Samson, because we can have him here.'

Jamie rubbed his face. 'Really?' he said.

'No problem. And we could go further.' Finian's imagination began to tick. 'If she wants to get rid of him, then why don't we get rid of her?'

Dizzying prospects unfurled in Jamie's mind's eye.

'Let's plan it,' said Fin. 'I'm starving. Have you had breakfast

91

yet? OK, then come and have it with me, and we can talk.'

Jamie thought of his tear-streaked face, and of Jess. He hung back, but it was as if Fin could read his mind. 'It's OK,' he said. 'No one's about, except Bella. Ma's taken Ganna to church, and Jess is still in bed. The baby kept her awake half the night.'

Jamie followed Fin into the farmhouse. In a matter of minutes the wasted desert of his mental landscape had begun to bloom again. He had cried in front of Fin, and it didn't seem to matter. Samson would be saved. And maybe they'd be seeing the last of Pippa. Jamie's confidence in his friend knew no bounds.

# CHAPTER TWELVE

'You'll be all right then, Fin? You can heat up that shepherd's pie if you can't wait till we get back.'

'Sure thing, Ma.' Fin was pleased to have a few hours alone in the house – alone, that was, except for Bella. He was looking forward to formulating his new plan for getting rid of Pippa Watts-Davison. First he had to decide which code to write his notes in. He was fluent in several.

Martha took Sibyl's arm and led her to the car. Martha taught art part time at the college of further education; the theme the examining board had set was 'Innocence and Experience'. After racking her brains – for she would have preferred a more concrete suggestion – it had struck her that her mother-in-law's face expressed a marvellous mixture of both. Persuading Sibyl to sit for the class had been easy. In her youth she had sat for artists like Meredith Frampton and Dod Procter, and to be asked again stirred her dormant vanity. She chuckled when Martha told her about the theme. 'And which do I represent?' she asked. 'Or shall we leave that for the students to decide? I don't know why they need a theme at all. Why can't they just paint what they see?'

Martha was inclined to agree. She tucked the tartan travel rug over Sibyl's knees. The day had been dank and lightless. At five o'clock it was already dark.

They drove through Broadhurst, where the only remaining signs of Saturday night's revelry were a few upper-storey windows still boarded up. Sibyl peered out. She hardly ever left the house these days.

'My dear, has Halland's closed?' she asked. 'What's that in its place? A laundry?'

Martha's heart sank. Halland's the haberdasher's had closed in the early 1970s. Sibyl's diagnosis of her own mental state seemed more accurate every day. 'It's a dry cleaner's,' she replied. 'You're rather out of touch with goings-on in Broadhurst, aren't you, Ganna? I should take you out more often.'

'Don't worry about me,' said Sibyl. 'I'm quite happy at home. I sit and arrange my mind – like clearing out a chest of drawers, in readiness. And besides, you've enough to cope with without exercising a broken-winded old nag like me.'

Martha laughed. 'Broken-winded you're not.'

'I'll tell you who is, though,' said Sibyl emphatically, 'and that is Jess. That girl is very low, Martha. Her zest for life has all but gone.'

This time, the old woman was echoing Martha's own fear. But still Martha's inclination was to dress the truth about Jess in its Sunday best. 'It's hardly surprising,' she said, 'since Louis keeps her awake so much. She needs more time away from him. She was quite different when she came back from the bonfire with the boys. I haven't seen her eyes shine like that for ages. Perhaps Nick is right – they should get a nanny. Then they could have some more fun together, as a couple.'

Sibyl's silence was meaningful.

'Don't you agree?' continued Martha. 'You always had nannies and nursemaids, didn't you? Wasn't it a good thing?'

'Not entirely, no. Of course it was far more restful for the mother, and yes, one could have "fun" with one's husband, if that was what one wanted. But I wonder, sometimes, whether Leo's – *weakness* – could have been prevented if Hugh and I had had more influence on his early upbringing. Nanny Wilkes was a treasure, as people said in those days, but Leo was, frankly, indulged.'

'Better than being repressed by some sadist,' said Martha. 'Don't blame yourself, Sibyl. Children have their own tendencies. They arrive in this world with a lot of luggage, and most of it gets unpacked sooner or later. Parents can only affect things to a limited extent.'

'I'm quite prepared to blame myself.' Sibyl's tone was tart. 'It seems to me that people these days are too slow to take blame for their decisions. But these tendencies, Martha – what are my great-grandson's tendencies, would you say?'

Martha smiled. 'Little Louis? Little Louis is a tyrant. He wants Jess all to himself, and when he gets her, he gives her a hard time. I never knew a ten-week-old with such a ferocious will. And he's very bright, too – and a charmer.'

94

'Just like his father, then?'

Martha pulled up in front of the college. 'Yes, just like his father. And like his grandfather too, perhaps.'

The next half-hour was lost in the bustle of greeting the students and setting up the easels and installing Sibyl in an upright armchair draped in black. Martha was amused to discover that beneath her coat Sibyl had exchanged her usual heather mixture for a quilted jacket of brilliant red. 'To make them think about the title,' she explained. 'The blood of the innocent or the scarlet woman?' Against the dark drapery the effect was striking, as was the nobility of the ancient head, the fine hair piled high like spun sugar. Martha felt a surge of admiration. A little forgetfulness was nothing; the unbowed spirit was what counted.

But when the students had settled down and the only sounds were the whisper of charcoal on paper and the wheezing of the elderly blow heater that was turned in Sibyl's direction, Martha found herself with time to think. It *was* worrying that Nick saw so little of Jess and Louis; even more worrying, perhaps, that Jess didn't seem to mind. Sibyl was right; postnatal exhaustion couldn't fully account for the defeated set of Jess' shoulders. She had always been dreamy, of course, but lately the dreaminess had turned to numb withdrawal. For all her talent, Jess had never really made a life of her own. Unlike Eliza and Finian, she had always been dependent, trusting other people to do things for her and rewarding them with unstinting affection. Poor girl – she had lost her father. Was she about to lose her husband too?

Martha considered her family and their future. Bella was as she had always been; she was predictable in her unpredicability, but one was never free of her. Sibyl, getting older fast, needed help now with most aspects of daily life. Eliza, autonomous in Oxford, but bitter about her father, and manless – puzzlingly manless, in Martha's view. Jess, adjusting to the aftermath of the earthquake that was childbirth with only the most basic support from her husband. Finian – Fin was marvellous, apparently as happy as the day was long, but he stood fatherless on the brink of adolescence, and Martha thought that the spell would soon break. And Leo – gone. No word from him yet.

And herself? Middle-aged, hard-up, solely responsible for the welfare of people and animals and birds and buildings, abandoned by a husband who had broken her heart so many times that the pieces would never quite fit back together again. How did Martha Antrobus feel about her own future?

'Mrs Antrobus?' A voice shattered her reverie. 'Could you give me a hand? I can't seem to get the shoulders right.'

The light caught Sibyl's jet earrings as she moved ever so slightly. How long old women's ear lobes grew! Martha could see from the slight bowing of her shoulders that she was beginning to tire. The betrayals people perpetrated on each other, she thought, are nothing to the way your own body betrays you. She moved to help the student. She thought, I'll manage without Leo. That's all there is to it.

Susan Chandler picked up the telephone.

'Suze? Tony here.'

Suze! The sudden familiarity could only mean he wanted something from her.

'Yes?'

'Suze, I'm ringing about the dog. Is James within earshot?'

'No, he's working in his room. Why?'

'Good. Well . . . it's a sensitive subject, I know, but Pippa doesn't really feel we should have the dog at weekends.'

'Why on earth not?'

'Well, he climbs on the furniture and . . . and messes things up rather.' Tony sounded apologetic.

'I can't believe my ears, Tony. You want me to look after Samson every weekend so that he can ruin my furniture instead of yours?'

Tony almost said, 'It's not your furniture,' but he stopped himself just in time. He said lamely, 'Would you mind? You have him in the week, after all, so it can't make much of a difference.'

There was a silence while Susan struggled to find the words with which to express her contempt. She failed.

'Suze? You still there? Look, I know it sounds silly, but there's a disease you can catch from dogs and –'

'Ah!' The light dawned. 'She's pregnant!'

'How did you guess?' Tony was put out.

Susan's hands were shaking. She tried to keep her voice

steady. 'Let me get this straight, Tony. Pippa's pregnant, so she wants to avoid the very remote risk of catching whatever-it's-called from poor old Samson – who, incidentally, is kept spotlessly clean, as you very well know. So you think it would be a good idea to deprive Jamie of his dog, who is the one real friend he has, for the sake of the baby. Do I really need to spell out for you how that would make him feel about the baby?'

'Susan, please keep your voice down. He doesn't know about the baby yet.'

'Then I'll tell him.'

'Please – please don't.'

'If you want me to keep Samson at weekends, I'll tell him.'

'Oh, Christ! Look – give me time to think about it. I'll ring you back.'

'Perhaps you should have thought about it before you picked up the telephone. And Tony – is Pippa in the room?'

'Yes –'

'I hope she can overhear me when I tell you that I didn't believe anybody could be so monstrously selfish as you, but it looks as if I was wrong. You've met your match.'

Susan unplugged the telephone. She longed for a cigarette – two years since she gave up, and she still suffered these pangs. Instead, she poured herself some whisky, which she didn't much like. It was still lingering in the decanter from Tony's time. She thought she had removed every trace of Tony, but still she kept stumbling over reminders of him.

Nursing the drink, she stood by the French window, gazing at the drab November garden. It was almost dark; the black twigs of the cherry tree, shaken by the wind, snatched at the dull purple sky. From the clump of laurels in the corner rolled two cats locked in combat, too intent on their battle even to yowl. The hard paving stones seemed to bring them to their senses; they shook apart and backed away from one another, backs arched and tails stiff. And then the noises began. How could such guttural, blood-curdling threats issue from such small, soft throats?

Susan pulled a cord; the curtains shut out the night. She had chosen the curtains, as she had chosen nearly every nice thing in the house. They were a deep, sombre violet; a rich, subdued colour that gave a point of focus and feeling of solidity to the high-ceilinged, white-painted drawing room. The colour was echoed in the patterned border of the carpet that had been specially woven for the room. Susan hated fitted carpets; round the edge of this carpet you could see a good foot or so of polished oak floorboards. She wondered about Powdermill Barn. She was sure that Pippa would be a fitted carpet enthusiast.

She ran her hand along the back of the *chaise-longue* that she had picked up for a song in Portobello Road and reupholstered herself. The concealed lighting, the purpose-built bookshelves, the leaping horse carved out of a lump of translucent alabaster, the Matisse lithograph of a bathing girl formed from one single, elegant fuzzy line – all had been designed or chosen or positioned by her. She did have a talent for these things. The Gascoignes were delighted with the work she'd done on their Islington house. On Saturday she was to drive with Polly to meet some more potential clients, who wanted something very grand and expensive done to their eighteenth-century house on Downshire Hill.

Jamie, though quiet, seemed a lot more settled at school. His half-term report cards had been satisfactory. Tony seemed to have stopped threatening to put her house on the market – probably only because house prices were so low at the moment, but still, it was a useful reprieve. So why, when she had thought she had regathered her scattered strength, did this news of Pippa Watts-Davison's pregnancy fill her with such dizzying despair?

She finished the contents of her glass in one swallow, and moved to the decanter tray for a refill. Then she sat upright on the edge of the *chaise-longue*, staring unseeing at the blank white wall.

In his attic bedroom at the top of the tall white house, Jamie inched his way through his homework. He'd finished geography, which was easy, and was about to give up on maths, which was impossible. He would give Matthew Fellows a ring later – he was quite good at maths. All that remained was English. Jamie usually dreaded English, because he never had any imaginative ideas, but tonight there would be no problem. Mr Furness had told them to write a chapter of their own autobiography, in a fictionalised way, as if it came out of a novel. Jamie knew exactly what he was going to write about. He put the date and his name at the top of a sheet of A4. Then on the title line he wrote BITCH. He wrote it in capital letters and he underlined it three times.

In Sussex, Finian was also busy. He lay face down on his bed with a ginger cat draped across the small of his back, filling his notebook with ideas for the removal of his friend's inconvenient stepmother. He had chosen his Greek code – the letters of the Greek alphabet, but shifted along one place to foil intruders, so that A was beta, B gamma, and so on. Finian was quite pleased with some of his ideas. His favourite was, admittedly, not original – he'd read about it somewhere. But it was practicable. He and Jac would sew prawns into the hems of the curtains of the barn, and perhaps shove a few into that king-sized mattress as well. However much Pippa scrubbed and fumigated the house, she'd never get rid of the smell because she wouldn't know where it was coming from. So she wouldn't want to come to the barn any more. Simple.

Ideally, she'd have a big row with Jac's father about the smell, because it would be driving both of them mad. Then they would split up, and Jac and his father would come on their own – the prawns would then, of course, be surreptitiously removed. Finian had to admit that it might simply drive both adults away – but then he'd just invite Jac to come and stay at the farmhouse. He could come on the train, with Samson on a lead. And if that didn't work – well, he had twenty-three other ideas written down.

He dislodged the cat, closed his notebook, and padded downstairs in his socks. Bella was in the kitchen, cutting up newspapers. Fin was hungry, but that shepherd's pie looked like something somebody had chewed up and spat out. He cut himself two thick slabs of bread and spread them with golden syrup. Then he took up his accustomed perch on top of the Aga.

Bella pasted her cuttings into an exercise book. She had showed Finian these books before, but he'd never been able to work out what the cuttings had in common. Reports of weddings from the local paper were favoured – 'The bride wore an ivory silk dress with lemon piping and carried an S-shaped bouquet of mixed lemon silk flowers. The chief bridesmaid wore burgundy.' Anything about lifeboats was also seized upon, especially those that had encountered disaster. The Kennedy family were there, but so were apparently random notices about charity concerts and lost cats. Perhaps Bella, too, had a code. 'Revenge is sweet, Bella,' he said, biting into his sandwich.

She looked at him and gave him one of her rare smiles.

'Revenge is sweet,' she echoed, and carried on pasting.

Sibyl hadn't 'sat' for six decades, but she hadn't forgotten how. She settled her muscles into comfortable shapes at the beginning, then detached her mind and let it drift far beyond the draughty, paint-spattered confines of the studio. Within seconds she lost all awareness of the squinting students measuring her up with their pencils, became oblivious even to the presence of her dear, patient, stoical daughter-in-law, the rock that shored up her tottering eighty-year-old existence. The smell of turpentine and the dusty air carried her back to a time before Martha, before Leo, before Hugh, even. She was eighteen years old, naked on a couch, long and white against the green velvet drape. Her head was thrown back, her hair flowed down to the floor in a pale-gold waterfall. She remembered the cracks in the plaster ceiling, remembered making them into faces and animals in her mind's eye. She didn't mind being naked at all.

The artist was a Pole, an angry little man. She couldn't remember his name now, though he had been something of an *enfant terrible* in the art world at the time. He had told her he was in love with her, many times, but she had taken this as a figure of speech, and she never remembered him laying a finger on her. The innocence of those days! Despite the declarations of the Pole and several other men, she was a virgin when she met Hugh. And when Hugh had said to her, once they were engaged, 'Look, darling, no more modelling. I just can't stand it, I'm afraid,' she had gladly complied, because he seemed so anxious about it, but even then she didn't fully understand why.

Hugh was a dear. Intelligent, fastidious, kind – a man with sensitive moral antennae who put his principles into action. Those early years of their marriage had been so calmly happy, a strongly woven fabric of shared tastes and interests and lively, like-minded friends. She had really been very, very lucky. But it wasn't until the birth of Leo that she had known the depth of love – churning, trawling, fear-laden love, that thrilled and filled you and could never let you be.

Such emotions alarmed Sibyl. She suppressed them as best she could; such intensity could not be good for the child. She wanted to press him to her, to bury her fingers in his curly head, to hide him away from the outside world and all threat of taint and harm. Instead she entrusted much of his daily care to kind, sensible Nanny Wilkes. The steady beam of Sibyl's interest and affection shone on Leo throughout his childhood, but only very rarely did he catch a glimpse of the hidden savagery of her passionate love.

He was a happy child, eager, confident, beguiling. She and Hugh often congratulated each other on the excellent foundations they seemed to have laid for the handsome, proud edifice that would be his adult life. How could they have missed the flaw, the faulty seam that had now cracked his marriage and his family apart?

Perhaps that weakness just hadn't been there in childhood. Hugh died when Leo was poised on the cusp between childhood and adolescence; in her grief and bewilderment, perhaps Sibyl hadn't noticed a certain falling away. Leo had seemed so strong, so self-sufficient. Everyone told her how well he had taken the shock of his father's death. She drew reassurance from this at the time; could that longing for comfort, for a smooth route out of the dreary, tangled thicket of mourning, have blinded her to the state of Leo's condition?

It was the same with young Finian now. Nobody worried about Finian. He ran at will through the countryside, with no apparent care in the world. Martha's face would always soften when Fin was mentioned. 'That's one person I don't have to worry about, thank God,' she would declare. Sibyl jerked a little in her chair as she thought, I must tell Martha. I must warn her to take more care of Finian. Because Leo was just such a golden boy. And now look . . .

Leo's face superimposed itself on Finian's, and Sibyl's thoughts blurred with the ache of loss. Her mind scrabbled for escape, and soon found refuge in the inexhaustible subtleties of colour. It was a lifelong habit of Sibyl's, at moments of stress, simply to contemplate colour. She thought now of Powdermill wood, for so many years a favourite walk but now for ever out of reach of her old limbs. She imagined the toadstools that would be scattered like improbable furniture, the dull-bright colours, purple, yellow, burnt orange, dirty pink. She thought of a November sky, grey clouds pressing down through the gaps in the trees. Some trees would be almost bare, some still thick with colour, fox colour and fire colour burning through the still, moist air.

When the life class ended and Martha installed her into the car again, the memory of a memory ruffled her equilibrium. She touched Martha's shoulder and said, 'I have something very important to tell you, my dear,' but for all her groping she couldn't open the right mental door. 'Tell me later, Ganna,' said Martha. 'I'm sure it will keep,' and by the time they reached the farmhouse, Sibyl had fallen asleep.

# CHAPTER THIRTEEN

Jamie didn't see Finian for several weekends after Bonfire Night. As Colin the builder had predicted, Tony and Pippa found their enthusiasm for the barn waning as the weather grew colder. They had some entertaining to catch up on, so they organised a couple of dinner parties in Tony's Dolphin Square flat. Jamie was allowed to choose how he spent his weekends, so he stayed with his mother and Samson in Holland Park. Tony, not wishing to let his rights over his son lapse, offered to take him to the Natural History Museum, but Jamie said, 'No thank you. I can go on my own.' And did.

The museum had been Jamie's favourite expedition since he was five years old. He minded frantically when the layout was changed, and it often had been in the last few years, as the authorities strove for ever more gimmicky and alluring displays. Jamie wasn't particularly interested in virtual reality and information at the touch of a button. He liked to wander from one glass case to another, bringing the stuffed occupants to life in his imagination. If he stared long enough he could make eyes blink, wings extend, muscles twitch.

He loved the size of the place, too. The vast, vaulted spaces made him feel diminished, insignificant. No one would notice him surrounded by such grandeur. When he could get rid of the sense of his physical self, Jamie could set his mind free. The dull mustard colour of the ornate carved sandstone had become for him the colour of thought itself.

So far, nothing had come of Pippa's threat to get rid of Samson. That Sunday, the day of his pact with Fin, Tony, coming upon Jamie alone in the kitchen, had cleared his throat as if about to give utterance to something important, but Jamie had simply bolted. He rightly guessed that Tony would be unlikely to bring the subject up in front of Pippa, so he had kept close to her as much as possible, though it pained him to do so. And now they wouldn't be going to the barn until the end of term, so he had a breathing space. In his pocket he had a letter from Finian full of proposals for Pippa's dispatch, but he couldn't read them yet, because they were in code, and Fin was sending him the code under separate cover. Every time he touched the letter he felt powerful and guilty, like a terrorist about to plant a bomb, he supposed.

Jamie always avoided the dinosaurs. They were far too public and too fantastical, too long gone to stir him. He made for his favourite corner, and there amongst the pinned butterflies, so delicate, so fresh that one had to forgive the barbarity of their executioners, he took stock.

He didn't know what Fin meant when he said he could get rid of Pippa. He knew he didn't mean murder; Jamie knew that hot thoughts of doing harm belonged to the blind black magic mindset of childhood that he had left behind him. Fin probably intended to put Pippa off; tell her something about his father, maybe, that would send her scuttling back to the prissy little world she'd come from. Jamie was sure that Pippa was only after his father's money. Why else would a blonde who might – he had to admit – be described as attractive by some people choose to live with a man with a bald patch who was twice her age? Surely most people of Pippa's age wanted to go to parties and have lots of boyfriends, not stodge around every weekend cooking sickly meals, fussing about what colour the duvet covers should be and cooing over his father and his boring, ancient friends. The money had to be the attraction. It was amazing that Dad, as a lawyer, hadn't noticed. Jamie and Fin would be doing him a favour if they could get rid of her.

Suppose, just suppose that Fin's plot, whatever it was, got discovered, and Dad was so furious that he banned Jamie from coming to the barn any more? The thought made him quail, but he remembered the ready welcome that Fin had offered to Samson, and he felt a small, warm assurance that the same welcome would be there for him, too. If he was chucked out of the barn, he'd just go to the farmhouse.

And besides, Dad wouldn't chuck him out. Dad always held on to things that were his, and Jamie was the only child he'd got.

Four o'clock on a wintry afternoon. Patrick Furness stood at the

104

Common Room window, looking out at the group of boys exercising in the school yard. These were the cross-country runners, deprived of a proper run by the sudden demise of the minibus. Instead they were being forced to circuit the yard at various speeds, breaking for press-ups every so often. Despite the flurries of sleet that whisked horizontally across the yard, the boys were not allowed to wear track suits. Their mortified flesh glowed pink and white through the gloom.

The cross-country runners were always a dismal lot, too uncooperative or uncoordinated to shine at football or rugby, too unadventurous to take up one of the more unusual sports, like fives or fencing. Cross-country, despite its ferocious regime, gathered the weak, the lazy, the friendless and the clueless into its embrace. Even when ordered to take a break, they made no attempt to fraternise, but stood gasping, hands on hips, puffing out steam into the biting air. Patrick Furness, sipping his tea, smiled in pity and contempt. His eye rested on little Chandler, his dark face damp, his bony knees trembling. He stood alone, the picture of dumb misery.

Patrick looked round the Common Room. He'd been meaning to do something about Chandler for a while now. Since half-term, the boy's written work had changed from numbingly dull to graphically confessional. It could be simply that he was imitating something he'd read or seen on television, but Patrick didn't think so. The last three essays had been as poorly constructed as ever, but there had been a desperate, driven tone to them that made them seem like something more than mere schoolboy melodrama.

Few of the armchairs ranged round the edge of the room were occupied; those that were had newspapers held up like 'No Trespassing' signs. But Patrick could tell from the legs and the shoes that Duncan Nethersole, Chandler's form tutor, was not there. Patrick poured himself another cup of tea and loaded a plate with cheese sandwiches and a custard tart. He studied the noticeboard, waiting for Nethersole's return from whatever godawful physical activity he had been involved in that afternoon.

When Patrick Furness had first arrived at the school, his relative youth and lack of superfluous weight had caused him to be pounced on by his heartier colleagues, who were convinced that he must have some sporting skill up his sleeve. It had taken a while to shake them off. Now he had wriggled himself into a comfortable niche as master in charge of 'leisure swimming'. All this entailed was rounding up his small group, escorting them to the sports centre to make sure none of them stopped on the way for a cigarette or worse, ticking their names off on a list and then reading a paperback while they meandered up and down the pool. The leisure swimmers were an even less impressive bunch than the runners; boys with serious weight problems or peculiar allergies were herded in, along with the run-of-the-mill weeds. Patrick sat on the side, looking up occasionally from his Conrad or Faulkner or Henry James to give them a vague smile of encouragement. He was supposed to escort them back to school but he tended to let them drift off on their own. He felt that by then they'd earned their cigarette.

Duncan Nethersole puffed into the Common Room and headed for the urns. His large, mottled thighs shook slightly as the warmth of tea and radiators began to take effect. Patrick wished, on aesthetic grounds, that his colleagues would change out of their kit before heading for the feeding trough, but he couldn't blame them if they didn't. A few hours on a windswept games pitch set you yearning for doughnuts and fondant fancies.

Patrick allowed Duncan to consume a couple of each before cornering him. Eventually he sidled over.

'Duncan?'

'Mm?'

'Is Chandler one of yours? I thought so. I'm a little concerned about him.'

Duncan Nethersole's brow creased. He had a kind heart, and worried if his charges had problems, though he rarely knew what to do about them. 'He's always quiet,' he said tentatively.

'Oh, I know, lacks confidence. And being in a form with loud-mouths like Webster and Ahmed doesn't help. But it's his writing I'm worried about.'

Duncan scooped a streak of doughnut jam off his plate and licked his finger, Patrick longed to tell him that a blob had lodged in his sandy beard. 'You think he might be dyslexic?' Duncan asked.

'Oh no. His spelling's not great, but no, it's not that. The thing is, the last three preps have all been about bumping off wicked stepmothers. I set three quite different topics, but he's managed to bring them all round to the same point. And they're becoming increasingly gruesome. It started with ground glass in the tea, then we had sawing through the brake lines and getting splattered across the windscreen. And in the latest one we've got some torture thrown in.'

The form tutor looked alarmed. 'Sexual?'

'No – adventure book stuff. He's pretty pre-pubescent. But it's not very nice – and it's not remotely like anything he wrote in the first half of term.'

Duncan Nethersole rubbed his beard and encountered the blob of jam. 'Hmm. Well. It does figure. You know his parents separated quite recently?'

'I didn't, no.'

'And the father has a girlfriend – Jamie spends his weekends with them.'

'Poor little sod. Only child?'

'Yes, and a bit of a loner.'

'He sits with Fellows and Wilson.'

'Oh, I don't think he's particularly unpopular. But Fellows and Wilson wouldn't be the best confidants if you were really down about something, would they?'

Patrick, calling to mind their flat voices and dust-coloured hair, had to agree. 'He lives with his mother, then?'

'In the week, yes. I've only met her briefly, but she struck me as the cold, neurotic type. Thank you for telling me, Patrick. I'll keep an eye.'

'I'll let you know if anything else comes up. There's a parents' evening soon, isn't there?'

'Yes, but it wouldn't necessarily be a good idea to say anything. The parents are at each other's throats. We don't want to make more trouble for the poor kid.'

Patrick nodded and moved away. Nethersole's caution was typical of the school's approach, in his opinion. When it came to anything unpleasant they kept their heads buried in the sand. Sympathetic ostriches but ostriches nonetheless.

The comments he had written on the stepmother stories had

so far been guarded. He would set them a tempting title this week, and if Jamie Chandler reverted to his theme then he would feel justified in taking positive action. This was only Patrick's third year in teaching, and some of his ideals were still intact.

What title, though?' 'Revenge' – that was sufficiently general, and sufficiently adaptable. 'Revenge' it would be. Patrick tipped the contents of his pigeon-hole into his bicycle bag and turned up the collar of his overcoat, ready for the chilly ride back to his flat.

'It's lovely, really perfect.'

The Islington house was ready at last. Jess, Nick and Louis were to move in on Saturday. Now, on this cold Tuesday after-noon, Susan Chandler was taking Jess through the house to double-check on all the details.

They stood in the little back room that was to be the baby's. The walls had been painted dusty blue – 'A sleepy sort of blue, I hope,' said Jess – and a frieze of golden stars and crescent moons had been stencilled above the dado rail. The curtains, thickly lined, were of deeper blue, studded with more stars.

Jess ran her hand along the rim of the antique wrought-iron cot, freshly repainted and fitted with a new mattress. 'I can't believe he's actually going to sleep in this enormous thing. He's still so tiny.' Louis, warm in his sling against his mother's chest, was, for once, asleep.

'But they grow so fast,' said Susan. 'It seems incredible to me that I've got a teenager now. In some ways it's flashed by. And yet in other ways Jamie's babyhood seems so long ago, like a dis-tant dream.'

Jess plumped the cushions in the window seat. 'Did you mean only to have one?' she asked.

Susan was surprised but not offended. Jess had a way of talk-ing – a simple, direct way – that made it impossible to take offence.

'I just got cold feet, really,' she replied. 'I must admit I found the pregnancy and the birth quite difficult – quite horrible, in fact. And Jamie was premature. He only weighed three pounds. It was all so gruelling. I kept putting off deciding about having a second until . . . well, until it was obvious that it wasn't the sort of marriage you should bring another child into.'

'Oh?' said Jess. 'And when did you *know* that? I mean, how can you ever be sure?'

Susan considered for a moment before replying. 'I was going to say,' she said at last, 'that it was when I found out that Tony was unfaithful. But that isn't quite true. It was when I realised that I no longer cared whether he was unfaithful or not.'

Jess said nothing. Her eyes were fixed on the dirty grey clouds that crowded the sky like stuffing spilling out of a giant toy.

'Tony never wanted another child, in any case,' Susan went on. 'Though it seems he's changed his mind now.'

Jess looked round. 'Oh, she's pregnant, is she? Bella thought so.'

'Bella?'

'My . . . my cousin, sort of. She lives with us. She's got a sense for these things.'

Susan notices that Jess still referred to herself as living in Sussex, but she didn't comment on the slip. 'Shall we carry on?' she said. 'You haven't seen those bathroom tiles yet, have you?'

'Not yet, no. But Susan –' Jess manoeuvred herself and the sling through the narrow doorway. 'How do you feel about that baby? That must be so strange, knowing Jamie's going to have a brother or a sister and –'

'I try not to think about it,' said Susan, holding open the bathroom door for Jess, 'because I'm ashamed of how bitter it makes me feel. Surprised and ashamed.'

Jess looked at the tense face with its angled cheekbones and fine, narrow nose. 'I'm sorry,' she said, 'I shouldn't ask so many questions.'

'Don't worry.' Susan laid a hand awkwardly on Jess' arm. 'I don't mind at all. I should talk more, I think. I'm not very good at talking.'

'But you're absolutely superb at decorating!' Jess was delighted by the elegance of the bathroom, the last room to be finished. 'The grey and white together – it's like being in a Brunelleschi church. If that's not too ridiculous a thing to say about a smallish bathroom in N1.'

Susan laughed, delighted by Jess' enthusiasm. I'll miss her, she thought. I really will.

'I won't dare take a bath, though,' continued Jess. 'It's far too smart. Let alone shave my legs or whatever. It looks like something out of a magazine.'

'Thank you,' said Susan. 'But I hope it'll feel like home, too. I very much want you to feel happy here, all three of you.' She put as much warmth into her voice as she knew how. Jess noticed.

'I'm sure we will,' she said. 'It's just all so new to me. I can't quite believe that I'll ever live in such a perfect place.' She turned away, because she didn't want Susan to see that her eyes had suddenly, unaccountably, filled with tears.

'So let me take you out, Polly.' Susan was emphatic. 'Somewhere nice. You've been such a terrific help, and I'm thrilled to have finished the Gascoignes' place. I just wish you could see it.'

'Maybe I can wangle an invitation. Though I don't know that I like him awfully. He's a cold fish,' said Polly.

'Oh, but she's an absolute sweetie! Anyway, tomorrow night? Estrelia says she'll stay with Jamie.'

'Lovely. I'm going to a private view in Bond Street, but I can leave early and meet you somewhere near there.'

'I'll try and book Agostino's. That's not far.'

'Agostino's?' Polly shrieked. 'My God, Suzie, can you afford it?'

'Thanks to you, I can. I'll book now, and ring you back.'

The completion of the house had given Susan a glowing satisfaction she hadn't felt for years. And thanks to Polly, there were a couple of other jobs in the pipeline, including this magnificent house in Downshire Hill.

Susan opened her wardrobe. She felt like dressing up for the first time in ages, and all her good clothes had been neglected for so long that they'd be bound to need an overhaul. She thought it was Freud who said that love and work were the only two effective therapies. Well, he was right about the work bit. She held up a grey jersey dress against herself. As for love – she'd been there, done that. And now she was free of it, and glad.

The dress was smart, but too sombre. There was hardly any colour in her wardrobe at all. There hadn't been for years, she realised. She'd give herself a day off tomorrow, and take her credit cards to Knightsbridge to rectify the situation. She felt like a lizard rubbing off its shabby old skin. It was time to reveal the new, shining one underneath.

'Suzie! What a dress!'

The waiter disappeared with their coats and Polly took a few steps back to admire her friend. Susan was draped in flame-coloured knitted silk. It complemented her olive skin; its clean, fluid line suited her angular body. Her short dark hair, newly cut, was teased into wisps to frame her small, sharp face, and a narrow black choker emphasised the length of her sinewy neck. Beside her, Polly, her face flushed with the wine she'd had at the private view, her voluminous dress enlivened with one of her characteristic silk scarves, looked like an overstuffed sofa. And knew it.

'Darling, are you trying to undermine my confidence by turning up looking like Jacqueline Onassis?'

Susan laughed. 'Of course not, just trying to bolster my own. But seriously, does it work? Do you like it? I got it this afternoon in Harvey Nicks. I could always take it back.'

'It's absolutely wonderful. It must have cost at least half of what the Gascoignes paid you.'

'Well, it wasn't cheap.'

'And this meal will cost the other half. That's the spirit, girl. Live dangerously.'

They lowered themselves into the chairs the waiters held out for them, Susan arranging her folds with care, enjoying the pull of the heavy fabric that was like soft chain mail. There was a vase of anenomes on each table, their jewel colours glowing in the candlelight. Iced water was brought, so cold that Polly mimed getting her lips stuck to the glass. She decided on carpaccio with char-grilled artichoke hearts. Out of old habit Susan handed her the wine list.

The plates were lopsided ceramic slabs, a white one on top of a larger black one. Susan's pasta blackened with squid ink and decorated with yellow blobs of saffron sauce looked so artistic that it seemed a pity to eat it, but it was utterly delicious. She handled it expertly. Polly dabbed olive oil off her scarf.

'It's sickening,' she remarked, 'the way not one single drop of that sauce will land on your immaculate front, while I can't even

111

capture an artichoke heart without making a pig of myself.'

'Don't say that! Now I'll be bound to drop it,' said Susan, but she didn't.

They chatted about work, the food, mutual friends. Then Susan said, 'I didn't tell you, did I? She's pregnant.'

The great thing about Polly was that she wouldn't have any trouble working out who 'she' was.

'Is she now? The little minx. So she's nailed him.'

'Do you think so?'

'Oh yes. A girl like that won't stand for having a child out of wedlock.'

Susan sipped her wine. 'I suppose marriage was inevitable, since he bought that barn as a cosy nest. But I believed him when he said he didn't want to get married again. Why did I keep on believing him?'

'I don't know. Probably because you're really quite nice. But does it matter, anyway? I mean, you didn't want him back.'

'God, no. Not any more.' The main course arrived. Black plates on white this time. A fan of guinea fowl breast, a golden triangle of polenta for Susan; calves' liver sautéd with spirals of wild fungi for Polly.

'Very pretty,' said Polly, 'but not much of it. Dare I ask him to refill the bread basket?'

'I suppose the reason I mind,' continued Susan, 'is that he'll be going through with her what he went through with me, only he'll be thinking that she's doing it better. If it was just another affair, then I wouldn't compare it to what we started out like. But with a baby . . . Oh dear, I'm not making any sense.'

Polly refilled her glass with Barolo, dark and thick and oily.

'Yes you are,' she said. 'Perfect sense. Marriage is special, even when it fails. You had ideals when you were first married. You don't like the thought of him dusting down those ideals and presenting them to the minx as if they were brand new.'

'That's right, yes. This baby and – and marriage will give her status, too. And I don't want that little cow to have status – especially not as Jamie's stepmother.'

'Does Jamie like her?'

'I've no idea. He's rather given up talking recently.'

'Just to you?'

'To everyone, I think. I'm a little worried. There's a parents' evening at his school soon. I'll talk to his form tutor or whatever they call it.'

'Will Tony go? To this parents' evening?'

'He won't know about it.'

Polly wiped her plate with a hunk of bread and licked her fingers. 'Could you ever imagine getting married again?'

Susan shook her head. 'I actually think marriage is a terribly bad idea, for almost everybody,' she said. 'Maybe it's just because I wasn't very good at it. But it seems to me that men just – mess things up.'

'Only men?'

'Yes, usually. Because they're naturally promiscuous, aren't they? So the whole thing's fake. The wife sits at home pretending she doesn't notice, and the husband sleeps around pretending it doesn't matter.'

'But Susan, promiscuity isn't the only reason marriages fail. John wasn't remotely promiscuous.'

'What was wrong with him, then?'

Polly sipped her wine. 'He was just dull. Dull, dull, dull.' She smacked her lips. 'I wasn't any good at being a wife, either. Poor John. But there are happy marriages.'

'Name one.'

'Well, those young Gascoignes you've been working for. He's bright, handsome – not my cup of tea, but a force to be reckoned with. And you say she's lovely. Sweet baby, expertly decorated house –' She winked.

'She's not happy, though,' said Susan.

'Isn't she? Probably just postnatal what's-it.'

'Maybe. I don't know him very well – you've seen more of him than I have. But she seems dazed by the whole business of being married. It's as if she's pining for something, but I'm not sure what it is.'

'Her freedom.'

'Not exactly. I tried to make the house as nice for her as I possibly could, because I got to care about her.'

'In such a short time?'

'Yes. It's funny, but she seems – I don't know. Vulnerable, and trusting. The way she talked about the house, it felt like she

113

was relying on me to make everything perfect for her.'

Polly picked up the dessert menu. 'Sounds a bit annoying to me.'

'Oh no. She's not annoying.'

'Coffee soufflé with butterscotch sauce – yeah, why not? Though I bet their cheese is good.'

'Have both.'

'Even I couldn't manage that.'

Susan rose. 'Just going to the Ladies'.'

'Aren't you having anything?'

'Oh yes . . . could you order for me? Mango sorbet in a praline basket – you can eat my basket.'

'The sorbet will match your dress.'

Susan took her evening bag with her. She knew her lipstick would have worn off by now, but she would never reapply it at the table, even when it was only Polly. And the urge to look her best had not left her.

Nick Gascoigne laid his credit card down on top of the bill. His meal had started early; he would have time for an hour or so at Dominique's flat before getting back to St John's Wood. Dominique was in the Ladies', a sure sign that she was expecting to go to bed with him. Jess would be asleep by the time he got back, but even so . . . He knew he was running risks seeing Dominique midweek like this, like a fox raiding the chicken house by daylight, but that only seemed to heighten the pleasure.

From the corner of his eye he saw a female figure shimmying past his table in a remarkable orangey-red dress. Out of old habit he scrutinised her. Not bad. Over forty, probably, and wishbone thin, but elegant in that clinging material. The austere haircut, the immaculate but understated make-up – she looked classy. And familiar. He knew her. Oh, Christ.

Susan looked full at him. He returned his attention to the bill, but it was too late. 'Hello!' she said, all smiles. 'I enjoyed being let loose on your house. I hope you're pleased.' She rested her hand on the back of Dominique's empty chair.

'Very pleased, thank you.' He waved at the waiter. 'I'm sorry, I'm in a bit of a rush.' With luck, Dominique would take her time, and they could slip out when the decorator woman's back was turned. But luck was not forthcoming. Dominique, fragrant and freshly coiffed, gave Susan a look of cool enquiry as she returned to her seat.

Susan's face hardened. She didn't wait for an introduction. 'Don't look now,' she said when she got back to Polly, 'but I've just encountered proof of my theory about men and marriage.'

'A friend of yours?' Dominique asked Nick. 'That's a superb dress.'

Nick shrugged. 'An acquaintance. Shall we go?' He knew that he would have to act quickly now. That woman would tell. He knew from her face that she would tell. But after all, it didn't really matter.

'How do you know?' said Polly, who had looked. 'It might be a business meeting. You've got to give him the benefit of the doubt.'

'Oh, Polly,' sighed Susan, 'I'm surprised at you. I saw her in the Ladies', spraying No. 5 down her cleavage. The benefit of the doubt is one thing you must never, ever, ever give a man.'

# CHAPTER FOURTEEN

On Friday night Nick didn't come home.

Jess didn't realise at first. Nick was still spending his nights on the sofa-bed. Louis was unusually calm that night, only waking once, at about two. He didn't stir at six, which was when his day normally began. Jess woke, out of habit, and lay still, trying to revel in the fact that Louis was still asleep, trying not to assume that that meant there was something wrong with him. She could hear the little grunts from the Moses basket, so she knew he was alive, but what if he was ill? What if he'd fallen into some kind of coma?

Willing herself not to get up, she propped herself up on the pillows, and looked long and hard at the nude self-portrait that dominated the end wall. She'd done no work for months – a few quick sketches of Louis as he slept, that was all. Perhaps she should give in to Nick about having a nanny. If she had time to herself she could force herself to work. There was a room at the top of the new house waiting to be turned into her studio. It was the one room that Susan Chandler had had no hand in – it was painted white, no curtains, no carpet, nothing. In that swept, simple space, Jess could make a fresh start.

She didn't like the self-portrait much any more. She was glad she had kept the face half shrouded in hair, so that she couldn't watch herself. When they moved – and today was the removal day – she hoped she could persuade Nick to relegate it to some obscure spot. That slim, sunlit girl looked silly to Jess now – boastful and naïve. And badly drawn, too. They definitely had to have that nanny. It was high time she pushed her art in new directions. Nick would be pleased she'd changed her mind. It would be nice to tell him something that would please him, for a change.

Still no movement from the Moses basket. Jess got out of bed. She hung over the sleeping baby, one hand on the tiny velour-clad chest, checking its rise and fall. All was as it should be.

Now she was up she felt restless. She longed for a cup of tea but didn't want to disturb Nick. He'd been out the night before at one of his business dinners; he never got back from them before midnight. It was half past six. On six hours' sleep Nick would be very grumpy all day, and since they were moving house . . . Jess deliberated, standing barefoot in her fine lawn nightdress that buttoned up the front for ease of midnight feeding. She tugged at an uncomfortable bra strap. It would be absolutely wonderful not to have to wear a bra in bed any more. Maybe that was why she didn't like the self-portrait. She thought, I'm jealous of that naked, unencumbered creature. She hadn't felt unencumbered for months and months.

She decided against tea because of the noise of the kettle, but she would risk fetching some orange juice and something to eat. Breast-feeding made her feel hungry all the time. She pushed open the bedroom door as gently as she could, and slipped into the living room.

It wasn't quite dark. The blinds hadn't been drawn. Dawn had barely begun to break but the orange streetlamps filtered into the room. Jess felt the emptiness like a weight on her shoulders. The sofa bed was untouched.

Why did a deserted room feel like a haunting? And how did she know that he had gone for good? In those seconds of realisation, Jess's future flashed in front of her.

A wail from Louis jolted her into action. She picked him up and bared her breast with automatic movements. 'You should have slept on, little Louis,' she said aloud, settling his triangular red cat's mouth into place. 'There's no hurry. Your father's left us, you see. So we're not going to be moving to Islington any more.'

'You're not going out, then?' asked Graham, stuffing his trouser cuffs into his socks. He never seemed to get over the fact that, for Eliza, Saturday night might have no special significance.

'Probably not. Have a good time.'

'Cheers.' She could hear him outside, whistling as he unlocked his bicycle.

Eliza said 'probably not' but what she meant was 'definitely not'. She always prevaricated a little with Graham because of the unlikely but chilling chance that if she said no, she was absolutely going nowhere, he would offer to stay and keep her company. His own arrangements were, after all, flexible. He was only going to a pub where various like-minded Green activists were wont to gather.

Some weekends Eliza made the effort. She cooked for friends, she went to the cinema, she went out in a group for a cheap meal, Indian or Italian. She even sat in pubs sometimes, though less often now – there was nothing more calculated to make one feel one's age than spending Saturday evening in an Oxford pub. Her social life was modest but satisfactory; she had no complaints. But now, in December, that most ancient time of year, it seemed appropriate to retreat to the dependable comforts of a fire and a good book and a warm cat. Eliza filled her teapot and opened a packet of digestive biscuits. She tweaked the fire into life – Graham provided little grey blocks of recycled newspaper which were always loath to burn. Eliza supplemented them with the twiggy bits she collected in her bicycle bag on solitary walks. When at last a flame was licking with interest at the frail pyramid, she kicked her shoes off, curled her legs under her and patted her lap in invitation to Sylvia.

Sylvia circled, kneading Eliza's legs, half wondering whether there wasn't a more comfortable lap elsewhere. From a kitten, Sylvia had expressed profound discontent with her lot; she had been named after the poet, Plath. Eliza had chosen her from one of the many Powdermill litters; she felt an affinity with the creature's restless, querulous idiosyncrasy. Sylvia settled at last. Eliza sipped her tea and stroked the cat's head, determined to force a purr out of her. Her Iris Murdoch lay unopened on the arm of her chair.

Like the rest of her family, Eliza rarely closed the curtains. She rather agreed with Ruskin that there was no such thing as bad weather, just different kinds of weather. Even on this winter's evening the weather interested her. It was snowing, but not in a way that meant anything. Little bunches of hard snowflakes would rush at the window and rattle it like handfuls of gravel, but it wasn't going to settle. The wind was up, and moaning in the chimney. Eliza loved that sad, primeval sound.

People passed in front of the window, coat collars turned up, scarves over their mouths. They shouted at each other, cheerfully. People in Oxford used their city. They walked, they cycled, they called on one another, they yelled greetings or even whole conversations the lengths of their streets. Eliza liked it; she liked the fact that it took more than a few snow flurries to dampen the town's spirits. And the street noises intensified the cosiness of her little house.

The headlights of a slowing car arched across her ceiling. A taxi – she heard the exchange at the window, and the sound of the car driving off. Then a knock at her door, and a voice through her letter box.

'Lila! Oh, please let me in.'

Jess had Louis in his sling, and a bag in each hand. Eliza hauled her into the narrow hall.

'My God, Jess, you've come to stay.'

She took the bags out of her sister's hands and looked her in the face. 'You've left him, haven't you? You've run away.'

Jess shook her head. 'Other way round. Oh, Lila, thank goodness you're here.'

Eliza propelled her into the living room. 'Tell me about it later. I'll get you some tea. Here, sit down. Hop it, Sylvia.'

Jess unhooked Louis and laid him on the tiny sofa. She started to cry.

'I knew you'd cry,' said Eliza. 'I just hoped you'd wait until I'd got some food inside you.'

Jess wiped her face on her scarf. 'I'm not crying because of Nick,' she said, 'I'm crying because of the fire.'

'The fire?'

'It's because it's so wonderful to see a real fire.'

'Not very real. It's made of those horrid recycled things. Here –' Eliza handed her sister a handful of kitchen towel – 'stop it. There's not much to eat, but . . . would cheese on toast do?'

Jess sniffed, nodded, and tried to smile.

'You can have my bed,' said Eliza, finding strength in practicalities, 'and I'll sleep on the sofa cushions in my study. But I don't have anywhere to put Louis.'

'That's OK. He can come in with me. I wanted to bring the Moses basket, but I didn't have enough hands. But we can go on the floor, Lila.'

'Rubbish. Do you think I would let anyone else sleep in my precious study?' Eliza clattered in the kitchen, slicing cheese, laying a tray. Louis woke, but lay quiet, transfixed by the flickering firelight.

'He's calm here,' said Jess. 'He knows it's a good place. He was never calm in St John's Wood. See, he loves the fire.'

'Hm. Less of that sentimental New Age talk, please.' Eliza set the tray on the floor and handed a plate to Jess. 'Now tell me, why did you come here? I thought you'd go home.'

'What do you mean, you thought? You didn't know Nick would –'

'No, I thought *you* would. It was only a matter of time, Jess. But I assumed you'd go to Powdermill.'

'Why was it obvious to you if it wasn't obvious to me?'

'I was there at the birth, remember.'

'So was I, actually.'

They both laughed.

'We were going to move today,' Jess continued, dreamily. 'The house was finished. It's sitting there now, waiting for us. It doesn't know we've let it down.'

'Not you, Jessie. Nick.'

Jess shook her head. 'Both of us. I've been going round in a fog, paying no attention. I deserve this.'

'Well . . . we won't argue about it. But what did he actually say?'

'He rang. He didn't come home last night. He rang, and said he'd be letting the new house, and staying in the flat for the time being. And could I please leave as soon as possible? And he'd paid some money into my bank account so I'd be all right for the moment.'

'Does he know you're here?'

'I expect he thinks I've gone to Powdermill. That's one reason I didn't go – just to thwart him, in some small way. And because I didn't want to dump yet another disaster on Ma. And because –' Jess paused.

'Because what?'

'Because I knew you wouldn't fuss me, Lila.'

Eliza smiled her twitching little smile. 'There's no drink in the house,' she said, 'but there is my emergency supply of Fruit and Nut. Shall we indulge?'

# CHAPTER FIFTEEN

'REVENGE', wrote Jamie. His heart thudded. On the desk in front of him was Finian's letter, now decoded. Samson lay across his feet, keeping them warm.

'Richard Jones was a sucesful lawyer. He was 48,' he wrote. Then he remembered that Mr Furness had told them to use more interesting names in their stories. 'I'm sick of reading about John Smiths,' he'd said. Jamie also felt unsure about how to spell successful. He tore off the sheet of paper and started again.

'REVENGE. by J. A. Chandler.'

He scanned the row of school books for inspiration for names.

'Roger Thesaurus was a rich lawyer. He was 48. He seperated from his wife because he met another woman. He had two sons, Zack and Fergus. (Their mother was the wife). They lived with their mother in the week, and spent their weekends with their father, Roger.'

He paused. What name was stupid enough for Pippa? What name summed up a silly fat blonde woman who didn't like animals?

His mother knocked softly at the door. 'Supper in half an hour,' she said, looking in. 'How are you getting on?'

'Fine. I'm writing a story for English. What's a really stupid woman's name?'

'Oh, goodness. I can't think. What about Fifi?'

'Yeah. OK. Thanks.' He started writing again. Susan retreated.

'The woman Roger had met was called Fifi. She was his secretory. She had fair hair but she wasn't as pretty as Roger's wife, though she was younger. She was very selfish and was only intrested in one thing – money.

'Now Roger did not know it, but Fifi wanted to marry him for his money.

'Zack found out. He –' How did he find out? Jamie doodled

121

on the discarded sheet of paper, sketching the outline of a nightjar. How did people in books find things out? Oh yes – eavesdropping. He continued:

'He heard Fifi on the telphone, talking to her boyfriend. She was saying how she would get hold of Roger's money and then kill him.'

Too extreme. Mr Furness complained about stories being 'melodramatic'. Jamie didn't understand why; he thought it made them more exciting. But he crossed out 'kill' and wrote 'leave' instead.

'Zack told Fergus, and they planned to get rid of Fifi.'

Now for the good bit. Jamie could feel himself smiling like a maniac as he wrote: 'They bought some prawns and sewed them into the curtains of Fifi's bedroom, at the bottom.' He eased his feet out from under Samson because he had pins and needles, and reread what he'd written so far. It seemed a bit bare. Mr Furness didn't like too many adjectives, but it needed a little padding.

'The prawns were large and juicy and orangey-pink. The colour of the dawn sky. As time past they slowly rotted away. The smell was terrible but Fifi did not know where it was coming from. She got really paranoyed because however much she cleaned the flat the smell never went away.

'The smell put Roger off. Every time he visited Fifi he wanted to throw up. He started to think about his old wife and how clean she was. Eventualy he got back together with Sarah, his first wife.'

'Supper!' called Susan, from the landing. 'Coming,' yelled Jamie, scribbling fast.

'Zack and Fergus had saved their father from Fifi's evil scemes. Her other boyfriend left her because she failed to get the money and she was so depressed that she comitted suicide, by drinking all the cleaning fluid that she got to clean the flat.'

Jamie laid down his pen. He would have liked to describe Fifi's agony as the cleaning fluid tore through her intestines, but Furness would say it was over the top. And supper was ready, and he was starving.

'It looked as though you were working hard,' commented Susan, setting a dish of lasagne on the table. 'You always used to hate English.'

'I like it a bit better than I did at Fossett House. Furness is better than Mrs Eachus.'

'I haven't met Mr Furness. What's he like?'

'Paddy?' Jamie shrugged. 'I dunno. He's quite young for a teacher. He wore black jeans once but they must have told him off because he never wore them again.'

'Why is he called Paddy? Is he Irish?'

'Irish? He might be. His name's Patrick. What do you want to know about him for, anyway?'

'Just interested. You seem to take more trouble over your English than you used to . . .'

'Yeah, but I'm still no good at it.' Jamie sought for a way of changing the subject. He didn't want his mother to ask to read this particular essay. 'I'm getting better at biology, though. I was third in the last test.'

'Were you, darling? Well done!' Susan lingered over her own small portion of lasagne and ladled out seconds for Jamie. He was in an unusually communicative mood. Most evenings he bolted his food and then went to watch television. One of the few rules Susan had insisted upon was that meals should not be eaten in front of the television; Jamie observed the rule, but it meant that most meals were over in under five minutes.

Tonight things seemed different. Susan was emboldened to broach the subject that was almost never mentioned between them. 'Jamie,' she said, 'about Dad and Pippa.' It pained her to use the name like that, but one had a duty to be civilised. 'How would you feel if . . . I mean, suppose Dad wanted to get married again? What would you think about it?'

Jamie laid down his fork. He stared at his mother for a moment. Then, 'Don't worry about it,' he said, 'because it's not going to happen. Believe me.' He shovelled in the last few mouthfuls, and looked at his watch. 'Time for *Deep Space Nine*.'

'All right. You go, I'll clear.'

'Thanks,' he said briefly, and was gone.

As she loaded the dishwasher Susan pondered, not for the first time, on the inscrutability of her only child. How was it possible to give birth to, feed, wash, cuddle, watch over an infant, and then find not so very many years later that you had so little idea of what was happening inside its head?

* * *

Patrick Furness took his academic gown down from its peg and swiped at it to get rid of the chalk marks. This not very effective gesture was his only concession to the fact that it was the First Year Parents' Consultation Evening. Most of his colleagues spent a few minutes in the lavatories, running combs through thinning hair, straightening ties and brushing dandruff from shoulders, but Patrick looked down on all that. He disliked the private school's sycophantic attitude towards parents as much as he had disliked the hostile indifference towards them that he'd encountered in his first job, at a state school. From his own observation, having money didn't make parents any more caring or effective. Or any less.

He made his way to his teaching room, carrying his mark book and a folder of recent essays. Brandishing written work under the noses of parents, particularly fathers, reassured them that something was actually being achieved. He was a few minutes early; he occupied himself by trying to reactivate the Blu-Tack that was failing to keep up the corners of a poster about the history of the Globe Theatre. He noticed some graffiti about the alleged sexual appetites of the head of music; it was written in felt-tip pen on the laminated surface of the book cupboard, and a wetted finger soon removed it. He reflected that he'd never seen any graffiti about himself; did that mean that he was popular, or merely insignificant? Or perhaps the graffiti was there, but he just didn't see it. Maybe the brain had a self-censoring mechanism to give protection against whatever might be hurtful. It certainly didn't do to dwell on the subject. Teachers, Patrick reminded himself, needed to keep their guard up. Thinking about your standing in the pupils' eyes made you either neurotic or smug, depending on how you interpreted the signs. Either case made you less effective.

A shadow fell across the frosted glass pane in the door; the first parent had arrived. Patrick shook out his gown and settled himself in his chair before calling, 'Come in.' He liked to guess which parent belonged to which boy before they announced themselves. In this instance it was easy; here was the rounded, sandy face of little Alasdair Scott, coarsened and sunk in flesh, stripped of whatever cherubic charm it might have possessed.

124

'Take a seat, Mr Scott,' said Patrick expansively. Mr Scott looked startled and impressed at being named. His intention to take this Furness man to task over the unsuitable nature of some of Alasdair's half-term reading matter melted in the face of such authoritative familiarity.

Parent after parent followed in a relentless procession, but Patrick found the evening energising. He was interested in his pupils – the job would be dreary if he were not – and meeting the parents often explained a lot. By the time Susan Chandler arrived he was well into his stride, and radiating a kind of concerned confidence.

Here was another one who it was easy to guess. The angular body, the small-boned face, the fine dark hair, the olive skin that suggested some Mediterranean blood somewhere – mother and son were so alike that it was difficult to see what the father could have contributed. But the shared anxiety, which young Chandler had got under control so that he appeared to spend most of his time in a dream-like state, was more clearly evident in his mother. Patrick noticed that though her hands were carefully manicured, the skin on her knuckles was almost raw.

He was about to greet her as 'Mrs Chandler', but stopped himself just in time. He wasn't sure whether she was divorced or separated, but in either case she might well regard that name as no longer applicable. Instead he half rose from his seat and held out his hand. 'Hello. You must be Jamie's mother.'

Susan smiled. She had just done the rounds of the maths and science teachers, and though they had confirmed that Jamie was not actually struggling, she had received no feeling that any of them had a sense of her son as a person. 'Chandler, ah, yes,' they had said, running the end of a pen along a row of figures in a mark book. 'Test results show some improvement. About average. Conscientious worker,' and she had wondered why she had come out on a freezing foggy night to hear things that could more easily have been put down on a piece of paper. But this young Mr Furness seemed different.

'I'm very glad you came,' he said, pressing the tips of his long fingers together, 'because I've been a little concerned lately. Not with the quality of his work,' he added hastily, seeing her face fall. 'No, on the whole that's improving, though his style is still

125

a little – immature. But the content of his essays shows some signs of . . . well, of disturbance, I suppose. Do you ever read what he writes?'

Susan shook her head. 'I don't like to intrude. Jamie has become very – very private lately. But I'm disappointed by what you say. He seemed to have been so much more enthusiastic about his English. He's been putting a lot of effort into it.'

Patrick leaned forward a little. 'He has. Oh, indeed he has. But for the last four preps he's been dwelling on a theme and – well, I think you should know about it. It may be just a lively imagination at work, or it may express some real anxieties. Here, this is the most recent.'

Susan took the two sheets of A4. 'Revenge', she read. Her eyes travelled swiftly over the story. Her lips twitched when she read the bit about the scheming Fifi being less pretty than her predecessor. She handed the sheets back. 'He can't spell, can he?' was all she said.

Patrick fixed her with a level stare. 'As I say, the last four pieces of written work have all harked on this wicked step-mother theme. Now, I don't wish to pry, but it's possible that Jamie is crying for help. He is expressing his powerlessness about the home situation and –'

'Mr Furness,' cut in Susan, 'I don't want to listen to a load of psychobabble.'

Patrick's voice hardened. 'I wouldn't call it psychobabble. More common sense. If he was my child I would be worried about him. But I've said enough; I really don't wish to intrude.'

'If you must know,' said Susan, as coolly as she could, but with a shake in her voice, 'yes, I am worried about him. And I didn't mean to be rude; I appreciate the fact that you're taking him seriously. The thing is that his father is a bullying, selfish, dishonest bastard who only wants to have Jamie visit him to spite me and –' She tried to stop herself but it was too late. 'I'm sorry,' she gasped between sobs, 'I really hate crying in front of a stranger.'

Patrick was aghast. 'I'm the one who should apologise. I had no business . . . Here, let me find you a tissue or something.' He tore a hank off a roll of the soft paper that was used to clean the whiteboard. 'That's all I've got, I'm afraid.'

Susan dabbed at her face. They both glanced at the door, where figures could be seen through the glass panel and impatient coughs could be heard. They looked at each other like conspirators. Susan liked his face – pale, a little gaunt, with thick, floppy hair and deep-set blue eyes. Celtic, she thought.

'You could leave by the fire door,' said Patrick. 'There's a Ladies' at the end of the corridor, I think. Just down a few steps, to the right.'

'Thank you,' said Susan. 'That's very thoughtful.' She picked up her handbag and stood up. 'Please let me know of any further developments.' Her voice was steady now. 'Your input could be very helpful.'

'Of course,' he said. 'Here.' And he wrote his address on a scrap of paper. 'Any time,' he said.

He opened the fire door for her. As she left, he gave her shoulder an almost imperceptible pat. 'Jamie's a great boy,' he said. 'He's very like you.' She gave him a swift glance, whether of reproach or gratitude he was not sure. Then she was gone, and he wondered what had made him say that.

Eliza didn't sleep well. The sofa cushions on the study floor were fine – she could curl her small frame comfortably into the most unlikely corners – but her thoughts were racing, and she'd heard a distant bell toll two o'clock, and three, and four . . . Towards dawn she'd dozed, and fallen into jumbled dreams about cats and babies. In her last dream Jess was telling her that she'd have to go back to Nick because she'd run out of toothpaste, but this one never reached its denouement because the thin cry of her nephew cut through Eliza's sleep like a cheesewire.

She propped herself up on her elbows. Half past six. The crying stopped; presumably Jess was feeding him. It was still dark outside, but there didn't seem any point in not getting up. She made tea for herself and Jess, not bothering to muffle the sounds she made; the lodger had come in late and drunk and in her opinion deserved scant consideration.

When she gently pushed open the door of her own bedroom and saw her sister lying on the narrow bed cradling Louis, her hair spread fan-like over the pillow, her eyelids lowered, her

127

skin waxen in the half-light, Eliza felt, of all things, a pang of the ancient envy that had never quite been rooted out. Even when she'd apparently lost so much, it seemed to Eliza that Jess had really lost nothing. Jess was unassailable; sad she might be, frightened too, but still she was shrouded in the aura of specialness that throughout her life had made her the exception to every rule.

Jess raised her eyelids and smiled, and Eliza swallowed her sour thoughts. She sat on the edge of the bed, and set Jess' mug of tea within her reach. She watched Louis' small hand pushing against the veiny breast as he sucked, and remembered the Powdermill kittens, kneading their mother's side in rhythmic contentment. 'What's it like?' she asked. 'Do you feel like a mother cat?'

'I think so.' Jess replied. 'You know how the cats purr and mirrup at the same time when they're being suckled? As if it's quite uncomfortable but they know it's the right thing to do? Well, it's like that. Except the cats are better at it than me.'

'How can you be good or bad at it? That's like saying you're good or bad at eating. Surely it's –'

'Just instinctive? Oh no, it's hard work. I'm used to it now, but at first it was awful. I thought that after he was born I'd get my own body back to myself, but if you're breast-feeding you're still possessed.'

'Possessed? You make him sound like a devil child.' Eliza stroked the back of Louis' dark head.

'Well, that's how I felt. And he is a devil child, but I think he's becoming tame.'

'"Bound and weary I thought best

To suck upon my mother's breast",' quoted Eliza.

Jess detached the infant fiend and, wriggling into a vertical position, draped him over her shoulder. She ran a hand up and down his back, rocking slightly, and looked at Eliza with troubled eyes. 'Lila, what is it about the women in our family that means we get left?'

Eliza bridled. 'Only you and Ma,' she retorted. 'Don't tar us all with the same brush.'

'What about Oliver?'

'What about him?'

128

'Oliver left you.'

'No. That's not so.' Eliza got up and tightened her dressing gown belt.

'Sorry,' said Jess dreamily, 'I thought he did. And Bella – she was left.'

'Jess, Bella's insane.'

'But she wasn't then.'

'So we were told. But I think she must have been, a bit. I don't believe that being jilted at the altar sends you mad.'

'It might. Look at Miss Havisham.'

'Exactly. Look at Miss Havisham – an entirely improbable fictional creation. I'm going to get dressed.'

'But Lila, you haven't answered my question.'

Eliza was at the door, but she looked back briefly. 'That's because I don't know the answer,' she said.


It was amazing how time just seemed to fizzle away when there was a baby around. It seemed to Eliza that they had achieved almost nothing beyond eating toast and tidying up a little, and it was already half past eleven. Eliza thought a walk would be a good idea, but it was a blustery, cold day, and Louis had no pushchair. Jess seemed content to sit by the fire and flick through the Sunday papers that Graham the lodger had left scattered about, while Louis, propped on a bean bag, exclaimed at the flames.

Eliza needed to assuage her restlessness. 'I'll go out and get something for lunch. The corner shop will have to do,' she said, but as she spoke there was a ring at the door. Tom Winchcombe stood on the threshold, Eliza's cat in the crook of his arm.

'Sylvia!' Eliza exclaimed. 'But you're carrying her!'

Tom smiled his gap-toothed smile. 'I certainly am. She got stuck in my tool shed, God knows how.'

'Thank you – thanks very much. But she never lets a man get near her, let alone pick her up.' Eliza, scooping the cat out of his arms, noticed how relaxed Sylvia's wiry little body felt.

'Perhaps she likes the smell of this jacket,' said Tom. 'The most gardeny of my gardening jackets.'

'Come in,' said Eliza, 'and have some coffee or something. It's too cold to stand out here. Fancy Sylvia getting into your tool shed! I didn't know she was so adventurous – she's normally such a stay-at-home. Perhaps she feels ousted.'

'Who's ousted her?' Tom followed her into the narrow hall.

'Louis. My nephew. He's staying here.' Eliza opened the living room door. 'My sister Jess,' she said. 'This is Tom. My neighbour – our neighbour, I should say.'

Jess put aside a colour supplement and smiled at him. Louis, on his beanbag propped between her feet, stared. All her life Eliza had been used to sensing the warm little tremor that ran through men when they first set eyes on her sister; she wasn't surprised to feel it now. What did surprise her was to find, suddenly, that in this case she minded.

When she came back with the coffee, Tom was on the floor, entertaining Louis. He's at her feet, she thought. Quite literally at her feet. She tried to quash the bitter little reflection, but when she had taken the cat from him she had felt the warm roughness of his jacket and the strength of his arm beneath it, and that was not something she either could or wanted to forget.

# CHAPTER SIXTEEN

Martha, leaning on her elbows at the parlour table, totted up the sums again. If she reduced last year's Christmas card list of ninety to a hard core of fifty, and sent them all second class . . . No, it was still disproportionately expensive. Martha always made her own Christmas cards – a lino-cut or a woodcut, usually – but there were still the materials to pay for, as well as the postage. Perhaps she could trim the list a little more, get it down to thirty, even . . . but deciding who to abandon was a hateful business. Better just drop them all at once.

She ran her eye down last year's list, written in blotchy Biro on the back of a large brown envelope, and miraculously pre-served amidst rolls of Sellotape, spare batteries, rusty pastry cutters and loose bits of binder-twine in the drawer of the kitchen dresser. The list could be divided into various cate-gories. The largest group consisted of their friends – Leo's friends really. Londoners, mainly; people Leo had charmed during the course of his life but with whom he had never had to do business. Martha shuddered as she thought of the friend-ships, even the kinships, that had bled to death as a result of Leo's efforts to remain in employment. These people for the most part belonged to some literary or artistic or theatrical milieu; they had often been to stay at Powdermill, less fre-quently in recent years. But though Martha enjoyed their witty, energetic company, they were not her people. They had come for Leo and the house and the break from London; they had embraced Martha on arrival and brought her drinks as she cooked for them on Sunday mornings, but not one of them did she miss. And the thought of telling them all, 'Leo and I have decided to . . .' No, best leave it. It made little difference.

Then there were the family – Martha's mainly. O'Hares and Reillys, sprinkled thinly over the British Isles, with a fair few still rooted in County Antrim. Some of these Martha hadn't seen since her marriage – since her girlhood. She'd only been back to Ireland once; when Jess was a baby, she and Leo had taken the little girls on a kind of royal progress to meet the relatives. A few had made their way to Sussex over the years; one first cousin in particular corresponded amusingly if intermittently with Martha, but Shelagh lived in County Durham now and had plenty of domestic ties of her own. And of course Bella made a difference. People would write at Christmas, sending cordial wishes to Bella; one uncle even sent postal orders from time to time, which Martha dutifully paid into a tiny savings account in Bella's name. But since Martha had taken Bella in at Powdermill, the relatives had kept their distance. Or perhaps, thought Martha more charitably, it's not Bella; perhaps they've just been keeping distance from the horrible tension between Leo and me. Who can blame them?

She would write to Shelagh, Martha decided, and tell her all about Leo. Shelagh sat at the centre of a web of family gossip and intrigue like a large and fairly amiable spider. She could be relied on to disseminate the news. It seemed odd to Martha that she hadn't thought about telling people earlier, because of course it had to be done. Or did it? There was no hurry. She'd write to Shelagh after Christmas; she was too busy now. Such a letter had to be worded carefully. And there was still the possibility that Leo would come back.

The rest of the list was made up of local people: friendly neighbours, helpful tradesmen, former employees from the days of the family's prosperity. The family doctor, now retired, who had been so good to them about Clare; Finian's favourite teacher from infant school; a couple of ex-pupils of Martha's from the art college. These people were real, she decided. They were a part of life. Most of them would know, or would have guessed, about Leo; a card signed 'from the Antrobus family' would do no harm. She counted them: eighteen. Even she could afford eighteen Christmas cards.

There wasn't much else she could afford, though. It wasn't until now, in the run-up to Christmas, that Martha felt the pinch of poverty. For Christmas dinner they would have one of their own geese – she had steeled herself to kill and pluck her own birds years ago – and there was a large Christmas pudding left from last year in the larder. It should be all right, but she'd

132

better give it a poke, to see. She would have no compunction in raiding what was left of Leo's wine cellar. The house would be decorated with greenery cut down by Finian; in the past he'd always been Leo's assistant woodsman, but this year he'd have to be in charge. The girls wouldn't expect big presents, but she'd fill their stockings as usual; they still liked those. The children made stockings for Ganna and Bella, and for Martha herself. But Fin – she'd like to get Fin a decent present. He never asked for new clothes, never compared his lot with that of his schoolfellows. He did odd jobs for the farmer and raised his pocket money that way. About his missing father he had said not a single word.

Martha tried to remember what Leo had been like with his son, but could only summon up images from Fin's infancy. Leo had professed delight when this last, late child turned out to be a boy, but in actuality he'd never shown as much interest in him as he had in the girls. Leo needed to be flattered, constantly. He was like a quick-burning fire that needed continuous feeding. The girls had fanned the flames with their admiration and adoration, even though in Lila's case it was tempered with disapproval, but Finian provided no such stimulus. Finian had always gone his own way. He was affectionate, but not passionate, at least not about people. His nature was strong and simple, he took people for what they were, and was never ingratiating, never demanding. Martha thought of the few activities that farther and son had shared – splitting logs for firewood, playing chess or Tri-Tactics by the parlour fire, occasionally taking the dog hare-coursing. It seemed to her that Fin had accepted his father's presence with equanimity but had never sought him out. Perhaps his departure had really not made much difference. She had always felt that Fin brought himself up.

Now, what to get Fin for Christmas? Something interesting, not useful, but what? To give Leo credit, he'd always been good at choosing presents for his son – and for all of them. Last year he'd given Fin binoculars, a second-hand pair in perfect working order in a beautiful old case of smooth chestnut leather. Would he send presents this year? she wondered. She'd heard not a word since that August night.

Martha rose and stretched. She was chilled, sitting hunched

133

at the table so long, to so little effect. The parlour fire was unlit; Sibyl felt shaky and was spending the morning in bed. Martha, buttoning her Aran cardigan, walked to the window. The winter garden was hushed, ashen. What would Christmas be like without Leo? Nick would be there – or so she assumed, she hadn't asked Jess – and the baby would be a great distraction. And Nick and Jess would bring things. Whatever Sibyl thought about him, Nick's wealth and love of luxury couldn't help but be a cheering influence at Christmas time.

A drowsy bumble bee crawled along the windowsill, draped in thick cobwebs like a tiny, groping bride. It'll never survive at this time of year, thought Martha. I ought to put it out of its misery. She raised a thick book to crush it, hesitated and laid it to one side. The bee stumbled on. 'I can't do it, I'm afraid. You'll have to sort yourself out,' said Martha, aloud.

Upstairs, Finian also contemplated a list. At the top it said, in code, 'Christmas presents – F. Antrobus'. Underneath, '£27.80' was boxed in a doodled frame. This figure represented the total of Fin's savings. When he'd first counted his money he'd been quite impressed; the tin money-box shaped like a thatched cottage that one of his Irish cousins had given him on his sixth birthday had been pleasantly heavy. But the list of names written underneath was growing longer, and it seemed that, after all, it wasn't going to go very far. The list was also in code.

Ma
Ganna
Bella
Linford
Pharaoh
Lila
Jess
Nick?
Louis
Jac
Dad

134

it said. None of the presents had yet been brought, but Fin started to fill in suggestions. Next to Pharaoh's name he wrote 'X-strong mints'. Pharaoh, the Antrobus' pony, was twenty-two years old now but still rideable. Pharaoh had a thing about mints. He was a mild-mannered beast, but if you had a packet of Polos in your pocket he would shove and push and nuzzle until he got one – or several. Fin smiled at the thought. He was off school today, feigning sick; he wondered how soon he could stage a recovery and go out for a ride. He'd chewed up digestive biscuits and spat them out into the lavatory that morning, to convince his mother he'd been sick, but he probably needn't have bothered. Ma didn't seem to mind about things like missing school any more. She'd most likely just be pleased that Pharaoh was getting some exercise.

He returned to the list. He wrote 'new collar' next to Linford's name, then crossed it out. A good leather collar would take up virtually all the money. He wrote 'Good-boy choc drops' instead. Unoriginal, but Linford wouldn't complain.

The women were easy. 'Soap,' he wrote, by his mother's name, and put ditto marks underneath for his grandmother and Bella. Lila and Jess? Yes, soap again, why not? They couldn't get jealous of each other if they all had the same thing. But what about Nick? Nick had never been with them for Christmas before. He'd been Jess' boyfriend last year, but he'd spent Christmas in New York for some reason. Fin remembered long telephone calls at odd times of day. But now they were married, and he was Fin's brother-in-law, so he ought to have a present. He could always share Jess' soap, Fin supposed, but if it had a flowery scent it might not be suitable. Finian embellished the doodles he'd already made. Nick was rich, and aloof – what could you possibly give to someone like that? He'd have to consult someone. Louis – now Louis was easy. Fin wrote 'rattle' next to his name with a flourish.

There were just two names left on the list. Jac – no problem. Jac, incredibly to Finian's way of thinking, didn't have a penknife. Finian's own multi-bladed specimen had been his constant companion for so long that he felt it had a character of its own. He'd get one, just a little less fancy, for Jac. It would cost a lot – it would be the most expensive present on the list –

but that was OK, because it would definitely be appreciated.

Finian's own knife had been given him by his father, at least three Christmases ago. Fin drew a squiggly line under his father's name on the list. Dad. He'd probably show up for Christmas. He'd never missed it before. It might be awkward with Ma, but Finian didn't understand why the fact that they didn't get on meant that Dad couldn't see the rest of them. Fin had hated hearing his parents shouting at night, and had been glad when his father had left, but as time went on he had found himself expecting a letter, or a phone call. It wasn't that he missed Leo, he told himself, but he thought he might write. It was strange, not knowing where your father was, even.

What if something had happened to him? Ma thought he had gone abroad; he could have caught a disease in a far-off city and died without telling anyone his name. He could have crashed the car on the night he went away. No – they would be able to trace it. But what if he'd deliberately driven it over Beachy Head?

Dad hadn't remembered Eliza's birthday, or Ganna's. He hadn't been back to collect any of his clothes. He hadn't even seen Louis. Surely, if he was alive he'd have been to see his only grandchild, at least? Fin's eyes smarted. He wiped them hard with the back of his hand, then scribbled over his father's name until it was quite obliterated.

When Rufus brought women back to the Hammersmith flat, Leo had to make himself scarce. That was the only condition Rufus laid down, and it was fair enough; Leo was not wholly oblivious to the fact that living rent-free in a comfortable flat for an apparently indefinite period was considerably more than most people in his position could expect. But it was luck, and Leo believed in luck. To him, life seemed to be ruled by luck, or its opposite.

At the start of his sojourn, when the weather was warmer and his host was going through a relatively celibate phase, this one condition had posed no great problem. But in November Rufus had taken up with a copper-haired croupier, a married woman who worked most peculiar hours. Though her marriage was said to be on the wane, her own home was still a no-go area for Rufus, so all their assignments had to be conducted in

Hammersmith, usually in the middle of the day. Leo had only himself to blame. He had introduced Rufus to his favourite gaming club, and that was where Rufus and this Paula had met. She was a furtive, mercenary woman with a short, hard laugh, and Leo was surprised that the liaison had survived the first couple of encounters, but Paula obviously had an appeal that eluded him because Rufus seemed quite smitten. And that meant that more and more often Leo found himself out on the wintry street, wrapped in his cape, with little money in his pocket and, frankly, at a loose end.

Just before leaving home, Leo had, unbeknownst to Martha, received a fairly hefty royalty cheque. He'd been living off that, even managing to augment it with a few successful games of blackjack and poker. He was going to get down to work soon – he had plenty of ideas, it was just a question of getting people interested in them – but as long as he had any money at all he found it impossible to focus his mind. He would stop drinking soon, too; the drink and the money would end together. And then he would knuckle down and get working – or maybe he would just go home.

One Saturday morning in December he heard Paula sobbing at the door, very early, and he heard Rufus's voice, urgent and welcoming, offering her a haven from whatever fresh crisis had cast her adrift. So he rolled out of bed and pulled on his clothes – which were Rufus's clothes, mainly, things he'd got too fat for – and was out of the house before that grating mixture of distress and consolation could really unsettle him.

It was so very early that everywhere was closed. He stopped at a workman's café, housed in a shack near the flyover, and took his place with the navvies and truck drivers. Eggs, sausage, beans, fried slice and as much tea as you could drink for £1.50. Leo, rubbing at his unshaven chin, aware of the dishevelment of his wiry curls, wondered if he was distinguishable from the rest of the clientele. There was only the cape, he thought as he lit his first cigarette, only the cape to tell him apart.

The tea was thick, dark orange, and tasted of brick dust, but he downed three mugs. The heat of it running through him was good, like the heat of the smoke as he inhaled. He liked to think of the scalding liquid scouring his insides, of the tobacco fumes blasting, scorching his lungs. Hollowed out. That was how he wanted to feel.

He pressed his cigarette out on the tinfoil ashtray and rose to go. Christmas shopping, he thought, apropos of nothing. I'll go to Harrods. Only a few stops on the underground, but he preferred to walk. All at once, everything seemed childishly, joyously simple. He would go to Harrods, buy them all presents, surprise them all by turning up at Christmas. He would spend whatever money he had left on the family he loved, and then start again. A new year, a clean slate. He didn't know why he hadn't thought of it before.

The doorman at Harrods, tightly encased in his bottle-green livery, looked just slightly askance at him, and indeed Leo's shabbily romantic appearance could hardly have contrasted more strongly with the rest of the sleek, purposeful shoppers queuing at the doors at opening time. But Leo was just as purposeful in his own way, despite the absence of a Rolex watch or an astrakhan collar. He had thought hard about presents on the long, cold trudge from Hammersmith, and thinking about what he would buy them brought his family clearly to mind. He felt warm, expansive; he would bear no grudges. Martha's present would be practical rather than romantic, certainly, but she would be treated as generously as the rest.

He stood in the middle of the ground floor, simply breathing, basking in the unfamiliar odours and opulence. Then he made his way to the lifts and travelled up and down, up and down, deciding where to start. He thought of Babar the elephant revelling in the lift on his first ever shopping expedition – 'Sir, this is not a toy. You must get out now, and buy what you want.' He remembered reading the story to his little girls, one on each knee, the warm, wriggling weight of them.

He made his mind up, and got out. Two hours later his cheque book was empty and his arms were full. He was well pleased with his purchases. For Martha a warm knitted jacket, made of sober grey-green wool that would suit her colouring and protect her from the cold without seeming in the least bit intrusively glamorous. For Finian a neat little chest of drawers for storing the shells and bones and feathers he loved to collect. For Eliza a set of the novels on the Booker prize list, hardbacks of course, handsomely wrapped. For Jess a silver bracelet, plain and solid – he could just see it setting off the golden grace of her smooth arm. For his mother an audio edition of *Bleak House* – she found reading for any length of time quite tiring. And for Bella – well, it was impossible to buy Bella anything that she would actually use. So he'd got her some boxes of candles, because he knew she liked hiding them away for fear of future shortages.

And finally, for the unseen, genderless grandchild, the most satisfactory present of all. A silver tankard, with a space for the engraving of date of birth and initials. A present for the future, thought Leo. A token of his commitment to the future of his family.

He couldn't wait for Christmas. Quite literally, he couldn't wait. He would call on Jess now, drop the presents at her flat. She could share his secret, the glowing secret of his intended return.

He staggered to the telephone kiosks, piled the parcels, scrabbled in his pockets for Jess' telephone number and some appropriate coins. Then he dialled, eager for the sweet shock of her musical voice. He waited. There was no reply. Perhaps he had misdialled. He tried again, still nothing. He counted a hundred and tried once more. No luck. Why had he assumed that she'd be in?

He felt suddenly deeply weary, and in need of a drink. His navvy's breakfast seemed a lifetime away. The pubs should be open by now. He hung the parcels and carrier bags from himself as if his wrists and hands were wooden props. 'Old clothes upon old sticks to scare a bird' – the line floated into his head, unbidden, unrecognised.

After three pints, a couple of chasers, and a bacon sandwich, Leo tried Jess' number again. But all it did was ring and ring and ring.

In Eliza's narrow divan bed, Jess slept. Eliza was in charge of Louis. Her intention had been to take him for a walk in the wintry dusk. Jess had been with her a week, and they'd bought a second-hand buggy through the local paper. Eliza had thought she might wheel him up to the gardens of St Saviour's, where

Tom Winchcombe worked; several times he'd urged Eliza to have a look round, and she never had. He'd mentioned it to Jess, too. 'It's a good time of year,' he'd said. 'Not much in flower, but you can see the sculptures more clearly. You can see the bare bones of the garden.' For Tom, Eliza had discovered, regarded the garden as a leafy exhibition space for the work of a sculptor friend of his. 'If the college start to complain I just drape a bit of plant over until they stop noticing,' he said. 'They don't complain in winter, because they don't use the garden. So I get away with quite a lot.'

Tom had dropped in three times in the last week, on what seemed to Eliza to be fairly flimsy pretexts. He would certainly become enamoured of Jess. Eliza had made every effort to resign herself to that inevitability. The baby might act as a deterrent to many men, but Tom seemed to find him an added attraction. 'That little bald patch at the back of his head,' he'd mused, quite misty-eyed, 'Dickon had one just like that. It's where they rub their head against their seats – it grows over once they can sit up properly.' Jess had been charmed.

'I rather like that patch,' she'd said. 'It's so square – like a little window.' Eliza snorted inwardly and removed herself to the kitchen, leaving the two of them sitting on the hearthrug, cooing over the bald patch. But now the thought of seeking out Tom in his icy twilit garden appealed to her. She thought she ought to let him know about Jess' circumstances, but another part of her mind wanted to see him in his work clothes, a solid shape in the mists of the grey and violet evening.

She laid Louis on the sofa while she fetched his quilted snowsuit. When she came back, he had fallen asleep. She hesitated, loath to disturb him, but reluctant, too, to delay her walk. Tom would surely knock off work as soon as it was dark, and the chance would be lost.

She stood gazing down at Louis, his pointed little features softened in sleep, his curled fist pressed endearingly against the round pad of his cheek. He was a scary little baby, with his sharp scream and his hard stare. And yet she really was beginning to love him.

A thunderous knocking at her front door made her jump. She was expecting no one, and that was no innocent neighbourly

140

knock. In a rush of protectiveness she tucked Louis' shawl round him, then hurried to the door as the knocks were renewed.

The man said, 'Lila,' and opened his arms to her. He wore his long black cape, and his whisky-laden breath coiled into the cold air. She stepped backwards. 'Dad?' she whispered. 'No, keep back.'

Leo let his arms drop. 'Oh, Lila,' he said, 'it's been so long.' The crack of tears in his voice disgusted her.

'Why?' she said, still holding the door. 'Why are you here?'

His long face was unshaven, his wiry hair greyer than she remembered. 'Where's Jess?' he said. 'I've been ringing them in London, but no luck. Have they moved? They were going to move. I want to see the baby.'

'They moved,' said Eliza, quickly. 'I mean, they're moving. I don't know their new number. I – I thought they were taking the old one with them.' Please, she thought, please Jess, please Louis, don't wake up right now.

'The baby,' said her father, swaying slightly, 'I haven't heard. Is it –'

'A boy. His name's Louis. They're fine. Everyone's fine.' She started to close the door. Leo's hand shot out and grabbed her wrist.

'Let me in, Lila. I'm your father, for Christ's sake.'

Eliza's eyes flashed. 'You've never behaved like one. Let me go.'

Leo tightened his grip. 'Lila, what can I do? I wrote to you – you stood me up. I've been ringing Jess – no reply. I can't ring Powdermill, but I'm desperate, desperate for news.'

A knot of pure anger formed itself inside Eliza. 'You gave up on your responsibilities long ago,' she said, her voice small and precise. 'You ran away, remember? So you've forfeited your right to any news. We're managing just fine without you, Dad. So let go of my wrist and get back to whatever hole you've been hiding in.' She tried to jerk herself free, but Leo clung on, and brought his face closer to her own.

'You're heartless,' he hissed. 'I'm talking about my family here. I've got a right to know – but you, you cold bitch, no wonder you could never get a man to stick with you –'

Leo's face was twisted. With his grey stubble and his watery eyes he looked like one of the vagrants who wandered round the coach station, poking in bins. His body was halfway through the door now. Any minute either Jess or the baby would wake, and then there would be no stopping him. Eliza looked him straight in the eye and then spat in his face. He lurched backwards. 'Will you go quietly now, or must I start screaming?' hissed Eliza, her heart thudding. Behind her staggering father a broad figure suddenly loomed.

'Having trouble, Eliza?' asked Tom. He laid a hand on Leo's arm. 'Come on, Mr Antrobus. We'll find you a taxi.' He propelled Leo, now slumped and unresisting, in the direction of the main road.

Eliza returned to the living room. There were stirrings from the sofa. She picked Louis up and paced the room, absently patting the squeaky bundle draped over her shoulder. Her head was spinning, but one clear thought rang out: Jess, tender-hearted Jess, must not know of Leo's visit. Eliza had to get to Tom to warn him before he said anything. She opened the front door and stood there, shushing the baby and waiting for Tom's return.

'Tony, this is a futile argument. Let's leave the choice to Jamie.'

'It was in the initial agreement that term-times should be spent with you, holidays with me.'

'Christmas isn't the same as other holidays, Tony.'

'Introducing the idea of choice will only confuse him. Just tell him he's coming to the barn with us, Susan – let's keep it simple.'

'And me? What about my Christmas?'

'You? Oh,' Tony sounded bored, 'you can suit yourself.'

Susan replaced the receiver. The conversation had made her more determined than ever to keep Jamie with her at Christmas. Half an hour until he got back from school. She picked up a nail file and fiddled at her nails. After her conversation with Patrick Furness she had no doubt that Jamie would want to stay with her. She thought of that story he'd written, of his scorn for the plump blonde invader, and smiled. She thought of Patrick Furness, of his floppy dark hair and the touch of his hand on her shoulder, and smiled again.

The telephone rang.

'Oh, hello, Mrs – er, Patrick Furness here. Jamie's English teacher.'

The coincidence made Susan feel faint. She replied, 'Yes, I know who you are.'

Patrick couldn't gauge her tone. He sounded less assured than usual. 'I'm just ringing to see – well, I thought I'd better find out if you were all right.'

There was a moment's pause as Susan fought to control the working of her facial muscles.

'I'm sorry,' said Patrick. 'You must think I've got an awful nerve. I shouldn't have made this call. I apologise.'

Susan found her voice. 'No, no, don't apologise. It's very thoughtful of you. I'm fine, actually, but I'm glad you asked.'

Patrick struggled to regain his professional composure. 'If you ever want to discuss Jamie's progress, please don't hesitate to contact me.'

'That's most kind.'

'Well, goodbye, then.'

'Goodbye, Mr Furness. And perhaps –'

'Yes?'

'Nothing. Goodbye.'

Perhaps we might meet again one day. That's what I nearly said, thought Susan. That's what I should have said. I keep forgetting I'm a free agent.

It had not escaped her notice that Patrick had rung her at a time when he could be pretty sure Jamie would not be in the house. She gave full rein to the childish grin that would keep trying to spread itself across her face, then went down to the kitchen to make a cup of tea and present a cosy, welcoming sight to Jamie when she got home.

She didn't have long to wait. He was whistling as he came through the front door – whistling something unrecognisable. Jamie had never been musical. 'Hi, Mum,' he called. He'd relaxed so much in the past few weeks, he sometimes seemed positively jaunty. He had got used to his new school, presumably. And accepted the break-up of his parents' marriage, too? Susan knew that Tony would eventually force the sale of the house, but she rigorously suppressed that thought. Take one

thing at a time, she told herself. He's quite bouncy at the
moment, so let's deal with Christmas.

'Hello, darling. Hungry?'

'Not really.'

'You usually are.'

'I had a Twix on the tube. But I'm thirsty. Is there any Citrus
Spring?'

Susan fetched him a can and a glass. She watched him drink
straight from the can and winced, thinking of bleeding lips. She
sipped her tea, and said levelly, 'Jamie, where would you like to
spend Christmas? With me, or with your father?'

He had a mouthful of fizz, and didn't reply at once. Susan
hurried on.

'Of course you don't have to make your mind up right away.
Give it some thought, if you like.'

'Oh,' said Jamie, 'I've already given it some thought. I
assumed I was going to the barn.'

'But darling, is that what you want? You don't have to go with
Dad and –'

'Oh, it's all right,' said Jamie airily. 'I'm quite happy to go
there. The barn could be quite Christmassy.'

Susan turned away. 'I see.' She pulled on her rubber gloves.

'Mum, you don't mind, do you?'

She said, without turning round, 'I just want you to do what
you want, Jamie.' I can be mature about this, she thought,
squirting cream cleaner on to the marble work surfaces.

Jamie said, 'Good. Is Samson in the garden?' The telephone
rang. 'Shall I answer that, Mum?'

'No, no.' Susan peeled off a glove. 'Get Samson.' Jamie was
gone. 'Yes?'

'Suze, it's Poll.'

'Oh, Polly –'

'Are you all right? You sound a bit –'

'No, I'm fine. Just in the middle of –'

'Well, I won't keep you. I just rang to tell you that you were
right about what's-his-face.'

'Who's what's-his-face.'

'That Gascoigne man. That night in Agostino's, remember?
Well, it's all over. He's left her, apparently, and neither of them

144

are moving into that house. He's going to let it. Can you believe it?'

'He's letting the house?'

'What a bastard, eh? It makes me hopping mad when I think of all that work you put into it, Suze. Look, I've got to dash, someone wants me on the other line. I'll ring soon – we must do lunch.'

The house, thought Susan as she scrubbed at the already spotless surfaces. The lovely, lovely house. She began to pull bottles and cartons out of the fridge. There's a bad smell, she thought. Something must have gone rotten in here. Oh, Patrick, you shouldn't have rung so early. You should have rung now. Because I'm not all right, not all right at all. It's too late to tell you, now, how very, very far I am from being all right.

Leo got back from Oxford, somehow. The details of the journey were hazy in the extreme, but he found himself standing outside the door of Rufus's flat at about eight o'clock that Sunday evening. He patted his pockets, searching for keys, but found nothing. He gave the door a half-hearted push, and was just sober enough to be surprised when it swung open.

Rufus was sitting at the kitchen table, looking anything but his usual genial self. With him sat two policemen. 'Anything the matter?' asked Leo.

'Of course not.' Rufus's tone was acid. 'These two kind gentlemen just dropped in for a chat.'

'Ah, Rufus, don't you start. Jesus, I've had a hell of a day.'

'I can't say it's been the best day of my life, either, to come back and find the place has been ransacked, all because you, Leo, forgot to double-lock this morning.'

The policemen exchanged embarrassed glances. 'Would you mind having a look around, Mr – er – and letting us know which of your belongings have been taken?' said one.

'Antrobus,' said Leo. 'And I don't have any belongings. Because I don't belong.'

'All the same, if you could just think . . .'

'Those parcels,' put in Rufus. 'All those bloody parcels you brought back from Harrods yesterday. They've gone, I'm pretty sure.'

Leo, accompanied by a policeman, went to look. Sure enough, the space by the foot of his bed where the parcels had been resounded with emptiness. The older policeman got out his notebook. 'Now, if you could just describe the contents . . .'

'The contents,' Leo repeated like an automaton.

'How many parcels were there, sir, and what did they contain?'

Leo opened his mouth to reply, then sank suddenly, heavily on to the bed. He stretched himself out, put his hands behind his head. 'Ah, sod it. It doesn't matter. I can't even remember.'

# CHAPTER SEVENTEEN

Jamie arrived at the barn as soon as his term ended, a week before Christmas. He had Samson with him. Tony Chandler had managed to sidestep any confrontation about the dog, and Pippa, busy with Christmas preparations, had put the issue on her mental back-burner. Tony was to commute daily this week. Pippa, who had given up her job as Tony's secretary with alacrity as soon as he had hinted that their relationship might make things difficult for him at the office, was determined to make this first Christmas at the barn one to remember. She bought a pile of glossy magazines and a special festive cookery book; soon all these were a-flutter with yellow Post-It notes.

Pippa had bought her presents in London, of course; there was nothing to buy in the country. The bread-and-butter presents had come from Peter Jones; her main gift for Tony she'd found at the Scotch House. A V-neck cashmere pullover, cherry red. Really Christmassy . . . she was thrilled with it. She kept all the receipts on her dressing table, held together by a papier-mâché clip shaped like a large butterfly.

The only present she wasn't sure about was Jamie's. She'd bought him a sweatshirt, decorated with a pattern of owls, because he liked birds. The thing was, the owls had nightcaps on, and were carrying guttering candles in their outstretched wings. Pippa thought they were sweet, with their bleary, droopy eyes, but she'd been having second thoughts about it. Jamie might think it was babyish. He was, after all, a teenager, though he didn't look or act like one. Pippa wanted to get it right with Jamie. She quite liked him – at least, she didn't mind him – and she had a feeling that if she got him on her side he could be a useful ally against his father. For Pippa was beginning to find that Tony could be quite difficult at times – like about the dog, for instance. Not that she would be enlisting Jamie's support on that issue, of course!

They'd decided to tell Jamie about the baby on Christmas

Day. It was amazing he hadn't noticed already, thought Pippa, running her hand with pride over her rounding stomach, but young boys might not be very alert about such things. It was five months now, wriggling away happily, and the nurse said at the last scan that she thought it was a girl. Pippa was going to have the little bedroom at the barn done out in pink. That was one of the things she was going to organise in the New Year.

Jamie, too, had bought his Christmas presents in good time. His father had given him an extra £50, telling him to get something decent for his mother and Pippa. Jamie had tensed at the way he'd mentioned them in the same breath, but the money was welcome. His mother was difficult to buy presents for, because the way things looked mattered so much to her. She always said she liked what he gave her, but Jamie noticed the way some things seemed quickly to disappear . . . Now she was doing this interior decoration work it seemed easier. He found a lavishly illustrated book about doing up houses, and bought her a card to go with it. 'Happy Christmas, Mum, love from Jamie,' he wrote on the card, and then, because that looked a bit bare, he added, 'Sorry me and Samson won't be there.' He didn't like to think about his mother's Christmas. She had said airily, 'Oh, I expect I'll go to Polly's'; he hoped that was true.

The book was expensive. Pippa's present was certainly not going to be as nice as that, even if his father was supplying the dosh. He came across a pretend champagne bottle filled with chocolate truffles. 'That'll do,' he thought. 'Fat pig.' And she was, too – she seemed to get fatter every time he saw her. She never even tried to wear jeans any more.

Still, it was good to be at the barn. As he helped unload the car, a couple of pine cones pattered down at his feet; he looked up and saw Finian, grimacing at him from a vantage point halfway up a tree. Fin was mouthing something at him; Jamie could guess what it was about. The prawns. In their last coded exchange of letters, they'd agreed to lay their trap at the earliest opportunity after Jamie's arrival. That way, the stench should be good and pungent by Christmas Day. Women, Fin pointed out, were always ratty on Christmas Day anyway because they had to do all the cooking, so what with that and the smell of prawns there should be a good chance of a bust-up.

As time went by, Jamie had become less convinced that anything mere boys could do would truly dislodge anyone as limpet-like as Pippa, but he was willing to have a go. If nothing else, the plotting was fun, and brought him closer to Fin. Fin was the reason why he'd chosen to spend Christmas at the barn. It gave him a little twinge of guilt to admit that, of his mother and Fin, he preferred to be with his friend, but that was indeed the case. He would get all his unpacking done straight away, put everything in its proper place the way Pippa liked him to do, and then he'd slip off and find Fin, and the holidays would truly begin.

It was Bella who answered Jamie's knock at the back door. She did not greet him, but called out in her high, toneless voice to Fin, 'Finian! Visitor for you, young man.' Fin scrambled down from the Aga. 'Hi,' he said, 'I've got the stuff.' He waved a dripping plastic bag tied with a knot. 'I went to Southbourne yesterday with Ma. I got them from one of those stalls on the sea front, while Ma was looking for presents.'

Jamie, alarmed, rolled his eyes towards Bella, but Fin mouthed, 'It's OK. She won't tell.' Aloud he said, 'When are your folks going out? I can't wait to get started.'

'It's only her. My dad's coming down on the train tonight.'

'Well? Is she going anywhere?'

'Yes, thank God. Her mother's coming at three and she's going to take her to Sissington Springs to look for wallpaper.'

'But you've got brand-new wallpaper already.'

'I know. But she's decided she wants to change the little bedroom. Don't ask me why.'

'Well, it's good news. Sissington's miles away. It'll take them all afternoon.'

'Shall I make a pot of tea for your visitor, Finian?' put in Bella, her voice the distant echo of a bright social tone.

Finian mouthed, 'Say yes.' Jamie said, 'That would be lovely, thank you.'

'She wants to talk to you,' Fin explained quietly, as the noise of Bella filling the kettle drowned the sound of his voice, 'but she won't do it directly. She has to go through me.'

The kettle, which was not electric, took ages to boil. It was a huge cast-iron one, and Bella had filled it to the brim. Jamie was

149

in a fidget, anxious to get away. Whatever Fin said, he didn't feel able to discuss things freely with Bella's ghostly presence hovering.

Jamie had not quite got used to the squalor of the farmhouse kitchen. The Aga, which ran on solid fuel, wafted out a fine pinkish dust that settled on everything, including uncovered food and drink. And food and drink did often sit about, uncovered, on the two massive tables made of pale, unpolished wood, their surfaces crisscrossed, scored by countless knives. Jamie didn't know much about cooking but he found it odd that the Antrobus women never used chopping boards. But he liked the way there was a cat on every surface. The ironing board, always up but rarely used, was a favourite roost for the ginger tom. The fluffy tortoiseshell coiled herself inside a rusty baking tin that had taken up permanent residence next to the Aga; the little grey, the last of the tortoiseshell's spring litter, favoured a pile of newspapers at the end of the settle. They were calm cats by day, hardly lifting their heads even when Jamie brought Samson in; at night, though, you could hear them yowling and screeching at unseen enemies in the thick undergrowth round the stables.

Bella brought the teapot, cups and saucers, sugar and milk. She arranged everything unnecessarily on a tray. She poured for them; a stream of steaming water, tinged only very slightly brown from the inside of the teapot, filled the cups. Finian fixed his eyes on Jamie, signalling, 'Don't say anything.' Bella peered at the cups, her pale face furrowed in concentration. Then she fetched a tea-strainer and laid it on the tray beside the teapot, saying, 'Ah!' as if the solution to a problem had been found.

Finian said, 'Great. Thanks, Bella,' and pretended to sip from his cup. Jamie followed suit. Bella gave one of her vague sweet smiles and wandered off into the cold depths of the house. If she had wanted to talk to Jamie, the idea had dissolved into vapour. Fin said, 'Quick,' and snatched Jamie's cup, along with his own. He emptied both into the sink.

'It's no use telling her,' he said. 'It would only upset her. One time she gave us raw potatoes for lunch and we had to hide them in our napkins.' He fondled Samson's head. 'Come on. It must be gone three by now. Let's get going.'

Jamie rose with alacrity, but when they reached the barn his

150

heart was beating uncomfortably fast, and he almost hoped that Pippa and her mother had changed their minds about their wall-paper hunt. But no, the place was deserted, and there was a note on the breakfast bar held down by a ceramic hedgehog. 'Jamie,' it said, 'see you about six. Have fun! Luv, Pips.' The dot above the i in his name was shaped like a heart.

Finian ripped open the plastic bag. There lay the prawns, a pound and a half of them. Jamie hadn't expected to see them whole like that, with their stiff orange whiskers and bobbly black eyes.

'Let's get going,' said Fin, 'in case they decide to come back early. In here?' he gestured towards the living room.

The curtains were thick and luxuriously lined. They had deep hems, almost like pouches. It was child's play to poke the prawns in through the gaps in the stitching. When they'd finished, there were still quite a few prawns left. Fin, squatting on his haunches, said, 'Where else? The bed?'

Jamie hesitated. It seemed so much worse to contaminate his father's bed than the living room curtains, which were in a way public property. He was about to suggest that they call it a day and share the rest of the prawns between the two dogs when a whine from Samson, shut as he now had to be in the cold utility room, changed his mind. 'Sure,' he said, 'the bed.' And he led the way upstairs.

The room had changed immeasurably since the hot afternoon when Finian had lain trapped beneath the bed platform. Now there were ruched curtains at the windows, cream with apricot-coloured flowers on them. The way they were gathered up reminded Fin of when Bella's skirt sometimes got caught in her knickers after she'd been to the loo. The bed itself was draped with an apricot-coloured quilt and piled with lacy white cushions. A pair of teddy bears, one dressed in a pink sweater, one in a blue, sat entwined amongst the cushions.

'We'll have to remember how everything went,' said Jamie, 'otherwise she'll notice.' They stared hard at the bears and the cushions. 'It's quite complicated,' said Finian. 'Does she do it like that every day?'

'I think so. I never come in here.' Jamie began to lay the cushions carefully on the floor.

The mattress, new and seamless, had no suitable hiding places for the prawns. 'We could just put them underneath,' said Finian doubtfully. 'But it's so thick, the smell might not come through.'

'And if she changed the sheets she might move the mattress and find them.'

The boys sat on the stripped mattress in silence. Then Fin jumped up.

'I know!' he said. 'The rails!'

'What rails?'

'These ones. They're hollow.' He reached up to the curtain rails that ran round the top of the bed and began to unscrew them.

'How did you know that?'

'I saw this bed being made. I saw everything in this house being made.' Finian was about to tell Jamie the story of how he had got trapped beneath this very bed, but then reflected that it might not be in very good taste. 'Look!' He'd detached the rail from the bedpost, revealing a perfect, prawn-sized space.

Jamie was anxious. 'I hope you can fit it all back together again. Otherwise we're going to have to think of a pretty amazing excuse.'

'No worries.' Fin stuffed a prawn in, and screwed the pieces back together. He moved on to the other corner. 'I'll just leave it a little looser than it was, so the smell can get out. Do you want to do the end one?'

They had just finished, and were re-entwining the teddy bears as the final touch, when the telephone rang. Jamie started guiltily but picked it up.

'James? Is Pippa there? No? Well, tell her that I'll be back earlier than I thought – she should meet me at seven ten. Everything all right? I'm looking forward to being there, I must say.' Tony Chandler, mellowed by the lunchtime office party, was at his most genial. 'OK, my son? I'll see you later.' The warmth in his voice made Jamie think of the time before, the time when he hadn't known that he belonged to an unhappy family. When he hung up, he averted his face so that Fin wouldn't see the regret that he had to struggle to suppress.

\* \* \*

152

The van had difficulty negotiating the ruts in the track that led up to Powdermill Farm. 'This'll kill the suspension,' the driver grumbled to his teenage son, who was learning his father's trade.

'Jesus! What a dump!' The boy took in the dilapidated front of the house, the slipping tiles, the overgrown holly bushes that darkened the windows, the bleached bones of the wisteria that in May smothered the walls with its hazy, sweet-scented, grape-like clusters, but that now clung, brittle, to the rusty wires that Sibyl had put up for it so many years ago. A couple of hens skittered round the doorstep, squawking at some real or imagined affront, but there was no sign of human life.

'It could be haunted,' said the boy.

'Don't be daft, son. You don't believe all that rubbish.'

The boy was about to launch into one of the many true tales of the paranormal with which his friends regaled each other late at night after a few beers and a couple of spliffs, but thought better of it. He was supposed to be impressing his father with his maturity, so that he could bunk off most of what remained of his time at school and help with the delivery service instead. He swung himself down and opened the back doors of the van.

Bella, peeping out of the attic window, caught the young man's eye as he heaved a large packing case towards the front door. She started backwards and went to find Martha, but not before her image had implanted itself in the fertile soil of his imagination. 'Christ, you should have seen it,' he was later to tell his mates. 'Long, straggly hair, kind of colourless. Like cobwebs. And it had these staring eyes, that looked like they've never been shut. It looked right through me. Then it just vanished. I'm not going up there again, man, I tell you, no way.'

Martha answered the driver's knock. 'Special delivery,' he said. 'Sign here, love, all right?' Martha signed, and as she looked at the pile of parcels her heart thumped. Leo, she thought. It must be Leo. I should have known he wouldn't forget Christmas.

The handwriting on the labels was unfamiliar, but that didn't mean much. The way the packages were done up looked professional; he must have got the shop assistants to do it for him. The man and the boy carried it all into the hall, then she dismissed them with a quick smile and a 'Happy Christmas'. As she

153

investigated each box in turn, she realised they were all addressed to Jess.

What could this mean? Would a similar delivery, equally lavish, arrive for each member of the family? Or had Leo's preference for his adoring second daughter, which he had sometimes made so painfully obvious, taken over to the point where he felt able to cut the others out altogether? One thing was certain. Martha was not going to have Jess sitting there on Christmas Day opening parcels while Lila and Finian looked on. She tore at the fastening of the largest item, a quite substantial packing case.

A folded buggy. A foam mattress. The sides of a dismantled cot. Martha was puzzled. Leo had a strange idea of a present, to be giving the baby things that he would obviously have already. And all this would amount to a quite un-Leo-sized sum of money. Unless, of course, his fortunes had taken a sharp upward turn.

Then she noticed the buggy wheels. It had been used. Not very much, but it certainly wasn't new. She opened another parcel. Baby clothes, lots of them. Babygros, carefully washed and aired, soft like second skins. Navy, white, emerald green, jolly orange stripes. White vests, with poppers between the legs. Miniature denim dungarees. Warm hats, with ear flaps. And a blanket. A purple blanket, knitted by hand, badly.

She ripped at the paper of the remaining packets. Toys, cot sheets, more clothes. Even a bottle of baby lotion and a half-used packet of nappies. Martha stood surrounded by her infant grandson's fixtures and fittings, complete to the last detail. Still holding the bath duck in her hand, she moved to the telephone and dialled Jess' number. Not for the first time that week, there was no reply. She gave Jess a chance – she might be feeding, or changing him. She counted thirty rings, then forty. Then she rang Eliza.

# CHAPTER EIGHTEEN

'Do you think there'll be a second post today?' Finian wandered round the kitchen, fiddling. Eliza glanced up from rolling out the pastry.

'On Christmas Eve? I shouldn't think so. And I think if there was, it would have come by now.'

'Oh,' said Finian, poking in the mincemeat jar with a wooden spoon. 'Just wondered.'

Eliza pressed the cutter down on to the pastry and gave it a little twist. Deftly, she transferred the floury disc to the baking tin and patted it into place. 'Were you expecting something particular in the post?' she asked, without looking at her brother.

Jess, settled in the rocking chair by the Aga, transferred Louis from the right breast to the left. 'Were you hoping to hear from Dad, Fin? I was wondering about that too.'

'Not really. Not hoping. Just – you know, it's weird not knowing where he is at Christmas time.'

'I agree,' said Jess. 'You'd have thought he'd have made some effort to get in touch. Not a word for four months – it's unbelievable.'

Eliza kept her eyes on her pastry. 'Ma thinks he's left the country,' she muttered.

'But you can still write. You can still ring, even. There's just no excuse – unless he's orbiting the Earth in a space shuttle.'

Finian laughed. 'He'd be a crappy astronaut,' he said. 'He never could keep still for ten seconds.'

'Like you, Fin,' remarked Eliza, as he circled the table for the fourth time, pulling off and eating fragments of raw pastry as he went.

Finian stopped in his tracks. 'Don't say that, Lila,' he said, his blue eyes flashing. 'He's not remotely like me.' Both sisters looked up in surprise at his vehemence. He made for the door. 'I'm going to decorate the tree. Anyone who wants can come and help.'

As the door closed the sisters exchanged glances. 'He misses him,' said Jess, rocking. 'But he won't admit it. I miss him too, I think. It's going to be a strange Christmas.'

Eliza placed a dollop of mincemeat at the centre of each pastry circle. 'He's not worth missing,' she said, scooping up a few spilt drops of the spicy brown ooze with a fingertip. 'I'm glad he hasn't been in touch. We're better off forgetting about him, and getting on with our lives.'

'That's what you think about Nick, too, isn't it?'

'It certainly is.'

There was a silence. Gently, Jess detached Louis, who had fallen asleep mid-suckle. 'If you've loved somebody, you can't just forget about them,' she murmured, more to herself than to Eliza. 'What was once there is always with you.'

Eliza flung open the oven door and shoved in the tray of pies with unnecessary force. 'Well, perhaps I wouldn't know about that.'

Jess ignored the bait. She laid Louis in his re-acquired Moses basket. 'Will you watch him, Lila? I'll go and help Fin with the tree.'

Eliza nodded, and rolled up the remains of the pastry to begin the next batch. She thought of her father's sour, drunken breath in her face and closed her eyes. The person I love isn't there any more, she thought. If I ever loved him.

She looked up at the cuckoo clock that still kept time though it had long since ceased to cuckoo. She remembered how as a child she had loved to imagine the cuckoo's little house, hidden deep in the clock somewhere, with tiny beds and tables and a Mrs Cuckoo and some babies.

Half past five. Just time to finish the mince pies before they all went over to the barn for a drink and a little seasonal *glasnost* with the Chandlers.

Once, she had climbed on a chair and peeped inside the cuckoo clock to see nothing but a dull dark space. I'm right not to tell them that I saw Dad, she thought. No one else needs to know that there's nothing there. In her pocket was a letter, addressed to her in a shakier version of her father's familiar hand. She hadn't read it, hadn't opened it. The best thing, she thought, would be to burn it without a glance. But she hadn't

156

done that yet. She shook flour over the table and set about her rolling once more.

Meredith Watts-Davison stood in the middle of the living room, sniffing. Christmas Day had dawned drear and lightless; a sleety drizzle was now falling, but for which she would have flung open the windows to get rid of the peculiar odour. She had been banned from the kitchen, where her daughter Pippa was putting the finishing touches to the festive meal. Tony, to whom she referred, with more optimism than accuracy, as her son-in-law, was setting out champagne and glasses on a tray, and young Jamie had been sent to change after getting himself covered in mud on his morning's walk with that farm boy and the dogs. Samson was shut in the utility room, which in Meredith Watts-Davison's opinion was just as it should be. She didn't see the point of big dogs. For many years she had kept Pekes.

A bowl of pot-pourri sat in the centre of one of the coffee tables; she lifted handfuls of the stuff and let it trickle slowly down, hoping its musky fragrance would banish the taint of whatever-it-was. What was it? She inhaled again. It reminded her of the smell cut flower stems made when they had been left to stand in water for too long, but the only flowers in the room were artificial peonies, made of silk. Perhaps some animal – a mouse, or worse – had died under the floorboards and was slowly decomposing. She opened her handbag and wrote, 'Suggest Rentokil Dec. 27th' in the notes section of her engagement diary. Pippa wouldn't think of it herself, but it would be tactful to wait until after Boxing Day before mentioning it. Meredith prided herself on her tact.

Possibly – even probably – the smell had something to do with the visit of that dirty family the evening before. It had been sweet of Pips and Tony to have them in for a drink, but Meredith didn't think they should bother again. The two young women had just about passed muster, though the one with the baby looked dishevelled, and the one with spectacles hadn't bothered to change into a skirt. The old lady had said little. She had looked dignified enough bolt upright in her chair by the fire; Meredith smiled, remembering Sibyl's astonishment at noticing there was no ash. She had obviously never come across one of those tremendously clever gas fires that looked almost like the real thing, but without the mess and the inconvenience. Meredith's smile faded as she thought of the dark patch on the seat of the old lady's tweed skirt, only visible when she stood up to take her leave. Meredith just hadn't been able to say anything to Pippa, but she'd had a surreptitious scrub at the chair after they'd gone. Poor old dear. She clearly couldn't help it, but somebody ought to let her know that it was no longer appropriate for her to accept invitations to drinks in other people's houses. Meredith thought with irritation of Martha Antrobus, to her mind the most culpable and offensive of the group. The woman's manners were those of the barnyard. Her clumpy lace-up shoes were spattered with mud, her fingernails were dirty, and she hadn't put on a scrap of make-up. Her only offering had been a very obviously home-made Christmas card and a jar of plum jam, also home-made. 'From our own plums,' she'd said, as if she was proud of her penny-pinching gift. She was the one who should have kept the old lady away; they gathered that the simple-minded one had stayed at home, so the poor old thing would not have been alone. Martha Antrobus, too, was the one who should have got her son out of his patched jeans and into something a little more respectable. Socially, the Antrobus woman clearly hadn't got a clue. And the way they'd sat there drinking Tony's mulled wine and eating Pippa's mince pies – well, Marks and Spencer's mince pies actually – and not making one positive remark about the way the barn had been done up . . . Yes, Meredith thought, this sickly, rotten smell might well have something to do with their visit.

Tony, carrying the tray, pushed the door open with his foot. 'Ah! Meredith!' he exclaimed. 'Pips is ready at last. Time for a drink. James!'

Meredith started. She had not quite got used to the way Tony raised his voice by several decibels when summoning his son. Pippa bustled in, pink-cheeked and smiling. She encircled her mother's waist with her arm and gave her a little squeeze. 'I had a bit of trouble with the bread sauce, but I've sorted it out. I think it's going to be perfect.'

Tony beamed at her. 'I'm sure it will be, darling. Meredith, aren't you proud of her? Her first Christmas dinner, and she's managed it all by herself!'

They act as if she was seven, not twenty-whatever-it-is, thought Jamie, slouching into the room. He wanted to look as inconspicuous as possible, but it wasn't easy, with only three other people there. He could smell the prawns distinctly, and was amazed there hadn't been any comments yet. He was beginning to regret the whole thing. When he'd planned it with Fin he'd never envisaged having to face the consequences alone.

'Ah, James! Good!' Tony unpeeled the gold foil and eased out the champagne cork with his thumbs. Despite his care it shot up and hit the ceiling with a crack. Foam gushed down the side of the bottle; Pippa squealed.

'Hand the drinks, James,' said his father with just a hint of reproof in his voice. He'd been told before what order to give people drinks in, but now he couldn't decide who had precedence, Pippa or her mother, so he tried to hand them out both at the same time. He took his own half-inch and retreated to the corner of the sofa.

Pippa started to sniff. 'I can't believe it,' she said. 'I gave this room such a good clean-out yesterday morning, but the smell's still here.'

'It seems a little better to me, darling.'

'That's because you've got your nose buried in your champagne glass. It's worse. What do you think, Mums?'

'Well, darling, I must admit –'

'You see. What can it be?'

Meredith swallowed. Since she'd been asked a direct question, she was going to give a direct answer. 'Pippa, love, I did wonder about those people.'

'People?'

'Last night. For drinks. They seemed a little –'

Jamie's ears burned. He longed to yell out a defence of Fin and his family, but he didn't dare. He busied himself with his champagne, swirling it round and round in his glass and trying to count the bubbles.

'Grubby?' Tony finished Meredith's sentence for her. 'You can say that again. I didn't want to invite them in the first place, but Pips insisted.'

'Tony, don't be mean.' Pippa bridled. 'They're our neighbours. It's our duty to have them over. And they're Jamie's friends,' she added with what she hoped was a sweet smile. Jamie wished she hadn't said anything.

'Well, never mind.' Tony was conciliatory. 'This bloody smell can't be anything to do with them, though, because Pips was cleaning the room in the morning, long before they set foot in the place. It's got to be an animal of some sort. Something's crawled off and died somewhere.'

'But it's upstairs too,' squealed Pippa. 'We both noticed it in the bedroom last night, didn't we, darling? It kept me awake, actually.'

'Could be another animal, then. A rat, I suppose. Country life, I'm afraid.'

'Ugh! Tony! No! Not a rat in the bedroom! Don't say it.'

'I wasn't going to mention it, because it isn't a very easy subject,' put in Meredith, 'but I do think Rentokil –'

'Sure, we'll ring them on Tuesday.' Tony picked up the champagne bottle. 'And now, who wants a refill? Because we've got a much more Christmassy subject to talk about.'

'No more for me, darling.' Pippa covered her glass with her hand and flashed a meaningful smile at Tony.

'No. Indeed.' He cleared his throat. 'A drop more for you, Meredith? And for you, my son, because we need to drink the health of your new baby brother or sister.'

'Sister,' put in Pippa, firmly.

Jess raised his head. Of course! Why hadn't he realised it before? He put a mental feeler out, cautiously, to see how he felt. Like probing an aching tooth with your tongue.

The feeling wasn't too bad. He managed to smile at Pippa. 'Congratulations,' he said, raising his glass. They all seemed to be looking at him expectantly. He racked his brains to think of the right thing to say. Ah! He had it! 'When's it due?' he asked.

'April. April the eighteenth,' replied Pippa. There was nothing she like discussing more, nothing she felt more certain about than this forthcoming baby. 'It's a girl, Jamie, so we're going to change the wallpaper in the little bedroom to pink. And –'

'Darling, we can't be sure. They said they couldn't be certain.'

'Oh, but they hardly ever make mistakes these days.'

'I'm glad it's a girl,' said Jamie. He didn't care, actually, but it seemed to be the right thing to say. All three of them beamed at him.

'Ooh!' Pippa leapt up with a little squeak. 'The potatoes! Come next door, everyone; Tony, you'd better start carving.'

As she left the living room, Meredith took one final sniff. Jamie, noticing, sniffed too. Then it dawned on him. Prawns or no prawns, the baby meant that there would be no getting rid of Pippa now.

The goose had shrunk significantly in the cooking. It was also overdone. Martha had told herself over and over again to take extra care this year. With Leo and Nick gone, the last thing the family needed was a dismal dinner, but despite her resolutions it looked as if a dismal dinner was that they were going to get. Sibyl, Jess and Bella were already seated; Fin and Eliza were bringing in plates of vegetables from the kitchen. Martha saw Eliza take one look at the goose and disappear, to re-emerge with a loaf of brown bread.

The dining room was rarely used. It was small, and panelled with dark oak; there was a large open fireplace that smoked. Leo was the only person who'd ever been able to lay that fire properly. Finian had done his best that morning, but the room was already dim with smoke.

The windows were tiny and diamond-paned; the walls were hung with mirrors in an attempt to create more light. Sibyl had framed the mirrors herself, years ago. The frames were made of driftwood and decorated with painted shells and stones. After more than five decades they still looked fresh and original – and incongruous, really, in the land-locked Tudor darkness of the raftered, low-ceilinged dining room. At the far end, opposite Martha, hung a sketch of Leo aged about fifteen. His ebullience and optimism were captured in just a few deft charcoal lines. It hung over the place where he used to sit – where, Martha realised, Finian was going to sit today. Someone had decked the mirrors with trailing ivy and yew, but the portrait of Leo was unadorned.

Everything necessary was now on the table. Finian and Eliza

161

sat down and folded their napkins. 'It smells good,' said Finian loyally. Martha dashed the carving knife against the steel before sinking it into the goose's withered breast.

Sibyl had been more than usually quiet all day. Now the sight of the knife and the issue of steam from the punctured bird seemed to rouse her. 'Where's Leo?' she said, her deep voice cutting through the chatter around her. 'Where *is* Leo? He should be here to carve.'

It was Eliza who broke the silence. 'He's left us, Ganna,' she said, gently but firmly. 'And he's not going to come back.' They all looked at the handsome old face, its strong bone structure defying the powdery folds of flesh.

'Ah yes,' said Sibyl, 'I remember now. How could I have forgotten? Young men don't come back in wartime, not even for Christmas. But Martha dear, how clever of you to manage such a magnificent meal on the rations.'

Finian murmured to Jess, 'She's putting it on. She must be.' But Jess only shook her head.

'I'm sorry,' said Martha, doling out stuffing. 'The goose is overcooked. I should have taken it out before I put the sprouts on.'

'Well, I wasn't going to mention it,' said Fin, 'but it does remind me of that man they dug out of the peat bog. Just a bit.'

Everybody laughed, gratefully. Martha set the remains of the goose on the trivet in front of the fire to keep warm. When she straightened up her face was wet. 'It's the smoke,' she explained, wiping her eyes on her napkin. 'Just the smoke. Fin, darling, you need to lay the logs in more of a pyramid shape. Pointing backwards.'

'I did,' said Fin.

Louis, lying in his basket, woke, and wailed. 'I'll hold him if you like,' said Eliza. She bounced him on her knee. 'Next Christmas he'll really know what's happening, won't you, little man?'

But Ganna won't, thought Martha, pushing a potato round her plate. If Leo doesn't come back soon, she won't know who he is. Maybe it's better that way. Maybe.


'Pips, that was absolutely delicious.' Tony turned the fire down a little and sank on to the sofa, legs stretched out in front of him.

He longed to loosen his belt, but the presence of Pippa's mother was inhibiting.

'Was it really, darling?' Pippa dimpled and smiled. 'I thought I cooked the sprouts for a little too long, but –'

'No, really, sweetheart. First class. The best Christmas dinner I've ever eaten.' In truth it hadn't been too bad. Pippa had relied on the good St Michael to provide her with stuffings and sauces, and though the sprouts had been a soggy khaki mess, everything else had just about held together. Sitting round the fire like this was really very pleasant, with black coffee, and brandy for him and Turkish delight for the others.

This is what family life should be about, thought Tony, warming his glass between his hands to release the fumes. This is what it's all for.

'Pippa dear, do have a little rest.' Meredith patted the cushion beside her. 'You've been waiting on us all too much. You've got someone other than yourself to think of,' and she smiled at the tight little drum wherein her grandchild lay.

Jamie sat on a straight-backed chair, apart. He was waiting for a chance to escape. They'd opened the presents that morning – he didn't know what he was going to do about that gross sweatshirt, but he'd said thank you as neutrally as he could – and he couldn't think what they were going to do with the rest of the day. It was only half past three. He wouldn't mind watching television, but he knew that his father wouldn't approve. So he couldn't be the one to suggest it. He stared out of the window that stretched from floor to ceiling. The sleet had stopped; light was already draining from the iron-grey sky. A few sheep huddled in the corners of the fields, though the leafless hedges could provide little shelter. Such colours as there were – green and brown and grey – all looked muddied, like the residue of a child's paint-mixing experiment.

Jamie said, 'I'd better take Samson out. It'll be dark soon.'

Pippa, her lips dusted with icing sugar from the Turkish delight, said, 'Ooh, poor Samson! I'd forgotten about him. Bring him in here, Jamie, why don't you?'

'In *here*?' Samson was never allowed in the living room.

'It's Christmas Day. Let's give him a treat. He can have a biccy. Mummy, where's that tin?'

She's in a good mood, thought Jamie, as he went to fetch the dog. Must be because Dad praised the dinner so much. The best he'd ever eaten! What crap! Jamie had thought briefly of Susan when his father had said that, but he'd quickly pushed the thought away.

Samson bounded into the living room, grinning and salivating. He sniffed Meredith's lap; she recoiled, but he wasn't very interested. Pippa offered him a biscuit from a festive assortment, and caressed his great head, but that didn't seem to be the right thing either. He snuffled along the floor like a bloodhound, his tail wagging frantically.

Pippa lost interest. 'More coffee, anyone?' she said, uncurling herself and brushing the icing sugar off her chest. 'James,' said his father meaningfully, and Jamie jumped to attention, carrying the adults' cups to the coffee pot for a refill. It was a couple of minutes before their attention returned to Samson. A couple of minutes was all Samson needed.

'What *has* got into him?' asked Pippa, a little irritated that he had refused her advances earlier. 'Why is he playing with the curtain? Hey, Samson, you'll tear it – oh my God! Ton-*ee*!' Samson, rolling on his back, was worrying at the curtain with teeth and claws, uttering little growls of pleasure and effort.

By the time Tony had his hands through the dog's collar and was hauling him in the direction of the door, the bottom of the curtain had been reduced to wet shreds. 'For Christ's sake, Jamie,' Tony roared, 'can't you keep this animal under control?'

'Don't beat him,' shouted Jamie. 'It wasn't his fault. Don't beat him, Dad!'

'Don't be a fool, Jamie. He needs to be beaten, to teach him a lesson. It's because you're too soft with him that this has happened in the first place. You and your mother.'

Meredith said primly, 'I'm afraid your father's right. Animals have to learn the hard way,' but Jamie hardly heard her. He flung his arms round Samson, who was now cringing away from Tony. 'Beat me instead,' he cried. 'It's my fault. I can explain – just give Samson a chance.'

Tony was holding a broom. 'Get off,' he ordered. 'Leave this to me.' But the boy wouldn't let go, so he was obliged to beat only the back end of Samson with the broom handle.

164

Pippa was too absorbed in examining the wrecked curtain to pay much attention to the mingled sobs and whines. 'Mummy, look,' she called, 'there's something in here. It looks like – it can't be.'

'Shellfish?' said Meredith, studying an orange tail. 'Prawns? In the *curtain*?'

'The smell! That's where the smell came from!' The two women, kneeling on the floor, stared at each other in blank bewilderment.

# CHAPTER NINETEEN

Polly Cruse always held an anti-Christmas party. While many of her friends and relations were snugly provided for on 25th December, there remained a significant and, apparently, growing number of people she knew who were cast adrift, rejected by or rejecting of tinsel joviality and fireside cheer. Polly lived in a penthouse flat in Maida Vale; she had one immense and airy studio room and very little else. Her friends often speculated about where she slept, for though there was a narrow kitchen and an even narrower bathroom, there was no bedroom nor even any sign of a bed.

On Christmas Day Polly transformed her studio room and held open house. The place was always thoroughly decorated, but the decorations owed nothing at all to the festive season. This year the theme was loosely Turkish; the room was draped with swatches of cloth, maroon and saffron, and there were little mirrors and tinkly bells hung up on strings. The usual furniture had somehow been disposed of, and giant cushions and kelims provided the only seating. The food, always plentiful, was spread about on low tables covered with gold foil. There were concoctions of aubergines and yoghurt and walnuts, sticky triangles of filo pastry drenched in syrup, bowls of dried figs, raisins and dates. Polly was highly organised; the little kitchen was piled with carefully arranged trays of replenishments, for the people who would drop in in the late afternoon in flight from earlier family duties.

Susan Chandler had never been to one of Polly's anti-Christmas parties. For the first ten years of her married life they'd alternated between going to her mother's or going to Tony's. Then both grannies had died within a year of each other, and Tony had suggested that they go away instead. So Tony, Susan and Jamie had spent Christmas at a ski resort three times in a row. It wasn't very domestic but she hadn't minded; it was something to do. It was better than staying in London and cooking a turkey for the three of them to eat in gloomy silence, or worse, sharing it with friends who would comment in the car on the way home on the visibly widening cracks in the marriage. Jamie didn't seem to mind not being at home either. He quite liked skiing, though Susan had felt for him when Tony shouted at him when he made mistakes. Jamie didn't like putting Samson in boarding kennels, but he accepted it when it was only for a week. And at ski resorts there were always people around – strangers with whom you could be cheery, and put on a temporary act as a lively, attractive, cohesive family. It had been the best solution at the time.

But now Susan was free, free for the first time in her life to do what she wanted with her Christmas, and the obvious thing was for her to go to Polly's. Polly clearly thought so. 'You must come first and leave last,' she said. 'And you *must* wear that dress. I won't let you in if you don't.' On the 23rd Susan reclaimed her dress from the dry cleaner's. On Christmas Eve she tore off the plastic wrappings, hunted down and removed all the safety pins, and hung it on the outside of her wardrobe where she could feast her eyes on the way the rich colour reverberated against the white-painted door. She had wallowed in a deep, scented bath, and now lay in her lilac wrap sipping white wine and telling herself that this party could be the beginning of the rest of her life. All was in readiness: the dress, the jewellery, the bouquet of Thai orchids standing in water downstairs – Polly had said no Christmas presents, but surely flowers were all right? Nothing stood between Susan and a magnificent day, chatting and laughing, consolidating old acquaintances and initiating new ones. Susan envisaged herself as others might see her, standing in the middle of Polly's party, slim and poised, looking like the kind of controlled, independent woman she herself had so often admired. You just had to think yourself into a role, Polly would say. And Polly was right. You should be able to turn yourself into anything you wanted to be.

Lying on the bed, Susan could see her reflection in the wardrobe mirror. In the lamplight her eyes were dark pools, her skin soft, her shadowy cheekbones high. She refilled her glass, and wondered how Patrick Furness would be spending his Christmas.

* * *

Polly drew the cork out of the twelfth bottle. She only had red wine – making sure that white was chilled was too complicated, and spirits were not a good idea because some people she knew tended to get sick at parties, even when they were on the less middling side of middle age. The wine she'd chosen was delicious, a rich Lebanese Syrah, spicy and aromatic. And the colour! Like the colour of a bead of blood, welling on a pricked fingertip. It was not cheap, but it was worth the price for the colour alone. Polly unwound the cork from the corkscrew and breathed in the scent. Corks were beautiful things. She hoped no one ever invented a better way of stopping a bottle.

She wandered round the room, tweaking things, impatient for the party to begin. She had hoped Susan would arrive early; there was no better way to start a party than to fuss around a bit with a girlfriend. And she wanted to brief Susan on some of the people who'd be coming. There were a couple of men, forties, divorced, who might take an interest . . . Polly saw herself as a free spirit as far as men were concerned, but that didn't stop her urge to matchmake on behalf of her friends.

She thought with satisfaction about the progress she had already made with Susan. Just a few months ago she'd been a poor, pale, helpless thing, miserable with her husband but not capable of imagining life without him, emotionally dependent on her son but unable to communicate with him in any real way. And now – Susan was managing. She was more than managing. She looked good, she kept the house looking good, she picked up the telephone. She was beginning to talk about thwarting Tony's plans to sell the house – plans that were only rarely mentioned but that were surely growing quietly, like bramble roots under paving stones. She had made an excellent job of Nick Gascoigne's house – pity the Gascoignes weren't going to live in it, but you couldn't have everything. And she was coming to Polly's party today, to make the most of a child-free, husband-free Christmas. The next step could well be a no-strings-attached affair, a harmless confidence-booster. As Susan's manager, Polly smiled to herself, and popped a date into her mouth.

The doorbell buzzed, and several voices shouted through the entry phone. The party had begun.

When Susan woke on Christmas morning, alone in her wide white bed, the light filtering through the curtains had such a peculiar opacity that at first she thought it had snowed. She went to look, but there was no snow, just jostling grey lances of sleety rain filling the space between her house and the one opposite. She wrapped her dressing gown more tightly round herself. How silly to think, even for a moment, that there would be snow on Christmas Day!

Last night's bottle of wine, three-quarters empty, stood with the used glass on the bedside table. The sight mirrored Susan's morning mood, sordid and forlorn. She picked them up. The flame-coloured dress, still hanging on the outside of the wardrobe, looked brash and out of place, a silly shout of colour in a monochrome world. She carried the glass and bottle down to the kitchen, avoiding her reflection in the mirror.

She prepared her usual cup of boiled water and lemon but turned in revulsion from the muesli packet. She padded round the house, barefoot, restless and afraid. She turned on all the lights, for comfort, or company.

On the living room mantelpiece stood a row of Christmas cards. Not as many as usual; the break-up of the marriage must have caused complications in the etiquette of card-sending. Most of the cards were tasteful reproductions of suitable Old Masters, sold in aid of charity; fat candles, even fatter robins, and cheeky drunken mice seemed to be things of the past. Susan picked up one or two and glanced, unseeing, at the messages. She'd sent none herself this year.

On the table, next to the poinsettia that Estrelia had given her and that Susan had been hoping would die a natural death, lay her present from Jamie. She had forborne from opening it before, imagining that saving it for Christmas morning would give the day more meaning. She had been wrong. Sitting there waiting for her it emanated a pathos that was almost repulsive. But to leave it unopened would make matters worse. She slid her forefinger under the sealed flap, easing the Sellotape so as not to spoil the paper. She didn't know why she did that, since she always threw wrapping paper away.

The book was shiny, expensive. She turned to the inside

cover to check the price, but it had been snipped out. Perhaps Tony gave him the money, she thought, not daring to feel touched. Jamie's card was tucked inside. She opened it, and read the message. 'Sorry me and Samson won't be there.'

She thought of another Christmas Day, long ago. Jamie would have been about five. They were staying with his Chandler grandmother; no one had helped him to buy his mother a present, and he was distraught. He'd taken one of his grandmother's ornaments, a Staffordshire figurine, and wrapped it in newspaper. 'It's for you, Mum,' he'd said. The figure had got chipped, and Tony had scolded him. She remembered the hectoring voice: 'It's not yours to give.'

She left the book on the table, took down the Christmas cards, and left them in a neat pile. There was no point in crying now.


'Oh, Poll!' said Susan, trying to giggle. 'I don't *want* another man.'

'Don't be silly, girl. I'm not talking about marriage, just a few nice dinners and a bit of fun.'

'Which one is he, then?' Susan felt awkward, conscious of the sharp angles of her shoulder blades. Mutton dressed as lamb, she told herself. A scarecrow in an orange frock.

'He's not here yet. He's about five feet ten, with a black moustache and –'

'A moustache! Ugh! Polly, how could you?'

'I know, I know. But it suits him because he's quite exotic-looking – Iranian, I think. Or half.'

The man with the moustache worked at the same advertising company as Polly. He was forty years old, a bachelor, a happy, light-minded man who loved putting smart-looking women into his smart-looking car and squiring them round in London. Not a long-term prospect, Polly would be the first to admit, but someone to lift the spirits, perhaps, at this grim time of year. But the man had not yet arrived. Susan plunged into conversation with Polly's downstairs neighbour, a retired actor named Gordon with a kind smile and a spotty bow tie, whom she knew slightly. She was reserving judgement on the moustache and its owner, but she wanted to be actively engaged when he arrived.

170

She couldn't help feeling like a wallflower, but she could avoid looking like one.

'Polly!' The voice was warm, husky. There were embraces. Susan peeped, and saw a flash of white teeth beneath the moustache. 'I've brought Nick Gascoigne,' said the husky voice. 'I knew you wouldn't mind. He's on his way. He just stopped to get – ah, here he is.'

Susan stiffened, and fixed her eyes in earnest absorption on the elderly actor's face. She did so in the hope that Polly would sense how little she wanted to talk to Nick Gascoigne. But she was not to be spared. She felt a hand on her arm.

'Suze, I want you to meet Kemal. Kemal, Suzie's one of my dearest friends.' Polly left them to it.

Kemal appraised Susan Chandler with practised speed as he exchanged a few remarks with her. Elegant, he decided, but too thin. Not his type, but too good to waste. He hailed his friend, who was on his way back from fetching himself a drink. 'You must meet Nick Gascoigne,' he said, 'a recent refugee from the marital war zone.'

Nick nodded, coolly. Susan said, 'We've met.' Nick raised an eyebrow and cocked his head on one side. Susan thought, I'm not playing this game. 'Don't pretend you don't know me,' she said, quite loudly. Kemal rolled up his eyes and looked for a chance to slip away.

'Remind me,' said Nick, with an impatient, twitchy, challenging smile.

I can't believe this, thought Susan. He's rewriting his own life, and he wants me to collude with him. She cleared her throat.

'My name is Susan Chandler,' she said in a high, loud, strained voice. 'You paid me to decorate your new house in Islington. The one you were going to live in with your wife and child. I loved the work. I made it beautiful for you. I'm on my own, but I loved to think of the three of you living there, in the perfect setting I'd created. No, don't interrupt please. But then, you see,' she turned to Kemal, 'you see, your friend abandoned his wife, who is very lovely and very young. He abandoned his wife and child, and that beautiful house will never be a home now. So all my effort was for nothing. No, don't go.' She gripped Kemal's arm, her hand like a curved clamp. 'Don't sneak off. I want you to watch.' She looked at Nick's irritated, disgusted face, took careful aim, and flung the contents of her wine glass at him.

The glass was full; Nick's white shirt was drenched, dyed with a spreading mauve stain. He gasped and spluttered and ground at his face; the wine stung his eyes. The party noise ebbed away as awareness of the drama spread. Polly bustled up. 'Suze –' she began.

'I'm sorry, Polly,' said Susan in the same hard, carrying tone. 'I've spoiled your party. I'm not really fit to be let out yet, you see. You shouldn't have tried.' She made for the door. Polly laid a hand on her forearm but with a quick twist she freed herself, slippery as a fish. 'Don't follow me,' she said, her eyes like torches. Polly, nonplussed, hesitated, and she was gone.

'A joke?' roared Tony. 'What the hell do you mean, a joke?' he paced up and down the kitchen, running his hands through his hair. Jamie crouched on the floor, soothing the trembling Samson, his face averted. He said nothing.

Tony came to a halt in front of the boy. 'Stand up,' he ordered. 'Let go of that brute.' Jamie complied slowly. 'Now kindly explain the humour of the situation. The house has been stinking for days, and brand-new curtains worth several hundred pounds have been torn to shreds.'

Silence from Jamie. From the living room came the sound of the two women fussing over the ruined curtain.

'It takes two to make a joke. That Antrobus boy was involved, wasn't he? They're like wild animals, that family. You can forget about seeing him again this holiday.'

There was a slightly less silent silence, as Jamie cast about for a way to exonerate Fin, and Tony ransacked his brains for a way to bring this appallingly unfestive scene to an abrupt and satisfactory close.

'Now lock that dog up, and go to your room until you can apologise.'

'I'll apologise now,' said Jamie, 'because I'm really sorry about the curtains. But I'll go to my room anyway. Come, boy,' and he led Samson away.

Tony rejoined the women. The sight of his potential mother-in-law's broad tweed-covered rump as she bent to sweep up fragments of chewed prawns was not a happy one, and he felt a twinge of sympathy for his self-banished son. He laid his hand on Pippa's shoulder. 'We don't need to take this too seriously,' he said. 'Just a boyish prank that got out of hand. That Antrobus boy was the instigator, of course. I'll have something to say to his mother in the morning. But now, don't let it spoil your Christmas, darling.'

Meredith straightened up and carried the full dustpan into the kitchen. 'I'll make us all a cup of tea, shall I?'

'Excellent idea.' Tony settled himself into the sofa, coaxing Pippa down beside him. He stroked her smooth head. 'I expect those curtains can be mended, Pips,' he murmured consolingly.

Pippa's head shot up like an otter's. 'Oh *no*,' she exclaimed. 'They're completely ruined. We'll have to get new ones.' She snuggled against Tony once more. 'But as you say, darling, we won't let it spoil Christmas.'

Susan stumbled through the empty, twilit streets – twilit, although it wasn't even four o'clock. She had wandered half a mile from Polly's flat before she noticed the absence of her coat. She slapped at her thin arms; as soon as she thought about the cold, it made her shake. Never mind; she had her little black bag, still slung over one shoulder. There was ten pounds in it. She would find a taxi, and get home.

But she couldn't find a taxi. A wind got up; it blew her dress back at her. The fabric sucked at her legs, trying to pull her down. She hobbled on. Her high, strappy black shoes pinched her frozen feet. She took them off, and threw them over an area railing. She would walk home in stockinged feet. At least it was a different kind of pain.

She tried to think about the route, but she was too cold to think. It couldn't be far. She had driven it so many times. She would stop somewhere – somewhere warm – and think it through. Ahead of her a church loomed, its windows dimly lit. Its bulk heaved up at her through the gloom like an ocean liner.

The doors were open. She slipped in. Electric bar fires dangled incongruously from the walls; Susan worshipped them.

173

A cooling cup of tea and a slice of Christmas cake on a thick, chipped white saucer sat on top of a row of hymn books. Susan gulped them down. It didn't occur to her that they were intended for someone else.

She sat in a pew at the back, flexing her sore feet, and opened her bag. Her wallet was there, but no A–Z, of course. Why bring an A–Z to your best friend's Christmas party? And there was another thing missing – her bunch of keys. She remembered the feel of them now, in the pocket of her coat. She could recall the weight of them, knocking against her leg.

She could break into her house. No, she couldn't. All that money and effort she and Tony had put into making it entirely burglar-proof – bars and alarms and special glass – she hadn't a hope. She went through her wallet. Money, receipts, dry-cleaning tickets – and a folded piece of paper, bearing Patrick Furness' address. Kilburn. She had a vague feeling that Kilburn wasn't far.

A quiet cough made her look up. A vicar, bespectacled, thinning hair, an understanding smile. A kind of identkit vicar. 'Can I help?' he asked, as if he was coaxing a kitten down off a rooftop.

She showed him the scrap of paper. 'If you could just tell me where this is – I was going to see a friend of mine, and I lost my way.'

'And you lost your coat, too. Well, you're not far. I'll walk with you.' There was half an hour to go before the next service, and the vicar had been looking forward to getting himself and the church in good order, but this strange arrival in his church surely provided an opportunity to act in the true spirit of Christmas. The thought made his heart beat a little faster. He fetched a cassock and wrapped it round the stranger's shoulders.

Susan rose. 'It's very kind of you,' she began, 'but if you just tell me the way – Oh!' She clapped her hand to her mouth in sudden realisation. 'It was your cake I ate. I am so terribly sorry.'

The vicar gave what he hoped was an encouraging little laugh. 'I like to think that's what it was there for,' he said. He noticed her stockinged feet, thought for a moment, and fetched a pair of Wellingtons that someone had mysteriously left in the vestry. He handed them to her without comment. 'You're sure

174

your friend will be at home now?' he said when they reached the house. 'I can't see any lights.'

'Oh, he'll be there,' said Susan, with a confidence she did not feel. She longed to be free of her kindly guide.

'On Christmas Day?'

Susan had forgotten about Christmas. 'Oh yes,' she improvised. 'He's Jewish.' She handed back the cassock and slipped out of the Wellingtons. 'I'm most grateful. Do please go. You must be very busy, today of all days.'

The vicar retreated to the end of the terrace, crossed the street, and peered back round the corner. He watched Susan, her dress glowing through the purple evening, her white arms luminous, as she tried the door, first a ring and then a knock. He saw her bend and lift the flap of the letter box, and then he saw her suddenly slump, crumpled on the doorstep. He was on the point of returning when a tall, dark-coated man, his collar turned up against the chill, rounded the corner and caught sight of the orange bundle by his front door. He heard Patrick's wondering expletive, watched as he gathered Susan in his arms. Then he scurried back to start the next service, at which his address, he felt afterwards, was more than usually inspired.

# CHAPTER TWENTY

Jamie lay face down on his bed, his pillow over his head. It was imperative that none of them should hear him crying. If they left him alone he'd be able to stop, soon, and make plans. He allowed himself five more shaking sobs, and then started to breathe slowly and rhythmically to get them under control.

Downstairs, to his surprise and relief, he heard the sound of the television. His father had always said that only vulgar slobs watched television on Christmas Day. Jamie managed a tight little smile at the thought that his father had set up house with a vulgar slob, without realising it.

He rolled over and sat up. He knew exactly what he was going to do. He and Samson were going to hide. Fin would help him – he had said as much. They would hide in the stable until the end of the holiday, and then – then they would go back to London, he supposed. Back to Mum. Mum showed no great enthusiasm for Samson, but she would never tell him that he had to go, even if he did chew up her curtains. He wondered if his mother had opened her present yet. He had expected her to ring him, despite Pippa, seeing as it was Christmas Day. Perhaps she still would. It was only five o'clock.

He began to pack. He had a rucksack; that was ideal. It would be his pillow as well. He packed all his thick jerseys and some thermal underwear his mother had made him wear for skiing. What luck that he had brought it to the Barn. He'd decided that London could never conceivably be cold enough for it.

He packed his skiing socks, and his Walkman. Then he took that out again, in case the scratchy little sound it made gave him away. It would be boring without it, though. He was sick of his Gameboy, and that was noisy, too. For lack of anything else he picked up the books that Mr Furness had given them to read over the holidays and that he had not yet opened. He would take a torch from downstairs, later.

It would be fatal to disappear now, during daytime. They'd

176

all start looking for him, and they'd find him before Fin had a chance to come up with a plan. No, he'd act normally until bed-time, and slip out when Pippa's mother had gone and Pippa and his father were asleep. They wouldn't be able to get rid of Samson until Boxing Day, at least. Samson would only have to endure a few hours of boredom in the utility room, and then he and Jamie would be set free.

Polly stood dithering at the top of the stairs. It was unlike her to dither. It was also unlike her to obey anyone else's command, but there had been something in Susan's face when she said 'Don't follow me' that had kept her rooted to the spot. Behind her, the noise of the party swelled and hummed, like a hive full of bees. She'll be all right, thought Polly. She'll go home in a taxi. Are there any taxis on Christmas Day?

Nick Gascoigne, holding his wine-soaked head under the shower, decided that making light of the incident was the most face-saving strategy. He whistled as he rubbed his hair dry. Polly handed him a clean T-shirt. 'I am sorry,' she said, 'I just didn't realise about poor old Suze.'

'Realise what?'

'That she was so -well, so frail.'

'She seemed pretty tough to me,' said Nick with a careless laugh.

Polly avoided his eyes. 'Your poor shirt –'

'Oh, I've plenty of shirts. I expect I deserved it.' Without waiting for this remark to be taken seriously, Nick strode off in search of food and drink.

The evening passed pretty successfully. Jamie managed half a turkey sandwich, though it had been like chewing paper, and he'd had to down each mouthful with a swig of Coke. He had mumbled further apologies, and his father had asked no more questions. Nothing further had been said about Samson, who, conscious of his disgrace, lay silent in the utility room, wagging his tail only the slightest bit when he was fed and allowed out to stretch his legs, as Pippa put it. Jamie noticed that action had been taken about the curtains in his absence. They had been taken down and put away somewhere. He didn't comment.

177

Meredith Watts-Davison left straight after supper, with much effusive praise to Pippa and Tony, and a few remarks to Jamie, not unkind. Jamie helped clear up; he said that he was tired and would go to bed early.

'Good idea, James,' said his father, giving Pippa's shoulder a squeeze. 'Us too, eh, Pips?' Though with his stomach full of turkey and Pippa's stomach full of baby, Tony hardly felt in the mood to do his festive duty by her.

Jamie had a bath. It might a long time before he had another one. He allowed the water to cool round him as his thoughts churned over and over. As the night deepened and grew more silent the prospect of the stable seemed less and less welcoming. I could just hang on for another couple of days and then go back to London, he thought. Samson would be perfectly safe there.

But there was Fin to consider. Fin would never forgive Jamie if he didn't run away to him. Fin would have Samson's best interests at heart in a way that even Jamie's mother couldn't manage.

And besides his mother hadn't rung him, even though it was Christmas Day.

Polly scrabbled absently in a bowl of cashew nuts as she let the telephone ring and ring. She had waited over two hours before phoning; she had felt sure Susan would be home by now. The party had dwindled to half a dozen die-hards slumped in corners on sagbags. She felt no compunction about ignoring them.

She counted the rings; thirty-five, forty. However deep her mortification, it was unlikely that Susan would refuse to answer the telephone on Christmas Day, in case it was Jamie. Susan was an awkward parent, but she was not an indifferent one – indeed, Polly had at times considered her overconscientious.

Where else could she be? Who would she turn to – who would there be to turn to, today of all days? Susan was stiff with natural dignity. Polly couldn't imagine her blundering tearfully into the midst of anyone else's Christmas.

Oh well. She was an adult. Polly would just have to assume that she could take care of herself. She started to tidy up, clattering and rustling things, more than ready to speed her remaining guests on their way. They took the hint, sorted out their coats and bags, and embraced Polly with hot, winy breath. It was when the last of them had gone that she noticed the one remaining coat. Black cashmere, Nicole Farhi, good condition. Susan's? Polly rummaged in the pocket for confirmation, and brought out a bunch of keys.

No coat, no house keys, a thin party dress, and an unstable mental state. Night gathering; the temperature dropping. At what point, wondered Polly, would it be irresponsible not to call the police?

The stable at Powdermill was divided into two. Pharaoh, the old bay cob, occupied one side; Martha liked to bring him in from the paddock on winter evenings. In the other half there were bales of straw and buckets and old tack. Here Fin's dog, Linford, slept on his chewed-up blanket.

Pharaoh had snickered in surprise when Jamie drew back the bolts, but he knew them, and when Jamie spoke a few calm words he resumed his sleeping stance, heavy head hung low, one front hoof resting on its iron-shod rim. Linford was no problem either. He and Samson were old friends now. They greeted each other with an interrogatory 'wuff', but they soon realised that no meal or walkie was forthcoming and settled down to sleep, flank against flank. Jamie pulled the bales of straw to make three sides of a square and spread out the old horse blanket that he found hanging on a nail. He laid his head on his rucksack and closed his eyes, but he was neither warm nor comfortable.

He sat up again and opened the rucksack. He put on two of the sweaters, and the skiing socks. He wanted the long pants, badly, but he couldn't bear the idea of taking his trousers off to get them on. He couldn't think why he hadn't put them on before setting off, instead of packing them as if he was going on some idiotic weekend trip.

It hadn't occurred to him, either, that there would be little chance of alerting Fin that night. In his imaginings he'd seen Fin opening the stable door and shining a torch at him and saying, 'Jac! It's you!' but why on earth should he, at half past eleven on Christmas night, with Linford and Pharaoh long since fed? He'd be there in the morning first thing, though, to let Linford out. Jamie tried to comfort himself with this thought.

Like all the Powdermill buildings, the stable was falling to bits. Through a gaping hole where the tiles had slid off and the plaster had crumbled away Jamie could see a patch of sky. The weather was clearing; the wind scoured away the clouds to reveal the face of a crazy moon.

In the next stall Pharaoh sighed and shuddered. Jamie couldn't see him but he could picture the shudder rippling across the horse's skin like wind in long grass. He thought of a legend he'd read somewhere, about hobgoblins stealing horses from their stables to ride about at midnight. In the morning the horses would be found, sweating and tired almost to death, their manes and tails matted with elf knots. But it was Christmas night, and that was holy. Evil forces couldn't operate on such a night, could they? Or did it work the other way? Did Christmas night bring them out especially? Samson whined, and cocked an ear. What had he heard?

Jamie didn't want to be in the dark any more. It felt frightening to move, but it felt worse not to. He took out his torch and one of the unread books. *Great Expectations*. It was very long. Could Furness seriously expect them to read this?

Thinking about school and working up a little boyish indignation was cheering. Jamie propped himself against a bale and forced himself to read.

'Put this on.'

Patrick Furness held out his largest, thickest sweater to Susan, who stood, shaking, in the middle of his living room. When she made no move to take it he hung it carefully round her shoulders and went to boil a kettle.

He took a long time over making the tea. He needed to think. So far he hadn't been able to get a coherent word out of her, but clearly there'd been some crisis, and it was to him that she had turned. To him – on the basis of one meeting and one ill-advised telephone call. He had thought about her since – thought about her to an extent that surprised him. And what surprised him even more was to find that she must have been thinking about him.

When he'd returned from a pleasant, harmless Christmas lunch with his parents and his married sister, he'd been expecting to relax at home for an hour or two, have a bath and do a bit of reading, before going on to a friend's party south of the river. Patrick, who was accustomed to privacy, valued it. When he saw the orange bundle shivering on his doorstep there had been a nugget of irritation at the heart of his concern.

With her thin white arms and her smudged dark eyes she reminded him of photographs of Dr Barnardo's orphans, spike-haired Victorian urchins in ragged adult clothes. He could see her ribs through that extraordinary chain-mail dress; he could see her chest rise and fall with the horrible fragility of an injured bird. When, as a boy, he'd found little birds like that he'd never known what the hell to do with them.

He carried in the tea, a slopping mug in each hand, and a half-full bag of sugar scrunched under his elbow. Susan still stood and shivered. He set the mugs down and guided her gently into an armchair – guided her, without remotely embracing her. He turned the gas fire up as high as it would go. She stared at the purple heat bubbling over those little white structures that had always reminded her of skeletons. Patrick sat opposite. 'Well?' he said.

Susan told him some of it. She told him why she was locked out of her house; she told him that his address had been the only one in her wallet. She told him that she'd had a row with some-one at a party and couldn't possibly go back there. She didn't tell him about the pathos of Jamie's present, or that this was the first Christmas she'd ever spent on her own. Or that it was Patrick she'd been thinking of, lying on her bed on Christmas Eve night on her own with a bottle of wine. She would have told him, quite easily, but she needed him to ask.

He didn't ask. He looked at her pinched face and saw it change, as she spoke, from bruise-eyed urchin to sunken-cheeked hag, and back again. He recoiled from the enormity of her unspoken pain. He knew he could have asked, could have said or done any-thing he liked, but he didn't. He asked for Polly Cruse's telephone number instead, dialled it, listened to Polly's exclamation of grat-itude and relief, and arranged to collect the coat and keys.

Susan didn't want her coat or her keys. He had picked her up off his doorstep. All she could think of was the pressure of his strong arms. She wanted him to ask her to stay the night, even

181

if it was only under a rug on his book-strewn sofa. She concentrated her whole being on willing him to make the offer. But he didn't.

He took the mugs through to the kitchen, rinsed them, and donned his coat and scarf. 'I shan't be long,' he said. 'Help yourself to anything you want.' She shot him one look of yearning reproach. He caught it, and held her gaze. 'I think it's better if you go home tonight, don't you?' he said. 'This flat's very small, for two people.' She nodded and he left her. He double-locked the door behind him.

Susan listened to his footsteps going down the communal stairs. She could still hear them when he closed the door and strode off down the quiet winter street. She heard him begin to whistle, loudly, as if to keep out the cold. He was whistling the 'Ode to Joy'.

Her limbs felt stiff and cramped. She stretched them, awkwardly, as if someone was watching, then paced the flat. Beyond the living room was the only bedroom. The single bed was unmade. A chair, a lamp, a small chest of drawers. A pair of discarded jeans sprawled crookedly across the chair. She picked them up and held them to her face.

The bathroom had no window. It was a bachelor's bathroom; scentless soap, no bath mat, a ring round the rub. Susan opened the small mirrored cabinet. Disposable razors; Elastoplast; Lemsip. Nothing stronger.

The kitchen was dirty. That morning's toast crumbs still lay scattered. The bread board had been used as a plate; it was streaked with smears of butter and marmalade. A stub of butter, still in its tattered paper, leaned against the heel of a loaf.

Susan opened the fridge, the freezer compartment, the kitchen cupboards. She didn't know what she was looking for until she found it under the sink. Cleaning fluid, J-cloths, a used Brillo pad. Bleach. She shook the bottle. Nearly empty.

'No gloves,' she said aloud. 'Patrick, I would clean your flat for you, but you have no rubber gloves.' She unscrewed the bottle of bleach, poured it into a glass. There was only half an inch of liquid. 'Oh well,' she said, and squirted the cleaning fluid into the glass. She filled it to the top with water and held it up to the light. I've heard about this somewhere before, she thought.

182

Death by cleaning fluid. She was too tired to remember. She stirred the mixture, and then she drank.

Jamie had never read so fast in his life. He galloped through the opening pages of *Great Expectations*; the mist, the bleak, marshy landscape, the cows that loomed up monstrously to terrify small, pale Pip – all these rolled past Jamie's mind's eye as if glimpsed from a railway carriage. He would read until dawn, he decided. There was no way he was going to sleep that night.

The food Pip stole for the convict haunted him more than the graveyard. He could see it so clearly – the meat pie, the slabs of bread and butter, solid like a child's building blocks. He could feel the satisfying weight of them in his stomach. He had never tasted brandy, but he could feel it running hot down his throat. He thought with infinite regret of that evening's half-wasted turkey sandwich. He had nothing to eat in his rucksack, nothing at all. Such imaginings had to be banished. He read on, greedily.

Bella never closed her curtains, except on Bonfire night. She sat in her rocking chair, knitting at first, then just listening, absorbed in its rhythmic squeak. From her window she could see the stable. Each door was edged with a thin rim of very palest orange. And the holes in the walls and roof winked weakly, like stars.

Bella was not surprised. It was Christmas night; anything could happen on Christmas night. On Christmas Eve the animals could kneel, and talk; she'd been down a few times, hoping to catch them at it, but they'd always heard her coming. But it seemed they'd got the day wrong, this year. She would try again. She went downstairs, noiseless in the plastic sandals that she wore whatever the season.

When Jamie heard the stealthy approach of footsteps and the cautious hand on the latch, he was not afraid. Linford opened and eye and cocked an ear, but didn't bark, so Jamie thought not of convicts but of his saviour, Fin. He felt a warm surge round his heart.

Bella swung back the top half of the stable door. Jamie clicked off his torch, but there was moonlight enough to see by. 'Fin's friend,' said Bella. 'You're hiding.' Her voice, usually flat, was exultant.

'They won't let me keep the dog.' Jamie tried to keep his voice steady.

'It's cold here,' said Bella. 'Follow me. Leave the dog. Fin will see to him. Come,' she said when Jamie didn't stir, 'come on. I won't hurt you.' She held out her hand.

He rose, a little shaky. 'Bring the bag,' she ordered, dropping his hand. He followed her across the stable yard, through the gate that had to be opened slowly to stop it from squeaking. Though she walked ahead of him, he could still feel on his hand the shock of her touch.

She led him through the sleeping house, up a wormy ladder, into an attic where moonlight slanted through a bleary skylight. Rows of apples were arranged on wooden crates, carefully not touching. The air smelt thick, spicy.

'I'll bring you things,' said Bella, vanishing. Jamie looked round. Piles of old magazines – he shone his torch at them. *Punch*, *Paris-Match*, the *Observer* colour supplement. He looked at the dates. 1966, 1968. And in the corner a black-spotted mirror, the kind that stood on a dressing table, hanging askew on its painted wooden frame. Catching sight of his white face in it spooked him. He turned it to the wall.

Bella returned with a sleeping bag, a bottle of milk, and a cake tin. 'Don't turn the light on,' she said, 'there's cracks in the floorboards. You'll see Fin in the morning.' And she was gone, without waiting to be thanked.

Jamie opened the tin. It was full of mince pies. He ate seven, and drank half the milk. Then he wriggled down into the sleeping bag, his head resting on his rucksack. Bella was right; Samson was better off in the stable. Getting him up that ladder would have been a nightmare. Jamie knew, suddenly, that after all he would be able to sleep.

# CHAPTER TWENTY-ONE

'Don't apologise,' said Polly. 'I'm just so glad you found me. I was about to call the police.' She drove Patrick fast through the empty streets, needing no directions.

'You know this area well,' he remarked.

'Me? Oh, yes. I know most of London well. London's my playground. I've often thought I could be a taxi driver if all else fails.'

But all is not likely to fail in your case, thought Patrick. He stole a look at Polly's strong, blunt profile. He found her certainty restful and reassuring. She would whisk Susan home in her new black Golf and Patrick could bathe and change and carry on with his Christmas, absolved of worry.

'She has no shoes, you said?' asked Polly, digesting the information Patrick had given her earlier. 'Why no shoes? She must have had them on when she left.'

'I've no idea. As I said, she wasn't very forthcoming. I hardly know her – my address just happened to be the only one in her wallet.'

A likely story, thought Polly. He's just trying to shuffle off his responsibilities. What is it about men that they always do that? Aloud she said, 'Poor pet, she must have been in a state. Do you think she should see a doctor?'

'I wouldn't have thought it was worth calling one out today. A hot bath and an early night will probably sort her out.' As Patrick spoke, he winced inwardly at the bland inadequacy of his recommendations, but he could feel himself being pulled into a dark forest of emotional entanglement, and it seemed imperative to resist the pull. 'We're here,' he announced with relief. 'Number thirty-one. With the green door.'

Polly bounded up the stairs in front of him with a speed that was surprising, given her size. She started calling before he'd unlocked the inner door. 'Suzie! It's me. I've got your coat.'

Patrick led the way into the main room. 'She's not here,' he said, taken aback. He looked round quickly. Nothing had changed. The chair cushions where they had sat still bore the imprints of their bodies; the gas fire wheezed quietly on.

'Suze!' No one could have failed to hear Polly's voice, but there was no reply. Patrick opened the door to the kitchen, and then to the bedroom. Something smelt sour and fetid, like rotten fungus. 'I double-locked,' he whispered, 'and all the windows are closed. She can't have got out. There's only the bathroom left.'

'She's having a bath, then.'

'I don't think so. The boiler makes an incredible racket.'

Polly rapped on the door. 'Suzie? It's only me. Can I come in?'

Silence.

Polly and Patrick looked at each other. 'The door doesn't lock,' said Patrick, colouring slightly. 'The bolt's broken, and I never bothered to fix it.' He backed into the kitchen as Polly turned the handle.

Polly's scream was long and loud. Her hand flew to her mouth. For a split second it crossed Patrick's mind that she looked comical, like a cartoon of a fat woman on a chair shrieking at a mouse. The next moment he was pulling Susan Chandler to her feet for the second time that day, only this time her legs buckled under her and her head lolled, unseeing, against his shoulder. From the round red hole of her mouth strings of bile swung.

Patrick staggered into the living room and almost threw her on to the sofa. 'She's breathing,' he said, 'but I don't think she's conscious.' As Polly reached for the telephone he dabbed at the red blisters, like burns, that had formed on her lips and chin.

'Poison,' he heard Polly say into the telephone, 'or something. I don't know. Oh, please hurry.' Patrick reminded her of the address, and she repeated it.

'Five minutes, they said. And we're to do nothing. Just keep her warm.' Polly knelt down by Susan's side while Patrick fetched his duvet.

'What is it, do you think? What did you have?'

Patrick's face was white and miserable. 'Nothing, I can't think of anything. There wasn't even anything to drink.' He

186

peered at the raw, weeping patches. 'It looks like acid, doesn't it? Batteries?'

'Could be, I suppose. There must be some remains, somewhere.' Polly's large jewelled hand stroked Susan's forehead rhythmically.

'I'll look,' said Patrick. He entered the bathroom with relief. He examined the puddle of vomit dispassionately. He would rather have looked at anything than the stricken shape on the sofa.

The ambulance was prompt. The men wrapped her like a mummy in white blankets and negotiated the narrow stairs with practised ease. 'She don't weigh much,' said one. 'You next of kin?'

Polly and Patrick shook their heads and exchanged glances. It was strange, thought Patrick, that though they were strangers they should be united by a sense of complicit guilt. They stood side by side as the men slid Susan on to the couch and swung shut the doors of the ambulance.

'Anyone to ring?' asked the driver as he climbed into his seat. 'We'll take her to the Royal Free. Come along later, see how she's getting on.' He revved the motor, and winked at Polly. 'Cheer up, love. She'll be all right. We handle this kind of thing every day.' The ambulance moved off.

'And people die of overdoses every day,' said Polly, to no one in particular. She didn't like being called 'love', and she didn't like being winked at.

'What now?' Patrick declined to follow up her remark. He hunched his shoulders up to his ears and wrapped his arms round his chest; it was cold, standing in the dark street.

'We'll have to tell people,' said Polly. 'Tony, I suppose. I've got her keys – I can go over there and find his number, I'm sure. It'll be up to him whether he tells the boy.'

'Is Tony the husband? Yes, you'll have to ring him, but poor sod – what a thing to hear on Christmas Day.'

Polly's face set in a grim smile. 'I would be only too delighted to spoil Tony Chandler's Christmas, if I thought I could. My fear is that this news will make very little difference to him.' She set off up the steps to Patrick's flat. 'I'll just pick up those keys, and then I'll be off. No need for you to come,' she added, a little stiffly.

Patrick hesitated. He had a party to go to. But into his mind's eye came a picture of Jamie Chandler, skinny and trembling in his PE kit. 'Of course I'll come with you,' he said. 'Just let me get my coat.'

Tony Chandler undressed slowly. Pippa was already in bed, her shoulders plump beneath her lacy nightgown, her face shining with a Vitamin E cream especially recommended for use during pregnancy. Tony thought she looked as if she'd been buttered.

'The smell's still there,' she said. Tony tied the drawstring on his pyjamas. It would be more comfortable to sleep naked – Pippa liked to have the central heating on high – but he didn't want to give her ideas. He sniffed obediently. 'Are you sure, Pips? You're not just imagining it?'

'Of course I'm sure.' Pippa sounded quite snappish. 'Check the curtains, darling, please.'

Tony patted and prodded the frilly apricot bunches. 'Nothing. I'll try these,' and he investigated the hems of the flimsy drapes that framed the bed. 'Absolutely clear. Satisfied now?' He climbed into bed.

Pippa snuggled up to him. 'Thank you, darling. But I really can still smell it. It's making me feel queasy.'

Tony stroked her hair. 'It's because you're pregnant, darling. Everything smells and tastes different. You've told me that yourself. There aren't any more mouldy prawns, I promise you.'

'Why do you think he did it, Tony? I know he said it was a joke, but it was a very thoughtless one. Do you think he did it to upset me?'

'Of course not, darling. You get on rather well with him, don't you? I think it's fun for him to have a stepmother who's so close to him in age.'

'But why –?'

'Well, boys will be boys. But he's got to learn. The dog will have to go.'

Tony folded his arms behind his head. Pippa laid her head on his chest. He tried to ignore the incipient heartburn that seemed to affect him more and more these days. 'Comfy?' he asked.

'Mmm. Tony?'

'Mmm?'

A small hand crept under his pyjama shirt. 'Do you know what I'd really like?'

Oh Christ, he thought. 'Mmm?' he repeated.

'Some Ovaltine. With sugar in it. Would you mind?'

'Of course not, sweetie.' He planted a kiss on the top of her head and sprang from the bed with relief. 'Anything else, while I'm there?'

'Well . . . I could do with a nibble. What about that Turkish delight?' Pippa rearranged herself in the centre of the bed and picked up a copy of *Homes and Gardens*. 'Mummy said she put on nearly four stone when she had me, and she lost it again quite quickly. Well, she lost most of it.'

In the kitchen, Tony measured milk into a saucepan and poured himself a small brandy. It might wash away the heart-burn, he thought. He was spooning Ovaltine into Pippa's favourite mug, which was decorated with red hearts, when the telephone rang. Jesus! At this time on Christmas night! It had better not be a bloody wrong number.

'Tony? Polly Cruse here. Listen –' He listened. At the end of the story, keeping his voice down so that Jamie wouldn't hear, he said, 'But she's not in any danger, you think?'

'I'm going to the hospital now, to find out. I'll ring from there.'

'Look, Polly, ring me in the morning, would you? Unless of course –'

Polly slammed the phone down. The boiled milk formed a mushroom cloud over the pan and flowed like lava over the ceramic hob. 'Shit,' said Tony.

Upstairs, he told Pippa what had happened, in whispers. 'No need to tell James yet. He'll only worry. We'll sort it all out in the morning.'

Pippa clung to his arm. 'Oh, how dreadful. Poor Susan. Was it sleeping pills?'

'They don't know. But she's not in any danger. Just a plea for attention, really. Typical of her to do it on Christmas Day.' Except that even as he said that, he knew it wasn't typical. 'Now don't you worry, darling. You've got to get a good night's sleep, for the baby's sake, remember? I'll get you that Ovaltine, and then we can snuggle up.'

Tony shoved the burnt saucepan into the sink and mopped up some of the mess. A proper clean-up could wait till morning. He boiled more milk carefully, and drank his brandy in two swallows. Telling Jamie was going to be the worst part. He definitely needed to sleep on it.

He put the Ovaltine and the box of Turkish delight on a little tray and crept upstairs, anxious not to disturb his son who, he imagined, would be sleeping by now. He set the tray down on the bedside table, then sat down heavily on the edge of the bed. There was an unfamiliar rattling sound. They looked up, and the rails above their heads fell apart. Pippa, entangled in curtains, shrieked. Tony grabbed the rail as it fell. The reek of decaying prawn filled the air; the Ovaltine poured on to the carpet, where it lay in a thick beige puddle.

'Oh, Jesus Christ!' Tony exploded. 'What the fuck is going on round here?'

Even as Pippa unwound herself from the curtain she thought how awful it would be if Tony used language like that once the baby was born. But now was not the time. She made a mental note to mention it in the morning.

Boxing Day morning was as chill and drear as the day before. Eliza lit the parlour fire early. Sibyl dozed beside it while Martha and Eliza knelt on the ragged turkey carpet smoothing out yesterday's wrapping paper for re-use.

'Fin really liked his present,' Eliza remarked.

'Did he? Oh good. I was afraid stick insects would be too babyish. They don't take much looking after.'

'That'll make a change in this house.' Eliza rolled her eyes meaningfully towards her grandmother, whose chin nodded forward on to her chest. Martha reached over and gently removed the bifocals that were in danger of slipping to the floor.

'Ma, you know what she said yesterday? About the war? I mean, does she really think – ?'

'I don't know, darling. She does sometimes, yes. It's very common, you know. She thought Fin was Leo the other day.'

'Wasn't she just muddling the names? Lots of people do that.'

'No, because she talked for some time about him going to

boarding school. It was rather pathetic – she kept saying, "I never thought you'd leave me, Leo."'

'How did Fin react?'

'He just kept repeating, "I'm Fin, not Leo." I think he was quite upset; he was very quiet afterwards. But you never can tell with Fin.'

'He nearly flew off the handle when I said he was like Dad.'

'That's interesting. He never mentions him to me.'

Eliza snipped the scraps of old Sellotape off each sheet of wrapping paper. Keeping her eyes on her work, she said quietly, 'It would be best if Fin never saw him again.' She paused. Martha said nothing. 'Don't you think?' She felt the colour rise to her face, and bent still lower over the pieces of paper.

It was some time before Martha said, 'No, I don't think that.' She shook out a tartan rug and draped it lightly over the sleeping figure. 'But what I want, above all, is for Ganna to see Leo again, before it's too late.'

Eliza said nothing.

'I really thought,' Martha's voice was heavy, 'I really did think he'd be in touch at Christmas.'

'But –'

The telephone rang. Martha rose to answer it. She left the parlour door open, and Eliza heard her say, 'No, I haven't. But then I haven't looked. Now don't worry – he'll be with Fin somewhere. They never go far at this age. I'll ring you back.' She came back into the parlour. 'Tony Chandler. He's lost his son.'

Eliza threw the scraps into the fire, where they bloomed into flowers of lime green and electric blue, then died. 'Serve him right,' she said. 'He doesn't deserve to have a child.'

'Lila,' said her mother gently, 'everyone deserves to have a child.'

'Even Nick?'

Martha hesitated. 'Probably. But it's not for us to judge.'

Eliza exploded. 'Ma, how can you be so bloody *passive*? If it isn't for us to judge, then who can? Nick is a monster – why does a monster deserve a child?'

'Darling, calm down. I wasn't talking about Nick. I was talking about Tony Chandler.'

'He's just as bad. That poor little boy –'

'That poor little boy will be all right. But I ought to go and look for him.'

'What happened, anyway?' Eliza's tone was quieter, sulky.

'They had some ghastly argument about the dog. You know the way these things always happen on Christmas Day. They thought he was in his room, but he wasn't, and they don't think the bed's been slept in. And the dog's gone, of course.'

'I expect Fin's hiding them somewhere.'

'Quite. But they're worried. And the mother's ill.'

'The one Jess knows? What's wrong with her.'

'He didn't say. I said I'd look – could you see to lunch, darling?' Martha left the room.

Eliza put the folded paper away in a bureau drawer. She turned to put another log on the fire and found her grandmother's watery eyes meeting her own. She started.

'Oh, Ganna, I thought you were asleep. Shall I make your coffee?'

'Eliza,' said Sibyl, 'does it serve me right, that I've lost my child? Did I not deserve to have one, either?'

Eliza was startled into a bold answer. 'It's the other way round,' she said. 'Your child didn't deserve you.'


'Has Fin turned up here yet?'

With Christmas Day over, the Antrobuses reverted to eating in the kitchen. Eliza was picking bits off the goose's carcass and arranging cold stuffing round them to make it look as if there was more than there was. Jess, with Louis under one arm, set out cutlery on the large deal table with her free hand. They looked up, alert to the tinge of anxiety in their mother's voice.

'I've been looking for him for over an hour, trampling all over the farm. And I got back to find both dogs in the stable. But no boys.'

'They won't have gone far without the dogs, Ma. They'll be in the house somewhere.' Eliza took the lid off the bread bin. 'Not much left. Is there any more in the freezer?'

'Should be. But there were two whole loaves out at breakfast time. It's unbelievable, the way you lot get through things.'

'However much I tweak this goose, it isn't going to go very

far. Shall we have cheese, too, with the baked potatoes?'

'Whatever you like.' Martha was distracted. 'Tony Chandler obviously thought Jac had run away. Would Fin – ?'

'Not without the dogs.' Eliza, having tried the fridge, looked in the larder for cheese. 'They'll turn up when they're hungry,' she said firmly.

'It's not like you to worry, Ma.' Jess slid Louis into his bouncy chair. 'Fin will be sulking in solidarity. Did you try the attic?'

Bella said, 'Not the attic.' She tilted the baking sheet she was carrying and three of the potatoes bounced on to the floor. Eliza darted over to save the rest. 'These'll be all right,' she said, scrutinising the fallers. 'The floor's quite clean. Relatively. But Ma, I'm sure we had a big block of Cheddar. It's not in the larder.'

'I thought we did, too. But obviously not. Why not the attic, Bella?'

Alarm flickered over Bella's usually unreadable face. 'Not the attic,' she repeated, 'there's no one in there.'

'If I put the mince pies in to warm now, they'll be ready by pudding time,' said Jess, opening the cupboard. 'Where's the tin? It always lives here, doesn't it?'

'Aha!' cried Martha. 'The light dawns. Bread – cheese – mince pies. Not the attic, eh, Bella?' She turned smartly and strode off. Bella wrapped her arms round herself and rocked on her heels. 'It wasn't me,' she moaned, 'it wasn't me who told.' Her face twitched and glistened. Jess put her arm round the thin shoulders and tried to halt the rocking.

'Of course it wasn't you, Bella. But they need to come out. They –' She cast about for a reason that would appeal. 'They can't get the dogs up the ladder. So they've got to come down.'

Bella stopped rocking and slipped free of Jess' arm. She disappeared upstairs.

'That'll be one fewer for lunch, then,' Eliza remarked.

'But there'll be two others. I have a feeling young Jac Chandler could be here for the duration.'

# CHAPTER TWENTY-TWO

Expense had not been spared at this clean, hushed, sunlit clinic. Bright curtains glowed at the windows. Glossy magazines, as tempting as unopened chocolate boxes, were arranged in fan shapes on low tables beside deep armchairs. There was not a scrap of lino; the floor was entirely covered by a carpet of a gentle pinkish-grey. The usual hospital smells of disinfectant and dinner trolleys were replaced by a faint scent of musk rose, some kind of essential oil, no doubt. Classical music – a piano concerto – tinkled from the walls, but seemed only to intensify the quiet. There was nobody in sight.

Jamie and Eliza stood, undecided, by a pair of swing doors. The girl at reception, politely understanding, like an air hostess, had given them directions, but neither had listened properly, Eliza because she assumed there'd be the usual helpful little arrowed signs, and Jamie because he was about to visit his mother who had had a mental breakdown and he was trying so hard not to think about what she might look like that he could-n't possibly attend to anything else. But there were no little arrowed signs. Eliza pushed the door open; two young women were approaching. She assumed they were nurses. They weren't wearing uniform – nobody did, in this place – but they were wearing bright, enquiring smiles, presumably to distinguish them from the patients. How tiring, thought Eliza, to keep those smiles going all day. How much easier just to wear a starchy little white number and a jaunty cap.

'Susan Chandler? Yes, of course. Is she expecting you? She's already got a visitor, so I'd better just check – wait here a moment, would you?' One nurse unfolded and spoke into a tiny mobile phone. Eliza stole a glance at Jamie and their eyes locked. 'Don't leave me,' he said, louder than he meant. He turned his head away, mortified. 'I won't,' said Eliza. She stood close to him so that the sleeves of their coats just touched.

It had been Eliza who had insisted on this visit. Ever since

194

Jamie had been coaxed down, shamefaced, from the attic, Eliza had championed his cause. Not that it needed much championing amongst the Antrobuses. 'Of course he can stay here,' Martha had told the vehement Finian, 'but I am going to have to talk to his father. Once I've done that, you can sort out the blue room for him. But don't move one item until I've come back from the barn, otherwise –' Her sentence meaningfully unfinished, she marched off to negotiate with Tony Chandler.

Tony put up a few token objections – as a lawyer, he liked to stake his claim at the outset of any deal – but his chief feeling was one of relief. Let James simmer down for a bit over at the farmhouse. That would keep the dog out of Pippa's way, perhaps even until the end of the holidays. Even Tony could see that disposing of Samson and telling the boy that his mother had tried to kill herself on Christmas Day should not be allowed to coincide.

In the event, though, Tony didn't tell Jamie about the suicide attempt. There appeared to be no need. The hospital identified the substance Susan had taken – some sort of cleaning fluid – and treated her accordingly. It seemed she hadn't managed to swallow much of it before staggering off to vomit, so the physical harm done wasn't tremendous. They cleaned her up and sorted her out and packed her off to a psychiatric clinic within a week. A mental breakdown, they said. No delusions, no voices, nothing like that. Just a giving-up on life. How long? Impossible to say; probably months rather than weeks.

It was a private clinic. Tony had made it clear that he would make no trouble about footing the bills. He thought he could get it all on insurance; after all, Susan was still legally his wife. Knowing that she was in a private clinic helped. When Tony thought of her pathetic, bungled gesture, the weakness of not being able to finish what you'd set out to do, he felt disgust and anger rise in his gorge like a bad taste. He told people that she was getting the best treatment money could buy, and that helped him not to think about it.

Martha Antrobus announced, in that abrupt way of hers, that she was not going to say a single word to James about Susan until Tony gave her the green light. Fair enough. It was a parent's role. When Tony told James that his mother was in a

195

clinic, he began with the words 'Have you ever heard the expression, mid-life crisis?' and ended by saying, 'So we'll forget all about those curtains, eh, son?' Nobody could accuse him of shirking his responsibilities.

Jamie didn't ask to see his mother. That idea didn't enter his head. He didn't think about much, those first days in the farmhouse. He just let his senses get used to the new, old place. The house was damp and cold, with a few pools of strong heat, so different from the dry, even warmth of the barn. The distinction between indoors and out was much less clear at the farmhouse. Bella let the back door stand open even on frosty days; Finian sat on the Aga until you could smell his clothes singeing. If you put your hand up to the door frames you could feel the sharp draughts that ran through the hollow walls like electric currents. On New Year's Eve it snowed a little. Jamie woke to find the white powder lying on his windowsill; it had blown through the gap where the window didn't fit. It hadn't melted. It didn't melt all day.

Then there was the dirt. Jamie had never lived with dirt, but here, the patch underneath each piece of furniture was quite a different colour to the rest of the floor. In the cracks behind sofa cushions one found used handkerchiefs, old crumbs, dirty teaspoons, crumpled and abandoned bank statements. Books once pulled out of bookcases never seemed to return, but lay scattered on every surface, their covers ringed by coffee mugs. On a scallop shell next to the kitchen sink a cracked bar of soap sat in a gluey puddle, stained brown because of the Antrobus habit of slooshing the teapot out with more vigour than care. And the teapot was emptied and refilled, emptied and refilled, without cease throughout the day. Jamie could hardly believe that people could drink so much tea. None of the Antrobus women seemed to be able to function unless they had their hands wrapped round a steaming mug.

Jamie got used to sharing bathwater, to sleeping with his socks on, to prickly horsehair sticking through his mattress. Life at Powdermill had the allure of novelty, and besides, as antithetical to the style of Pippa, he admired it. He soon learned that there was never enough meat to be had and that it was wise to stock up on thick slices cut from the brown loaf that made its appearance at every mealtime. And potatoes. There were always potatoes, with black bits in that you had to cut out. The women had formed a sort of unofficial rota, and meals perked up considerably on the days when Eliza and Jess had control. Martha didn't seem to consider lumps of gristle or wildly contrasting temperatures as problems, and having Bella as her chief assistant didn't help.

But Jamie also discovered with relief that to the Antrobuses food was never a big deal. With Pippa, every dish exacted its toll of thanks and praise. Whereas at the farmhouse, Finian could say, 'Ma, this mince isn't cooked. It's red,' and Martha would say indifferently, 'It's just the tomato in it, I expect,' and Eliza would chime in, 'No, Fin's right. It's horrid. I'll put it back in the Aga for ten minutes,' and no one would take offence, and no one would have to eat raw mince out of politeness. Nobody commented on what Jamie did or did not eat; nobody pressed unwanted second helpings on him as both Pippa and his mother were so inclined to do. Without thinking about it much, Jamie became quite happy at the farmhouse.

By day he had little time to think about his mother. Fin was, of course, his constant companion, and Fin was always busy. The tottering tenements that housed Martha's poultry were in desperate need of attention after twenty years or more of constant use, so Finian, aided by Jamie, set about them with hammers and pliers and rolls of wire netting. The two boys worked in companionable ease. Jamie didn't notice the smell after a couple of hours, and he loved the close, incurious proximity of the birds. The boys usually worked in the morning; in the afternoon, before light faded, they would saddle the quietly reluctant Pharaoh and Fin would teach Jamie to ride. At five there was tea and toast, and things that Jamie never had at home, like fish paste and Swiss roll. Then there was the baby to play with, and sometimes they'd lie in front of the parlour fire and play Monopoly or Cluedo with Eliza – Jess too, if she could be prevailed upon, but she was utterly hopeless at games. In Monopoly, all she wanted to do was to collect the sets in her preferred colours, without a thought to the financial wisdom of such decisions. To Jamie such heedlessness was the essence of feminine charm. He didn't play very sensibly himself, sometimes, because of watching her small hands, bare of rings now, as they jiggled the dice, and because of the way the two curtains of thick hair would sweep down across her face as she played. Jess usually chose the hat as her token. Fin let Jamie have the dog, although he would have liked it for himself. Eliza was always the iron.

So it wasn't until he was in bed that Jamie was ever really alone. And then, as he lay concentrating on the battle between the waves of warmth his body was sending out and the clammy chill of the sheets, thoughts of his mother would creep into his mind. His bedroom was next to Bella's. He could hear the squeal of her rocking chair and the flap of her plastic sandals – even if he woke in the early hours he could often hear them. At such times he would try to conjure up an image of his mother's face, but the details were lost, and all that he could think of was Bella's pallor, and Bella's wandering stare.

So he hadn't asked if he could visit his mother, and when Eliza told him that she had found out the whereabouts of the clinic from his father, that she thought Jamie ought to visit her, and that she was happy to take him, he didn't know whether to feel grateful or the reverse. On the train to London he buried his nose in *Catcher in the Rye*. He'd finished *Great Expectations*, amazed that in a few days he'd read a book at least three times longer than any he'd read before. Eliza, who was reliable in that respect, took the hint, and opened her own book; their conversation was minimal. But he hardly read a single sentence. Here he was, on his way to visit his mother, and he didn't even know what was wrong with her. He chided himself for his astonishing lack of curiosity. Mental breakdown – what did that mean? His secret, night-time fear was that she would have turned into Bella. But she was in hospital, and Bella wasn't. He clung on to that difference. Hospital was where you went to be cured.

At the station Eliza said, rather gruffly, that if he had any money perhaps he ought to get his mother some flowers. He surveyed the florist's barrow in despair. Mum was so fussy about flowers; he'd spent thirteen years with her, and he still couldn't remember what she liked. All he could think of was that she had a thing against chrysanthemums because they made her think of funerals. Virtually everything on the barrow had a label saying

'C'mums' stuck into it. Just about the only things he could see that were definitely not chrysanthemums were sheaths of roses, dull red, their velvet heads tightly scrolled. Roses were what lovers gave on Valentine's Day. Even he knew that.

He settled for some white carnations. The notice, 'Cars £1.95', confused him, but they definitely weren't C'mums, and his mother liked white. Or used to. How did he know, now, what she did or didn't like? They took the tube to the hospital. The longer he held them, the more pointless and bereft the flowers looked, paltry in their soggy-tipped paper cone.

When the nurse said, 'She's already got a visitor,' Jamie didn't take it in properly, and it took him a few seconds to recognise the tall man in the heavy overcoat who jumped to his feet when Jamie and Eliza went in. Out of context and out of his teaching clothes Mr Furness looked young, awkward and unplaceable; it was only when he said, 'Hello, Jamie,' in that slightly gravelly voice of his that Jamie felt the warm, safe sense of the familiar surge through him like a delicious taste.

Jamie said, 'Hello, sir,' and then, idiotically, 'I've read one and a half of those books you gave us.'

Patrick smiled and said drily, 'Oh good.' His eyes met Eliza's and caught the tiny tail end of a suppressed smile. They both glanced almost guiltily, towards the bed, and both took a step or two back. Eliza gave the smallest kind of cough, and Jamie moved to the bedside.

Susan Chandler lay flat on her back. The room was warm – too warm – but she had the white blankets pulled right up under her chin and tucked tightly in. Her face was puffy, almost bloated, and she had mustard-coloured circles round her eyes like fading bruises. Against the pillow her hair looked very black and spiky, almost jagged. Her pale skin was pimpled and scabbed with purple and red. It wasn't much more than two weeks since he had seen her, but . . . It's because she hasn't got any make-up on, he told himself. Her eyes were open, but they didn't turn in his direction. 'Hello, Mum,' he said, trotting out the sentences he'd prepared on the tube, 'I hope you're feeling better. I brought you some flowers.' He held them towards her.

She lay still, without reaction. Jamie hated the way he couldn't see her arms. He longed for her to put out a hand, even

199

if only in a movement of rejection. But she didn't. Jamie braced himself, leaned over and kissed her cheek. Like a clockwork puppet, Susan jerked away from the kiss and closed her eyes.

The nurse hurried up. 'She's still heavily sedated,' she explained to Eliza. 'I'm afraid we haven't been able to get her to talk yet. But don't worry –' she turned her bright smile on Jamie ' – we will. It's only a matter of time.'

'Shall we go and get something to eat?' said Patrick. 'There's a reasonable café downstairs, I believe. Jamie?'

'Good idea.' Eliza smiled with relief. She took the flowers out of Jamie's hands and gave them to the nurse. 'Could you put them in a vase? For when she wakes up?' She was awake all the time, thought Jamie, but he didn't say it.

The café was clean, expensive, empty. They helped themselves from the perspex cabinets. 'Have what you like,' said Patrick, 'I'm paying.' He managed not to say 'It's my treat' just in time. Poor little chap, he thought. This is not what the Christmas holidays should be like for a thirteen-year-old.

They carried the loaded trays to a table by the window. The food was good; wholesome, fresh, temptingly presented, but the plates and cutlery were made of bendy plastic. Eliza's knife buckled as she spread butter on her poppy seed roll. 'You'd have thought,' she remarked, 'that in a posh place like this they could afford decent metal cutlery.'

'Oh, it's not the cost,' said Patrick, 'it's what people might do with it. Look at the windows.' He tapped one. 'Unbreakable.'

'Oh,' said Eliza, and shot him a look of horror. But Jamie hadn't listened. 'I'm just going to the toilet,' he said. The adults smiled and nodded. Eliza covered his spaghetti to keep it warm. 'Now, who are you?' asked Patrick, when he'd gone.

'I was about to ask you the same question.'

They had longer for their explanations than they expected. Jamie sat on the floor of the lavatory for some time. His head swam, and his face felt cold and tight and sweaty all at once. He tried to hold it back, but as soon as he lost the battle not to vomit he felt considerably better.

When he got back they had finished eating. Eliza moved up for him without comment. Patrick took a packet of cigarettes out of his coat. 'Do you mind, either of you? I won't if –'

'Sir! I didn't know you smoked.'

Patrick chuckled. 'Rumbled at last,' he said. 'I don't, much. But there are times –' He held the packet out to Eliza.

'I don't much, either,' she said, taking one. 'But there are, as you say, times.'

Jamie smirked at Patrick. 'I won't tell,' he said. Patrick winked at him. Jamie took the lid off his spaghetti. He was suddenly, wonderfully, hungry. It wasn't until they were going home on the train that it occurred to him to wonder what Paddy Furness was doing in his mother's sick-room.

The one and only bath at Powdermill was a vast, claw-footed monster, almost six feet long and so deep that Jess had to kneel upright by its side in order to keep a grip on Louis, who at four months old was too big for his plastic tub. The baby-care manuals showed appealing illustrations of parent and baby sharing a bath, indulging in lots of bubbly bonding fun, but the cooler water Louis required made such behaviour unthinkable in January in the unheated bathroom.

Jess squirted in liquid and swished the water to make the bubbles come. Because of the cold, clammy air the stripping of Louis was left till the last minute. Martha held him in her capacious lap. She had on one of the rough towelling aprons she had made for her own children's bath-times. Louis tugged at the fat locket she always wore, trying to get it into his mouth. In childhood this locket, tarnished silver with entwined enamel initials, had held an almost mystical significance for Jess. For a treat her mother would let her release the catch to reveal two curls of hair, one red, one light brown. These locks had been taken from the heads of Martha's long-dead parents, and to Jess they had seemed like fairy relics of incalculable antiquity, the only tangible evidence of an enchanted, vanished land.

'Don't let him break that, will you?' said Jess. 'I should hate to see that locket go.' The water had reached the faint line that her grandfather Hugh had painted round the tub in wartime, when hot water was patriotically limited. That was deep enough for Louis. Jess straightened her back.

'Would you, darling? I'm so used to wearing it, I never even think about it. I wonder if I would miss it, if it was gone.' Martha gently prised off her grandson's exploring fingers and handed him to Jess. She took off the locket, pressed the little catch, touched the curls with a fingertip. 'I can't have looked at these for years and years.'

Jess looked. The curls fitted so neatly together, their colour scarcely faded. 'Were they happy, your parents?' she asked. 'Their hair looks so snug, it makes you feel as if they must have been.'

'Happy? I don't know.' Martha closed the locket, slipped it under the neck of her jersey. 'I was only twelve when Ma died, remember – not old enough to ask myself that question. But I should think they had their share of trials. I don't think that gamblers' wives are ever entirely happy. Da was a difficult man.'

Jess tugged at Louis' poppers. 'Are there any men who aren't difficult? Sometimes I think women should marry each other.'

Martha grunted, amused. 'That often seems to happen, more or less. That's what happened in my family, as far as I can remember. My mother, and *her* mother, and my Aunt Kathleen . . . and me, of course. And Da was elbowed out, I suppose. When I think of my childhood it's always the same scenes. The women in the kitchen with their gingham aprons on. Or Ma at the back door, feeding ducks out of a bucket. But Da –'

'But that's how I always think of you, Ma! Feeding ducks. But not gingham. I think of you wearing that old raincoat of Dad's, with binder twine round it instead of a belt.'

Martha laughed. 'I'm flattered that you have such a glamorous image of me, poppet.'

'I'm happy to say that you haven't an ounce of glamour in you.' Jess dunked Louis in the steaming water, her arm cradling his back, her hand gripping his upper arm. 'I'd hate to have a glamorous mother.'

'But poor little Lou here has got one.'

'Don't be ridiculous. I'm a wreck. Just look at this cardigan.'

'Cardigan or no, you just can't help it, Jess. Look at him, he's already in love with you.' Louis, his legs working like a clockwork frog's, was indeed gazing raptly at his mother's face, waving his hand and cooing and gurgling with the liquid sound the wood pigeons made, hidden in the new tree.

'All babies love their mothers,' said Jess, smiling and cooing back. 'They've got no choice.'

'That's true. But Lou isn't the only one. Men won't keep away from you for long, darling. You're not like me or Lila. You know that, don't you?'

Jess frowned. 'I'm not looking for anyone. Nothing would persuade me to have Nick back, now. Louis is plenty for me.'

'Oh, I didn't mean Nick. No, I don't see him as a man who changes his mind. Ganna said he treated you as a possession, and she was right – and possessions are easy to dispose of.'

'Ganna said that?'

'A long time ago. She was worried. I told her it was nonsense, but it wasn't.'

Jess was silent, touched and startled by the idea of discussions about her welfare taking place in her absence. Living for the moment as she did, she had never been able to grasp that she existed independently in the minds of other people. After a while she said in a small, brave voice, 'I like being on my own.'

'I'm not saying you should pair off again, Jess. I'm just saying that you will. As a fact. Some people –'

'I'm hardly likely to meet anyone, am I, living here with a small baby.'

'Louis won't always be a small baby. And you won't always live here.'

Jess cast her mother a stricken look.

'Oh, my darling, don't think I don't want you – either of you. You'll stay here as long as you feel the need. But you're young, my love. You can't imagine it now, but the sap will rise again. And you'll be off, and that's how it should be.'

'Ma, how can you be so sure about everything? You and Lila – you always *know*.'

'Does Lila always know?'

'She thinks she does.'

'Not quite the same thing.' Martha spread a white towel on her lap. 'Here, pass him over. The water must be getting cool by now.' She wrapped the towel round the slippery, protesting baby so that only his small fierce face was showing. 'My little monkish grandson,' she said fondly. 'Cistercian, I think.'

Jess rolled her sleeves down, flexing her aching arms. 'Was Lila right to take Jac to see his mother today, for example?'

Martha considered. 'Yes and no. Yes, in that no one else was

203

going to make it possible for him, and no, because she – and he – hadn't the faintest idea of what they might find.'

'But you didn't try to stop her.'

Martha unveiled Louis and rubbed his damp-darkened curls. 'No, I didn't. She's twenty-eight.' She paused. 'Jess, why do you think there's never been a man in her life?'

Jess thought about Oliver, married, charmingly selfish, casually cruel. Martha hadn't known about Oliver. Few people had, because of Eliza's strong and proper sense of shame. 'Because of Dad, I suppose,' was all Jess said.

'Ah.' Martha's gaze wandered to the dark, uncurtained window, furred by condensation. 'Because of Leo. He's got a lot to answer for. Not that I suppose he ever will answer for any of it.'

Jess longed and feared to hear more, but the thud of Finian's feet on the stairs intervened. The bathroom door was flung open to admit Fin and a blast of colder air. 'They're back,' he announced, 'Lila and Jac. And Jac's starving. So am I.'

'How did it go?' Martha asked.

'Fine. He's OK – I think. Can we finish the Christmas cake?' Fin looked at Louis, who was resisting insertion into vest, nappy and babygro with every atom of his four months' strength. He surveyed his sister's struggles with unhelpful amazement. 'You might as well,' he remarked, 'try to make a squid wear a bathing costume as do that.'

Jess pulled a face. 'Thanks, Fin,' she said. 'You're a pal.'

# CHAPTER TWENTY-THREE

Pippa and her mother found the most gorgeous little shop in Sissington Springs. It was called Humpty Bumpty, and it was stuffed with really clever maternity clothes and cuddly toys and hand-painted nursery furniture. Pippa's waistline had reached the stage where really none of her old things would do, and the lure of the post-Christmas sale prices was irresistible. Mother and daughter made three separate trips there in the week Tony went back to work.

'That's so clever!' exclaimed Meredith as Pippa adjusted the floppy black satin bow at the neck of a tartan dress. 'The way that bow takes attention away from – well, makes one focus on the neckline. But I'm not sure about red on you, darling. They've got it in green.'

Pippa pouted. 'I haven't decided about it, anyway. I want to try that mauve needlecord – the one with the paisley pattern.'

'It's rather busy, don't you think? That navy smock is nice.'

'Navy's so boring.'

'But it suits your hair.'

The assistant, hovering, squashed a small yawn, converting it into a twitch. 'Shall I bring them both for you to try?' She ran a practised eye over the Watts-Davison women's well-shod feet and reputable handbags and surmised, correctly, that all three dresses would be purchased.

'I can always bring them back,' said Pippa as she presented her credit card.

'You can't bring sales goods back, darling.'

The assistant smiled confidingly. 'Not usually, no. But we can make exceptions for regular customers. Would you like to take a catalogue?'

Pippa frowned a little as she signed her name. She didn't like writing 'Philippa Watts-Davison' any more, but the day when she would become Philippa Chandler seemed further off than ever. Her mother seemed to read her mind as they headed for the café across the road. 'Any more news about –' She paused. She didn't want to say 'Tony's wife' because saying it seemed to fix that fact more firmly, and she didn't want to say 'Susan' because she'd never met the woman and never wished to. She amended her sentence. 'Any more news from the hospital?'

'That Polly Cruse woman rang last night. Apparently she's not to have any more visitors.'

'Tony wasn't thinking of visiting, surely?'

'Well, I did rather ask him to go, because I think we should be getting on with the divorce. But if she's not well enough, I suppose we can't.'

Meredith pushed open the glass door of the café. 'A window seat, please. For two.' She spread their carrier bags – made of stiff pink paper, with such pretty ribbons for the handles – in a wide semicircle like a charm to ward off other customers. 'Darling,' she said once they were comfortably settled, 'it's sweet of you to think about her health, but the fact is that at this rate you're not going to be married before the baby's born.'

Pippa's eyes welled. 'It's not my fault, Mummy. Tony's not going to do anything while she's in hospital.' She gave a squeaky little sob. 'I never thought it would be like this.'

Meredith laid a consoling hand on her daughter's plump pink paw. 'I know, darling, I know. You're not the type to be an unmarried mother; everybody knows it's not your fault . . . Perhaps it would be better in any case to wait, and have the wedding after you've got your figure back. But there are other things Tony could do.'

Pippa sniffed enquiringly.

'He could buy you an engagement ring, for instance. I'm quite surprised he hasn't done that already. And he could sell the Holland Park house and buy somewhere else for you in London. That little flat won't be suitable at all once the baby's born – no garden, and only one bathroom. And no spare room. You might want a nanny to live in, you know.'

'I don't think I will. Those foreign girls people have – I'm sure they're very nice and everything, but they'd get on my nerves, the way they eat all the time and run up huge telephone bills.'

'You'd just have to be strict, darling. You can put a meter on the phone. If you get a nanny from a reputable agency –'

'But I want to have the baby all to myself!'

Meredith compressed her lips in a smugly knowing smile, and changed tack. 'We'll see, darling. But about the house. Tony's always intended to sell it. She's known that from the start. It's an absurdly large house for a woman on her own.' Meredith had never visited the Chandler marital home, but she did not allow the fact to dilute the strength of her opinions.

'There's Jamie,' began Pippa, without much conviction.

'I thought you said he was to board at school. And you and Tony have him in the holidays, don't you?' Meredith put on her reading glasses to scan the menu. 'Spicy chicken wings – no thank you. There's hardly any meat on a chicken wing. Deep-fried potato skins. Why skins? *I* throw potato skins away.' She looked at her daughter's troubled face. 'Darling, I know what you're thinking. The boy will kick up a fuss, initially. But they're very adaptable at that age. Pippa, Tony must put that house on the market. You've simply got to stand up for your rights.'

Pippa hadn't been thinking about the difficulties of selling the house. She'd been thinking about an engagement ring. What she'd really like would be a square-cut sapphire surrounded by diamonds, but that was what Princess Diana had had, and it didn't seem to have brought her much luck. Inside her, the baby stirred. The first bubbly flutterings had hardened into definite prods and jerks. She squinted at the blackboard where the specials of the day were chalked.

'I'll have salmon roulade,' she said. 'Salmon doesn't count as seafood, does it? I'm not supposed to have seafood.'

'In my day,' said her mother, 'we didn't go in for all these food fads. It was a pint of milk a day, and plenty of what you fancied.' She took off her glasses. 'I'll have a word with Tony if you like, darling. I just don't want you to have to worry about a thing.'

'No, Mummy, I'll do it.' Pippa was increasingly aware that the less direct contact Tony and her mother had, the easier it was for them to sustain a bland and cordial demeanour. 'I'll have a word with him tonight. You're quite right. That house has got to go.'

It was Susan's choice to have no more visitors. It was first and virtually the only response she gave to the insistent, patient questionings of the nurses and doctors. 'Don't let anybody in,' she said after Jamie's visit, her dark eyes scanning the kindly face that bent over her. 'Nobody at all. Please.' Then she turned her head and closed her eyes, longing to drift back into that pale-grey doze that lapped her like a lukewarm mist.

Polly came, so she was told, and brought flowers, but they didn't let her in. They let the flowers in, though. White lilies with red throats and tongues, their edges peeled back like wounds. Susan tried to keep her eyes shut so that she didn't have to see them, but she still had to breathe their smothering odour. She fingered the blooming, rotting wounds on her own face; perhaps the sickly smell was the scent of her own decay. She thrust her hands back under the covers again, held her arms close by her sides. She liked the tight white blankets that swaddled her as if she were a baby. She left her meals untouched on the bedside table. If she refused to eat for long enough, they'd have to feed her like a baby too.

She knew what they thought, but it wasn't true. She remembered exactly what she'd done; she hadn't forgotten a thing. She had desired one man, attacked another, swallowed poison. She wasn't fit to be a mother, or a lover, or a friend. The only thing to do was to clean it all away, wash away the guilt and the shame. If she could become a baby once more, then everything could be cleansed, remade.

The school were very accommodating about taking Jamie as a boarder at such short notice. There wasn't a space for him in any of the dormitories, so a sick-room was made ready. 'I hope you won't be lonely, sleeping in here on your own,' said the matron, but Jamie was relieved. To enter a junior dormitory with its term-old hierarchies and rituals would be to be set down in a foreign country with no phrasebook and no local currency. On his own in the sick-room he could preserve his invisibility intact. The matron apologised for the fact that he could stick nothing on the walls, but Jamie was grateful for this enforced anonymity. He stowed his clothes in the chest of drawers, his schoolbooks on the small shelf; the room was too narrow for the storage of larger possessions, so it remained a quiet, monkish cell, a soothing place that made no demands.

Polly Cruse had taken Jamie back to the Holland Park house before term began so that he could collect anything he needed. In her forthright way she asked him whether he was sad about boarding, whether he would miss home – 'because it'll be some time, you know, before your mother can come out of hospital –' but he was able in all honesty to say no, he wouldn't miss it. The house felt unreal, like an empty stage. Polly, or Estrelia, had tidied and cleaned it so that it was as impersonal as a hotel. He collected very few of his own belongings – just his uniform and a few books he needed. He hovered over the Wildlife Fact-Files, but left them where they were. He would miss them, but an instinct for self-preservation told him that they belonged to the past, and his past was dangerous. He must live, now, with no past and no future, just treading water, with no thoughts beyond present survival.

Polly insisted on taking him out to lunch. He wished she wouldn't. He enjoyed the deep-dish pizza and crispy french fries – after the erratic catering at the farmhouse it was good to have something reliably hot and savoury – but her robust questioning made him ache with embarrassment time and again. She encouraged, almost demanded, complaints about Pippa and his father, and he was tempted to sink into the soft luxury of grievance, but he struggled to maintain his reserve. He had had a narrow escape with the prawns episode; his mother's condition had diverted attention in the nick of time. Pippa was pregnant; there was no dislodging her; indifference was the only course open to him.

'So, Jamie, tell me. How are *you*, truthfully?' Polly laid a large hand lightly over one of his. He quashed the urge to flinch and produced as natural a smile as he could muster.

'I'm fine,' he said. 'I think boarding will be fun.' He wondered whether he dared withdraw his hand.

Polly's eyes searched his face for a few seconds, then she leaned back. 'Well, if you're sure . . . but you know you can get in touch with me, whenever?'

Jamie nodded. 'That was delicious,' he remarked.

He just doesn't have a clue, thought Polly. She picked up the menu. 'Got room for a pud?' she asked 'Death by Chocolate. That sounds pretty amazing.'

Jamie assented. He was longing to leave, but normal school-boys were supposed to have huge appetites, and a normal schoolboy was the role he had to act. Samson was to stay at the farmhouse; Jamie would endure boarding, because every week-end he would have Samson, and Fin. Jess, too – just to look at, of course. He never dared even to imagine that he could ever matter to her.

# CHAPTER TWENTY-FOUR

'What are you doing with those candles, Ma? Has there been a power cut?' Jess, pink-cheeked and sniffing from the February air, unbuckled the backpack and eased it off her shoulders.

Martha set down her pewter candlesticks on the hall table and relieved Jess of her burden. 'He's asleep, bless him.'

'So he should be. I walked for miles. Right through Powder-mill Wood and back by Compass Lane. Ma, have you ever noticed how the buds of the honeysuckle leaves are like little praying hands?'

Martha smiled as she worked Louis free of the straps and struts. 'There's no power cut. It's Candlemas. Ganna wants candles lit in the parlour. Would you sit in there with her, Jess? I've got to get on, and I'm worried she'll set fire to herself if I leave her.'

'OK. I'd like to sit by the fire. I'm frozen.' Jess clapped her mittened hands. 'The pond's rock solid – I must tell Fin. It's definitely skateable.' She took Louis from her mother. 'How does Ganna know it's Candlemas, when half the time she can't even remember her own name? What's Candlemas for, any-way?'

'Something to do with presenting Jesus in the temple, I think. I'm ashamed to say that I can't quite remember. But Ganna's very insistent.'

Jess bore the still sleeping Louis into the parlour. Her grand-mother, leaning on two sticks, gazed out at the frostbound gar-den. A solitary magpie gripped the thin bough of a stripling ash. Against a colourless sky its black and white shape stood out clear and strong, larger than life, like an illustration from a medieval Book of Hours.

Sibyl looked up, and at the sight of Jess with Louis in her arms her face was transformed, shaken by joy. 'Ah, he's come!' she cried. 'A light to lighten the Gentiles. Give him to me.' Then a troubled bewilderment flooded her. Her face sagged, and she dropped her outstretched arms. 'But it's not him, after all,' she muttered, turning back to the window. The magpie stretched and dived, grazing the frozen tussocky lawn with its skittering bounce. Then it vanished, leaving nothing else to look at in the featureless weave of brown and dun and grey.

'I've brought you candles, Sibyl,' announced Martha in that cheery tone she hated to hear herself use. 'Where do you want me to put them?'

'Don't humour me. I don't need candles in the daytime.'

'But you wanted them for Candlemas.'

'Ah yes. To lighten the darkness. That the thoughts of many hearts may be revealed.' The old woman twisted her head on its slow lizard neck. 'The sun shall be darkened, and the moon shall not give her light. After the tribulation of these days.' She staggered; Martha caught an elbow, and guided her into her accustomed chair. Jess sat opposite, cradling Louis, her clear grey eyes meeting her mother's in perplexity and alarm.

'There, and there.' With her stick Sibyl indicated the positions of the candles, on either side of Jess. 'Light them, light them. Then leave us.'

'Ganna,' said Jess when her mother had gone, 'who do you think I am?'

Her grandmother peered, her face sour with suspicious doubt. 'I can't be certain. You might be my son's mother. She had hair like yours. You can't be my daughter, of course. I never had a daughter.'

'Ganna, listen. I'm Jessamine, your granddaughter. *You* are your son's mother. You must try to remember that.'

'Oh no.' Sibyl smiled a secret, superior smile. 'I can't be. My son's mother's gone. But the son will come again. In the clouds of heaven, with power and great glory. And then I can depart in peace.' She closed her eyes. 'I could sleep now. Why don't you rest too, dear? Everybody says you're looking so tired.'

Jess sat for a long time. There was no sound except for the hiss of the sappy logs in the grate and the sighing breath of the two sleepers, the infant and the ancient. She let the candles burn, feasting her eyes on the blue and orange flames that were weakened by the daylight but still provided spots of pure pleasure in the monochrome, enfolding world of a frozen February.

Sitting there amidst the stillness, Jess could almost hear the soft knocking of her own heart.

As the candle flames collapsed and died, Martha came back into the parlour with tea on a tray. She smiled down at the old woman. 'I knew she would,' she said. 'She can hardly keep awake for more than a couple of hours. Like a new-born baby.'

'Ma,' said Jess, 'she thinks I'm her.'

'Yes, I know, love. It's the hair, I think.'

'And the baby. She thinks he's' – Jess stumbled over the disused word – 'Dad.'

Martha was silent. She poured the tea. She groped for words that would comfort and reassure, but none were forthcoming.

'If he doesn't come back soon –' began Jess. She blew on the surface of her tea, holding the mug gingerly above the sleeping baby. 'How can we find him, Ma? There must be a way.'

'I don't know, Jessie.'

'Have you rung anyone? Any of his old friends? What about his agent? Somebody must know.'

'I haven't rung anyone.'

'But you must. It's urgent. He doesn't know about Ganna. If he knew, he'd be here, like a shot.'

Would he? wondered Martha. He knew about the baby. He knew he had three children and an eighty-year-old mother. He never let those considerations stand in the way. Aloud she said, 'Jessie, is it just for Ganna's sake you want him back?'

'Of course it is,' said Jess with a flare of unaccustomed anger. 'And for Fin, a bit. But as far as I'm concerned – well, I don't care. I really don't.'

Martha looked at the three faces – Sibyl's creased like an unironed linen sheet; Louis' round smooth apple of a head, plumped out now at five months old, his delicate eyebrows and lashes giving new definition to the softness; Jess' half hidden as usual by the canopy of hair, her cheek flushed by the fire, her brow contracted by the thought of her father. She was still so young – it was easy to forget about Nick. Jess fitted nobody's image of a wife. And yet, thought Martha, when I was her age I'd had the first two, and a third on the way.

She stared into the sluggish, wheezing fire. My third, she thought. My lost baby. Sometimes, at night, when the wind was

213

up, Martha could hear the child Clare had never been clawing at the windows, crying to come in.

She banished such thoughts. 'Lila doesn't want him back,' she said. 'She'd be furious if we tried to find him.'

'But what do *you* want, Ma?'

Martha let out a deep, sighing breath. 'If he comes at all, I want it to be of his own accord. Ganna or no Ganna, I can't chase him.' She looked at her daughter's yearning, disappointed face. 'And he will come back, darling. In the spring. You'll see.' Saying it made her almost believe it.

Jess accepted her mother's words of comfort like a soft pillow. Through long habit she relaxed into belief in Martha's fathomless adult understanding.

'There is something I do want,' said Martha in a brighter, firmer tone. 'There's something I want you to do for me, Jess.'

'Of course. What is it?'

'I want you to draw. I want you to let me take Louis off your hands so that you can draw properly again.'

Jess' bubble of optimism burst. 'Oh, Ma, I can't. Don't ask me to. How can I, when there's nothing *to* draw?' She uncurled herself from the chair, laying Louis without disturbing him in the warm hollow her body had made. 'Watch him, will you, Ma? I'm going to cook some carrot for his tea.'

Martha nodded her acquiescence. She remained motionless when Jess had gone, gazing at the baby but seeing nothing. If he doesn't come back, she thought, I'll never forgive him. But if he does, could I forgive him then? Her tea grew cool beside her, and her heart ached with love and pain.

Patrick Furness clenched his shoulders against the moist, congealing cold. He glanced again at his watch; the Oxford coach was, uncharacteristically, late. Patrick had been an undergraduate at Oxford and had done his teacher training there; his first job had been at a middle-brow comprehensive on the edge of Blackbird Leys. Several of his close friends still lived in or near Oxford, and he went down to visit for a couple of weekends every term. The journey itself was a chore, even on this new, improved 'Oxford Tube', but when the coach finally reached the St Clements roundabout and Magdalen Tower reared up ahead, heralding the unrolling of the red carpet of the High Street, his spirits never failed to rise.

He paced the length of the bus queue, arching his cold toes inside his thick leather boots. A straggly group had formed, composed mainly of bleary-looking student types, with a couple of even blearier tramps asking for small sums of money. A slight young woman in a duffle coat stood at the head of the queue. Patrick, staring at the clear, precise line of her profile, thought there was something familiar about her. One of the tramps approached her; he was a rich chestnut colour all over – hair, skin, clothes, teeth, all of a uniform shade. He spoke to her; she shook her head and spread her hands as if to show they were empty. Then he grabbed her arm, and hissed out some kind of curse. Patrick stepped forward, but to his astonishment the girl whirled round and knocked the tramp down.

She stood, gasping and apologising to the man who sprawled unexpectedly at her feet. Some members of the queue moved as if to help him up, but when they got close enough to smell him they hesitated. The girl stretched out her own hand to him just as Patrick heaved him up from behind.

'Oh!' said Eliza as they manoeuvred him towards the nearest, hurriedly vacated bench. 'It's you!'

'The hospital. Of course. I was just trying to place you when –'

'When you saw me indulge in a piece of completely gratuitous violence. You must think I'm very odd.'

'He shouldn't have touched you,' Patrick replied gallantly, though her reaction had indeed alarmed him.

'No, he shouldn't. But I only meant to push him away.'

'You just don't know your own strength,' said Patrick, smiling, as he installed the tramp on the bench. To spare the man's feelings he fought the urge to wipe his hands straight away, though in truth the slumped figure seemed too dazed to notice such niceties. Eliza bent over him. 'Have I hurt you?' she asked, raising her naturally quiet voice. She was answered by a slow shake of the head, and an indecipherable grunt.

She turned to Patrick, biting her lip. 'Here comes the bus. Don't miss it. I'm in no hurry – I came up for a party last night, and I'm only going home. Nobody's waiting for me but the cat.

Do go. But the thing is, I really don't have any cash and I ought to get him a cup of tea or something. Could you possibly let me have a pound?'

'I'm in no hurry either. The buses are every half-hour, aren't they? I'll get him a cup of tea – wait here.'

Patrick returned with a polystyrene beaker for each of them and a sausage sandwich for the tramp. They sat either side of him as he drank, perched on the arms of the bench like carved sentinels. He pocketed the sandwich and lumbered off with a grunted farewell, embarrassed, confused, or drunk.

'I should have got him some fags,' said Patrick. 'I have a feeling he wasn't overimpressed with that sandwich.'

'He seemed to be OK, didn't he? I mean, I couldn't really have hurt him?'

'Of course not. You just took him by surprise. He's well padded, anyway. But tell me, do you make a habit of attacking people in the street?'

'No, I don't. Though for some time I've felt I'd like to.' And to the surprise of both, Eliza recounted the story of her father's pre-Christmas visit to the little Oxford house. Her voice stayed clear and level, and her eyes dry. As she spoke, she realised that she had described this incident to no one; she had never even discussed it with Tom Winchcombe, despite his deft rescue of her on that occasion.

'And how did your mother react?' Patrick asked.

'She didn't. She doesn't know. This is a real cliché, but you're the first person I've told.'

'A cliché?'

'Yes – going on a journey, and confiding in a stranger. But look, if I've embarrassed you, I'll wait for the bus after this one.'

'Don't be ridiculous. I'm getting quite used to encountering women in bizarre situations.'

'Are you going to elucidate?'

'Well, you know about Susan Chandler.'

'I don't know much, actually. What little I know is filtered through a far from disinterested source, namely her ex-husband. Who I would not trust further than I could spit. Not even as far, actually – I'm quite good at spitting.'

Patrick laughed. 'I can believe it. Look, here's the bus. I'll tell

216

you about Susan Chandler on the way.'

'Are you sure you don't want to read?'

'Positive – I've got a stack of marking to do and I'll be only too happy to put it off.'

By the time they reached the green and cream Hoover factory, Patrick had told her all about his connection with Susan Chandler, including his guilt and self-disgust at having, as he put it, 'totally ballsed it up'. By the time they passed the turn-off to High Wycombe, Eliza had filled him in about Nick and Jess and her mother's household of dependants; as they crossed Magdalen Bridge Eliza, now apprised of a sketchy resumé of Patrick's career and love life (two serious relationships, both mutually concluded; three or four other, more fleeting liaisons; one early broken heart from non-requital), had decided that he would be the perfect match for Jess. But how were they to meet? Jess had spoken, vaguely, of returning to Oxford for a visit, but by the time that was organised, Patrick would be gone.

They parted at Gloucester Green.

'You're going back tomorrow night, then, are you?' asked Eliza, so casually it sounded almost rude.

'I am. But I'll be down again in a couple of weeks, for half-term. A mate of mine's moving house and I'm going to give him a hand.'

There was a pause.

'Well,' said Eliza, 'goodbye, then.'

'Can't I have your telephone number?' asked Patrick. 'Here's mine – you might need me for a witness, when you get done for assault.'

'Very funny. But yes, let's – meet.'

They exchanged scraps of paper. Eliza unchained her bicycle from the rack where she had left it the night before. She rode off with a jaunty wave and no backward glance. Patrick stood there until she had disappeared from sight, watching and pondering.


'Fin, keep *still*.'

'I was.'

'No, you weren't. You shuddered.'

'Well, anyone would shudder. It's bloody freezing in here.'

Jess laid down her pencil with a theatrical sigh. 'OK, let's have a break. This drawing's useless anyway. I'm only doing it because Mum wanted me to.'

'Mum wanted a drawing of *me*?' Finian looked, fleetingly, pleased.

'No, not particularly of you, you arrogant brat. She just wanted me to start drawing again.' Jess looked up and caught the tail end of a look of disappointment crossing her brother's face. She softened. 'But when I said I was going to draw you, she did say, "Oh, good."'

Fin rotated his head to ease his cramped neck. 'Let's have a look, then.' He peered at Jess' work, resting his chin on her shoulder. 'It's not a bad drawing,' he said after a while, 'but it doesn't look much like me.'

'No,' she agreed, 'it doesn't.' An unvoiced judgement hung in the air between them.

'You've made me look . . . older,' said Fin.

'Sorry,' said Jess. 'Back in your pose now. I'll try and put it right.'

Fin fidgeted. 'Must I? I've got tons of homework to do.'

'Fin, that's a lie. You know you never do any homework.'

'All right, it's a lie. But can I go anyway? Per-lease?'

Jess laughed. 'Go on, then. I'll fiddle with it on my own. Or maybe I'll just scrap it.'

'Scrap it,' called Fin over his shoulder as he bounded down the stairs in search of food and warmth. 'Draw Ganna instead. She keeps much stiller than me.'

Jess propped the unfinished drawing against her dressing table mirror. She had made the face longer, the hair curlier, the nose crooked and more prominent. 'I've made him look like Dad,' she said aloud. 'Why the hell have I done that?' Then she folded the paper and tore it across and across and across.

# CHAPTER TWENTY-FIVE

'And remember we're talking about positive pain.' The class leader's voice was deep and musical, her lungs expanded to their full capacity after years of teaching breathing techniques to first-time mothers. She was gigantic – just how huge it was difficult to tell, because the loose smock top, brightly patterned with stars and moons, was so voluminous, but she had several rolls of chin, and that smooth, blooming complexion that makes it difficult to guess the age of very fat people. Her baby-fair hair was coiled in a bun on top of her head, and maintained its neatness miraculously whatever position she chose to demonstrate. And her weight didn't seem to affect her suppleness; her short legs in their tight black leggings were as bendy as plasticine.

She was sitting on the floor in a half-lotus now, addressing the semicircle of eight anxious couples. Her name was Brigitte, she had the merest trace of a Scandinavian accent, and her warm and welcoming smile never flickered.

Pippa looked down at her hands. The others were asking questions about how much it would hurt, and she didn't want to know. She wasn't keen on pain, positive or otherwise, and despite all the relaxation techniques they were learning to help with 'pain management', she privately intended to demand an epidural at the earliest possible juncture, or even a Caesarean. That didn't sound too bad – full anaesthetic, and being forced to stay in bed for several days afterwards. The only thing was, it might leave a scar on her tummy. She was worried that might put Tony off.

She flexed her fingers, admiring her nails, painted pearly pink by the manicurist that morning. Even more, she admired the sparkle of her engagement ring – one enormous diamond flanked by two smaller ones, set in platinum. She'd been a tiny bit disappointed not to get the sapphire she'd always wanted, but this ring was gorgeous and Tony had chosen it all by himself. He'd given it to her on Valentine's Day, cunningly hidden inside a box of chocolates. She'd teased him and called him a soppy old Pooh Bear, and it had taken the utmost effort of will not to ring her mother then and there and share her moment of triumph. But no, she'd waited until he was safely at the office next day, and then she'd indulged in a lengthy and highly satisfactory telephone conversation. She smiled at the memory. She glanced up at Tony, who looked bored and cross. Poor old darling – it was sweet of him to come along to these classes, when it wasn't his kind of thing at all.

There was a general shuffling and murmuring all around them. Pippa realised that she hadn't been paying attention for several minutes. The mats were being unrolled, and everybody, men as well as women, was taking up positions on them. Pippa tugged at Tony's sleeve; he shook his head. 'Please,' whispered Pippa. 'Everyone else is.' This was true. Tony complied with a reluctant grunt.

There was a lot of talk about closing your eyes and imagining white sand and blue seas. It made Pippa think of St Lucia, of how ardent and attentive Tony had been in those days, of how ingenious he was about finding devices for getting Jamie out of the way so that they could have time to themselves. Things had fallen off a little since then, but Pippa wasn't worried. She knew she didn't look her best, with this great humpy mound of a tummy. Never mind; there would be plenty of time to make it up to Tony after the baby was born. She stroked the back of his hand with her fingertips, but received no answering pressure.

Tony wasn't thinking about St Lucia. He was thinking about what a fool he must look lying on this mat in his work suit – Pippa had been insistent that there was no time to change. He was ravenous – in the hushed room they would all hear his stomach rumbling – and he needed a drink. He didn't remember going through any of this tomfoolery when Susan was expecting James. One thing he had to admit about Susan was that when it came to women's business she handled things on her own. Even now, with this nervous breakdown or whatever it was, she'd had the guts to say no visitors, no letters, no gifts. You had to admire that.

Pippa, though – Pippa had had him tied to her side throughout this entire pregnancy. He'd been forced to live through every symptom, every purchase, every fear. What did he think of this new changing mat; what did he want for the snacks he was to eat while he watched her in labour; she thought she might have piles, would Tony mind taking a look? Yes he bloody well did mind, though he didn't say so. She was young, he kept reminding himself; young and scared. She'd learn. But then there was her bloody mother . . .

Brigitte's mellow voice infiltrated into his reverie. 'Now we need to do something about those pelvic floor muscles. Men, you too; you need to share this with your partners. I want you all to imagine inserting a finger – a clean finger, of course – into your vagina. Now clench . . .'

'Oh, Jesus Christ,' said Tony, all too audibly. He sat up. A couple of the other men raised their heads and shot him sympathetic glances. Brigitte's kind smile only widened.

'Any problems over there?' She beamed.

'No, we're fine,' said Pippa, beaming back. Under her breath she hissed, 'Tony, lie down and do as you're told.'

After a second's hesitation, Tony lay down. He would go through the motions. But he wasn't going to clench anything for anybody.


The minute Eliza stepped through the front door of her little house on the day of her encounter with Patrick, she knew that something was different. She sniffed, but it wasn't exactly a question of smell. There was just a feeling in the air. It didn't take her long to find out. There was a note, propped against the bread bin. Graham the lodger was in love.

'Ros has this really big flat in Cowley,' he'd written, 'and we agreed, the two of us, that I might as well move in straight away. I hope this isn't too inconvenient for you. Please find enclosed the rest of this month's rent. Cheers, Graham. P. S. Fed the cat, Sat a.m.'

Eliza let out a whoop of joy and punched the air like a footballer. She snatched up Sylvia and bestowed a kiss on her protesting furry head. She had known, of course, about Ros, who had appeared on the scene about three weeks earlier; despite the big flat in Cowley, she and Graham had consummated their passion all too audibly in the house on numerous

221

occasions. Eliza had thought dark thoughts about Ros, but would do so no longer. She had taken Graham off her hands, and Eliza felt giddy with gratitude.

She tore round the house, flinging open doors. Graham had removed every trace of his existence, save for constellations of Blu-Tack marks that made the wood-chip walls of his bedroom look like maps of the heavens. No oozing shaving foam in the bathroom, no odour of trainers wafting from the bedroom, no Birdseye Menumasters in the freezer compartment. Eliza piled the fire as high as the tiny grate permitted. When the blaze was established she pulled off her boots and installed herself with the cat on her knee and the customary pot of tea by her side.

'Just you and me again, eh, Sylv?' she murmured. 'Now what could be better?' She thought of that December evening when her precious solitude had been so dramatically broken by Jess and Louis. They'd talked in the weeks that followed of the possibility of living together on a more permanent basis, but the presence of Graham had made the idea impracticable. 'There's no room, Lila. We'd really get on your nerves,' Jess said. 'It's best if I go back to Powdermill for a while. Until I get something sorted out.'

Over the Christmas holidays it had become clear to Eliza that Jess was not going to get anything sorted out in a hurry. Where was she to go, and what could she live on? Her marriage to Nick had estranged her from most of her old friends, and though some money from Nick appeared in her bank account each month, it was barely enough to set up a separate establishment. Eliza, angry on Jess' behalf, had tried to push her into a quick divorce and a proper financial settlement, but Jess resisted. 'Not yet, Lila,' she had said, raising troubled, tired eyes to her sister's face. 'Maybe one day but – I just can't think about anything now. Don't you understand?'

Eliza didn't understand, but she had to accept. She turned her mind to Jess' own talents – despite the baby, surely a fit young woman should be able to earn her own living? But, somehow, Jess never had got round to putting her abilities to profitable use, and Eliza had to admit that in her present state the chances of Jess gaining employment were slim. Jess had always been so slow – the opposite of the short-tempered, decisive

Eliza. After school Jess had drifted about for years, doing nothing in particular – she was over twenty before she finally applied to the Slade. And then when Nick came along, everybody said how wonderful it was that there was somebody making decisions for her. It was no coincidence that, since the arrival of the all-powerful Nick, Jess had hardly put brush to canvas. Eliza winced; her aversion to Nick still produced a physical reaction every time she thought of him.

Now dreary Graham had taken himself off, there was no practical reason why Jess and Louis should not live here in Oxford. They'd have to share a room, but it would be a while before that was a problem. Nick's money would help pay the rent. It would ease the burden of dependency that Martha carried on her broad shoulders. And with Jess under her gaze, Eliza would have a better chance of protecting her from the two things she feared most for her sister – the return of her father and the return of Nick.

For Jess was so passive, so trusting – so weak, one might say – that Eliza could not be certain that she would not, in time, fall back into the arms of one of those two imposters. And imposters they were – a sham father, a hollow husband. Jess did not let go of love easily. She lived for love, and love of a mother, a sister, even a baby son, might not be enough.

The best idea was to get another man on to the scene. Eliza had long since despaired of turning her sister into the kind of woman who could live independently of men – the kind of woman she believed herself to be. This Patrick Furness seemed eminently suitable. Bright, thoughtful, unattached; handsome in a skinny, untidy sort of way. He would return to Oxford at the end of February, he said. Eliza would have Jess installed by then, and she would invite him over for dinner. It was simple. He would not be able to resist Jess. What man could?

Eliza loved her solitude, but she would sacrifice it in her sister's best interests. She would ring her very soon and persuade her to move to Oxford. But first there was just one thing she would do for herself. She would make one all-out attempt on the affections of Tom Winchcombe. If she failed, she failed – but she owed it to herself to try.

# CHAPTER TWENTY-SIX

'Tony?'

'Yes, honeybunch?'

'Mummy thinks we should definitely have a nanny.'

'Fine. If that's what you want.'

'Tony, if we're going to have a proper conversation, would you mind putting the newspaper down?'

Tony sighed, and folded *The Times*.

'And please, darling, don't breathe like that.'

'Like what?'

'You know. Through your nose.'

'Am I supposed to breathe through my ears?'

'Oh, don't be cross. You know what I mean. So do you agree then? That we should have a nanny?'

'Sure, but you used to say you wanted to do everything yourself, and that a stranger would get on your nerves.'

'I think I've changed my mind. Everyone says it's so tiring. And you can always change them if you don't like them.'

'Change what, the baby or the nanny?'

'Tony, don't be fa – what's that word?'

'Facetious?'

'Yes. Don't be it. But darling, if we have a nanny, we'll have to get a bigger flat.'

'Why? There's room for the baby here, and we can have a daily nanny. That's what you used to talk about.'

'Oh no. They're much less reliable. Everybody says so. And if you have a live-in, then you can go out in the evenings whenever you want to.'

'Well, I'm afraid it's just not on, Pips. I can't afford to move. What with paying extra to James's school now he's a boarder, I'll be fully stretched.' Tony set his mouth in what he hoped was a firm line and reached for *The Times* again, but Pippa laid her hand over his before he could reach it.

'You could sell the house, Tony.'

'Sell the *barn*?' Tony was incredulous.

'No, no. Holland Park. You could sell the Holland Park house. You know that was always the plan.'

Tony looked at her for several seconds, but under his gaze she neither blushed nor turned aside. An image flashed into his mind of the way she had looked on the day he interviewed her to be his secretary. Only three years ago, but it seemed like a different era. He remembered how she had shaken her blonde fringe at him like a little pony, and how she had cast a glance from her blue eyes up at him, so clear, so frank, so beguilingly free of guile. Well, appearances could be deceptive.

'That was always what you were going to do,' she repeated.

'Don't you think,' he said levelly, 'that the situation has changed somewhat? Susan did, after all, attempt to kill herself. She is, if you remember, still in hospital. Has it crossed your mind that selling her home while she is in a fragile mental state might be – how shall I put it? – tactless?'

Pippa pushed out her lower lip. 'Ooh, Tony, I do hate it when you're cross. We'd find somewhere else for her to live, of course. It wasn't good for her to be rattling around in that great big house, all alone. I wouldn't be surprised if that wasn't what pushed her over the edge – the loneliness. She'd be so much better off in a cosy, manageable flat. Like this one.' Her face lit up. 'Hey, we could just swap! You and I could move to Holland Park, and –'

Tony slammed his hand down on the coffee table. The gesture wasn't as impressive as he hoped, because the surface was littered with magazines, which muffled the sound. But still, he made Pippa jump.

'We are staying where we are,' he said. 'The subject is closed.' He got up and strode over to the small kitchen area to make a drink, for want of anything better to do. In a flat this size there was absolutely nowhere to go.

Pippa picked up a magazine. She flicked through it for a few minutes in silence. Then she said, 'Darling, I think it would be a good idea if Mummy was with me during labour as well as you.'

'They wouldn't allow it,' said Tony.

'Oh, I've checked at the hospital. You're allowed up to two

birth partners. I'm meeting her for lunch tomorrow – shall I tell her you think it's a good idea?'

'Are you getting a replacement for Graham, then?' Tom Winchcombe asked. He straightened up, brushing crumbs of frozen earth from his corduroy-covered knees. The Botanical Gardens were hardly looking their best this frosty February morning but Tom found much to interest him in the ragged, twiggy clumps poking out of the hard, churned beds. Eliza stood by his side, watching the slow shifts of muted colour in the silent river. Five-year-old Dickon ran up and down the gravel paths, apparently content with imaginary victims for the many ambushes he sprang.

'Sort of,' replied Eliza. 'My sister needs a home. It's all a bit much for my mother, so –'

'Jess! Ah, I'm glad Jess is coming back.' Tom's eyes smiled, as if at a secret memory. It's no use, thought Eliza. I can't win. He's never going to go dreamy like that at the mention of my name. And nor, for that matter, is anyone else. She said, a little tartly, 'It won't be permanent, of course. Just until she sorts her life out a bit. It's difficult to work with the baby crying, and the mess –'

'When Linda first left me, I missed all that so much,' said Tom. 'I longed for the sight of a line of washing, or a few toys scattered over the floor. It's ironic, because Linda never liked those things. She's organised. She came home from work, once, and there were forty baby wipes scattered round the room – Dickon decided that all his soft toys needed their nappies changed at the same time. I thought it was funny, so I left them there for her to see. But she just burst into tears.'

'Maybe you should have been the one to keep him.'

'Oh, I wanted to. But Linda was adamant, and I didn't fight it. They favour the mother, you know, the powers that be. And fighting over it would have been the worst thing for Dickon.'

Together they looked at the small warrior, brown curls flying, cheeks flaming as he careered along his war-path. Eliza laughed. 'He's considerably more war-like than you.'

Tom agreed. 'Oh, we never gave him guns, but he'd aim a banana at you from two years old. They're born with their characters, you know. They'll go their own way, whatever their parents try to do.'

'I didn't believe that,' said Eliza, 'until Louis was born. I had no idea twenty-odd inches of flesh could have such a powerful will. He was a terrifying baby.'

Dickon changed direction in favour of the river bank. Tom and Eliza followed him. The sun, a burnished shield, hung heatless at the rim of the sky. A pair of swans slid down the river towards it, their dark webs paddling secretly beneath the water's surface.

'They seem to be looking for something,' said Eliza, 'but at least they're both in search of the same thing.'

Tom did not reply. He opened his arms for Dickon, who ran into them, screamed with delight as he was tossed in the air, and ran off again with ululating whoops, flourishing an imaginary tomahawk.

'I'm glad he's always on the side of the Indians,' said Tom. 'I was, too.'

'And me,' said Eliza. 'And when you had to choose Oranges or Lemons I was always Lemons.'

They strolled on. 'And your father?' asked Tom, out of nowhere. 'Has he been back?'

'He has not.'

'And have you heard from him since?'

Eliza thought of the letter, unopened, that she had preserved since before Christmas. 'I don't know where he is,' she answered truthfully. She touched Tom's arm. 'Tom, I never told Jess he came. You won't –'

'Of course not,' said Tom. He didn't ask a reason, but Eliza rattled on. Her father was a gambler, Jess needed protecting, she would trust anybody, their mother had enough to worry about, and –

'So he's never seen his grandson,' said Tom. 'Poor sod.'

'All this stuff from the Government about family values.' Eliza adopted the clipped, academic tone with which her tutorial pupils were familiar. 'Families need fathers, et cetera. What a load of rubbish.'

'The Government got it all wrong,' said Tom. 'They make it all sound like a punishment. And it's not. I don't know whether families need fathers, but fathers need families, that's for sure.'

Dickon sprang out of nowhere. 'Dad, can we go to the green-house?'

'It'll be warm in there. Suit you?' he asked Eliza. 'You look as if you're perishing with cold.'

As they walked towards the great palm-filled glasshouses, Eliza found a mitten-clad hand gripping her own.

'Dad, can you and Eliza swing me?'

Flushed and laughing, they swung him in out of the cold.

# CHAPTER TWENTY-SEVEN

The letter on the mat was addressed to Jess at Powdermill, redirected in Martha's large, firm hand. Eliza wasn't aware of ever having seen Nick Gascoigne's handwriting, but she knew instantly. She carried it through to her sister, holding it by the corner as if it might burn or stain.

Eliza wished she could conceal this letter, or at least vet its contents before allowing whatever poison it contained to contaminate Jess. But she would not tamper with it. She thought of herself as an honest person; honest people did not interfere with the mail. That letter from her father, though – that pre-Christmas letter that lay like something festering in a drawer beneath her carefully folded shirts. That letter was addressed to her.

Jess and Louis had been living in Oxford for nearly two weeks, and a rhythm had established itself. Louis was a much easier proposition now; he ate regular meals, took two naps a day, sat up, mouthed toys, laughed a lot, clapped his hands. He could play peep-bo and pat-a-cake, and could twirl balletically in the bouncer that Tom had nailed up for them in the doorway between the kitchen and living room. Eliza felt that he had truly joined the human race, though sometimes, when he gazed at the fire, or listened intently to street noises after dark, she could catch a glimpse of the old witch-baby, the fierce-eyed tyrant who hadn't asked to be born.

They had come to behave, she and Jess, like a married couple over these last two weeks. Eliza made breakfast, which they ate together on Jess' bed. At half past eight she left for the college, Jess in her dressing gown waving goodbye at the door. Eliza worked in the library all day between tutorials, then she'd pick up some little treat for supper on her way home. Jess would have tidied up a bit, done the routine shopping, walked Louis by the river, taken a load to the launderette. They'd bathe him together and then Eliza would make supper while Jess gave him his last feed by the fire. After supper they'd read, or talk, or Eliza would work and Jess would dream. It was never hard to work with Jess in the room. She had a wonderful talent for keeping still.

Three or four times Tom Winchcombe dropped in and they cleared the toys off the other armchair and drank coffee and wine. He showed no favour to one or the other of them, but Eliza wondered if he'd have called as often if she'd been there on her own. Sometimes, as she worked on comparative feudal systems in the library, she wondered whether Jess was wheeling the buggy in the direction of St Saviour's garden, and she would be shot through with the pain of the old jealousy, but it didn't last long. Patrick Furness was bidden to dinner the following Saturday, and she felt a warm and growing confidence that he and Jess would be just right for each other.

But now the Saturday had come, and with it this letter from Nick, hurled in to shatter their peace like a petrol bomb in a shopping centre. She carried it slowly, but there was no point in delaying. Jess knelt on the floor, helping Louis to tear up old magazines. He delighted in the noise the paper made, and in the discovery of the potential of his own small strength. Eliza handed the letter over without comment.

Jess' colour changed. She tore it open, read it through twice, and then handed it to her sister. 'He's going to America,' she said. 'He thinks we can still be friends.' Eliza scanned the note. New job in Chicago – house and flat both let – could be contacted at this address. Sorry he'd let things slip a little – not cut out for family life – couldn't see why they shouldn't stay in touch – how about dinner before he left?

Eliza handed the letter back. 'Well?' she asked cautiously. 'Is dinner on?'

Jess gave a short laugh. 'I hardly think so,' she said. 'After all, as he puts it, he has let things slip a little.' She pushed the letter into Louis' clutch. 'Here, Louis,' she said, 'shred this.'

Eliza turned to the window. She didn't trust herself to say the right thing, didn't want Jess to see her broad, exultant smile. She hardly dared believe that the spectre of Nick had been so soon laid to rest.

'Lila,' said Jess after a few minutes, 'could you look after Lou for me for a while this afternoon? Not if he'll be in the way, but

– I just really fancy getting some drawing done. I haven't done anything for – well, I couldn't draw at Powdermill. But I think I could here. Do you mind?'

'Good idea,' said Eliza. 'No problem. He can come shopping with me. OK, little Lou?' Her voice, like her sister's, was breezy, matter-of-fact, but inside, her heart was bucking like a March hare.

'Well?' asked Eliza, thawing her numbed hands round a mug of tea after her three-hour shopping expedition with Louis. 'Did you draw?'

'I did, I did.' Jess was beaming. 'I drew solidly the whole time. Do you want to see?'

'Of course.'

Jess produced her largest sketchbook. There was an arrangement of pots, pans, apples and oranges, boldly and simply executed in coloured chalks.

'Colour!' exclaimed Eliza. 'Very Cézanne. I like it. The way that orange is sitting in the shadow . . . brilliant. But why my old saucepans, Jessie?'

'I just felt like looking at something absolutely plain and functional. I'm really, really sick of strings attached.' Jess removed the sketchbook. 'I'm glad you like it. I was really pleased. It's such ages since I achieved anything at all.'

Eliza pointed at Louis, still strapped into his buggy. 'You achieved him.'

'Yes, but not on purpose. He was kind of thrust upon me.'

'Well, babies are.' They both giggled. Jess started to pull Eliza's purchases out of their carrier bags. 'I'll start on the salad, shall I? We may as well get as much done in advance as possible.'

'My God, Jess, you're a changed woman. Usually it would be midnight before it occurred to you to wash a lettuce.'

Jess smiled. 'I know. It used to drive Nick mad.' She rummaged in the kitchen drawer for the sharpest knife. 'What he really wanted was a proper old-fashioned wife, dinner on the table at eight sharp, buttons sewn on before they'd even considered falling off, that sort of thing. But he never admitted it. He always thought he wanted a sex goddess. Poor Nick. I fell absolutely between two stools.'

231

'Poor Nick, indeed! That way madness lies, Jess.'

'Don't worry. I can say poor Nick because I have no intention of seeing him again if I can possibly avoid it.'

They fell silent. Eliza sipped her tea while Jess chopped and sliced. Rarely, thought Eliza, had she felt in such peaceful accord with anyone. This must be what a good marriage felt like. Not that she had any experience of that.

'Lila,' called Jess suddenly. 'Why did Tom's wife leave him?'

'I thought you'd know.'

'Why would I know?'

'Well, you always seem to be having cosy little chats with him.' Eliza tried to keep her tone neutral, and failed.

'So do you. He's just a cosy chat sort of a person, I suppose. That's why I can't think why she left him. I mean, he's just so – nice.'

'Ask him tonight.'

'All right, I will.'

The supper party was a success. Dickon had to come with Tom, of course, but he was no trouble. He bought a supply of small armoured vehicles, played with them on the hearthrug, clambered on to his father's knee for a bedtime story, then fell asleep in Eliza's bed, a plastic tank still held in one furled hand. Louis, too, was impeccable. He stayed up for half an hour, charming in his snug sleepsuit with his dark hair damp and curly from his bath. It was good, Eliza felt, that Patrick should be fully aware of his presence, but good, too, that Louis should be on top form, all grins and gurgles and emitting none of those glass-shattering screams by means of which he ensured that none of his desires were ever thwarted. Like Dickon, he went to sleep quite cheerfully – drowsing over his evening breast-feed, then carried, warm and lolling, upstairs to the repainted second-hand cot. Eliza wondered as she stirred the cream into the mushroom soup whether Patrick might find the breast-feeding a little alarming, but then that, like Louis, was a vital part of the whole picture. It was unusual to meet, as it were, your girlfriend's breast before she even was your girlfriend, but – well, it was one way of doing it. And Jess herself was in vibrant mood. The destruction of Nick's letter and the afternoon of drawing seemed to have charged her with new energy. Eliza hadn't seen her shine like that since – when? Since the early days with Nick, she supposed. The very early days.

There was a certain reserve about Patrick that made it difficult to judge, but Eliza was pretty sure he was struck by Jess. The soup was followed by pasta with a chicken liver sauce; Eliza, assembling it in the little kitchen while the others talked, took her time so that she could watch them. Really Patrick was perfect. The long, thin fingers, the husky voice, that intriguing scar like a small question mark just under one cheekbone . . . and the way he paid attention to what people said, that impression one always received of a listening allegiance. Now, as she watched, she admired the way he turned to Jess and Tom in turn, his own contributions a balanced mixture of questions and comment. How perfect it would be, after Nick, for Jess to have this fair-minded, perceptive, considerate man!

Patrick turned, and saw her looking. He smiled, and held her gaze. Confused, she turned her attentions to the salad. It would not do for him to suspect that she had any designs on him.

When she brought the food through they were talking about parenthood, Jess listening earnestly to what Tom had to say, her head cocked to one side in a way that Eliza recognised as indicative of full concentration. 'But didn't you want to just take him?' she asked. 'I mean, it wasn't your fault if Linda left you for someone else. Why should it be you who had to lose Dickon?'

Tom swirled his wine. 'I didn't lose him,' he said, 'and he didn't lose me. I did think about fighting it, yes. But that would have been just for me. And the main thing was that Dickon should lose as little as possible. He still has a mother and a father, you see.'

'Apparently,' put in Patrick, 'about half of all fathers completely lose touch with their children within a year or two of the family splitting up. That statistic's given me the uneasy feeling that fathers can't be all that important. It's good to meet someone who discredits that idea.'

'I don't know,' said Eliza, serving out. 'There are exceptions, of course, but overall I don't think fathers *are* very important. Not like mothers. Oh, sorry, Tom. I meant you to be one of the exceptions.'

'I suppose,' said Patrick, 'that they're as important as they choose to make themselves.'

There was a pause. Tom refilled the glasses. Then Jess spoke.

'When Dad first left,' she said, 'I tried to convince myself that he didn't matter at all. I thought bad behaviour cancelled out all the – well, all the love there used to be. But as time goes on, I think of him more and more. I'd give a lot just to know where he is.' She turned to Tom, with a beseeching, confiding gaze. 'He's never seen Louis, you see.'

Eliza fixed her eyes on her plate. 'He doesn't deserve to see Louis,' she muttered. 'As Patrick says, he's as important – or unimportant – as he chooses to be. He could have been there for us, but he opted out of all that.'

'He was there for us, once,' said Jess simply.

'For you, maybe,' said Eliza, 'but not for – all of us.' She turned to Patrick. 'My father had his favourites, you see. But all this family history must be very boring for you. I'm sorry.'

'Don't be,' said Patrick. 'As the product of a boringly stable middle-class marriage, I find it all quite fascinating.' But Eliza noticed, with gratitude, that he deftly turned the conversation to a less personal topic, with a question to Tom about Dickon's passion for war games.

Over the years Eliza had become quite adept at assembling palatable meals from cheap ingredients, but when it came to puddings her imagination tended to fail her, and she never got much beyond stewed apple. So she'd bought three kinds of cheese from the covered market, and clementines, grapes and walnuts, and Patrick had contributed a bottle of port. Jess, who still suffered from broken nights, began to yawn and droop before midnight, at which point Tom tactfully retired next door, the sleeping Dickon slung over his shoulder like Father Christmas' sack. But Patrick stayed, talking and cracking nuts. Eliza, delighted, plied him with coffee. It was worth a bad night to get him firmly hooked. Jess reached the point where she could hardly keep her eyes open, and stumbled off to bed with apologies. But still he stayed. Eliza opened another walnut. She loved working the kernel out of its shell unscathed. Such a peculiar thing it was, like a toy brain.

'Are you doing anything tomorrow?' asked Patrick nonchalantly. 'Because I fancied a walk over Port Meadow. We could have lunch at the pub – I forget its name.'

'That would be nice, but I don't know if we could get the buggy across it. The path rather peters out, I seem to remember. But I could baby-sit, and you and Jess could go –' Oh my God, she thought, how unsubtle can you get? She felt her colour rise.

'Oh,' said Patrick. 'I meant just you and me.' And he caught her gaze once more, and this time she did not look away.

When he had gone, she left the debris of the meal where it lay, and hurried to her bedroom. From beneath her folded shirts she drew out her father's letter. It was written on headed paper filched from some club or other, in shaky, blotchy ballpoint.

'Dearest Lila,' it read, 'for very dear you will always be to me, whatever my deservings.' Then it rambled on, a maudlin mixture of apology and self-justification that she skimmed over in blear-eyed dismay. It gave no account of how her father had spent his time since his departure, but it did give a London address, one which Eliza did not recognise, as a base for any further communication. There were four sides of only fairly coherent outpourings, but the last paragraph of all stood out strong and clear. 'I know I am not welcome,' it said, 'so I will not trouble you again. But if ever you, or any of the others, can bring themselves to see me, then please, Lila, tell me so. Until then, be sure, my shame will keep me away.'

Eliza opened the window to let the night air cool her hot cheeks. There was a moon, nearly full, hanging like a sad face over the sleeping town. Except that Oxford, of course, never really did sleep. Even as she watched, a cluster of shouting teenagers rounded the corner, returning, presumably, from some club or party. A frayed cloud crossed the moon's face, making it look as if it were retreating behind a handkerchief, recoiling from the brash delights of the human world.

'It's always best,' said Eliza out loud, 'to make one's decisions by moonlight.' She shut the window, and, late as it was, found pen and paper and started to write. 'Dear Dad,' she began, 'I think I may have been a little hasty . . .'

In the next room Jess dreamed her sister was trying to suffocate her by drawing her hair across her mouth. 'It's all right,' the

235

dream-Eliza assured Tom Winchcombe. 'It's all for the best. She won't feel a thing.'

The fear jerked Jess awake. She lay till the movement had crept back into her petrified limbs. Moonlight seeped through the cracks between the ill-fitting curtains, falling on the small hump of Louis in his cot. It's all right, Jess told herself. It was only the moon that made me dream. And she rolled over and once more slept.

# CHAPTER TWENTY-EIGHT

One morning in early spring Susan Chandler woke up to a different world. She didn't know why or how her life had been remade for her, nor did she try to find out. She didn't dare probe too deeply in case her new-granted energy should prove a fragile illusion. All she knew was that on this day, without any warning, she found herself able to tear off her swaddling bands and grasp her future in her own strong hands.

The doctors advised caution. More than two months in the clinic, scarcely stirring unless bullied into it, had left her thin and weak. She swung her legs over the edge of the bed that first morning and wobbled like a new-born foal. She was in a fever to leave, but that was not allowed; she had first to reach a target weight, and temperature and blood pressure readings had to give satisfaction. It took five days, days in which she ate and talked and exercised – talked to the hospital staff, for her embargo on visitors continued. She wanted no memory of her invalid self to remain in the minds of those she cared about; she was about to relaunch herself into their lives.

Those she cared about! A short enough list it proved to be. From the pure silence of her months of stupor her feelings for people had emerged, miraculously refined and clear. Jamie she loved. She knew she would have to coax his love for her back, but right now she felt equal to the task. Polly – yes, Polly mattered. Polly and a handful of other friends, with whom she would now be able to communicate on an equal footing, not from a position of feeble dependence. Patrick Furness mattered not a jot. A decent young man, but one with no part in her life – he felt like nothing more than a distantly embarrassing memory.

And Tony – most marvellous of all was that Tony Chandler now belonged to a discarded past. If he figured at all now it was only as Jamie's less than satisfactory father. His part in her own life seemed so remote that when she thought of her marriage the scenes actually appeared in black and white, like an ancient ciné film. And, like a ciné film, such scenes were silent. She saw images from their courtship, their holidays, their rows, their break-up, but she watched them dispassionately. Nothing stirred.

On the fifth day the psychiatrist discharged her. He held back his misgivings, for he had no grounds on which to detain her. A taxi carried her and her very little luggage back to Holland Park.

She stood outside on the pavement for a few moments, looking up at the house. The March wind was chill, but she let her coat hang open; after the clinic's warmth it was thrilling to feel currents of cold air spiralling about her bones. Blinds or curtains covered all the windows but the house did not look abandoned. The black and white tesselation of the front steps looked newly swept, and the area in front of the basement windows was neat and free of litter. Both neighbouring houses sported window boxes full of shouting daffodils. Her own window boxes, of course, were empty, but the look of restraint pleased her.

She unlocked the door. Estrelia had come in every week, so two months' post was piled carefully on the hall table, and the house smelt as usual of bleach and air freshener. It was cold, though. She turned on the central heating and kept her coat on until it had made an impact. She prowled round the place, opening doors and drawers, lifting ornaments, an intruder in her own house. Every room was as anonymously clean as if it had been made ready for a letting agency. She plugged in the fridge; it shuddered into life. She ran the tap for a while to get rid of any rusty residue before filling the kettle; there was nothing to eat anywhere, but there were a few herbal tea bags – rosehip, and peppermint. She collected the stack of post, and slid it all into the kitchen bin.

Upstairs was the same as down – a shuttered dolls' house, waiting for its owner to impose a character on it. Only Jamie's room was any different. It seemed he had taken very little to school. His books, his clothes, even his Wildlife Fact-Files were as they had always been. On his desk there was a framed photograph of the three of them, squinting into the sun on a skiing holiday. Jamie had set the timer on the Leica, the first proper camera he had owned. Susan was glad he had left the picture behind. She turned down a corner of the counterpane. His bed was not made up.

She tiptoed downstairs, wary of the way the empty house gave significance to her every action. She poured boiled water into a mug and dunked a rosehip tea bag. A patch of scummy dust collected on the surface. She sipped. It tasted like Ribena without the sweetness.

The telephone squatted on the grey marble surface, sending out a silent challenge. She caught sight of her reflection in the glass door of a china cabinet – an imprecise image, as if glimpsed in a dark pool. She ran her fingers through her hair, making it stand up in spikes. She was startled by her own hollow-eyed pallor.

'Just do it,' she said aloud. Then she picked up the telephone. Tony's office number was still stored on one of the memory buttons.

'Who shall I say is calling?' asked Morag, Pippa's soft-voiced office replacement.

'It's a personal call.'

Tony came on the line, gruff, in haste. 'Yup?'

'Tony, it's Susan.' She didn't pause for a reaction. 'I wonder what your plans are for this house? You did talk of selling it at one point. Could you hurry that along, please? It's really an absurdly large house for one person.'

'Susan? Susan – my God –'

'I won't keep you, Tony. I know you don't like to be bothered when you're at work. Perhaps you could ring me when you've put it on the market. Bye.'

When she put down the handset she found she was trembling and sweating. She tipped the barely touched rosehip tea down the sink, then picked up her handbag. She double-locked carefully as she always did, then walked to the small supermarket round the corner, where she bought bread, eggs, tea – the things that campers need.

Tony, for once, was at a loss as to how to proceed. He reached for the telephone, withdrew his hand, stood up, circled the desk. He loosened his tie, checked his watch, sorted unseeing through the contents of one pocket. A major problem in his life appeared to have been sorted out at a single stroke, and he didn't like it at all.

'Is everything all right?' cooed Morag. It was only in the last few months that she would have dared ask such a question. Tony had employed her for her quiet manner and unobtrusive appearance, and for a long time had all but ignored her. But over time she had grown on him; he found her singsong lowland accent and careful little movements soothing. She had pretty eyes, too, and good skin – clear, pale and lightly freckled, which gave her a comfortingly countrified appearance. He never minded if she asked him questions. He'd told her a lot about Susan since Christmas. She was quite the little confidante, really.

'She wants to sell the house,' he said, sitting down. 'After all the fuss, it's her who wants to sell it.' He looked almost sleepily bewildered.

'So she's left the clinic, then?'

'I don't know. I think so. I didn't ask. She didn't give me a chance to ask. She just put the phone down.'

'She's always been a bit of a one for that, hasn't she?' Morag brought Tony a cup of coffee, placed it without comment near his elbow. 'I expect Pippa will be pleased,' she hazarded.

'She'll be delighted. She's been on at me for ages –' Tony slurped his coffee. 'But I'll have to talk to Susan. These things can't be done in a rush. She's been in an awful state, after all – she may not know her own mind.'

Morag uttered only a tiny, sympathetic mew.

'The market's very depressed,' Tony went on. 'Selling the house now could be foolish. And it's Susan's home. I can't see her settling in a new place.'

'What would James think?'

'James? Yes, quite. It's his home too – one of them. What can Susan be thinking of? You can't sell a house just like that.'

'It was your home, too. You'd miss it, wouldn't you, Tony?' Morag had never ventured so far before.

Tony looked at her, surprised. He sought her gaze, but she lowered her eyelids respectfully, bending her head over a file of letters. Her curly dark hair looked as though it would be springy to the touch. 'You might be right, Morag. It would be a bit of a wrench.' He stood up. 'Never mind, not your problem. Back to work, I suppose. Get me the correspondence on that Fowler case, would you?'

She obeyed. He watched her as she left the room. A slip of a girl – hardly anything to her. Nice little legs, though. And that dark-green suit looked good on her. Oh well.


'Yes, Polly, of course I'm sure.'

'But this lovely house! All the colours – the pictures – everything. You spent six months of your *life* tracking down those bathroom tiles.'

'That was six months wasted, then.'

'Suze, what's happening to you? Are you going to tell me that the way things look doesn't matter any more? What did they do to you in that clinic? Suzie – you haven't got religion, have you?'

Susan laughed and laughed. 'Oh, Polly, you are a hoot. But it's good to hear your voice again. Did you ever get the wine stain out of your carpet?'

'Come round and see. Or shall I come to you? Have you eaten yet?'

'I'm poaching myself an egg.'

'Well, bin it. Let's go out.'

'Great. I want to tell you what I'm going to do with the rest of my life.'


Tony still had the keys to the Holland Park house. He could see through the frosted glass that the landing light was on, so he rang the bell, but when no one answered he unlocked cautiously. He called Susan's name so as not to alarm her, but the house had that listening quality that houses have when there's no one at home.

There were evidences of recent habitation, but they were quite un-Susan-like. A carrier bag, plonked on the kitchen floor, disgorged its contents. An empty egg shell sat in a tacky pool of albumen by the side of the cooker. A used saucepan had been plunged into the washing-up bowl. Gobs of egg white floated on the surface of the water like tiny icebergs.

Tony climbed the stairs.

'Susan,' he called again. 'Susan,' but now his voice sounded almost pleading. He nerved himself to push open the bedroom door, as if he were expecting some horror. But all he saw was a tangle of clothes thrown on to the bed. Black leggings, a grey sweater. She must have bathed and gone out. Where? With whom? How long had she been home?

Did she have a lover, this stranger wife of his? That man who'd found her on Christmas Day – who was he? Polly Cruse had been vague, and Tony had never cared to ask. It hadn't interested him – until now.

He opened her wardrobe, looking for clues. There were none. Her sombre collection of clothes hung there much as he remembered, dark shapes shrouded in plastic. She put shoe trees in her shoes, stuffed spare leather bags with tissue paper. Susan had always been so careful with things.

His hunger to know grew. He turned to the dressing table. He wasn't sure what he was looking for – letters, a diary? He found neither. He thought of the bathroom cabinet, where she had kept her diaphragm, meticulously clean in its special plastic pouch. When he found it still there, he felt a surprising surge of relief. What the hell was the matter with him? It wasn't as if he wanted her back.

It suddenly enraged him that he could find no trace of himself in this house. He'd taken all his things, obviously, but there should be something, some token, some imprint . . . He bounded up to the top floor, to his son's attic bedroom. He used to come up here sometimes, read James stories when he was younger, help him with his homework. How long was it since he'd set foot in this room? Must be getting on for a year.

The framed photograph caught his eye. He picked it up, held it under the light. It wasn't a particularly good likeness of any of them; he wondered why the boy had bothered to put it in a frame. Then it occurred to him that perhaps there weren't many pictures of the three of them together. He put it back on the desk, next to another photograph, of James holding Samson when he was a puppy. Tony remembered taking that picture himself. James would have been about nine. Tony blinked back the unfamiliar discomfort of tears.

From his inside pocket his mobile phone began to bleat. Tony jumped as if it were a trapped insect. He unfolded it.

'Yes?'

'Darling, what's happened? Supper's spoiling. You didn't tell me you were going to be late. Where are you? It doesn't sound like the office.'

'I'm in a taxi, Pips. I'm on my way. Listen, I've got good news for you. I've talked to Susan about selling the house and she's really been very reasonable. She accepts that a smaller place would be more appropriate and –'

'Ooh! Tony! You are brilliant! Oh, I knew she wouldn't mind. She's out of hospital, then? Oh, darling –'

'Yes, yes, well, I knew you'd be pleased. Listen, the traffic's terrible. I'll be home in half an hour.'

In the Dolphin Square flat, Pippa changed the table setting. She got out the heart-shaped candle holders that she'd bought for Valentine's Day, and she changed the ordinary wine goblets for champagne flutes. Then she settled down to indulge in a half-hour telephone call to her mother.

# CHAPTER TWENTY-NINE

Pippa's baby was born two weeks before it was expected, but it was still colossal. The head was too big for a normal delivery so Pippa got the Caesarean she wanted. She didn't fancy being conscious for the operation, so she opted for a general anaesthetic. Tony was relieved; pacing the waiting room was much more his style than providing a reassuring commentary on whatever unspeakable things the doctors had to do.

When Pippa came round she felt drowsy and weepy, and she wasn't at all pleased when her son was placed in her arms. 'Oh, Tony,' she wailed, 'it wasn't supposed to be a boy. They've given me the wrong one.' Tony soothed her as best he could, and the nurse was understanding. 'They're often like this after a C-section. It's the anaesthetic. She's not herself, poor sweetheart.'

'It's such a funny colour,' sobbed Pippa. 'I thought it would be blond. Please call the doctor, I'm sure there's something wrong.'

'Baby's just fine, Mrs Chandler,' said the nurse, picking it up. 'And he's just the image of his daddy, aren't you, darling?' Tony peered at the be-shawled lump the nurse held out to him. He saw more resemblance to a Hallowe'en pumpkin than to himself, but he appreciated the wisdom of the nurse's line of comment.

'I think you're right,' he said brightly. 'Do you know, Pips darling, I think he's got my eyes?'

But Pippa wouldn't look. She tried to turn on one side and winced. 'I hurt so much,' she said. 'Do call the doctor, Tone. What's the point of going private if you can't have the doctor when you want.'

By the time Meredith Watts-Davison arrived with a blue and white bouquet and a brand new Liberty nightie for her daughter, Pippa had had a sleep and was no longer tearful, though still grumpy.

'I just can't believe it,' she complained. 'They said it was a girl at the scan.'

'They never said they were sure, darling. But he's absolutely beautiful. And he looks so like you. I'm sure he's got your eyes.'

The male infant slept in a transparent cot by his mother's bedside. His orangey colour had settled down into the lightly tanned look of postnatal jaundice; his eyes were tight slits folded in fat.

'He looks foreign,' said Pippa, shortly. Meredith patted her hand.

'They all look like that, darling. Sort of Chinesey. It goes in a day or two. Honestly.'

Pippa allowed herself to be distracted by her mother's gifts. She approved the nightgown, but when Meredith pointed out it buttoned down the front, she said, 'Oh, Mummy. I'm not going to breast-feed. There's absolutely no way.'

'It helps you to lose weight, darling.'

'I don't care. I just won't.'

'Just as you like. Bottles are much cleaner.' She looked round the prettily appointed private room. 'Is there a buzzer anywhere? I wonder if they'd bring me a cup of tea?'

Pippa pleated the hem of the sheet with irritated fingers. 'We'll have to have the room at the barn redecorated,' she said. 'It'll cost a fortune.' Her eyes filled again. 'Oh, Mummy, all that lovely pink. I think I should sue the hospital, don't you? It's not my fault it wasn't a girl.'


Jamie stayed at Powdermill for the Easter holidays. He could have stayed in Holland Park with his mother, but the 'For Sale' signs were up and Susan moved restlessly through the house changing things to make it look even more impressive, and Jamie felt uneasy there. Being with his mother wasn't as bad as he'd expected. She looked thin, but pretty and bright-eyed – there was nothing of Bella's clouded stare, to his unutterable relief. Mum was chatty, too, and cheerful, and she didn't seem to want to talk about embarrassing things. But it wasn't like being at home, somehow. It was more like staying with someone – a nice aunt, or even a sister. He felt at least as grown-up as his mother, now.

'Don't you mind your house being sold?' Finian asked as they carried buckets of feed to Pharaoh in the stable. The peacock followed them, his head cocked in anticipation, his new-grown tail glittering bronze and emerald in the spring sunshine.

'Not that much.'

'You've always lived there, haven't you?'

'Yeah. Well, since I was four. I can't remember much before then.'

Finian gazed back at the russet hump of the farmhouse, flanked on one side by a row of Scotch pines, their blue-grey tops like puffs of cannon smoke; on the other by wild cherries and chestnuts, just unfurling into life. 'I can't imagine this place being sold,' he said.

'It won't be. Will it?' asked Jamie with a pang of anxiety. He couldn't imagine such a thing, either.

'God knows.' Finian opened the stable door and slapped Pharaoh's dusty flank. 'It belongs to Ganna. That's how come Dad never got a chance to sell it. But if she dies –' He tipped the bucket; the contents swished into the manger. Jamie breathed in the dry, yeasty smell.

'Won't she just leave it to your mum?' he asked.

'Dunno. I hope so. But Dad is her son.'

'But he's –'

'Missing. Yeah. But he might turn up. If he's still alive.'

'Of course he's still alive!' Jamie was shocked.

'How are we supposed to know? He never got in touch.'

'But they trace people. If –'

'They trace them if they find the body. If they can identify it.'

Jamie thought of all those half-inch reports that ran in a column down the edge of the home news pages of a newspaper. A lot of people did just disappear. 'I'm sure he'll come back,' he said in a small voice that was meant to be consoling.

Fin buried his face in Pharaoh's neck. 'I don't care if he doesn't,' he muttered. 'This old boy could do with some exercise. Fancy a ride?'

On the way back to the house to collect Pharaoh's tack, Fin stopped in his tracks and grabbed Jamie's arm so hard that it hurt. 'Oh, Christ Almighty,' he said, 'talk of the fucking devil.'

Jamie was alarmed. Fin didn't swear much, not compared to

246

the boys at school. 'What? What is it? What have you seen?'

Fin pointed. 'The green car. That's the car Dad took. He's back.' He turned to Jamie, his eyes wide. He suddenly looked very, very young. 'What'll I do?' he said. 'I can't see him.'

Jamie's heart thudded. His emotions were in turmoil; Fin had never turned to him like this before. He thought quickly.

'We can get into the barn,' he said. 'I know where the spare key is.' He brightened. 'Hey, let's get the jacuzzi working. It'll take a while to heat up. But you always said you wanted to try it out.'

The front door of the farmhouse was never locked. From life-long familiarity Leo Antrobus knew how to open it so that it made no sound. He stood in the hall, uncertain, looking about him. Coats lay, flung as always, over the high oak settle; on the bare wooden floor there was a convocation of Wellington boots, some upright, some fallen, like a miniature Stonehenge. Attempts to train the family to leave their boots by the back door had always failed. He sniffed. Wood smoke, frying, damp dog. The unvarying smell of home.

There was a movement on the stairs; Bella, trundling her car-pet sweeper. Her dust-coloured hair, her plastic sandals. The blue bulge of a varicose vein on her bare calf. No change in Bella, either. He spoke her name, softly. She looked up and dropped the carpet sweeper; Leo jumped forward to catch it before it bumped all the way down the stairs. 'Bella,' he said, with gen-uine affection, 'how are you, old girl?'

'She's in the garden,' said Bella, and fled.

Leo opened the kitchen door. The usual pinkish pall of Aga ash thickened the air. It left a taste at the back of your throat. Cats, curled like muffs, occupied every surface. The fat tor-toiseshell unwound itself and pushed against Leo's leg, purring and dribbling. He fondled its head absently, then picked up a photograph propped against a toast rack on the dresser; a dark-haired baby with pointed features and vigilant eyes. He turned it over. 'L. G. 3/2/96' was pencilled on the back.

He was still holding the picture when Martha came in, whistling and stamping the mud off her feet. She wore an old tweed jacket of his with a pair of secateurs lolling out of one pocket, and her arms were full of daffodils. Moisture beaded her hair, more silver than ginger, strands of which fell about her flushed face. Her fingers were pink and swollen from picking flowers in the long wet grass. Leo couldn't move, couldn't speak. He was paralysed, overcome by the constancy, the splendour, the immutability of this red-cheeked whistling woman. You are my life, he thought, but he couldn't say it.

Martha dumped the daffodils in the sink, and then she turned and saw him. For one instant glad joy tore through her at the sight of the shape of him, so long known. He was like the missing piece of a jigsaw puzzle and her arm jerked out automatically to touch him. Then she remembered, and kept still.

'How did you get here?' she asked, and the effort to keep her voice steady made it sound gruff, accusatory.

'In the car. How else?'

'You haven't sold it then?'

'Oh Martha, is that all you can say?'

Martha turned aside, sorted through the daffodils as though they were surgical patients needing her utmost attention and concentration. She could scream at him now, she could shout, Why? Where have you been? Didn't you think about us? But she knew that once she started, years of control would be gone. So all she said was, 'Sibyl's in the parlour.'

'Will I shock her? Will she want to see me?'

'She wants nothing else.' She held up a fat bunch, shook the drops from the stems. 'If she knows you at all, that is. She's far gone, Leo.'

'Come with me, Martha.'

He always was a coward, she thought. But perhaps it would be best. 'All right,' she said. 'Just let me find a vessel for these.' It came back to him how she always said vessel, not vase, or jug.

He followed her to the parlour. They didn't speak. Sibyl sat by the fire, her rug over her knees. For once she was not asleep. Martha went up to her and touched her shoulder. 'Sibyl,' she said, 'prepare yourself. He's come back. Leo's come back.'

The old woman craned her neck. 'I know that,' she said, almost indignantly, 'I heard his footsteps in the hall.' She held out her two trembling hands. 'Oh, Leo,' she said. 'Oh, my son.'

Leo knelt beside her, clasping her hands. 'Forgive me,

248

Mother, forgive me.' His voice was croaky. He buried his face in her lap.

Sibyl looked up at Martha as if puzzled. 'I do apologise,' she said vaguely, 'for not getting up, but I'm not as well as I was. But my daughter-in-law will make you a cup of tea. You must be tired after fighting for so long.'

Leo raised his grizzled head. His blue eyes sought her face. 'Mother,' he whispered. 'I've missed you.' Sibyl scanned his face, frowning. 'I know those eyes,' she said. 'They took the baby away, you know.' Her expression changed to one of aggrieved suspicion. 'The baby was here, now it's gone. They thought I wouldn't notice.' She closed her eyes.

'Come on,' said Martha to Leo. 'Best leave her.' Her voice was still gruff, but not ungentle. She closed the parlour door softly behind them. 'She comes and goes, but she did know you.'

'I had no idea,' said Leo, shaking his head. 'I never imagined –'

'That's just the trouble,' said Martha briskly. 'You never imagined. For all your imagination, Leo Antrobus, you never did imagine.' She gave a little laugh. 'Shall I make you some tea, then? You look as if you need it. Your mother was right about that, at least.'

The jacuzzi proved satisfactory. After much trial and error Jamie got it working and they climbed in together; the pummelling jets of hot water got them warm to the marrow of their bones, a feat impossible to achieve at the farmhouse between September and May. They lay there for ages, talking; not about Fin's father, or anything difficult like that, but just drawing on their common store of jokes and references, concerning animals or ridiculous people at their respective schools or things they'd seen on television. They talked about girls a bit, too. Finian's attitude was fairly casual; he noticed pretty ones, but described them as if discussing the points of a horse. His school was mixed, of course, so he had a larger field of reference than Jamie, whose school only took girls in the sixth form. At the core of Jamie's heart burned the precious image of Jess, but this passion was at once too sacred and too absurd to be mentioned, so as a cover he enlarged upon the charms of one Alice Morrell, a leggy blonde who had appeared in the end-of-term play in a low-cut frock that became her well. Jamie hadn't even seen the play, but he'd heard Alice and her appearance in it discussed so often by his contemporaries that he felt as if he had. He rattled on, happy in the new-found understanding of how to do somebody a favour. All this idle chat gave Finian a breathing space before he had to meet his father, and he knew Fin was grateful.

But in the end it had to be faced, of course. They emptied the tub and dressed, Finian exclaiming at the size and softness of the towels. They'd made a bit of a mess of the bathroom carpet, slopping water all over it, but it didn't matter much. His dad and Pippa wouldn't be down for ages, not until after the baby was born. 'Hey,' he said to Finian, 'we can do that again. They won't be here for at least a couple of weeks. We could sleep over here too, if you like.'

The thought sustained Finian on the walk back to the farm-house. 'We could cook over at the barn and everything,' he mused. 'It would be brilliant. Would it be OK with your dad?'

'He wouldn't know,' said Jamie, daring and scornful. 'I wouldn't even tell him. It's my home as well. Supposedly.'

The green car was still in the drive. Finian had half hoped, half feared that it would be gone. The bright day had clouded over, and the light was on in the kitchen. He could see the heads of both his parents; they were seated at opposite ends of the long table, like book-ends. He flung open the back door, humming loudly. Leo rose to greet him.

'Oh, hello, Dad,' said Finian, shrugging off his donkey jacket with an air of nonchalance. 'I knew you were back. I saw the car. This is Jac Chandler. His father bought the barn. Remember?'

Leo hovered. He looked old, dithery, at a loss. Martha's heart smote her. She knew Leo must be yearning to hold his son in his arms, and the feeling banished, for the while, the knowledge that he had forfeited any right to do so. 'Come in, boys,' she said, warmly. 'Isn't it great to have Dad home? I'll run into Broadhurst and get something decent for our supper. What do you fancy, Fin? Lamb chops?'

Finian shot her a look of reproach and surprise, but the moment was cut off by the telephone. It rang extraordinarily loudly in the kitchen, and it always made the plates on the dresser rattle, and the little grey cat spring to its feet. Martha made for it, but before she could get there it was answered in the hall. 'Bella,' murmured Martha. 'She must have been listening, just outside.'

Bella emerged from the shadows. 'The baby's born,' she said, to nobody in particular. 'It's a boy.'

'Jac, it's for you! It must be your father.' Martha was delighted to have this harmless little drama to divert attention from the more potentially painful one in the kitchen.

'A boy? But I thought – oh, well.' Jamie went out to speak to his father. In his absence Martha sketched in Jamie's family circumstances for the benefit of Leo.

'So he's staying here,' Finian added firmly by way of conclusion.

'Oh yes,' said Martha, 'he's staying here, for as long as he wants.'

Jamie came back in. 'It's a very big boy,' he said, his dark eyes bright. 'She had it, you know, cut out. Dad wants me to be its godfather.'

'How lovely,' said Martha. 'I think you'll be a very good one.' Privately she thought, that's the best idea that ghastly man has ever had.

'What's he called?' asked Fin. He liked babies.

'Er – Tarquin,' said Jamie. Then he added hastily, 'But I expect I can change that.'

The butcher's was shut by the time Martha got to Broadhurst, so they had to make do with fish and chips. But the evening was a merry one. Leo checked the remnants of his cellar and brought out some Medoc; Martha watched his consumption anxiously, but he drank only a glass and a half. He toasted the health of Jamie's new brother with his old eloquence. The wine loosened his tongue, and he told anecdotes about his travels that kept them all amused. Bella and Sibyl ate with them; Sibyl said little, but from time to time her face would clear as if with the renewed pleasure of recognition. At least, Martha hoped it was that. Really, she thought as she drank her wine, it's just as if he's just come back from some extended business trip. We still don't know what the hell's going on.

The cats were shooed outside to squabble over the remains of the fish, and Leo played Monopoly with the boys while Martha put Sibyl to bed. Play money, thought Martha. That's all money ever has been to Leo. Does it really matter so very much?

The boys went to bed straight after the game. Leo and Martha stood at the bottom of the stairs, looking at one another. 'I'll make up your bed in the girls' room,' she said, with resolution.

Leo reached out, put his hand on her forearm. His touch was tentative. 'Why in the girls' room?' he asked. 'Please, Martha.'

She drew away, and shook her head. 'Not yet,' she said. 'Not yet.'

# CHAPTER THIRTY

Jamie's continuing presence in the farmhouse did much to make the first few days after Leo's return less awkward for Finian, and indeed for Martha. The boys carried on with their normal pursuits, Leo sometimes joining them when they walked the dogs or mucked out the stable. Leo, too, was grateful for this opportunity to renew contact with his son without the embarrassment of a tête-à-tête. Despite his air of nonchalance, Fin bristled with resentment; Leo sensed it, feared it, and hoped that time and custom would blunt the edges of such jagged emotions. He asked Martha, privately, how the boy had taken his absence. 'He hardly mentioned your name,' she answered in all simplicity.

'He didn't mind, then?' Leo dreaded the answer.

'I wouldn't say that. I think he just applied himself to learning to live without you. It'll be a hard lesson to unlearn, Leo.'

Jamie at first accepted with resignation Leo's presence in the life he and Fin shared, but, to his surprise, he soon found pleasure in his company. His friend's father was a far less fearsome figure than he had imagined; since he didn't know any other gamblers, he had modelled his idea of Leo on a sardonic, mustachioed rake in a Napoleonic drama series he'd seen on television, and the real thing proved far more humble and shambolic. There was an edge – Leo had a quick wit, and was a talented mimic – but the was eager to please, and seemed almost deferential towards his son. This irritated Fin, who addressed several sarcastic rejoinders to his father. Such sallies went unrebuked.

Guests were always so useful, reflected Martha, even quiet little boys who spent hours out of the house like Jac. Guests forced you to stick to a routine; you cooked, you tidied up a bit, you watched what you said in front of them. Having Jac there made it feel as if Leo was a guest, too; this was a good thing, Martha felt. Only time could tell whether he was or wasn't. Sibyl's rapidly increasing needs took up much of Martha's time, too; she and Leo were rarely quite alone. Leo had been shocked

253

the first time he saw her rinsing out rubber sheets, and suggested that they employ a nurse. 'And what'll I pay her with? Pony nuts?' snapped Martha, allowing herself the rare luxury of scarcely veiled reproach.

Susan Chandler rang most days. She repeatedly volunteered to have Jamie back; Martha and Jamie himself separately reiterated that they were quite happy with the existing situation. Susan felt guilty but relieved. She was busy, showing people round the house, and going to look at smaller properties that she might buy with her share of the proceeds. She was enchanted by an airy penthouse in Notting Hill, at the top of a large white house in a quiet street foaming with cherry blossom, but she tried to put it out of her mind because there was no bedroom for Jamie. Polly talked of giving up her job and proposed that she and Susan start up their own interior design company. The idea was exciting. Susan considered reverting to her maiden name, but then she thought that if she abandoned 'Chandler' Jamie's feelings might be hurt. It was, after all, his name too. She had not forgotten her resolution to put Jamie first, but remembering to do so was harder than she had imagined.

On the Wednesday after the birth it was decreed that Jamie should travel to London to visit his new brother. Fin promptly telephoned a couple of school friends, but they were both away; his face was clouded, and Jamie knew that he was racking his brain for a way of avoiding a heart-to-heart with Leo. 'Why don't you come with me?' suggested Jamie. 'Looking at the baby won't take more than a couple of minutes, and then we can go and do something.'

'Like going to the Natural History Museum?' Fin hadn't been since he was five, and he was curious to see his friend's holy of holies.

'Yeah? Why not?

And so it was arranged. Tony Chandler, extracting himself from a busy working day to escort his son to the clinic, felt a surge of irritation at the sight of that dirty, carroty-haired boy, a head taller than his own son, striding loose-limbed along the platform at Charing Cross, but he suppressed his reaction. He'd barely spoken to the boy since that ridiculous incident with the prawns, but now was not the time for recrimination. He greeted them both heartily, and squeezed his son's shoulder with what he hoped looked like a relaxed paternal gesture.

At the clinic, Finian, who was possessed of a certain amount of natural tact, stayed in the reception area, flicking through copies of *Hello!* magazine while the inspection of the baby took place. The child's name had been modified to Rory and his looks had improved immensely. He had a good round head and broad shoulders, and Pippa was beginning to feel quite proud of him; everybody kept telling her that he looked like Will Carling. A jocular debate had taken place between Tony and her consultant. 'He'll be a great prop forward,' remarked the doctor, and Tony had said, 'Prop forward? Rubbish. Fly half – that's the only position for my son.' My son! Hearing Tony say that made Pippa feel all warm inside.

Jamie, equipped with a musical box he'd bought for the baby with his own money, and a bunch of pink roses for Pippa towards which his father had steered him on the way, approached the bed with caution. Pippa was sitting up in bed, looking fat. He didn't know whether to kiss her. He never did kiss her, normally. So he just said, 'Hi,' and held the roses out.

'Ooh! How sweet of you! Could you put them – yes, there's fine, the nurse will sort them out. And a pressie for Rory, too! He's asleep at the moment – look, there – don't disturb him, will you?'

Jamie had no intention of disturbing the rather scary unknown quantity lying in the funny aquarium-like cradle. He looked at what little was visible – a cheek, a fist, a nose like a blob of putty – and struggled for an appropriate comment. 'He's very round, isn't he?' was all he could manage.

Luckily, Pippa laughed. 'He's a great big boy,' she said with pride. 'A healthy size. Not one of your skinny little weeds.'

This was probably not meant to be taken personally, and it certainly didn't register with Jamie. 'Nice flowers,' he said, looking at the offerings that were banked up on either side of the bed as if at the site of a road accident or unlawful killing. Then Rory Chandler woke, and his hiccoughy wail made them all start. 'Time for his feed,' said Pippa. 'He's very regular. Put them on a routine from day one, then you don't get any nonsense.'

Jamie's hackles rose in panic. She was going to feed him! He would have to watch her unveiling her breast. Why hadn't he considered this eventuality? But then a nurse appeared, bearing a bottle. She lifted up the very round baby and made shushing noises. 'Are you the big brother?' she asked. 'I've heard about you.' She was friendly, Irish. Jamie felt obscurely pleased.

'Would you like to feed him?' the nurse said. 'If that's all right with you, Mrs Chandler?' Pippa was quite happy. She liked the way this nurse always called her Mrs Chandler, despite evidence to the contrary in her medical notes. Jamie found himself settled in a chair with his brother's fuzzy ball of a head in the crook of his arm.

The nurse showed him how to hold the bottle. 'You tip it like this, see, so you don't get any air in. Easy now – that's it.'

The baby sucked and sucked. 'He's a good trencherman,' remarked Tony, looking on with folded arms. About halfway through, the baby paused, and opened his milky kitten-blue eyes. 'Hey!' exclaimed Jamie. 'He's looking at me.'

'He knows his brother,' said the nurse. She looked at Tony Chandler and winked.

Back in the waiting room, Fin asked, 'What's he like, then?'

'Great,' said Jamie. 'He's really nice. He feeds really well – he's already nearly regained his birth weight.'

'Sounds impressive,' said Fin, vaguely. 'He can be a friend for Louis when they're older. I'm glad he's a boy.'

Tony Chandler offered to take them out to lunch, but they both insisted there was no need. Relieved, he thrust a twenty-pound note into Jamie's pocket. 'Treat yourselves,' he said. 'I've a mountain of work to get through, I must admit.' They parted company at the tube station. 'Thanks, Dad,' called Jamie. 'See you soon.'

On the train bound for South Kensington, Finian said, 'Lila and Jess are coming next weekend. Did I tell you?'

'Don't think so.' Jamie hoped he sounded noncommittal.

'It won't be the first time they've seen Dad. He saw them in Oxford, apparently, before he came home.'

'That's good, then. Get it over with.'

'Yeah.' The train rattled on.

'So he'll have to move out of their bedroom, then?' Jamie

wanted to hear more about Jess, and thought talk of practical details the least hazardous route back to the subject.

'Yeah, and not only that. A man's coming with them, so God knows where they're all going to sleep. Ma said would you and me mind going on the parlour floor, if necessary.'

'Course not,' said Jamie, and took the bull by the horns. 'What man?'

'Oh, Jesus, I forgot to tell you! You know him. It's your English teacher. The one you think's all right. He's going out with Jess, I think.'

'Paddy Furness? No!'

'Yes, yes, it is. Christ, I really meant to tell you, Jac. It's weird, isn't it – your teacher ending up as Jess' boyfriend.'

It's worse than weird, thought Jamie. But Fin burbled on. 'Actually, maybe it isn't Jess. Maybe it's Lila. It's usually Jess who has the boyfriends, but Lila met this guy on a bus or something. Ma did tell me to tell you, but I can't remember which one it is.'

Jamie wished with all his strength that it would turn out to be Eliza. He remembered that visit to the clinic, one pallid winter lunchtime. He thought of the cigarettes, Paddy Furness lighting Eliza's. The memory stirred him for a reason he could not define.

The train lurched into South Kensington station. 'Look, we're here.' Finian chattered as Jamie led the way to the museum, but his replies were monosyllabic. His thoughts were in turmoil. Paddy Furness and Eliza – Jesus! It wasn't at all an unwelcome idea. He felt a furtive grin stealing across his face at the thought of appropriating just a little special attention for himself. Paddy Furness was a good bloke.

Jess, though. If it was Jess . . . Jamie looked up at the well-loved façade of the Natural History Museum, glorious against the tender blue of an April sky. I'll always love you, Jess, he thought. Even though you'll never know.

He turned to Finian with an air of authority. 'This is it, then. Which bit do you want to see first?'

When Sibyl took her meals, more often than not on a tray by the parlour fire, Martha draped her in napkins, and kept a damp cloth to hand. Leo had protested when he first witnessed this loss of dignity, but Martha was firm. 'She would hate to sit all day in filthy clothes,' she said. 'And filthy they would become. At least I can just take the napkins away afterwards.'

If Sibyl felt strong, she would totter into the kitchen, leaning on Leo's arm, and eat with the rest of them, but this was increasingly rare. Her food had to be prepared separately too; she could no longer negotiate bones, or lumps. She tended to eat early; the ritual of putting her to bed seemed to Martha to take longer each day.

One evening, when Leo sat in the armchair opposite, keeping up a flow of chat to divert attention from the stench and the slop of his mother's puréed cauliflower cheese, Martha took up a spoon and held it up to Sibyl's mouth. She had never fed her before. The old woman cocked a wary, watchful eye; then she opened her mouth and allowed the spoon to slide in. Neither woman made a comment, and the meal was finished in this manner. A door of memory swung open in Leo's mind; he saw Clare, her head hanging back, dribble trailing from the cave of her open mouth. Martha, spooning some mush in, gently closing the mouth to make sure it was swallowed. Dabbing at the small chin, where the constant trickle of saliva had made a sore red runnel. Repeating the process. Again. And again.

He stood up, put one foot on the fender, leaned his forehead against the chimney breast. 'I can go, Martha,' he said, 'if you think it'll be difficult when the girls come. I can always go somewhere else.'

A sound of protest came from Sibyl's throat, halfway between a cough and a sob. Martha said, 'Don't be silly, Leo. There's no question of your going.'

'No need at all,' said Sibyl unexpectedly, 'now that the war's come to an end.'

Later, when the boys were watching a late-night horror film, Ganna was breathing heavily in deep sleep, and the squeak of Bella's rocking chair, like a trapped animal, could be faintly heard, Leo and Martha stood at the foot of the stairs.

'Good night, then,' said Martha.

'It reminded me,' said Leo, suddenly. 'Seeing you feed her like that. It reminded me, that's all.'

258

Martha turned her head away. 'It'll be twenty years next week.'

'I know,' said Leo. 'Twenty years next Tuesday.'

Slowly she turned back to look at him. 'I didn't know you paid any attention.'

'You wouldn't let me pay attention, Martha. You shut me out.'

She tightened her lips and shook her head. Tears slid out from under her closed lids. Still she stood there, solid as a monument. Leo took her in his arms. 'Little Clare,' he whispered. 'Poor little girl. Poor little girl.'

Martha let vast sobs shake her, let herself be enfolded by him. Then she pushed free, gently, and smeared her wet face on the sleeve of her cardigan. 'Come, then,' she said. 'Are you coming to bed?'

They climbed the stairs, side by side.

*Also by Charlotte Moore and available in Arrow*

## PROMISES PAST

Sarah and Adrian Stanhope are taking the plunge. They are leaving London with their three small children to live in a small market town. Adrian will commute, the children will thrive and Sarah will too. But she doesn't. Is it the seven year itch? The reality of the rural idyll not measuring up? Or the downright attractiveness of the local GP?

Standing aloof is childless Claudia Prescott, devoted to her career and shoring herself up against all manner of hurt, from an errant husband to ubiquitous references to babies, while Hilary Nightingale, singular and translucent, paints murals and attempts to conduct a fledgling affair under the eagle eye of her teenage daughter.

*Promises Past* is a brilliant exploration of marriages in silent crisis, unlicensed desire, motherhood and childlessness, and teenagers presiding over their parents' lives in proprietorial vigil.

'A stunning first novel about marriage, guilty desire and family pressures. Highly recommended' PRIMA

# THE ANNIVERSARY

Ann Swinfen

The most evocative and compelling family novel since Rosamunde Pilcher's *The Shellseekers*, *The Anniversary* sweeps the reader into the fabric of a family, a community and an era.

It is June 11th 1994 in the depths of Herefordshire and Natasha Devereux's family and two hundred guests gather together to celebrate the fiftieth anniversary of St. Martins. From the vision of one woman who fled Bolshevik Russia and opened her doors to artists, musicians, writers and refugees from war-torn Europe it has become a sanctuary for five generations of a family who – over the course of one day – face marital crisis, impending birth, teenage trauma, a father's roving eye into forbidden territory, momentous news from the past, communal financial crisis, and a lost love from the summer of '57.

As the evening shadows spread-eagle across the lawn to the rambling house and the great old copper beech, Natasha comes to the fruition of her life's work, The kaleidoscope of memory has been shaken, decisions have been taken. There has been a birth, and a death, but above all a celebration.

# FACING THE MUSIC

Mary Sheepshanks

'There wouldn't be any trouble if only you had a wife,' Lady Boynton had said. But Flavia Cameron was not at all what she had in mind for Gervaise Henderson. Impossibly young, with a musical talent that could have been heard in concert halls around the world, the headmaster's new wife was beautiful and sparkling and she swept the Upper Fourth of their feet.

Until Ben Forbes arrived, with a father who saw Flavia not as a prodigy, a daughter or a wife, but, for the first time, as herself. It is a discovery that will throw her life into turmoil.

Perceptive and poignant, funny and touching, *Facing the Music* is a welcome new novel from the author of *A Price for Everything*.

Praise for *A Price for Everything*:

'Touchingly wise and extremely funny' THE TIMES

'Midway between the sexual candour of Mary Wesley and Joanna Trollope's sharp observation' MAIL ON SUNDAY

## Other B format titles available in Arrow

| | | | |
|---|---|---|---|
| ☐ | The Last Guests of the Season | Sue Gee | £5.99 |
| ☐ | Letters From Prague | Sue Gee | £5.99 |
| ☐ | The Morning Gift | Eva Ibbotson | £5.99 |
| ☐ | A Countess Below Stairs | Eva Ibbotson | £5.99 |
| ☐ | Passing Places | Amanda MacAndrew | £5.99 |
| ☐ | Breaking the Chain | Maggie Makepeace | £5.99 |
| ☐ | Telling Only Lies | Jessica Mann | £5.99 |
| ☐ | Plucking the Apple | Elizabeth Palmer | £5.99 |
| ☐ | Old Money | Elizabeth Palmer | £5.99 |
| ☐ | The Young Italians | Amanda Prantera | £5.99 |
| ☐ | One True Thing | Anna Quindlen | £5.99 |
| ☐ | A Price For Everything | Mary Sheepshanks | £5.99 |

ALL ARROW BOOKS ARE AVAILABLE THROUGH MAIL ORDER OR FROM YOUR LOCAL BOOKSHOP AND NEWSAGENT.

PLEASE SEND CHEQUE/EUROCHEQUE/POSTAL ORDER (STERLING ONLY) ACCESS, VISA OR MASTERCARD

☐☐☐☐☐☐☐☐☐☐☐☐☐☐☐☐☐☐☐

EXPIRY DATE .................. SIGNATURE ........................................................

PLEASE ALLOW 75 PENCE PER BOOK FOR POST AND PACKING U.K.

OVERSEAS CUSTOMERS PLEASE ALLOW £1.00 PER COPY FOR POST AND PACKING.

ALL ORDERS TO:

ARROW BOOKS, BOOK SERVICE BY POST, P.O. BOX 29, DOUGLAS, ISLE OF MAN, IM99 1BQ. TEL: 01624 675137 FAX: 01624 670923

NAME ............................................................................................................

ADDRESS........................................................................................................

....................................................................................................................

Please allow 28 days for delivery. Please tick box if you do not wish to receive any additional information ☐

Prices and availability subject to change without notice.